HOLLY WATT is an award-win
worked at the *Sunday Times*, the
before moving to Devon with her

@holly_watt

To the Lions
The Dead Line
The Hunt and the Kill
The End of the Game

THE LAST TRUTHS WE TOLD

HOLLY WATT

RAVEN BOOKS

LONDON · OXFORD · NEW YORK · NEW DELHI · SYDNEY

RAVEN BOOKS
Bloomsbury Publishing Plc
50 Bedford Square, London, WC1B 3DP, UK
Bloomsbury Publishing Ireland Limited,
29 Earlsfort Terrace, Dublin 2, D02 AY28, Ireland

BLOOMSBURY, RAVEN BOOKS and the Raven Books logo
are trademarks of Bloomsbury Publishing Plc

First published in Great Britain 2025
This edition first published in 2025

A catalogue record for this book is available from the British Library

ISBN: HB: 978-1-5266-6150-0; TPB: 978-1-5266-6151-7; PB: 978-1-5266-6148-7;
EBOOK: 978-1-5266-6145-6; EPDF: 978-1-5266-6147-0

2 4 6 8 10 9 7 5 3 1

Typeset by Integra Software Services Pvt. Ltd.
Printed and bound in Great Britain by CPI Group (UK) Ltd, Croydon CR0 4YY

To find out more about our authors and books visit www.bloomsbury.com
and sign up for our newsletters
For product safety related questions contact productsafety@bloomsbury.com

To Cressy and James
&
Iris and Hetta

PROLOGUE

In their different ways, they all saw it.

Maggie hunted it down at work, as if it were part of her job. A couple of minutes, that's all it took. Routine.

It popped up on Ollie's phone with a jokey, vicious caption. He laughed sharply, before realising.

It came in a briefing for Rory. Just one of the risks, one of the fears, one of the hundreds of threats buried neatly in piles of paper.

Some of them saw it on the bleaker news sites. Stills from the CCTV, that frozen split-second. Blurry. Solid black pixels blocked out the worst.

Ayda avoided all coverage for days and then dreamed about it anyway, waking to her own screams, the horror crushing her throat.

Jude painted it, a hellstorm of sharp edges and scarlet.

They all saw it.

The blaze of headlights filling the tunnel. A black shape, moving suddenly, horribly. Silhouetted for a second and falling almost gracefully. Disappearing in a nightmare jerk, the violence a punch every time.

In Maggie's version, there were giggles in the foreground. A babble of teenage girls waiting for the Tube. Off to Mile End, their laughter smashed by a horn blaring frantically, their screams dissolving in the wail of brakes.

You couldn't be sure. Not really. Not even with all the different angles.

A couple of the teenagers – their giggles long gone – swore that someone ran away. Shoving through the crowds before anyone else could react.

All eyes had been on the train, of course. It sat there, oddly prosaic. Halfway down the platform, as if it should still be moving, the horror hidden by oblivious steel.

The driver was shuddering with shock. 'I tried,' he said, over and over. 'I tried.'

Of course, someone might have run away because it was unbearable.

In the chaos and the hysteria and the crush of the platform, no one could quite be sure. Already the loudspeakers: *…an incident on platform two, please make your way to…*

No one sees you in a crowd.

In her office, Maggie watched the footage again and again. There was nothing gory in this particular clip. Nothing grotesque. Just three teenage girls, smiling for the camera. Cropped tops, flat stomachs, one of them had pink hair. The last few seconds of innocence. The camera was pointing away from the train as it roared along the platform, focused on the girls. Not on the passengers five-deep, waiting more or less patiently for a space on the rush-hour Tube. Then there was a sudden movement to the left. The footage jerked and blurred.

Tube lights, dazzling.

A flash of purple.

A patch of grimy platform.

Darkness.

When the phone's owner picked it up, there was a split-second of a young face, wet with tears. Then a fumble and the screen went black.

Days later, Maggie went down to the platform.

It was always busy this station, even in the slump of the afternoon. And there would have been hundreds of people at rush hour, thousands even, and only sketchy CCTV. Maggie walked from platform to platform, watching for cameras.

It was *possible*.

It was impossible.

It *was* possible.

The next day, Maggie went back to the platform again, waiting patiently as the trains grumbled past. There was no way of guessing what had happened here. No flowers, no candles; the spatter of blood hosed away in minutes. People hurried past. Nothing to remember, nothing to forget. Maggie stood staring at the advertisements. They had changed in the last few days, slip slap, London oblivious.

A woman stepped closer, 'Are you alright?'

Kind eyes, a hint of worry.

'I'm fine.' Briskly. 'Thank you. I'm fine.'

And as she walked away, the words echoed around her mind.

I'm fine, I'm fine, I'm fine.

1

It was mid-afternoon when Maggie reached Ollie and Elizabeth's road, her weekend bag rumbling down the pavement behind her. Elizabeth's road now, she corrected herself. A tote bag was sharp on Maggie's shoulder, clanking gently.

In the June light, the cherry trees glowed green and the Victorian houses smiled benignly. Clapham. Maggie had never liked it. She shook away a moment of apprehension, letting her excitement bubble up again. It had been so long since they were all together.

Together.

Maggie walked up the garden path and rang the doorbell firmly. A flurry of footsteps and the door was flung open.

'Maggie!' A squeal.

Pretty, blonde Elizabeth, barely changed twenty years on. She wore a white dress, mid-calf, flaring out from the waist and embroidered with tiny daisies.

'Come in,' Elizabeth smiled. 'Come in, come in, come in.'

Elizabeth stepped back. This was one of those houses an ordinary family might have lived in a few decades ago. Now, of course, it would cost millions. Four storeys, just south of the common. Unimaginable.

'Let's go down to the kitchen,' Elizabeth decided. 'I'm so glad we could all get together to scoot down, Maggie. We've got so much to catch up on.'

'Ayda said she'd be here as soon as possible,' Maggie said as she watched Elizabeth stride across the parquet flooring.

'Oh wonderful,' Elizabeth smiled back over her shoulder as she disappeared down the stairs. 'Now, what do you want to drink? I'm driving, so you can.'

'Anything,' Maggie felt a sudden awkwardness as she followed Elizabeth down the stairs. Gauche, almost. 'Whatever's open.'

The kitchen was a beautiful room. The glass doors were pinned open to the green of the garden and a breeze blew round the island. Outside, the earth had been gouged out for decking and a large seating area, with steps up to eye-height, manicured flowers and a fiercely pollarded willow. The garden was sunny, the right side of the road: Elizabeth's family would know.

'We're lucky that it's so lovely and warm. The weekend's meant to be nice too,' Elizabeth had her head deep in the fridge. 'Well, for quite a lot of the time. Champagne,' she reappeared with a flourish. But Maggie was staring at the kitchen table. Next to a vase of yellow roses was a slightly battered white envelope, the size of a folded tabloid newspaper. It was propped up against a large porcelain bowl, blue and white, Chinese scrolls.

That fizz of apprehension and excitement, again.

'Is that…'

Elizabeth put the champagne down on the countertop. 'Yes,' and for a moment, there was no emotion at all in her voice. 'That's it.'

'All of us, back together,' said Maggie. 'Every single one of us, for once.'

'Well, apart from…'

'Of course,' Maggie hurried. Not that. Not now. 'Of course.'

This is going to be *fun*, she insisted to herself. This is going to be *brilliant*.

The buzz of the doorbell made her jump, shattering the sudden silence. Stop it, she told herself. You're being pathetic. But she couldn't quite push away the memory of that phone call.

Maggie… Maggie, I'm scared.

'That'll be Ayda.' The smile was back on Elizabeth's face. 'You go and let her in, Maggie. I'll open the bottle.'

2

Maggie trotted obediently up the stairs. Beside the heavy front door, she could see Ayda's face peering in, red and green and twisted by the stained glass window. An Uber driver was hauling bags up the short flight of steps.

'Ayda,' Maggie hugged her with a burst of affection. 'It's so nice to see you.'

'How is she?' Ayda murmured.

'She seems…' Maggie shrugged. 'Just the same.'

'She always…'

'I know.'

As they came down the stairs, a cork popped in the kitchen.

'Ayda!' Elizabeth squealed, in the same tone as she had used for Maggie's arrival. 'Isn't this fun? I'm *so* excited to see everyone.'

Ayda thrust some lilies in Elizabeth's direction. 'They smelled so lovely.'

'They're gorgeous. Thank you. We can take them with us. How are you?'

Amidst the fluster of words, Elizabeth was pouring out two glasses of champagne and one glass of some sparkling soft drink. The glasses matched, which they wouldn't in Maggie's flat.

'I don't know where to start.' Ayda tried to make it a joke, but the years yawned open, quite sharply.

'I was trying to think when I last saw you.' Elizabeth handed her a glass and gestured them all towards the scrubbed pine kitchen table. 'You didn't make it down to Leatherhead in March, did you?'

'I think it might have been last summer?' said Ayda.

'Was it the Newtons' wedding?' Elizabeth hazarded. 'Down in Somerset?'

With a stab of regret, Maggie realised she hadn't seen Dan Newton since his wedding. That happened sometimes: the wedding, a tie that undid the rest.

'That was probably it,' Ayda nodded. Maggie could see she was agreeing without thinking. 'I hooked up with Dan's brother at that wedding.'

'But you and Maggie still see each other all the time,' said Elizabeth.

'Too often,' Maggie grinned sideways at Ayda.

'Not enough. Sorry about last week, Maggie, I just…' Maggie shrugged away Ayda's apology.

Ayda always cancelled now. Last minute. *Just a few more things I have to get done. I need to… Sorry, Maggie. Sorry.* She had always been highly strung. Unquestionably successful as she raced up the ranks of one of the biggest law firms in the world, her rivals realising the threat too late. Maggie was used to Ayda's slenderness now. She was no longer startled by the sharp bones, the angles. The fragile cheekbones and the shadows under the eyes: that was just Ayda. She still looked good, though. The clothes were understated and expensive. The dark bob was sliced long enough to flirt, short enough to boss. She always made it to the gym, no matter what, pounding away at classes with names that Maggie didn't recognise. *Bootcamp. SoulCycle. Barrecore.*

'Here.' Ayda nudged the bowl of crisps towards Maggie. 'I'm not hungry.'

'Thanks.'

'Was everyone able to come in the end?' Ayda asked brightly. 'Well, apart from…'

This time, the silence hung over the table for longer. For a second, Maggie allowed herself to remember. At once the grief was knife-sharp in her throat, a scar splitting open, sorrow smearing blood-red all over the marble countertops.

'Yes,' said Elizabeth firmly. 'Everyone.'

'And Ollie's driving down with us?' Ayda yanked the conversation forward. 'This afternoon?'

'Yes,' Elizabeth nodded firmly. 'Yes. That's all amicable now. Very amicable indeed.'

'That's *great*,' Maggie heard the ring of insincerity in her own voice.

Ayda caught her eye. She had messaged Maggie after hearing the plan.

Sodding TYPICAL that we have to drive down in gritted-teeth silence so E can make out that everything's hunky-dory.

'Ollie was meant to be driving down with Rory and Finlay tonight.' Elizabeth sat down at one of the kitchen island bar stools. 'But Rory had to visit somewhere in Somerset this morning, and Finlay decided to head down with him.'

Finlay and Rory were brothers, Rory the elder by eighteen months.

'It'll be so nice to see them all.'

Elizabeth stood up sharply. 'Hummus? Tarama?' Shrill. The doorbell was almost a relief. 'Sorry, Maggie,' Elizabeth was decanting salsa now. 'Would you mind grabbing that?'

'Course.'

Maggie hurried up again. That was one redeeming feature of her tiny flat, she supposed. Only a couple of steps to open the front door.

'Hello, Ollie.' He was standing there, a key awkward in his hand.

'Hello, Maggie.' He shoved the bunch of keys into his pocket with a half-laugh. 'I wasn't...'

'I know.'

Maggie stepped back to let him inside his old hallway. To her right, double doors opened onto a formal drawing room, all creams and blues and golds. The dining room was immaculate, as always. He had come straight from work, Maggie guessed, just over the river in Knightsbridge. He had loosened his tie, bright red with neat rows of horseshoes. There was a flush in his cheeks though. Maybe not straight home. And not his home. Not any more.

'We're downstairs,' said Maggie.

'Are we all ready to go?' Ollie dumped his bags in the hallway, next to Ayda's pile of luggage. 'It's fun escaping London early, isn't it?'

Ollie was losing his hair, Maggie noticed, and it was greying at his temples. The good-looking boy was quite abruptly middle-aged. With a shiver, Maggie wondered if he was thinking the same thing about her. Maybe there should be a maximum time between seeing people, so friendship didn't become a jolting reminder of age. Or maybe that was just friendship. He was still handsome though. Hazel eyes, even features, smooth skin. Brown hair with a hint of red in it. A thickening waist and a scar above one eye from an old rugby game. It gave his face some edge, but not much.

She imagined herself in his eyes. Maggie: same as usual. Brown hair, brown eyes, taller than most women. Too many Maltesers to meet all the deadlines, but made it to Park Run most Saturdays. Well, some Saturdays. Ordinary, basically.

Ollie straightened his shoulders. 'Shall we?'

As they walked into the kitchen, Maggie wondered if Elizabeth had been practising that smile. Elizabeth walked across to Ollie, right hand firm on his upper arm as she steered them into a cheek-to-cheek kiss. 'Lovely to see you.'

'Afternoon, Ayda.' Ollie spoke over Elizabeth's shoulder.

'Hello, Ollie.'

The silence elongated. Maggie stared at the wine cellar next to the French windows. Ollie had it installed just after he and Elizabeth moved in. *Bespoke*, he told Maggie, when he first showed it to her. *Designed just for us.*

The little cellar was circular, spiral steps leading down under a thick glass floor just in front of the bifolds. The wine bottles jutted into the stairwell like cogs, or teeth in an ugly mouth. It made Maggie think of an open grave and she always avoided stepping on the glass.

Ollie walked over to the kitchen table and stared down. 'I can't believe you kept it,' he reached out and touched the envelope. 'For all those years.'

'Of course I did,' Elizabeth's voice was brisk. 'We promised, didn't we?'

They had promised a lot.

'Maggie would have lost it,' Ollie laughed.

'I wouldn't!' She would.

'I haven't seen Ivo for months.' Ollie sat down at the table, his movements unconsciously familiar. *This is where I always sit.*

'Me neither.' Even as she spoke, Maggie felt that old rush of emotion. She pushed it away, quite deliberately. 'But he's barely ever in London these days, is he? It's all New York, Mustique, Shanghai.'

'And Zurich,' added Ollie. 'I suspect there is something quite sharp going on with Ivo's tax arrangements.'

On the kitchen wall, Elizabeth had hung a careful collage of dozens of photographs. Maggie's eyes flitted across. There he was. That smile, jolting as a camera flash and freezing her in time. Maggie stared at the dark hair, the slanting blue eyes. The golden boy caught in the middle of all the laughter, all the ludicrousness, all the joy of university life.

'It'll be nice to see him again,' she managed.

'So, how's everyone else getting there?' asked Ollie.

'Finlay and Rory should be there by now, actually.'

Elizabeth had always been the organiser. She was the one who had set up the WhatsApp group – of course there was a WhatsApp group

– Uni get-together, can you believe it's been 20 years? EEK! It had been buzzing away for days, giving them all a sense of intimacy, of familiarity, even if Maggie hadn't seen Ollie since March or Ivo since… was it last year?

It had been Elizabeth, too, who organised the painful Zooms during Covid. The tedious pub quizzes and, 'Finlay, you've bloody muted yourself again.' Those hadn't lasted.

'And the others?' Maggie asked. 'How are they getting down?'

'Jude is making her own way, not sure how. Then there's us. And, of course, it's Ivo's house now, so he may be staying there for a few days. Before heading off. Boston, I think he said?'

Ivo had said Boston.

'Amazing place,' said Ayda, 'to have all to yourself.'

'Since his father died,' Elizabeth pointed out.

'It'll be weird seeing Jude again,' Ollie wrinkled his nose. 'She was a complete mess the last time I saw her. Embarrassing.'

'She's fine,' said Maggie.

'No,' he said flatly, 'she's not.'

Jude had been veering further and further out of control for years. The chaos had been charming in her twenties, endearing almost. But her thirties were turning into a long morning-after her twenties. The gilt was wearing off, the joke running too long. There were hollows in her cheeks now, her teeth more prominent, her smile harsher.

'You still see her quite a lot, don't you?' Elizabeth asked Maggie.

'As much as I can. All a bit hectic at the moment.'

She couldn't remember exactly when she'd last seen Jude.

Ollie was fidgeting with the white envelope, tugging at a corner.

'Don't,' Elizabeth took it off him. 'After all this time, we have to wait for everyone to be together.'

'I can't believe it's been two decades,' said Ollie, almost to himself. He sat up. 'How's the journalism going, Maggie? I loved that interview with the Home Secretary last week.'

'Thanks, Ollie.' It had been a different member of the *Post*'s lobby team who had done that interview, but he was trying to be nice.

There was a pause.

'Right,' Ollie clapped his hands on his knees. 'Shall we make a move? The drive will take hours anyway.'

'It's time to go back to Wintercross,' said Ayda dreamily. 'All of us, together.'

I'm not sure... I'm not sure I'll go, Mags.
You have to! We all promised. It has to be all of us, together.
Maggie... Maggie, I'm scared.

The wave of foreboding flooded through Maggie all over again.

2

Finlay
Get a bloody move on, you lot!
We're getting stuck-in already.

Four hours, that's how long Elizabeth had said the journey would take. But the traffic put paid to that.

'Bring the rest of the bottle,' Elizabeth had urged as they left. 'There's no point in leaving it.' So, Maggie and Ayda sat in the back of the car, swigging champagne from the bottle and gossiping, hypnotised by the flash of headlights on the motorway.

'Ivo's messaged,' said Ayda as they reached Devon. 'Jude's run out of cigarettes, can we grab some on the way?'

'Sure.' Elizabeth was overtaking a lorry: mirror, signal, manoeuvre. 'Tell him it's no problem.'

There was still a glow in the sky as they drove through Chagford, the nearest town to Wintercross. It was pretty: pastel and stone houses around a squiggle of a square. The clock on the church was chiming nine o'clock as Elizabeth indicated left for Wintercross. There were still a few people standing outside the pub, their cigarettes glowing in the dusk.

'What's that?' asked Ayda. Down one of the dark streets that led off the square, a blue light was flickering. It was a police car, its siren switched off. The blue light was still revolving, glinting over the sleepy houses before the shadows swallowed them again.

'I can't see what's going on.' Maggie peered.

'Friday night, I guess.' Ayda stretched.

It was Maggie who went into the Spar for cigarettes.

'Do you know what that's about?' She gestured towards the blue flicker. The journalist, always.

The woman behind the counter was sixtyish, tired eyes, ready to clock off, 'Dunno.'

'Hope everyone's alright. I don't think I've ever seen the police in Chagford.'

'There's been a lot of police around the place,' the woman said grudgingly, 'for a while now.'

The woman turned away, rearranging the Calpol and the aspirin despite it looking neat enough already.

'Why—' Maggie began to ask.

A man stepped forward, plonking down a pint of milk and six cans of lager on the counter, and the woman's attention flicked towards him. After a couple of seconds, Maggie headed back out to the car.

'Do we need anything else?' Elizabeth looked at the sleeping shops.

'I've brought loads of wine,' said Ollie.

'Fine.' Elizabeth accelerated carefully. 'Let's go.'

The car crept down lanes that narrowed like bronchioli. They all cheered as they caught sight of the house for the first time, floodlit and magnificent, silhouetted against the last glow of the sky. The granite gloom of the moor loomed in the distance.

'God, it's such a beautiful place,' said Maggie. 'I can't believe this weekend is finally here.'

'I'm so excited to see Ivo,' said Elizabeth. 'And Finlay and Rory too. And Jude, even.'

'Over twenty years since we first came down here,' murmured Ayda. 'And it still looks exactly the same.'

'This place will look the same centuries from now,' said Elizabeth. 'The home of the Fitzwilliams.'

And again, Maggie felt that edge of foreboding, like a flicker of flame snaking up a scrap of paper. She pushed it away.

Too late now, you're here.

The front door opened as Elizabeth stopped the car, the light spilling across the gravel. There was a babble of voices, dark figures crowding through the big oak door, a dog barking hysterically.

'Rory!' Ayda waved frantically. 'Finlay!'

'You made it!' Finlay punched the air. 'We'd practically given up all hope.'

Finlay was holding a wine glass, Maggie saw, liquid spilling as he gestured. Blinking at the light from the hallway, she felt blurry from the hours in the back of the car; an animal emerging from a burrow, not ready for the arrival despite anticipating it for weeks. The others, however, were overflowing with excitement. As Maggie looked up at Wintercross's austere façade, she caught their mood and felt her own elation flood back.

Together.

'Get inside!' Rory shouted. 'Before Finlay drinks all the bloody wine. We've been waiting for hours.'

'The traffic was terrible as we joined the M5,' Elizabeth sounded defensive. 'And there was a crash near Bridgwater...'

Her voice trailed away – knowing she was being dull – as Ivo strode across the gravel.

'Miss Fletcher.' He mock-bowed as he opened Maggie's door. 'What a delight to see you again.' As always, his warmth lit up the whole group. He was a surge of energy, thrilled by their arrival, a broad grin splitting his face in half. Maggie unfolded herself from the car. As she stood up, Ivo was very close. She found herself looking up at his jawline, pale in the night. His black hair was chaotic and his blue eyes were laughing into hers. Happiness poured through her, flooding away her misgivings.

'Ivo,' she began, 'it's so lovely to—'

But already he was moving on, swerving round the car to welcome Ayda. 'My back,' Ayda was shouting as she emerged. 'I'll never stand up straight again.' Ivo was pulling Ayda into a bear hug. 'I'll rub it better, you gorgeous minx.'

Ollie was pulling suitcases out of the boot. 'It took advanced engineering to get everything in,' he was saying to Rory, over the babble of excitement. 'Tetris, basically. These girls never pack light.' It had been ages, Maggie thought, since anyone called her a girl. The word had been swept away by the tide of change at work: *problematic*. And no one else would call her a girl outside of work, not these days. For a moment she felt a pang, like the first time she was *Madame*, not *Mademoiselle* on holiday.

But then: 'How are *you*, gorgeous?' Finlay swept her into a bear hug.

'Look at *you*,' Rory was just behind him, 'you're looking wonderful, Maggie.'

'Oh, it's so lovely,' Maggie found herself saying. 'It's so lovely to see you all again. All of us, together, at last.'

Together.

They crashed into the hall, a swirling mass of noise and energy. Maggie picked up splinters of conversation.

'Not seen you for ages—'

'You're in the blue bedroom, just up—'

'What happened to that guy you were—'

'Shut up, Pagan—' This to the black Labrador who was capering with excitement, shoved away crossly as he jumped up at Elizabeth.

'Pagan?'

'He yowled all night when he first arrived as a puppy.'

'Who looks after him?' Maggie asked Ivo. 'When you're not here.'

'The Verekers have him,' Ivo answered, over his shoulder. 'They're in the gatehouse these days.' The gatehouse had glowed cosily as they passed it, the roar of their engine shattering the peace for a few seconds. The lane would have settled back to silence now, like snow in a globe.

'They took over from the Archers?' asked Maggie.

'Good memory,' Ivo nodded and Maggie felt her face flush. Every memory, carefully conserved. 'They retired at last, thank God. Mrs V is rather better at looking after the house than old Ruth.'

'She is indeed.' Looking around, Maggie realised that Wintercross had undergone a substantial overhaul. The entrance hall had been forbidding, with ancient wood panelling and a sweep of cold granite flagstones. Heavy oak furniture had crouched in corners, dusted with cobwebs, and there had always been a smell of damp and wet dog. Now the hall was immaculate, sprays of pink roses radiant in stylish vases. The armchairs were upholstered in blues and yellows, Colefax and Fowler at a guess. Elegant rugs were scattered here and there and, even in the middle of June, a fire flickered in the baronial fireplace. It looked, Maggie thought, as if someone had applied chic make-up to an already perfect bone structure.

'This place is looking incredible,' Ayda was saying. 'Transformed.'

'You must have spent a fortune.' Ollie said what they were all thinking.

'After my father...' Ivo shrugged. 'It was either let it fall down or allow Mrs V and her mob of interior designers to run wild.'

'They've done a wonderful job,' said Elizabeth. 'Exquisite.'

'Thank you, Elizabeth.' There was an edge of mockery in Ivo's voice. 'Now, drink first? Or shall I show you to your rooms?'

'Drink,' Ollie insisted. 'I need a drink.' They had been polite all the way down, Ollie and Elizabeth, but strained. As if they were morose parents, middle-aged, not fighting only for the sake of the raucous children in the back seats.

'We were in the kitchen,' Ivo led the way. 'Come in.'

Wintercross was a truly ancient house, patched together over the centuries. There were four main rooms at the front, two on either side of the high-ceilinged entrance hall. To the left, as they walked in, there were two vast drawing rooms, linked together by double doors. 'What a wonderful entertaining space,' Elizabeth had said the first time Ivo showed them around, a teenager testing out adult phrases.

On the right, there was a dining room, with a library beyond. The library was concealed behind a bookcase, the books sawn in half. Pressing *A History of the Fitzwilliams* let the bookcase swing open. Ivo's father had used the library as a study in a fug of cigar smoke. In here, there were busts of long-dead Fitzwilliams and dusty rows of gold-lettered books that hadn't been touched for decades. Past the library, there was a smaller billiards room. At the back of the house, two wings reached out to form a sort of C. The left wing contained the ballroom. The idea of a house having a ballroom had seemed ludicrous to Maggie; implausible even.

The right wing held a cosier sitting room – the snug, Ivo called it – which led into a large kitchen. Off the kitchen, there was a muddle of utility rooms and boot rooms, all festooned with wax jackets and wellingtons. A grand staircase rose up from the entrance hall to a string of elegant bedrooms above. There was a narrow second staircase that climbed out of the snug, up to the rabbit warren of rooms in the attics.

Maggie thought briefly of her parents' house. A nice semi in the suburbs, with a small garden, the grass clipped close by her father. *Nice*. It always felt disloyal to even think about it amidst the glories of Wintercross. And the moment she was here, it was the semi that seemed unlikely, like trying to remember snow in summer.

They followed Ivo towards the kitchen, cackling their way down the corridor into the snug.

'How are things at the *Post*?' Ivo looked back at Maggie.

'Oh, fantastic,' Maggie gushed. 'I'm deputy political editor now, and I just love it. Working out of the heart of Parliament is really—'

'Great, great!' Ivo was already moving ahead, grinning back at her, half apologetic. 'Rory, can you grab a couple more bottles of that red from the cellar?'

It always felt as if she were trying to hold his attention, a performing seal clapping her flippers. Maggie shrugged the feeling away. She was almost in the warmth of the kitchen, the table heavy with half-filled plates and half-empty bottles, when she felt a tap on her shoulder.

'Hello, Maggie.'

'Jude.' Maggie smiled a beat too late. 'It's lovely to see you.'

'You too, darling. You too.'

Jude was wearing a gold corset top and shiny black leggings. Ballerina tiny, her eyeliner was a pristine wing, blending perfectly into a coppery eyeshadow. There were a dozen gold bracelets on her wrists and a row of tarnished rings ran up the outside of her right ear. The mass of dark red hair was held back by an art deco headpiece made from black feathers. She looked beautiful, Maggie thought, a bird of prey surveying her domain. But then she always was stunning at the start of the evening. The ice cubes in Jude's highball glass clinked.

'How was the drive down?' Jude's eyes glinted towards Elizabeth.

'Fairly glacial.'

'Christ, I can just imagine. She's still fighting the Cold War, isn't she? Brezhnev in Boden.' Jude grinned. Her teeth were uneven and there was a gap between the front two. When she smiled, she put her tongue against the gap. Maggie felt a surge of almost-forgotten affection.

'It's great to see you, Jude,' she said truthfully. 'I got you your cigarettes.'

'Oh, thank you, sweets.'

There wouldn't be an offer to pay.

'How are things, Jude?' A throng of people carried them into the kitchen.

'Oh, you know, darling. Fine.'

Jude had always been instinctively evasive. It intrigued men and irritated women.

'What are you up to?' Maggie persisted.

'Oh, a bit of this, bit of that.'

All through university, Maggie and Lily had loyally traipsed to tiny theatres and pub backrooms to watch Jude storm and fury.

'Not my sort of thing,' Elizabeth had always been firm.

Jude had some success after university: the star in a couple of plays, fourth on the credits for a sitcom that was cancelled after two series. *Promising*, she was called. Ten years ago, people were delighted to be sat next to her at dinner: the glamorous one, with the glinting intelligence to boot. Now, Maggie watched people hesitate. 'Oh yes, I *think* I saw that.' Crushingly polite. A promise, broken. The partying hadn't helped. *It's networking*, Jude insisted, *meeting the right people*. But there was a wildness to it, the night turning into day turning into night.

'I'm so looking forward to having a proper catch-up,' said Maggie, not quite untrue. They had been good friends all those years ago. And even now, when Jude was in the right mood, she could make Maggie laugh more than almost anyone else.

'Me too, darling. Me too.'

They were all settling into chairs around the big oak table in the middle of the kitchen. This room had also been revamped. Before, the kitchen had been Mrs Archer's domain, food whisked straight to the dining room. Now, it was a room to be lived in. Or, at least, it was a room that might be lived in.

The early arrivals had already eaten. Elizabeth, bustling, cleared away dirty plates, stacking them in the sink for Mrs Vereker to deal with in the morning. Maggie found herself sitting between Rory and Finlay. Not next to Ivo, of course. Ayda and Ollie had manoeuvred themselves into those seats. Ivo was on his feet again in a moment anyway, pouring drinks, putting out crisps and nuts and dips.

'There's slow roasted lamb shoulder in the bottom of the Aga, too,' he said. 'Mrs V made it, so it should be safe. And jacket potatoes. Help yourselves.'

But no one did, crisps would be enough. Maggie had grabbed a sandwich when Elizabeth stopped for petrol and suspected that she smelled of cheese and onion.

The volume of noise rose again. Candles dripped wax onto the pine table.

'I see the phone reception,' Ayda was scrolling through her phone, always half-working, 'is as crap as ever. I always remember wandering around up by that tor, holding out our phones like water divining rods.'

'The Wi-Fi password is—'

'Oh, do put your phone away, Ayds.'

Rory turned to Maggie, kissing her on the cheek. 'Are we just going to agree this weekend is off the record?'

His voice was light but his eyes held hers.

'Of course,' Maggie lifted her glass to her lips. 'Can't imagine I'll remember much of it anyway.'

'Quite.' Rory was smiling, eyes still cautious.

'Don't worry,' Maggie nudged him. 'This weekend never happened, Rory.'

'Good.' He reached out for the bottle. 'Thank you, Maggie.'

'How are you?' Finlay turned towards Maggie. 'I don't think I've seen you since the funeral…'

The funeral.

'No.'

'And it was far too long before that…'

They had all seen less and less of each other, thought Maggie, especially in recent years. A few of them had turned forty recently, but their lives were too widely dispersed for milestones to generate big reunions. Maggie knew that Elizabeth, bruised from the divorce, had opted for some spa weekend in Hampshire for her fortieth, with only a small selection of her old school friends. Jude's party, on the other hand, was a rave in an east London warehouse with lots of people Maggie didn't know, wearing face paint and sequins, their jaws working too hard. Maggie had only lasted an hour. She had wondered – hopefully – if she might be invited to Ivo's celebrations, but she never heard anything. It had probably been a weekend on some tropical island or a few days skiing in Aspen. Discreet, expensive, nothing slapped up on Instagram, obviously.

Maggie's own fortieth had fallen just a few days after the funeral and she hadn't been able to face a big party.

'I know,' Maggie said lightly. 'We really must get together more often.'

'We must—' Finlay's voice faded into silence, his eyes going past her. Elizabeth was on her feet at the head of the table, and she was holding the white envelope.

'Twenty years,' Rory let out a whistle. 'Twenty years since we all sat down for that dinner. What the hell did we all write down?'

Maggie... Maggie, I'm scared.

And Maggie felt that thud of fear again.

3

> **Maggie**
> We should do something for Lily.

> **Ivo**
> Absolutely. I'll have a think.

'Twenty years ago,' Maggie could tell that Elizabeth had planned this speech, 'we sat down to dinner. And over the course of that evening, we all promised faithfully that we'd meet up again this month. And two decades later, here we are.' She smiled around the table.

'When,' Finlay howled, 'did we get so old?'

'We promised,' Elizabeth ignored him, 'that we would come together to read our predictions, to see what we got right,' she waved the white envelope, 'and what we got wrong.'

'A time capsule,' Rory said quietly, 'of us.'

Maggie stared at the envelope. It had yellowed slightly, crimped in places, but it was essentially exactly the same twenty years on: large, white, ordinary. She remembered it being sealed, carefully, in the flickering light of the candles. Elizabeth had kept it safe, just as she'd promised.

'Nine of us made eight predictions each,' Elizabeth went on. 'But we didn't make predictions about ourselves. So that is seventy-two predictions that we have to get through over the course of the weekend—'

'We're here for three nights,' Ayda interrupted. 'So that means we have to get through twenty-five a night or so. And then we can go and lie by the swimming pool during the day, or go on bracing walks.'

It was Thursday night now. They had originally planned to stay from Friday night to Sunday night. But then, Ivo had sent a message a few days ago.

> **Ivo**
> I've got to be in Boston by
> Sunday evening. Sorry, guys.

Elizabeth had messaged crossly, answering within seconds.

> **Elizabeth**
> Ivo! We're due to arrive late on Friday
> night. It'll be such a rush to get it all
> done by dawn on Sunday. Is it better
> to do it another weekend? We'll fit in
> around you, because it has to be all
> of us together.

And Maggie had wondered if, as the date had got closer, Ivo didn't want them there at all, really. Didn't want to waste a weekend with people he barely saw these days. But Elizabeth had persisted.

> **Elizabeth**
> That Thursday is exactly twenty years
> on from the dinner party, anyway. So
> it's the perfect time for us all to get
> down to Wintercross.

Eventually, they had all agreed to leave work as early as possible on Thursday. Taking Friday off made it feel like a holiday.

A celebration.

'I can't remember what I wrote at all,' said Ayda. 'Absolutely no idea.'

'I was trying to think,' Ivo agreed. 'But it's all so long ago now.'

Memory was a snapshot, thought Maggie, and it depended on the focus. Some parts were crisp and clear, others faded to a blur. For a moment, vividly, she remembered those young faces bent over the scraps of paper. Eyes gleaming as they glanced around and calculated each other's chances.

'Well,' said Elizabeth. 'We might as well get started.'

She looked around. Finlay reached behind his chair and grabbed a knife from a wooden block on the kitchen surface. With a flourish, he handed it to Elizabeth, presenting it flat across both his palms. Elizabeth picked it up slowly, ceremonially. For a moment, the knife caught the candlelight. In her flowing white dress, Elizabeth was a Druidess, standing over her sacrifice.

She moved the knife towards the envelope.

Maggie felt that surge of apprehension again, that flicker of fear.

They were different people now, the thought was sharp. These were secrets buried for a lifetime, coolly disinterred for a joke.

And one of them…

She glanced around the table and saw the misgivings reflected in several faces. Rory looked stern, his jaw clenched. Jude looked as if she might burst into tears, her mouth twitching, her eyes blinking. Ivo's face was still.

In one sharp movement, Elizabeth slipped the blade under the envelope flap and sliced it open. A beautiful glass bowl stood on the edge of the kitchen counter. Venetian, frozen starbursts of blue and green. Elizabeth brought it to the centre of the table. Then she upended the envelope sharply, a flurry of papers tumbling into the bowl. Elizabeth looked around, eyes burning with an odd defiance.

'Who' – it was a challenge – 'wants to go first?'

4

Elizabeth, on Rory: Well on his way to becoming
Prime Minister.

There was a flutter of cheers and catcalls as Ayda read out the words, the
tension dissipating at once.

'Call me Nostradamus,' smiled Elizabeth.

'Got that one right at least.' Finlay turned to his brother, a broad smile
on his face.

They had always been close, the two brothers, touchingly pleased with
the other's successes. These days, Rory was by far the more successful.

'Ridiculous,' Rory was shaking his head as he laughed. 'It's never going
to happen.' But there was a gleam in his eye, a hope he wasn't trying to
crush.

Ayda stroked the scrap of pink paper smooth on the table. 'It might,
Rory. It just might.' Rory had gone into politics straight out of university, landing a job as a special adviser almost immediately. *A bright boy*,
everyone said, *an exciting future. 'A Tory.'* Jude curled her lip.

Rory spent three years working for a junior minister, the pair of
them rising with well-matched vigour. The junior minister was a Devon
MP. Maggie had joined the dots years later, a neighbour of Ivo's father.
After that apprenticeship, Rory had spent a couple of years working at
a big management consultant – 'always a good idea to get a bit of time
in the real world under your belt,' Ivo's father again – before standing,
disastrously, in a seat in Yorkshire. 'Cannon fodder on this occasion,'

Mr Fitzwilliam had boomed. 'But it's all excellent practice. The party will remember your efforts.' Four years later, Rory stood again, this time in friendly Somerset, adding 2,000 votes to the already solid majority. Now he was racing up the ranks. He was good on television, with his wide-set, grey eyes and neatly cut, sandy hair. Good-looking, by political standards. He would listen intently to the interviewer, then nod briskly. *That's an excellent question, Leah*, before pivoting smoothly to his agenda, whatever it was that morning. Nothing to do with the question, quite often.

'Prime Minister.' Finlay lobbed an ice cube at Rory. 'God, the country's even more screwed than I realised.' The brothers were laughing at each other, Rory trying to chuck the ice cube down Finlay's T-shirt. Like many brothers, they looked alike until you knew them, Maggie thought. Finlay had the same grey eyes as Rory, and the same dark blond hair, but Finlay was taller, emanating an overwhelming sense of gym-built power. There was a will to survive there, a ruthless determination. *You'd want him on your side after the zombie apocalypse*, Ayda said once. Not a domesticated force.

Although he was the younger brother, Finlay looked older than Rory. His face was much heavier, the brow bones and the jaw more pronounced. His nose had been broken on several occasions: a bad-tempered rugby game, a punch-up on Suicide Sunday, a swan dive into a swimming pool, while drunk. He had been lucky to get away with that. And that was all before leaving uni. While Rory's hair was always the same, shaped to within a few millimetres of where it was tonight, Finlay's had been shaved, bleached, pony-tailed, anything. At the moment, his hair was cut very short, almost the same length as his stubble.

Tonight, Finlay was wearing old combats and a faded forest-green T-shirt. Comfortable. Practical. There would be a penknife in his pocket. Rory, on the other hand, was still wearing his suit trousers, the top button of his shirt undone, the tie discarded. An off-duty MP who could answer a call from *Newsnight* at any time, retying his tie as he scrolled through his notes.

'Whose prediction was that?' Ivo asked.

'Mine.' Elizabeth ducked her head.

It was typical of Elizabeth to have written on pink paper, thought Maggie. A memory flashed into her mind: Elizabeth tearing neat squares from her notepad, head bent, nipping her lower lip with concentration as her fountain pen shaped careful, indigo-ink italics.

'Were all your predictions like that?' asked Ivo. 'Generous?'

'I think so,' said Elizabeth. 'I used to be quite nice, you know.'

'Until life overtook us all,' Ayda was trying to catch peanuts in her mouth.

'I like your predictions,' Ivo decided. 'Let's open yours first.'

'But—'

'Yes,' Finlay drowned out Elizabeth's protests. 'God knows what the rest of them are like. We need some light relief to get started.' He leaned forward and grabbed another folded pink square and Maggie sensed them all bracing themselves.

5

Elizabeth, on Ayda: She will have made partner
at one of the Magic Circle firms.

'See,' said Finlay, with satisfaction. 'This is really cheering stuff. And spot
on, too.'

'Elizabeth,' Ayda grinned, 'I had no idea what I really wanted to do
then. How the hell did you know?'

Elizabeth looked pink with pleasure. 'Well, you were looking into
traineeships at the time, and you're bright, Ayda. I knew you'd suit the
law. I knew you'd do brilliantly.'

'But even I didn't guess back then…' Ayda hadn't known the depths
of her ambition back in that wintry June, thought Maggie. She did now.

'Plus, we all watched lots of *Ally McBeal* back then,' said Elizabeth.
'And you had the right legs for those skirts.'

Elizabeth had always watched people, thought Maggie. With her long
blonde hair and big blue eyes, she looked like a Sloaney cliché. But her
eyes glinted, watching people talk, people laugh, people argue. There
used to be a hint of awkwardness in it, as if she was trying to work out
why they were talking and laughing, as if she had had to learn. That had
been smoothed away, mostly.

Elizabeth could be kind, though, and thoughtful at unexpected
moments, occasionally. A card before an exam, brownies when you
were ill. Loyal, too. She was the one who had kept them all in touch
over the years. Remembering birthdays, congratulating successes,

keeping the fires flickering. Maggie had been quite touched by Elizabeth's determination to maintain their friendship.

'You've done brilliantly,' Elizabeth said to Ayda now.

Intellectual property, that was Ayda's specialty.

'It's valuing knowledge,' she had explained to Maggie once. 'Pricing intelligence.'

Those intangible rights: patents, trademarks, copyright. All becoming increasingly complex as the world accelerated.

'So you can't touch them?' Elizabeth had tried to understand once. 'Intangible, that means untouchable. They don't really exist?'

'Not physically.' Quite patient for Ayda.

'I don't get it,' said Jude. 'It's so limiting. Pinning thoughts like butterflies. Monetising ideas and dreams.'

'Maybe. But everything rests on those rights. And how else do creatives pay the bills?'

Ayda's mind always sliced through the intricacies with a ruthless brilliance. She had made partner four years ago, shockingly young. The nerves had only tautened since, thought Maggie, a rollercoaster winding higher and higher.

'Are you working on anything interesting at the moment?' Rory asked Ayda.

For a split second, Ivo's and Ayda's eyes met.

'Not this weekend!' Ivo was laughing.

'No,' agreed Ayda, smiling. 'Some guy joined Ivo's firm and his old company says he took some commercially sensitive info. with him,' she explained to the table. 'Throwleigh Pearce are representing SummerX.' SummerX was the hedge fund Ivo had founded, one of the biggest funds in the world.

'And did he?' asked Finlay. He was sitting next to Rory now. With his stubble and sun-tired skin, the younger brother looked like the elder's bodyguard. They were both sitting in the same position, chins resting on their right palms, and you would be able to tell them apart by their hands alone, thought Maggie. Rory's, clean and smooth. Finlay's, with the nails bitten short, calluses here and there.

'Well,' Ayda lolled back in her chair. 'Not according to the dream team of Throwleigh Pearce and SummerX.'

'We'll see.' Ivo grinned, closing down the conversation.

'But you enjoy what you do?' Rory persisted. 'We barely see you any more, Ayds. You're always working.'

'You're one to talk, Rory. And it is pretty relentless,' Ayda admitted. 'But it is fun, too. I enjoy it.'

'You don't want to miss out on life,' Jude said, 'locked up in your Liverpool Street tower. "Rapunzel, Rapunzel, let down your briefs."'

'I'm not,' Ayda snapped.

'Of course, you're not,' Maggie chimed in, always the peacemaker of the group. 'And, anyway, it makes you happy.'

'Exactly.'

'Sure, Ayda.' Jude's voice drawled. 'Sure.'

6

Elizabeth, on Maggie: She will have won her
first Pulitzer.

Maggie managed to keep smiling as Rory read out the words.

'I was never exactly likely to win a Pulitzer in the UK,' she tried for
flippancy. 'They're for American journalists.'

But she felt winded, as if physically jolted by her hopeful nineteen-
year-old self and the ghost of optimism.

'Or whatever the British version is of a Pulitzer,' Elizabeth waved her
hand. 'And you're almost there, Maggie.'

'Hardly.' Maggie felt her smile become fixed.

'You were always buried in the student newspaper office back then,'
Finlay remembered. 'Always scribbling in notebooks. We could never
get you to come out when you were close to a deadline.'

A head full of dreams in those days. That teenage intensity, raw with
ambition. Her stories would change minds, change laws, change the
world, she *knew* it. And one day, one glorious day, she would be the
Editor – definite article – with a glamorous blow-dry to boot. Now she
was a steady pair of hands. Could be trusted to knock out 800 words,
clean and fast. 'Very punctual,' her news editor had said in her annual
review last week. Bruising, that had been. And, of course, she never
had had to rush home in time to pick up the kids from nursery; which
mattered in journalism, even if they said it didn't.

She still enjoyed it, mostly. The interviews, drawing out information bit by bit. The race across the country to track down an MP who'd
gone off piste. She liked the big set pieces: the elections, the Budgets, the
drama of the occasion. Although she'd sat through so many of them now
that the excitement was leaching away. Election nights just meant 3 a.m.
in a sports hall in Nuneaton, or 4 a.m. in a leisure centre in Clacton, or 5
a.m. in a school gymnasium in Carlisle.

She'd watched so many bright young things rise – they always thought
their own rise was inexorable, that they would continue on this precise
trajectory forever – and fall, again and again. Everyone always thought
they were different, and these days the full circle could take less than
a fortnight. *These days.* When did that phrase creep into her vocabu-
lary? She still took pleasure in the elegance of the language, fitting words
together with the right cadence, the right tone. Although it was all more
rushed these days – several articles a day to feed the internet beast – so
no one noticed. And the sincerity, the idealism: that had disappeared,
long ago.

'I loved those articles you wrote in Afghanistan,' Ayda said loyally.
Afghanistan…

A war drifting into the history books over here, a bloody mess there.
In the corner of her eye, Maggie caught Finlay's flinch.

'That was at least a decade ago,' Maggie half-smiled at Ayda. 'But I'm
sure you found last week's read through on the Kempton by-election just
as fascinating.'

'Of course,' Ayda grinned back. 'Couldn't put it down.'

7

Elizabeth, on Finlay: Brigadier Finlay Adair, of
course.

The room fell silent. Finlay tried to smile, and Maggie realised what she
must have looked like just a few moments earlier.

'Not a bad guess, Elizabeth,' Finlay tried to make light of it.

Finlay had been the youngest person at that dinner, remembered
Maggie. His older brother's sidekick, a casual invitation. He was a first
year, when the rest of them had been at the end of their second years,
within touching distance of real life. On the cusp, when a year was
forever. Even before university, Finlay had wanted to be in the Army. The
Cadets had swallowed him up, his holidays spent mountaineering and
canoeing and parachuting. All the jolly games used to ambush the boys.
He'd talked a lot about the wilds of Canada, Maggie remembered vaguely.

She hadn't seen him much in the years after leaving university. He had
joined the Army properly as soon as he graduated, and began appear-
ing in perfectly polished brogues, immaculately ironed shirts. They had
caught up at Rory's birthday parties once a year: Finlay grinning, buying
drinks, getting wilder as the hour got later. Then he'd been away on oper-
ations and had missed a couple of Rory's birthdays. She hadn't seen him
for a few years.

She hadn't seen him until Forward Operating Base Larka.

FOB Larka was fifteen minutes from Camp Bastion in a Chinook. On the way to the base, the helicopter roared over the dusty Afghanistan countryside, its loading ramp jutting open at the back. Maggie had looked down at the patchwork of ochre and emerald, and felt the emptiness clutch at her stomach. She was strapped in, but the harness felt flimsy, insubstantial. Ridiculous to let your life depend on a few strips of nylon anyway. Especially when the whole world might explode into flames and flying metal and the vicious grip of gravity at any second.

As they approached Larka, the helicopter dived close to the ground. It was hot, the wind blistering the green of the fields and ruffling the slow drift of the irrigation canals. Maggie was aware of locals staring up as the helicopter juddered past; the aircraft a threat and a target all at once. Everywhere, the torn silk purple of the opium poppies fluttered defiantly. The Chinook jerked and Maggie's weight jolted against the nylon straps. For a second, she saw herself tumbling through the air, down and down and down. And then the helicopter pulsed on.

The soldiers had been in Larka for months by the time Maggie visited, hidden behind the sun-baked walls of the compound. Hidden for part of the time, that was. There were daily excursions into the chaos around the base, where the enemy waited, unseen. She was there as defence correspondent for the *London Post*. So young back then. Pretending to know what she was doing in her navy-blue flak jacket, PRESS front and back in big white letters.

The soldiers were so young too. None of them knew what they were doing either, not really. This was a *Swallows and Amazons* war, far away from the grown-ups. At first, they still thought they would be home for tea, and *then* they would find out what they were meant to be doing. Counter-intelligence and ink-spot strategy and air support: it all sounded as if someone somewhere knew what they were doing.

Surely, they did.

Surely.

They didn't.

The bomb exploded an hour after the Chinook had throbbed away from the base. A few hundred metres to the south of Larka, Maggie found out later, but even from that distance, the sound was a thud to the chest. On television, explosions are a spray of orange sparks, a puff of sooty smoke, over in a few frames as the hero sprints on.

This noise was solid. A roar transmuted. It swallowed everything and spat it out broken.

Slowly, the world began to move again. Maggie saw the urgency, men sprinting to their positions, their faces taut. There were rapid words over the radio, a series of codes she didn't understand.

Where are you, what's happened… Who? Who?

A siren howled. And there were screams out beyond the wall. In the distance, unreachable, no one can help you there, sorry.

Ludicrously, for a second, Maggie's mind filled with shoppers meandering around Oxford Circus. Bathers on the beach at Bournemouth. An ice lolly in Hyde Park at lunchtime. A blur of disconnected images, because how could it all be the same world?

It took hours to get the men back to the compound. Pinned down by a hail of gunfire, and pleading for Apaches that never came. She hadn't realised how desperate it was, clinging on to this small patch of earth, beside the goats and the poppies and the reed-choked irrigation ditches. Oh, the *arrogance*. She hadn't realised until then, not really, brought up to believe they were always on the winning side.

By the time the men were back, she knew.

This was a routine patrol, just one man caught in the blast. 'Life-changing injuries,' they call them, coyly. Wouldn't even make a news in brief. That meant all the flesh blasted away from the soldier's right leg. From knee to ankle, there were just shin bones gleaming white, a lump of foot dangling bloodily. They had to amputate, of course. The left leg wasn't much better.

Finlay was one of the last men back. Maggie saw him stagger into the compound, slumping to the ground as the gates slammed behind him. One of the men threw him a bottle of water as he lay against a rock, pushing off his helmet, dragging off the body armour. He was drenched with sweat, his face smeared with blood and dirt. Surrounded by the bustle of the camp, he sat very still, staring off into the distance.

After a few minutes, he sat up and looked around. Saw her across the dust of the base.

'So,' he said quietly, no hint of a smile, 'now you know.'

A few years later, he left the Army, and he never discussed it again.

Maggie looked towards Finlay. The forced smile had gone now and instead, his eyes had filled with a burning anger.

8

Elizabeth, on Ivo: Tycoon.

'You got that one right.' Maggie's laugh was too hearty, pushing away the last echoes of Larka.

'I wasn't sure how he'd do it exactly,' Elizabeth smiled down the table. 'But I just knew.'

We knew right from the start, thought Maggie. All of us.

From the first moment she had caught sight of Ivo, across the crowded student bar, she had known. Destined for greatness: it sounded trite. But he was. He had caught her staring at him on the second night at university, and grinned before she jerked her gaze away. He was tall, standing inches above the engineering students who were flocking around him.

'That's Ivo Fitzwilliam,' whispered the girl next to her. 'Isn't he gorgeous?'

In a room of people trying to forge their own identities – sloughing off the long years of school, the people who remembered when you cried, once, in Year Six – Ivo was utterly confident. Everyone knew his name at once. He'd done a gap year, hopping from Thailand to Laos, from Vietnam to Cambodia. He told self-deprecating stories about getting lost in Ubud, and draped beautiful rugs, ruby and amethyst and gold, over the scuffed magnolia of his student rooms. Only later did Maggie realise how clichéd that all was.

He was fun though, always. People lit up when they spoke to him. He had a sense of the ridiculous, a loud crack of a laugh. Bright, too, unquestionably. He was reading maths in a college renowned for its mathematicians. Perhaps he wasn't one of the absolute best there, but the absolute best won Nobel prizes, and swam in mathematics so abstract that only one or two other people in the world could follow their thoughts. At Trinity College, Cambridge, they treated Fields Medals like scout badges.

'Mathmo,' Jude mocked now. 'Nerd.'

There was nothing nerdy about Ivo, although Maggie suspected like many of them, he was happier at university, where he didn't have to hide his mind the way you had had to at school. Maggie still remembered her letter. *We are delighted to offer you a place...* Everyone at this table had got one.

'Some of that lot were such geeks though,' Ollie mocked now. 'Do you remember Mathmo Bob? He could barely make eye contact.'

'I bumped into him in Chamonix a few years ago,' said Finlay. 'He has a chalet there, works in Geneva. He was sitting in a hot tub, surrounded by blondes and drinking Dom Pérignon. Not such a bad life, it turns out.'

'No way,' Ollie pulled a face. 'Mathmo-sodding-Bob has a place in Chamonix?'

'Yes,' Ivo was laughing at Ollie's discomfort. 'Robert Chambers writes algorithms for Cyan Cap. I tried to poach him last year.'

'Bloody *hell.*'

After university, Ivo had briefly gone to work for Manatons – one of the biggest investment banks in the world – before spinning out his own hedge fund. SummerX was now managed in tax-friendly Zurich. Ivo commuted from his home in London. By private jet because his time was a lot more valuable than a Gulfstream's. SummerX was a quant fund with a trading strategy that relied on hugely complex algorithms. Ayda had tried to explain SummerX's modus operandi to Maggie several times.

'They build algorithms which decide how to invest the fund's money. Their software can make decisions a thousand times faster than any human, so it dives on any advantage in the market, right?'

'Right,' uncertainly.

Ayda took it down a notch. 'Basically, Ivo's computer systems look at information from all over the world and buy and sell shares off the back of that intelligence.'

'What sort of information?'

'Literally anything. They might use satellites, because during the pandemic, you couldn't trust any of the official data coming out of China, but you could track how many trucks were going in and out of distribution centres, and you could count how many cars were parked outside the shopping malls. And you could certainly tell when the crematoriums were running twenty-four seven.

'Or they might analyse social media. Because if all your employees are moaning on Glassdoor, your company's probably on the way down. If people are bitching about your hotel chain on Tripadvisor, you're definitely on your way down. And if everyone's slagging off your nappy quality on Mumsnet, you're totally fucked. Mums will know there's a problem weeks before the City has the faintest clue.'

'Okay.'

'Then there's credit card data or intel from websites selling anything from tomatoes to Ferraris. They can track the number of phones at a specific location – say a Tesla factory – and extrapolate that the number of people clocking in every night shift has gone up 30 per cent, so business must be booming. It's endless.'

'I see.' Maggie wasn't sure that she did.

'You just need to find a way of analysing all that information, and that's where Ivo's systems come in. They scrape that intelligence, process it and work out exactly what it means. Alternative data, it's called now, and pretty standard, but back when Ivo started, it was ground-breaking. Those algorithms – a way to analyse vast, vast amounts of data – were pioneering stuff twenty years ago. And because Ivo started ahead,' Ayda shrugged, 'he stayed ahead.'

All that really mattered were the millions. Hundreds of millions now, probably, for Ivo alone.

'Loads of people got hoovered into the City in our year,' said Jude slowly.

'And spat out again in the financial crisis,' said Ayda. 'We only had a couple of years of fun before the whole edifice began to crumble.'

'They were nerds though,' Ollie insisted. 'Do you remember that guy... Hui Fen or something? Those weird tracksuits he wore. What a freak. And, God, do you remember that bloke who—'

Jude stood up abruptly. 'Which room am I in, Ivo? I need to call someone.'

'I'll show you.' Ivo was on his feet. 'Shall I show you all to your rooms, by the way? So you know where you all are?'

'Let's do one more prediction first,' said Elizabeth. She was taking the lamb out of the Aga, the shoulder bone sticking up. She placed the lamb on the side and put her hand in the bowl. Smiling, she looked down at the piece of paper and her face froze.

9

Rory, on Finlay: God, I hope you're not in jail.

Silence, then the fire hissed and spat.

'What?' Elizabeth turned towards Rory. 'Why on earth would Finlay be in prison?'

The pause went on a second too long. Rory had a strange smile on his face. Then he rolled his eyes. 'You've all seen Finlay driving, right?'

'Yes. But…'

'Or Finlay dancing,' said Rory even more cheerily. 'Or, quite frankly, Finlay doing virtually anything.'

'Charming.' Finlay's laugh was forced. 'You're not exactly safe on the dance floor yourself, Royster. Do you remember that time in Zermatt when—'

'But jail?' Jude said uneasily. '*Jail*? What did you mean by that, Rory?'

'I thought we were still meant to be doing your predictions, Elizabeth.' Finlay was slightly too hearty. 'I was enjoying those a bit more, I have to say.'

'The pink ones.' Ivo picked up the Venetian bowl. 'There are still a few. You haven't picked one out yet, have you, Maggie? Your turn then.'

Jude was about to say something else. Maggie looked at the heap of paper and all at once the nondescript pieces of paper seemed threatening, menacing.

Don't be ridiculous, she told herself. *Don't.*

There were only three pink scraps left. Maggie reached in and grabbed one.

10

Elizabeth, on Lily: She will be a superstar consultant,
solving everything from AIDS to acne.

As Maggie read the words aloud, the room seemed to inhale. When she looked up, Jude's mouth was quivering, thoughts of Finlay and jail clearly forgotten. Ivo was staring up at the kitchen ceiling, eyes narrowed.

'We knew she would come up,' Maggie sounded as if she were protesting. 'She was *there*.'

'Lily,' breathed Elizabeth. 'Lily.'

For a moment, the air danced with memories.

Then Rory stood up. 'To Lily' – he raised his glass – 'To our beautiful girl.'

The words rippled around the room.

'I still don't understand,' Jude said quietly, 'what happened.'

The squeal of brakes filled Maggie's ears again. A black shape, falling. Screams and a train stopped short, halfway down the platform.

'She must…' Ivo wasn't able to find the words. 'She must have just had enough. Everything got too much and she… jumped.'

'We don't know that she did,' Ollie's voice was harsh. 'She could have been pushed.'

'They said it's pointing towards an open verdict,' Rory agreed. 'It was so crowded on that platform. Or she might have been knackered from working so hard. Just tripped.'

The teenagers were insistent that there had been a shove, a push, someone moving fast through the crowd. But they were teenage girls, and you know what they're like. The CCTV was too blurry and the scene was too crowded. February, cold, everyone in coats and scarves and hats. There were hundreds of people: it was impossible to know.

'But, of course, Lily hadn't been happy,' Rory said carefully. 'She hadn't really been happy for a long time, had she?'

Jude opened her mouth as if to say something. Finlay was staring down at his plate, his eyes unreadable.

'No, she hadn't,' said Ayda simply.

Unexpectedly, Maggie felt her eyes prickle with tears.

'It's such a waste,' she said. 'All that energy and enthusiasm and *life*. All gone, just like that.'

'You used to see her a lot, didn't you?' Elizabeth asked. 'Before she died.'

Maggie nodded wordlessly. They had always been close, her and Lily, but the bonds had tightened as others moved on with their lives. As everyone else got engaged and got married, and moved to Wimbledon or Walthamstow or Weybridge, and sprogged up.

As Lily and Maggie were left behind.

Maggie's friendship with Ayda had intensified too, although Ayda and Lily were both so busy with work that it had been rare for all three to meet up.

Memories of Lily flooded the room. Dark hair, wild curls, olive skin, blue eyes. It might be a phone call. 'Mags! Do you fancy Secret Garden Party this weekend? It'll be such fun!'

Or a work crisis. Maggie would go round to Lily's flat to find her cramming for one of her endless exams. Lying on the sofa, half-buried under textbooks. Stuffing her face with Bourbons, cackling at the hopelessness of it all. But she could be tough and brave and determined, too. Running a marathon with her hair scraped back, her legs splashed with mud, her face raw with cold. Dancing on a table afterwards, in the roar of a heaving bar, 'isn't this *amazing*, Maggie? I did it! I actually *did* it!'

Kind, too, mostly, and carelessly generous. When Maggie was dumped by one boyfriend – that relationship had been a long-term one by her standards, almost six months – Lily had turned up with a hamper and champagne and plans for a picnic on Box Hill. When Maggie was stuck in hospital with appendicitis, Lily visited every day with chocolates or silk eye masks or Jilly Cooper. But there were dark times, too. Lonely times. Demons. Times when Maggie banged on the door to Lily's flat and had been sure – *sure* – that Lily was in there. That Lily was in the dark silence, just inches away, unreachable.

A few days later – a few weeks even – Lily would reappear, with muttered explanations.

Work. A cold. A migraine.

Maggie knew that Lily told her about the small problems. The crashed car. The guy who didn't call. The flunked exam that could be retaken soon anyway.

But not the catastrophes. Those Lily dealt with herself, hiding away, buried deep, shamed.

'I can't believe she's gone either,' Jude's eyes were glittering. 'I keep expecting her to walk through the door with some crazy idea. Some mad plan.'

'She was special to you, wasn't she?' said Elizabeth. 'A terrible loss for you, Jude. I am sorry.' Jude inclined her head.

'We were lucky to have Lily in our lives,' said Rory, nodding his head. Politician earnest. 'And we will miss her forever.'

'I can't bear the thought that she killed herself,' said Maggie slowly. 'I can't bear the idea that she was so sad and that she didn't tell anyone about it. That I didn't guess how bad things were.'

'But do you really think she killed herself?' said Jude. 'Really, Maggie? I don't.'

Rory's nod froze.

Jude's eyes were sharper all of a sudden. Watchful. A silence grew and hardened.

'I… I don't know,' Maggie stammered. 'That's what the police seem to think, isn't it? They just can't be 100 per cent sure, because it was all so chaotic on that platform. I know she didn't leave a note or anything like that.'

I can't bear it, Maggie didn't say the words aloud. *I can't bear the idea that someone murdered Lily. It is not bearable.*

'When did you last see Lily before she died?' asked Jude.

'I hadn't seen her for a while,' said Maggie. 'She'd been working such long hours. You know what it was like. We were going to catch up soon though.' Maggie jumped awake some nights, going over and over the conversation that would never be. She had read their last WhatsApp exchanges again and again, as if they might reveal something new.

'I know what her job was like,' said Jude. 'But you're saying that she was completely fine when you last saw her? That there was nothing out of the ordinary?'

'No,' Maggie said. 'But you don't know, do you? You can't know what someone else is thinking. And Lily... she could be quite opaque. It could take her time to... what is this, anyway, Jude? The Spanish Inquisition?'

'So, Lily was completely fine when you spoke to her last?' Jude ignored the jibe. 'She definitely wasn't suicidal?'

The shortest of hesitations. 'Yes,' said Maggie. 'Yes, she was fine.' And it was true in as much as Lily hadn't sounded like someone who was going to throw herself under a train.

There was something close to disappointment in Jude's eyes. For a moment, Maggie thought Jude was going to ask something more, but then she picked up the bottle of wine, dismissing Maggie. There was a second or two of silence. Eyes met and flicked away. Slowly, the evening slid back to amiable chatter. At one end of the table, Ollie started talking about England's chances in some cricket series, Rory at least looked as if he was interested in the middle order selection. At the other end, Maggie picked up the piece of pink paper, Jude's words echoing in her ears.

'A superstar consultant,' Maggie murmured. 'She deserved it.'

Elizabeth shrugged. 'I almost put down violinist. The Berlin Philharmonic. The London Symphony Orchestra.' After the textbooks had been shoved under the sofa, Lily might play the violin, with the precision of a surgeon and a strange sort of magic. Eyes empty, swaying as the bow danced over the strings. Several of them played instruments; it was helpful for Oxbridge applications after all. Maggie hadn't touched her clarinet since leaving school, but for Lily, it was elemental. She started off reading natural sciences – 'my careers teacher told me I'd get in because they were so desperate for girls to do it' – but leaned towards music like a sunflower.

'You and Lily lived almost next door to each other when you were kids, didn't you?' Jude spoke to Ayda.

'We lived on the same road,' Ayda nodded. 'Went to the same school.'

'Weren't your mothers best friends or something?' Jude persisted. 'I thought you practically grew up together?'

'It must have been unbearable for her poor mother, the whole thing,' Elizabeth tried to redirect the conversation. 'Have you seen Lily's mother recently, Ayda?'

'No,' Ayda said. 'Not for a while. I don't go home very often.' Work. She didn't need to complete the sentence for them all. 'Maybe,' Ayda acknowledged slowly, 'I should.'

'How is your father, Ayda?' Maggie asked without thinking.

'He's…' Maggie saw Ayda's face and didn't need the answer. Ayda's father was dying. Cancer, the pancreas, that most agonising of deaths.

'I'm so sorry, Ayda.'

'I still don't understand,' Jude persisted, reaching out for the shred of paper, 'what happened to Lily.'

'Poor Lily.' Ivo, who had bored of Bangladesh's wicketkeeping woes, looked up.

'She said she was so looking forward to this weekend,' said Elizabeth. 'I hadn't seen her for ages, but we were emailing about this weekend not long before she died. She said she couldn't wait to see us all again.'

Maggie stared at her fingers. *No*, she thought. *No, that's not right.* And she fought the journalistic instinct. That urge to be first to speak, to say, 'no, no, *this* is what happened.'

Because of that last conversation with Lily. Those last words, just a few days before she died.

The voicemail first.

Maggie… Maggie, I need to talk to you.

But by the time Maggie had returned the call, Lily had clammed up.

Ignore me, babe, I'm just being daft, tell me what's going on with this new Health Secretary? Is she going to be even worse than the last one?

It was only at the end of the call, when Maggie was chatting cheerfully about Devon – *I can't wait to go back to Wintercross. It's been far too long* – that there had been another pause.

I'm not sure… I'm not sure I'll go, Mags.

You have to! We all promised. It has to be all of us, together.

Maggie, I can't. You don't know…

You'll have a lovely time, Lily. All your old friends.

I can't.

Why on earth not?

Maggie… Maggie, I'm scared.

11

Elizabeth, on Jude: She will have won at least
one Oscar, probably three.

'Well, I won't,' said Jude crisply. 'We know that now.'

The room was silent.

'Sorry,' Elizabeth murmured.

'There's no point in apologising,' Jude snapped. 'It was a nice thing to say twenty years ago.'

Maggie remembered her own apprehension. 'We can't be angry with each other,' she said quickly. 'Not about something we wrote on a whim two decades ago.'

Ivo's eyes were on her. 'Why?' he was laughing at her. 'What on earth did you write, Maggie Fletcher?'

'Nothing serious,' Maggie felt herself blush. 'I can't remember most of my predictions, to be honest.'

'Maggie's right though,' said Rory. 'It was all a long time ago. We can't get angry.'

'I'm not angry,' said Jude, who was angry.

Elizabeth had captured them all on the upswing back then, thought Maggie. The precise moment in the curve where the straight line led all the way to tycoon or Turner Prize, Pulitzer or Prime Minister. They all thought then that their rise would continue at that perfect angle, because getting to Trinity meant everything had been perfect so far, and they hadn't realised that there were a million ways to be knocked off that optimum line. And almost all of them were, in the end.

We were lucky, she told herself, *that we ever had the opportunity in the first place. Even if we squandered it, some of us.*

And she was glad, quietly, that they had almost reached the end of Elizabeth's predictions.

'I'll show you to your rooms,' said Ivo.

Maggie's room was exquisite. The interior designer had evidently been given a free rein. Tiny birds hopped among wild roses on the hand-painted wallpaper, and the huge bed was piled high with white linen pillows. Pale peach roses drifted petals on the dressing table, and a bunch of sweet peas on the fireplace wafted a delightful scent. Heavy, black beams criss-crossed the ceiling.

'The girls get the nice, big rooms,' Ivo had shown them to the spacious bedrooms on the first floor. 'Boys in the attics with Mrs Rochester.'

Maggie's bedroom was above the library. She lay on the bed for a moment, picturing the steps to Ivo's old bedroom. Left, along the corridor, down a couple of steps, then the last door on the left. Although he had probably moved into the master bedroom by now, looking out towards the high moor. It was nearly midnight. She could fall asleep this minute, surrendering to puffs of Egyptian cotton. But, 'back in the kitchen in fifteen,' Ivo had said, as she dropped her bags and admired the pretty curtains. And she couldn't miss a minute.

Maggie forced herself upright, wandering around the room. The ancient elm floorboards creaked under her feet, polished by the centuries. One window looked down the drive, back towards the gatehouse. The walls were remarkably thick here, leaving space for a deep window seat. The other window looked out over a small patch of flat roof. Some long-departed Fitzwilliam with a supreme indifference to Wintercross's medieval beauty had smashed through the granite to create French windows. Anachronistic iron railings had been added, enough to make English Heritage weep.

Maggie threw open the French windows, letting the smell of cut grass drift in. Beyond the balcony, the ground fell away steeply towards the river. There was still the faintest glimmer of blue to the north-west. She sat down on the bed and felt that sense of apprehension flare up again.

And there was something else, too. That sense of picking at a scab that would be best left well alone. She wondered about her own predictions. She couldn't remember everything she had written on those scraps of paper all those years ago, and was worried there had been snags of cruelty in her twenty-year-old self. Too quick, too sharp.

She picked up her phone and tapped in the Wi-Fi code that someone had helpfully printed out and left on the bedside table. It was almost comforting to be pulled back to everyday life. Another email from her news editor; didn't the man ever sleep?

You're in Devon for the weekend, aren't you? Fancy staying on for Sunday night? There's an inquest the editor wants covered. Some girl who died. His wife's a trustee of the charity she worked for or something. You okay to cover it? Tamsin'll sort a hotel.

Sure, Maggie messaged back. The blue gleam in the village square flickered again. *No problem.*

The news editor's message flashed back within seconds. *Arthur can fill you in on the case. He's been on it til now. But I need him in Woolwich for the start of that big terrorism trial on Monday.*

Arthur was the *Post*'s crime correspondent.

No probs.

Maggie peered in her dressing table mirror. Her make-up looked tired. She sent a quick message to Arthur – *I'm in Dartmoor for the weekend… near a dot on the map called Chagford. Ross wants me to cover some inquest on Monday? Says you've been covering it til now. Can you whack over everything I need to know? Cheers!* – and pulled out her make-up bag.

She was stroking on mascara when her phone buzzed. She tapped on Arthur's message. *Funny that you're in Chagford. That's right next to where they found the body.*

A cold finger ran down her spine. Maggie stared at the message, willing it away. *Found the body?* She typed slowly.

The message flashed up a few seconds later. *Yeah. That's what your inquest is about. A bunch of kids found a dead woman on Dartmoor, not far from where you are now.*

12

Jude, on Elizabeth: Elizabeth Randall-Page will
have a beautiful house, with fluffy towels and
everything matching.

Arthur wouldn't mind a call late on a Thursday night, Maggie knew.
He was the most determined of bloodhounds. She pressed buttons and
Arthur answered on the first ring.

'What happened to her?' Maggie asked, without a hello.

'It's not quite clear, pal.' Arthur was eating something. Probably crisps.
'She died back in the winter and you must know what it's like up on the
moors at that time of year. It was just exposure most probably. Or possibly it was a suicide. But she'd been dead out there for long enough that
it wasn't especially clear.'

'Grim.'

'Yup.'

'Where did they find her exactly?'

'Near to something called Barras Tor?'

Barras Tor. The name rang a distant bell. Not far from Wintercross,
Maggie remembered, but much deeper into the moor. 'Who found her?
A dog walker?' It was usually a dog walker. As she spoke, Maggie caught
sight of herself in a full-length mirror. She looked out of place in the
elegance of the bedroom.

'Some kids doing their Duke of Edinburgh hike,' said Arthur. 'They'd
got lost, so they weren't on the usual path.'

'Poor little things. Horrible to come across something like that.'

'Not nice. The parents went tonto, by all accounts, as if someone had left a corpse out there on purpose for them to stumble over.'

'Poor kids. Poor woman.'

Maggie could hear someone bounding down the backstairs. Finlay, it must be, from the speed and energy of the steps.

'The Editor's got a bee in his bonnet about the story because his wife's a trustee of the charity the victim worked for.'

'So don't fuck it up, you mean?'

'So don't fuck it up. And the other thing…'

'What?'

'The police seem a bit more interested in it than you'd expect.'

Maggie hesitated, her fingertips tracing the hand-painted wild roses. 'Weird.'

'Yes. Weird.'

'Send me everything you've got.'

The crisps crunched. 'Will do.'

The phone went dead. Maggie thought again of the blue lights flickering in the darkened square as they'd driven through this evening, of the sprawling bleakness of the moor. Then she scrolled back through the rest of the messages. As always, they were a babble of ideas and rumours and *I need 800 words on the Attorney General's statement asap!* London, two hundred miles to the east, seemed implausible. It was almost impossible to conjure up that ant heap of people.

Maggie peered out of the window. The police must have been up there when the body was first found, somewhere under the vast black sky. She imagined the forensics tent, the quiet busyness, the police tape catching the breeze. It seemed impossible that it had happened just a few miles away, so close to the glory of Wintercross. Maggie stepped away from the window and headed downstairs.

'Guys,' she said, as she walked into the kitchen. 'You'll never guess what.'

The room was a happy babble. Ayda was laughing at something Ivo had said. Elizabeth was at the Aga. Finlay was pouring out more wine as he looked up.

'What?'

'A few months ago, they found a body up near Barras Tor of all places. I just spoke to one of my work buddies about it. Do you remember? Barras Tor was close to where we went that time—'

Her words tore the contented chit-chat to shreds.

'A body?' interrupted Ayda. 'What? Whose? Up on the *moor*?'

'Who died?' asked Rory. 'When? How do you know, Maggie?'

'I don't know much about it.' Maggie faltered. 'The *Post* just asked me to cover the inquest on Monday. Our crime correspondent's sending me his notes.'

'Jesus.' Ivo spoke in a hiss. 'How awful.'

'It sounds as if whoever she was,' Maggie said hesitantly, 'she'd been up there for ages by the time they found her.' They were all frozen in the same position as when Maggie made her announcement. Finlay was still holding the bottle of wine in mid-air.

'Grim.' Ayda pulled a face.

'How utterly horrible,' said Elizabeth. 'How very sad.'

She was used to this, Maggie realised abruptly, and they weren't. To her a murder in Ilford, an arson attack in Sheffield and a multi-car pile-up on the M25 were all part of a normal day's work. She had spent years of her life trawling through the aftermath of death and destruction. Knocking on doors: 'Sorry to bother you…' Waiting for press conferences: 'We are sorry to report…' Sorry, sorry, sorry. To her, a body on the moor was intriguing, rather than shocking.

'It must have been pretty horrible for the kids who found it,' she admitted.

'The kids?' asked Ollie. 'What do you mean?'

'It was some teenagers doing their D of E award who found the body,' said Maggie. 'Apparently.'

'Was it an accident?' asked Elizabeth eventually. 'What happened?'

'Exposure, I think,' said Maggie awkwardly. 'I don't know much yet. Suicide, maybe.'

Elizabeth flinched at the word.

'Grim,' said Ayda again.

'How sad,' said Elizabeth, 'that nobody went looking for her as soon as she went missing.'

'I wonder how long she'd been up there before they found her?' said Finlay.

'It depends on where she was.' Ivo's usual bounce had disappeared. 'Some bits of Dartmoor are so remote that a body could lie undiscovered for years. In other places, a body would be spotted within hours.'

'Depends on the weather too, I guess,' said Finlay. 'There was quite a lot of snow last winter.'

Like a glacier giving up its secrets, Maggie thought, as the ice melted away.

'I would *hate* to find a corpse,' said Elizabeth.

'Horrendous,' Maggie agreed quickly. 'The stuff of nightmares. Those poor, poor kids.'

'They'll probably love telling people,' said Finlay. 'That anecdote would have been pure gold in my playground.'

'When did they find the body?' Ivo, who had spent most of his childhood up on the moor, looked distressed.

'A few months ago. They've just got to the inquest now. Apparently, the police were quite interested in it all. I saw a police car as we came through Chagford, so maybe that was something to do with it.'

'Is there any more red?' asked Ollie. 'That Malbec is quite something.'

But Ivo wasn't ready to go down to the cellar yet. 'It's awful.' His eyes were dark. 'So terrible. I wonder if it's someone local?'

'Have you heard of anyone going missing recently?' asked Finlay. 'That'll be the easiest way to tell, surely?'

'Not that I know of,' Ivo shook his head. 'But I'm not down here very much. I had no idea.'

In the entrance hall, Maggie could hear the walnut grandfather clock striking midnight. Ayda reached for the Venetian bowl and for a moment, Maggie wanted to say, 'no, stop, I've had enough.' Too many secrets, too many cruelties, unfolded one by one. Ayda looked at her as if she could read her mind and then unfolded the paper with slow deliberation.

'Right,' said Ayda. 'The next prediction.'

13

Elizabeth, on Ollie: Ollie will be an estate agent.

After the drama of the body on the moor, the words took a moment to sink in.

'An estate agent?' Ollie blinked at his ex-wife. 'Why the hell did you write that?'

Elizabeth met his eyes with an unwavering stare. 'I suppose I just thought it seemed likely.'

Ollie had gone into the City after university. Manatons, just like Ivo. He planned to move into hedge funds too. All the boys did back then, chasing the millions. And Ollie had made the move from Manatons to a hedge fund, eventually.

'The funds don't all perform though,' Ollie had told Maggie bleakly, drunk in some bar on the Fulham Road. They must have been in their late twenties by then; the faces around them starting to look young. 'Everyone thinks you automatically make a fortune when you work for a hedge fund. And we did raise a decent amount at first, but we were unlucky with a couple of things and now people are pulling their money out left, right and centre.'

'You've still done okay, Ollie.' Maggie had spent the day talking to volunteers in a food bank. To a mother, crying, desperate to feed her four-year-old. She didn't especially feel like holding Ollie's hand as he sulked into his £15 glass of wine. 'To be fair.'

'I mean, yes, sure,' Ollie admitted. 'But it's decent money, rather than spectacular...'

'And you spend it so fast.'

'Well.' A weak smile. 'I suppose so.'

A few weeks later, Ollie's fund closed down.

Ollie never meant to be an estate agent, but one morning, he put on his suit, picked out his tie, and that's what he was.

'But I didn't want to be an estate agent back then,' Ollie stared across the table at Elizabeth.

'I know.'

'Did you always think this is how I would end up?'

There was a glitter in Elizabeth's eyes. 'Quite obviously not, Ollie.'

For a moment, Maggie flashed back to Ollie at freshers' week. He had been wearing a football shirt on that first day, Chelsea blue. Maggie had never seen him wear a football shirt since, not once, not ever. That was Ollie: sharp-eyed. Changing overnight into someone who could almost – but not quite – blend in with the group who talked loudly about holidays in St Tropez or St Moritz or St Barths. The Old Etonians and the Old Wykehamists and the Old Radleians, who all knew each other and knew that Ollie didn't belong.

Grammar school: almost anyone else would have been proud. 'I'm the first,' Ollie admitted to Maggie, once, while very drunk. 'The very first of my family to go to university.'

Feversham & Cecil: that was the name of the agency where Ollie worked, operating in the heart of Knightsbridge. There was nobody there called Feversham or Cecil, and there never had been, but the names sounded right. Maggie had googled them once and their adverts flashed up on her computer for weeks after, the algorithm confused.

Meticulously renovated.

Grade I, stucco fronted.

Exquisitely proportioned, a landmark property.

Just the sort of place a hedge fund manager would buy.

'I hate it,' Ollie had told her at another of Rory's birthdays, three years ago. 'You're within touching distance of all these unbelievable houses, and yet you're nothing to do with them at all. You're constantly...' He searched for the word, 'on the periphery. Part of the bloody entourage.'

'It does sound miserable.'

'And all the rest of them' – Maggie guessed he meant the other agents – 'are so bloody pompous. They behave as if they're part of that world, and then they head home to their two bedder in Hounslow.'

'You're alright though,' Maggie said briskly. 'You and Elizabeth have the house in Clapham.'

Grumpily, 'It's Elizabeth's, really. Her great aunt left it to her.'

Ollie gestured imperiously at the waiter: more wine.

'Luckily for you.'

'It was a wreck when we got it. But I suppose so.'

'Stop feeling sorry for yourself, then.'

'How's work with you?'

'Oh.' A shrug. 'I've been made deputy political editor.'

'That sounds great.' He was kinder than she had been.

'It's okay.'

'You'd have been delighted with that, when we were back at university! Deputy political editor of the *Post*. It sounds so grand, Maggie.'

I would have been, Maggie thought. And didn't say aloud. *And I was when I first got the job. When I thought it was a step to the next thing, whatever that was.*

'Deputy political editor,' Ollie said again, admiring his glass of wine. 'That's great, Maggie. Really great.'

The worst thing was that the job suited Ollie. Maggie imagined him throwing open the double doors to another vast room, *and here we have...* just the right mix of veneration and pomposity. It suited him and that was what hurt the most.

14

Finlay, on Ayda: We'll still be superheroes together.

'What?' Ayda was laughing. 'Superheroes? What are you talking about?'

'Don't you remember?' Finlay had a mock-hurt expression on his face. 'That girl we rescued in my first term at Trinity.'

The body on the moor had disappeared. The room was full of laughter once again.

'Oh God, yes,' Ayda said. 'What the hell was her name? Katie or Katia or something like that?'

'She was so wrecked,' said Finlay. 'Completely out of it.'

'What happened?' asked Ollie. 'I never heard about this.'

'It wasn't a big deal,' said Finlay. 'Ayda, Lily and I were walking home from Cindy's or somewhere, and we came across this girl who was literally *in* one of the flowerbeds in Great Court. She'd been sick everywhere. Lily was also quite wrecked, so she just went to bed. But Ayda and I decided we were superheroes so we picked her up and worked out which was her room and tucked her up in bed. The End.'

'That was nice of you.'

'Yeah,' Finlay looked noble. 'And after that, Ayda and I had this joke about being superheroes. Which obviously meant nothing whatsoever to Ayda.'

'It did!' Ayda laughed at him. 'We can carry on being superheroes again, if you want.'

'If you absolutely *insist*,' said Finlay. 'I've actually brought a Catwoman costume down with me. I take it with me everywhere, in fact. You'll look smoking hot.'

And for a moment, it was as if they were all back at Trinity again. Giggling, mocking, playing at life.

15

Finlay, on Elizabeth: She will be a wonderful florist.

'A florist?' Elizabeth was half-laughing as she turned towards Finlay. 'A *florist?*'

'Well,' he was smiling, half-shrugging. 'I didn't know you very well. And I remember you'd done the flowers so beautifully that evening.'

All of a sudden, the flowers were sharp in Maggie's memory. They were exquisite that night. Maggie had been sent out for the flowers for the dinner party. 'Get lilies,' Elizabeth had ordered. 'White ones. Half a dozen.'

But at the flower stall in the station, Maggie had hesitated. The lilies wouldn't do for this evening. They were just buds, the narrow white heads still closed, blind as newborn puppies. They would need more time to open – slowly, oh so slowly – to their full, sculptural glory. Maggie had stood in the station, lost in flowers. She felt weighed down by the decision. Rebecca red roses. The spiky blue of an iris. A train pulled into the station and a flood of passengers, tired of London, swept past. A few stopped. Carnations for a birthday. Boisterous, congratulatory tulips. Guilty chrysanthemums for a missed train, a kissed lover.

'Can I help you?' The stallholder was tired of Maggie's hovering.

'I'll take the freesias,' Maggie said, coming to.

The flowers were wrapped in silence and brown paper, and Maggie turned towards the terraced house. The rain pattered down. This part of town had been colonised by university students years ago. She walked past rows of workers' cottages. Sullen brick houses filled – now, lifetimes later – with love affairs, and screaming rows, and sloppy, sick-spattered sprawling. What would they make of the students, those old working ghosts? Of the already-regretful half-night stands, and the takeaways and the glittering toothpaste-stained bathrooms?

When Maggie got home, Elizabeth's head turned with a speed that showed that she had been waiting all the time Maggie was out. They had decided to live together some time back in their first year. Ayda and Elizabeth and Maggie. Elizabeth had decided, really. She had found the least damp, least draughty, least woeful cottage and decided it would be their home.

'Where are the lilies, Maggie?'

'They weren't ready. I got these instead. They smell lovely.'

'Oh, Maggie. I asked you to do *one* thing… and God knows where Ayda's got to.'

'Sorry.'

Elizabeth was a flurry of pashmina, grabbing the umbrella that Maggie had forgotten.

'Could you at least tidy the sitting room and lay the table while I'm out?' There was impatience in Elizabeth's voice. Maggie had promised to tidy the sitting room this morning, yesterday, all term. Now Maggie fluffed cushions on the sagging sofa and piled-up books. Mountains of books. A library-full. A sprawling pile of knowledge and imagination, cluttering up the whole room and her whole mind.

'Not now, Maggie,' Elizabeth reappeared with armfuls of roses just as a book was opened, and the pages began to turn. 'It's getting late.'

Maggie sherpaed the books up the stairs and hid them in her bedroom.

The plates were mismatched. Blue and white Wedgwood, utilitarian cream, cheap chipped flowers. The table would sit eight, just, with elbowing and knocked over wine glasses. As Maggie dutifully folded napkins and looked for candles, Elizabeth clattered in the kitchen. The house smelled wonderful. Beef bourguignon? Maggie guessed, hopefully. Potato dauphinoise? Neither of those options would have occurred to her before she met Elizabeth. Maggie couldn't remember her parents ever hosting a dinner party.

Elizabeth poked her head around the kitchen door. 'Can you give the glasses a polish?' In her head, because she always drew a picture to enliven a dull task, Maggie became a housemaid: black dress, white apron, rushing to complete her tasks before her master – a Jane Austen vicar? A Dickensian lawyer? – got home from work.

'Could you do a table plan?' Elizabeth interrupted her thoughts again, definitely not a kindly vicar. Then, 'Don't worry. I'll do it.'

Elizabeth loved giving dinner parties. She enjoyed every step of selecting the guest list, and cooking and making the house as beautiful as it could be, which wasn't very beautiful.

Why the rush? Maggie wondered now. *Why were we always in such a hurry to get on to the next stage?* Because nowadays they ran away to Glastonbury, and drank too much and wore clothes a teenager would laugh at.

'And why the hell did we waste all those years thinking men in their thirties had any appeal whatsoever?' Ayda had grumbled once. 'When there were all those delicious eighteen-year-olds with six packs at our beck and call?'

Elizabeth always loved combing through recipe books, planning the starter and the canapés and the pudding. She loved arranging the flowers best of all. Blushing roses and pale blue delphiniums and fairy-tale tangles of sweet peas. The roses dominated the sitting room that evening: delicate, enchanting, perfect. Making up for the holes in the sofa and the stain on the carpet where Maggie had knocked over a bottle of red.

The freesias were dumped in the kitchen.

And then Lily – thoughtless, careless, generous Lily – had turned up with Jude in tow and spoiled Elizabeth's numbers.

'Jude was meant to go on a date,' Lily announced, when Elizabeth opened the front door, 'but she had a bit of a meltdown so I told her to come here instead.'

Just from her rear view, Maggie could tell Elizabeth was gritting her teeth.

'You must come in,' Rory had insisted. 'We can all squash up. It's lovely to see you, Jude.' And so, Jude had swept in, or been swept in, clutching a bottle of sambuca.

'A florist?' Elizabeth laughed at Finlay now. 'Why would I have been a florist?'

Ayda looked at her buzzing phone. 'I need to take this,' she said briskly. 'Singapore.'

'I'll have a cigarette while you're doing that,' said Finlay, who still smoked when he had drunk enough.

'Can I nick one?' asked Ollie. Elizabeth frowned, before remembering that she didn't care any more.

'Sure,' shrugged Finlay. The two men stood just outside the kitchen door, their smoke whisked away by the breeze.

'I need the loo.' Maggie stood up too. She climbed the stairs to her room, needing a moment of quiet. Out of habit, she flicked through her messages. Arthur had emailed all his notes. Instinctively, Maggie went to read them, but then forced herself to leave it. There would be plenty of time on Monday. Maggie looked out of the window again, gazing towards the moor and feeling a thud of sadness. That poor woman. All at once, her room felt airless and claustrophobic, despite its generous proportions.

Maggie nipped back to the narrow stairs that led down to the snug. Upstairs, she could hear Finlay and Rory mocking each other. As she reached the snug, she could hear laughter from the kitchen. She didn't feel like talking to the others just yet. Dodging the kitchen, Maggie slipped down the corridor to the entrance hall.

Outside, the air was cool, a breeze coming off the moor. At once, Maggie breathed more easily. From inside the brightly lit house, the sky had looked dark. But now the stars glittered as they never did in London. There was the Milky Way, so sharply clear. Maggie wandered away from the front door. Clouds scudded across the sky, but the moon was high, and so bright that Maggie cast a shadow as she crossed the lawn.

Slowly, she became aware of the English summer all around her, a relief after the roar of the capital. The hedgerow to her left was thick with Queen Anne's lace and the small pink rosettes of ragged robin. She caught a waft of honeysuckle. All of a sudden, she knew where she wanted to go. Past the hedges, planted to slow the wild Dartmoor winds. Through the maze-like rose garden. Past the sundial. Across a lawn. Around a corner.

Here.

To the north of the house, the ground fell away, plunging down to the river in its steep-banked valley. But here on a rise a couple of hundred yards to the south of the house, a huge granite boulder, thirty feet tall, jagged up through the lawn. A tor. Lion's Rock, the Fitzwilliams called it, for its strange profile. She knew they came out here in the evenings to watch the sun go down. Pistachios and gin and tonics and the easy digestion of the day.

Maggie clambered up the granite, finding handholds and scrappy footholds. At the top, she sat down and stared up at the stars. She thought she could make out Pegasus and Andromeda, Lyra and Arcturus, but she wasn't sure. The Plough, she knew: prosaic. For a moment, she thought about those ancient astrologers, trying to pin down the future from a flicker in the heavens. Staking it all on the stars.

She heard the sudden clatter of a helicopter. *It might be a police helicopter,* she thought. Maybe it had something to do with the body out on the moor. Although surely they would have everything they needed by now for the woman found months ago. She could just make out green and red lights as the helicopter headed towards Exeter, the sound fading as it thudded away.

Maggie looked towards the moor, imagining the pinpricks of light from the police torches. Although they would probably have brought in arc lights at the time, harsh brightness to light up any clue and blot out all the stars. She peered into the darkness but there was nothing up there now. A cloud blew across the moon and the darkness closed in sharply. A row of beeches fifty yards away disappeared, shapeless and lost in the night. Leaves rustled, the wind picking up. Maggie looked back towards the quiet glow of the house for reassurance.

A movement.

Maggie sat up sharply.

Something had caught her eye. A movement less random than the sway of a branch, or the flutter of a leaf in the breeze. Something somewhere between her and the house. Maggie's eyes swept the darkness again, but there was nothing to see now. The shadows closed in, swallowing her sight. She felt blinded, blunted, an edge of panic creeping up her throat.

Maggie... Maggie, I'm scared.

There isn't anything there, she told herself firmly.

Nothing at all.

There, again: was that a hint of a movement?

'Pagan?' she tried, hoping that the dog would come leaping across the lawn. But her voice disappeared into the darkness and no dog sprang into view. Overhead, the stars twinkled indifferently. There were no neighbours out here, no cheering glow in the distance. She thought she saw another movement. Were those eyes gleaming for a second in the dark?

Moving fast, Maggie slithered down the tor, scraping her elbows and jarring her knee against the granite. She crouched down as soon as she reached the ground. Another movement, even closer now, invisible in the dark.

'Who's there?' Maggie called hoarsely. 'Who is that?'

The wind whipped her words away.

'Is there someone there?' Her voice dissolved into the night, revealing only her fear. Her isolation. And her location. Maggie peered into the blackness. *There's nothing there*, she tried to convince herself. Just darkness, just that flash of old fear.

'Stop messing about,' she called out, trying to sound authoritative. 'I'm not in the mood.'

The silence stretched out. And she was just about to breathe, just about to give herself a shake, *you idiot, there's nothing there at all*, when she heard it. A noise, she was sure of it. Not the wind in the trees, not the cry of an owl. A noise: indistinct and alien to this place.

Someone was there.

Maggie began to walk towards the house. She forced herself to walk slowly, to stay calm. The house seemed so far away now, its lights insignificant under the vastness of the sky.

Not far though.

Not far, don't panic.

She was nearly at the rose garden when there was a sudden snapping noise ahead of her.

Maggie froze.

Someone was there, Maggie was sure. Someone was hiding in the shadow of the hedge, waiting for her to wander into a trap.

There can't be.

There is.

'Who's there?' Her voice sounded high-pitched, terrified. 'Who is it?'
No one answered.

Sudden footsteps, loud in the night.

Maggie ran.

In the darkness, in her panic, the rose garden was a maze. The bushes were thick tangles, looming up unexpectedly. Deep between the hedges, Maggie couldn't make out the lights from the house any more. Disorientated, blinded, she slammed into a line of roses. Thorns snagged her clothes, the scent of the roses were sickly sweet. For a terrifying few seconds, she couldn't go forward, couldn't go back, an animal in a snare.

Maggie forced herself to steady, yanked herself free.

More footsteps.

Now they sounded as if they were coming from a different direction. Surely…

Where…

'Go away!' she screamed. 'Leave me alone.'

Maggie sprinted away from the rose garden, ducking low as she ran across the grass. The ground was uneven under her feet, tripping her, trapping her. She knew she was too loud, too obvious, a blundering target. And now she realised she was further from the house. Further from the laughter and the safety and the friends she loved.

Who? Where?

More footsteps. And a figure, dark on darkness, chasing.

She scurried past another hedge, pushing away the sinking realisation that she was getting further from the house, further from shelter, because there was nowhere else to go in this shadow maze. She thought she heard footsteps just a few yards behind her, and sprinted. The lawn fell away slightly and she crashed to the ground, the roughness tearing at her palms. Then she was up again, racing on. Another hedge loomed up and she threw herself beneath it, surrendering to that animal instinct to hide. Were those footsteps in the distance? Was someone searching? Had they lost her? Maggie burrowed deeper under the hedge, shrinking in. She imagined her eyes, glimmering white in the night, and tucked her head to her chest, almost praying.

Pathetic.

Maggie… Maggie, I'm scared.

She tried to breathe quietly, to fold herself smaller.

No one called out. No, 'Maggie, you idiot, have you got a light on you?' No, 'oi, come on you, it's time for another prediction.'

You're only scaring yourself, she told herself. *It's just your imagination. It's seeing everyone. It's not sleeping.*

And it's Lily… Lily *dying*.

Wintercross does this to you.

Everything was still now, the breeze the only sound.

Or was it a deliberate silence? A careful search of the gardens?

Maggie forced herself to open her eyes. Her eyes were playing tricks on her now, the darkness moving and dancing. There were spots in her vision and it was impossible to tell if there was anything there at all. Maggie closed her eyes again, curled tighter. And just then, somewhere in the distance, she was sure that she heard an angry exhalation of air and the sound of footsteps turning away.

16

Ollie, on Finlay: He'll have shagged a lot of really hot
girls, which is really fucking annoying.

Maggie unfurled herself.

The night was quiet, empty.

She stood up, shaking the crumbs of earth from her trousers, and
listened.

Nothing.

Slowly, stepping clumsily, she made herself start back towards the
house. Nobody waited by the hedges, nobody loitered on the lawn.
Maggie found a gravel path and followed it back to the front door, her feet
crunching loudly. The door stood open; the entrance hall glowing, light-
house safe. Maggie stepped into the hall and collapsed onto one of the
armchairs. She forced herself to breathe slowly, staring at the fire while
she stroked the fabric, embroidered with pink and blue hydrangeas.

'You coming?' When Maggie looked up, Finlay was standing there.
'We're waiting for you.'

'Sorry,' she muttered. 'I thought…'

'You okay?' Finlay looked at her more closely.

She met his eyes for a second. Then, 'I'm fine.'

'Get a bloody move on then,' he grinned at her, turning on his heel.

When she reached the kitchen, they were all back in their places. None
of them could have… she was being ridiculous.

'There you are.' Ivo was pouring more wine. 'We thought we'd have to send out a search party.'

'Where were you?' asked Jude.

'I was just...' Maggie let the words fade as she slipped into her seat. 'Where are we?' she asked.

'You've got a bit of leaf in your hair,' Elizabeth swept it away.

None of the rest of them looked as if they had just been outside, although it was impossible to tell. Cheeks might be reddened by the wine or the cold, and she couldn't think of a way of asking: who wasn't here five minutes ago?

This was meant to be fun, she told herself again.

This was meant to be *fun*.

17

Ivo, on Elizabeth: Princess of Wales. Lady X,
at the very least. The power behind the throne.
And she deserves it, because she is very nice.

'It's so odd, isn't it?' said Jude. 'The idea of the power behind the throne.
All that "behind every great man" crap.'

'Only works if you're behind a great man, anyway,' said Elizabeth,
who was leaning against the Aga, never quite able to sit down and relax.
'Otherwise, it's all a bit of a waste of time.'

'Very nice, though?' Jude raised an eyebrow. 'Our Elizabeth?'

'Shut up!' Elizabeth protested, half-hurt. 'I *am* nice.'

'You are,' Ivo agreed. 'There's always been something old-fashionedly
honourable about Elizabeth.'

Maggie wondered if Elizabeth's charms were more appealing to men
than women. Elizabeth flushed with pleasure.

'You were always,' Ivo insisted, 'very kind to me. You were lovely when
Seraphine and I broke up. I'll always remember that.' Seraphine, Maggie
could remember the sting. Auburn hair, huge green eyes, Yeats quota-
tions floating in her wake. It was the only time she had known Ivo to
be truly heartbroken. He had been bewildered. Stunned that this could
happen to him.

Elizabeth had not been the only woman to appear with a trayful of
brownies.

18

Ayda, on Rory: Happily married, 2.4 children.

The politician's smile, fixed.

'Nearly got there,' he said lightly.

'I'm so sorry.' Ayda clutched her mouth.

'Don't be silly.'

Rory had married Genet just a few years after leaving university. A bit *young*, people would say suspiciously. That was until they met Genet. Genet was tall, carelessly graceful, always smiling. She had grown up in Ethiopia, and flown to England to do her A-levels.

'I did not expect someone like Rory,' Genet had said to Maggie, in mock horror over a coffee. Her pointed chin rested on both palms and long fingers framed her smooth face.

Rory hadn't expected someone like Genet either.

'Terribly *vibrant*,' they said in Somerset, without enthusiasm.

'He's so hideously English,' Genet insisted to Maggie, waving her cappuccino around. 'I expected somebody *fun*.'

But she and Rory were smiling at each other, and when they smiled at each other, it was as if they were the only two in the room. The end came fast. Genet was pregnant, twins. But one morning, Finlay called Maggie, panicking, trying to find Lily. *I need to speak to Lily. We're in hospital... But we need her. Can you come too, Maggie? Rory... I don't know...*

A heart attack, out of the blue.

'Peripartum cardiomyopathy,' Finlay recited in the waiting room when Lily sprinted in. As if the proper medical name might make it survivable, treatable. Although by then a doctor had come to tell them that she was dead, that there was nothing they could do. Dead, such a blunt word for the beautiful, laughing Genet. The twins might have survived if they had been able to operate fast enough, Maggie learned later. But they hadn't, so they didn't. The twins died with her.

'Her name meant heaven,' Rory said in his eulogy. 'And she could not have had any other name.'

Maggie had watched Rory speak, slowly, precisely. His eyes stayed on the organ at the back of the church for every word of his speech. Not once did he look at the congregation, and not once did he hesitate.

19

Finlay, on Jude: Still partying like a mad thing.
Will hopefully have grown back her hair.

The mood lifted.

'Oh my God, yes,' Ayda cracked up. 'Do you remember, Jude? You'd just cut off all your hair.'

'Was it for a part or something?' asked Ollie. 'I can't remember.'

'Not that you didn't look good,' said Finlay hastily. 'But, you know, you had such lovely long hair. And… well…'

Jude had shaved her head not long before that dinner, Maggie remembered. Appeared one day, with a chin-up defiance. They had all done idiotic things with their hair back then. The boys had experimented with misguided facial hair. Maggie had cut her hair short, hoping to look like a *Sliding Doors* Gwyneth Paltrow, and stared in the mirror with a sinking heart.

'Maybe I liked it like that,' Jude tossed her head and pushed back the mass of dark red hair that was coming loose from her feathery headpiece.

'You looked ravishing,' Maggie soothed.

'Do we think it's time for bed?' Elizabeth asked hopefully. Everyone ignored her.

'I always thought you were gorgeous,' said Finlay. 'The hair was just a shock.'

'My mother hated it,' Jude said bleakly. 'She looked up when I got home for the holidays and said, "Oh good, you've got a contraceptive haircut. That's one thing less to worry about."'

'She was a bitch,' said Ayda thoughtfully.

'She was,' Jude agreed. 'She really was.'

20

Maggie, on Ivo: Will still be too cool for school.

'Whaaat?' but it was a pretend outrage.

'Ha, you *were*, Ivo. You know it.'

Maggie remembered staring at the piece of paper on the wine-stained, too-small dining table, trying to think what on earth to write about Ivo. All those emotions swirling inside her, far too much for a scrap of paper. She had bottled it in the end. Picked something anodyne, unremarkable.

'Course you were,' Ayda joined in. 'With your *gap yah* wall hangings and all that weed.'

'We all took bloody gap years,' Ivo laughed.

'Almost all,' said Jude.

Maggie hadn't. She'd spent the summer before university working in a petrol station just off the M25.

'We *all* thought we were so cool back then,' Ivo was grinning.

Had they? Maggie didn't remember that.

'No, we didn't.' Ollie rolled his eyes. 'And the NatScis, the Mathmos…' Ollie always adored Cambridge slang. Natural Scientists, Mathematicians, but only for those who knew. 'That lot barely left their rooms. The engineers weren't much better.'

'Some of the mathmos were proper geeks,' said tough, physical Finlay.

'They really were.' Ayda, smug in her own coolness.

'Rob Chambers. Hui Fen,' Ollie listed them. 'What's-his-name – Aidan Gardiner – he's also made a sodding fortune. Rowan Parker. And…'

A sudden silence fell over the table. They all knew which name came next.

'And Mike,' Elizabeth's voice was quiet. 'Mike Jansen.'

The name fell into the silence.

Mike Jansen.

Everyone in their year would always remember Mike.

A mathematician, walking back to Trinity after a meeting with his supervisor. The meeting had been late, followed by a quick drink or two at a nearby pub. Then back through the common, along the river path. A bit drunk, probably; a bit naïve, definitely. An attack. An unusually brutal one, the police concluded later. Much later, that was, when his body was fished out of the river.

'They never found out who did it, did they?' Maggie felt the memory of that fear creeping across her throat.

'Town and gown,' Ayda said. 'There were always tensions, don't you remember?'

'Yes,' said Maggie. 'But never anything else like that.'

She remembered the shock as the story spread around the halls. *Have you heard? Did you know?* Girls weeping, although they barely knew him. *I was in the queue right next to him in the canteen the day before, you know? The girl in front of us got the last veggie burger.* Half enjoying the drama. Because no one *died* back then. They were teenagers, practically immortal. There had been one girl at Maggie's school. *Leukaemia, so awful, two years above me.* But basically, death happened to other people. So, for weeks, they talked about nothing else.

Death had given Mike a glamour he certainly hadn't had before. Gingery hair, a weak mouth, glasses. His photograph peered shyly from the student newspaper week after week. The dons eulogised his mathematics ability. *A once in a generation mind, would have changed how we understood...* Had he been that good? Maggie had been to the aftermath of a thousand tragedies now, and the superlatives were always the same. *He was the kindest man, she was my very best friend; RIP cheekiest chappy, never ever forgotten.* Do not speak ill of the dead, that oldest of superstitions.

For months, they had all imagined it. The shock, the punch. Down on the ground, screaming with pain and fear. Kicks to the kidneys, the stomach, the neck. Begging, 'why me, why me, why?' The creeping realisation: they're not stopping. You're not meant to survive this. Because now you're down, and now you're dying. The foot draws back, comes forward even faster, and the lights go out with a snap. They imagined it so often that they knew what had happened.

But also, they didn't know. Because the running club had gone up and down the river path at dawn, long before anyone made out the shapeless shadow in the water, and the police could never decipher the mangle of footprints.

Most of all: *it could have been one of us. I walk along that river path all the time, you know? It could have been* me. The whispers had gone on and on.

He was the first, Maggie thought, the first to fall off that perfect trajectory.

He was the first to die.

21

Maggie, on Elizabeth: Beth will regret not working.

Beth. Maggie hadn't used the nickname for years. Elizabeth suited her better.

There was hurt in Elizabeth's eyes as she looked towards Maggie. 'What did you mean by that, Maggie?'

'Nothing,' Maggie muttered. 'Nothing at all. I'm sorry.'

Trinity, she thought, had taught them to value intelligence above all else. Wit. Cynicism. All the way through, they had attacked each other with sharp humour. It was only later that they had learned to value kindness. And some of them still hadn't. The predictions had been a chance to show off their foresight, their acumen, and they had taken that seriously. None of them had given a moment's thought to the sting when they read it twenty years later. Twenty years was impossible to imagine anyway. Unthinkable.

'I never meant not to work,' insisted Elizabeth.

That was a lie, Maggie thought. Although it was possible that Elizabeth had believed her own lie. 'I'm sorry,' she said again.

Elizabeth had wanted to get married, all the way along. It was an old-fashioned ambition, and one she had kept to herself. But Maggie had known. Elizabeth wanted the rosy-cheeked children, and the crumpets for tea and the sound of the car in the drive: Daddy's home! Dinner at 7.30. A G&T waiting, with the ice clinking with promise. For Elizabeth, the dinner parties were a rehearsal for the lifelong performance that would start soon. A rehearsal dinner. She had read History of Art: long hours of staring thoughtfully at Monets and Turners and Vermeers, and modelling herself vaguely on one of the Wyndham sisters.

'Why did you come to uni at all?' Maggie had asked her once, when Elizabeth was quite drunk by her standards. 'If you don't really want to work?'

'I want to be educated,' Elizabeth answered. 'I want to *know*.'

'And it would be a safety net,' added Maggie, 'in case it doesn't work out.'

Elizabeth didn't answer. To her – the trapeze artist, smiling and swinging – falling was unimaginable. She didn't need a safety net.

Maggie had wondered if Elizabeth saw university as a distraction – *watch the birdie* – so she could never be accused of being a gold digger. Or maybe it was the hunting ground, and the long blonde hair and the pale blue eyes were her camouflage. Elizabeth hadn't gone out with Ollie at university. That privilege had been reserved for the scion of a Gloucestershire baronet. Aubyn or Aubrey? Something like that. But Aubyn or Aubrey had bolted not long after they all left university, probably after one too many hints. A few years later, Maggie saw the announcement in *The Times* of his engagement to the daughter of some French count, and felt a pang on Elizabeth's behalf.

'I worked after university,' Elizabeth persisted.

At Sotheby's, said no one aloud. Smiling sweetly at the prospective purchasers of a string of grand masters. The Sotheby's salary was pin money, but Elizabeth's parents always helped out. Still did, as far as Maggie knew. But there were no proposals. And Ollie, the Manatons banker, gained a certain appeal.

Several women from their year had stopped working now anyway, felled by little Otto and little Ava. They'd been told they could have it all, but not that it would kill them.

'Well, do you?' Jude asked bluntly.

'What?'

'Regret not working?'

'Of course not,' said Elizabeth. 'I'm very busy with my exercise and my volunteering and everything else. I'm very happy with my life.'

22

Lily, on Ayda: Our mothers will be comparing
and contrasting our grandchildren.

Maggie felt her heart twist as she caught sight of Lily's handwriting on the small piece of paper.

Lily had always teased Maggie about reading English.

Compare and contrast the presentation of love in the following poems…

Compare and contrast the Macbeth marriage with the relationship between Othello and Desdemona…

Compare and contrast the deaths of Ophelia and Juliet…

The great works reduced to formulaic essays, quotes to be ticked off.

The echo of the exam hall rang down the years.

Abruptly, Maggie was back in the library, Lily running in late, squeezing past a row of disapproving chair backs towards the empty seat next to Maggie.

'God, I'm *so* hungover that I couldn't face the lab this morning. But I've got *so* much to do.' Lily proffered a paper bag of penny sweets, picking out a miniature Coke bottle for herself with an untrammelled delight. Maggie grabbed a sherbet. 'What are you working on?' Lily hissed at Maggie, pulling a heavy biology tome towards her.

'*Lucky Jim.*'

'That's not *work*. Oh God, my head.'

'What were you up to last night?' Out of the corner of Maggie's mouth.

'Ayda's dad took us out to dinner.' Lily's voice was too loud, earning a glower from the librarian. She popped a bright yellow and white egg into her mouth. 'Bassel Nassar is so cool, you know? He took us out to the Marchmont and we had loads of champagne. Then me and Ayda went on to Toxic8, and… well.'

'Sounds fun.' Maggie wished she'd ignored her essay crisis and gone out too.

Living only a few hundred yards apart in Surrey, Ayda's family – the Nassars – had always been generous towards Lily's mother. Lily's father had disappeared before memory began, but the Nassars helped fill in the gaps.

Ayda's mother – Fiona, that was it – used to drive both girls back to university at the start of term. Mr Nassar might pick them up at the end of it. Bassel Nassar was a property developer, throwing up identikit houses at a safe distance from the expensive part of Surrey, where he himself lived in neo-Palladian splendour. Fiona Nassar had given up her job as a primary school teacher and now did a lot for children's charities. She wore her hair in an elegant blonde bob – not a strand of grey permitted – with large pearl earrings. On regular visits to Cairo, she suffered rather than enjoyed Bassel Nassar's large and boisterous family. Ayda was the treasured child, the golden girl who had triumphed at everything. Trinity was merely to be expected.

Lily's mother – always Stella, never Mrs Blake – appeared only occasionally in their university lives, always beautifully, if eccentrically, dressed. Maggie remembered Lily performing in a string quartet once with Stella weeping in the audience.

That day Stella had worn a long, violet dress, delicate as cobwebs, with masses of thin gold chains around her neck. As the music reached its zenith, Stella tried – somewhat ineffectually – to wipe away the mascara tracking down her cheeks. One of the fathers, a row away, whisked out a silk handkerchief. 'Keep it, I insist,' adoringly, and in that moment, Stella was all Maggie aspired to be.

Afterwards, Stella insisted on taking Maggie and Lily out for tea. They went to the only elegant cafe in Cambridge, with Stella perching on a little chair upholstered in pink satin. Stella insisted that Maggie and Lily had big creamy eclairs and exquisite little macaroons, but refused to touch anything herself.

'Il faut souffrir pour être belle,' Lily recited the words she had heard a million times, rolling her eyes at her mother, half-laughing. They had the same blue eyes, the same tilt of the head as they laughed.

You have to suffer to be beauty, Maggie translated laboriously in her head.

'I know that you're happy buried in your laboratory, Lily,' Stella shook her head pertly, 'but I, for one, appreciate beauty.'

'I enjoy beauty too,' Lily insisted. 'It's just that I like fun too.'

But they smiled at each other, enjoying each other's company. So alike, although where Stella's hair was elegantly styled, Lily's was allowed to bounce in cheerful corkscrews. Where Stella's make-up was immaculately painted on, Lily had slapped on some moisturiser and hoped for the best. Stella's nails were a perfect polished red. Lily's nails were bitten to the quick. Stella smiled at her daughter, with a look that was halfway between delight and disapproval.

Not that there was any chance of Stella's delicate glamour transmitting to Maggie either. On a student diet of Pot Noodles and Bacardi Breezers, Maggie thought of herself as robust, sturdy, with brown hair liable to frizz in the rain. Back then, she plastered on foundation to hide the occasional spot, and wore – she now realised – far too much eyeliner, unevenly applied. Looking back at old photographs, she was surprised by her own teenage beauty and wished she had recognised it at the time.

Of course, none of them placed any value in the allure of youth back then. It was a buyers' market for leggy, smooth-skinned dewiness. Everyone had it; it was quite ordinary.

'I hope there is a parallel world somewhere' – there was a shine in Elizabeth's eyes, unreadable – 'a different universe, where Mrs Nassar and Mrs Blake are comparing and contrasting their grandchildren.'

'She's *Miss* Blake,' Ayda's voice cut through the sentimentality. 'Lily's mother never married.'

'She's still beautiful now though,' Ollie reminisced. 'Lily's mother.'

'She even looked beautiful at the funeral,' said Elizabeth.

The crematorium in Leatherhead – 11 a.m. precisely – had seemed an unlikely final resting place for Lily. It had been one of those cold spring days, when it felt as if summer might never arrive. There were pools of dying daffodils along the crematorium drive and a shiver in the air.

They had chatted awkwardly in the car park, waiting for the 10.30 a.m. mourners to pour out the back door. There was an entrance and an exit, both firmly signed: a conveyor belt of grief to avoid an uncomfortable collision between pink balloons and coral tutus and long, black coats and veils.

In the crematorium, waiting for the service to begin, Maggie felt a flood of envy for the couples, sitting down around her. These were little teams – united – with partners to hold hands and sympathise. She watched Finlay put an arm around his girlfriend's shoulders, hugging her closer for a second as she nodded, teary-eyed, across the aisle to Rory.

They didn't all make it. Ayda: work crisis. Ivo: stuck in Hong Kong.

A moment later, Maggie felt a surge of shame for even thinking about her own loneliness as Stella walked to the front of the room.

Although Elizabeth had changed the locks on Ollie by then.

And Finlay and the girlfriend had split up a couple of weeks later, anyway. His girlfriends never lasted.

'Your parents didn't make it to the funeral, did they?' Elizabeth said to Ayda.

'They were away,' said Ayda. 'A cruise in the Caribbean. They were sorry to miss it.'

Although Maggie could never work out what Mrs Nassar and Stella Blake would have had in common anyway.

'It is so important,' Elizabeth said, 'to say goodbye.'

23

Rory, on Jude: Will live in a whirl of glamour
and will have found a way to be happy.

'Oh, thank you, darling.' Jude looked close to tears. She was drunk, Maggie realised. Heading towards maudlin.

'You were always going to live a glorious life, Jude,' Rory gave her a reassuring smile. 'Always.'

'Pure glamour,' Jude pouted. 'That's me.'

A memory flashed through Maggie's mind: Jude, nineteen, running through the rain in her May Ball dress, glitteringly happy. Wrapped in Rory's dinner jacket, with Great Court glorious around her, a perfect sort of glamour.

But that was twenty years ago.

'And I hope you are happy too, Jude,' Rory spoke earnestly.

'I am,' Jude insisted. 'I am, I am, I am.'

There was a brief silence.

'I'm exhausted,' said Elizabeth. 'I need to go to bed soon. Such a long drive.'

But no one followed her lead. Ivo had made some very strong coffee.

'I thought that we should have a bonfire,' Ivo said slowly. 'For Lily.'

'Now?' Elizabeth looked at the clock. It was almost two o'clock in the morning, the brief darkness of the summer night pressed up against the window. Nobody had bothered to close the curtains. 'It's a bit late, isn't it?'

'Let's,' Jude was on her feet. 'We need something to remember her. To commemorate.'

'Vereker cut back the hedges earlier in the year,' said Ivo. 'There's a massive pile of branches down by the old chapel. We could light them, watch them burn. We always had big bonfires at Wintercross. Do you remember when—'

Ivo's enthusiasm spread through the group. But Maggie could only remember the body out on the moor, the footsteps out in the night, and found herself cowering at the thought.

'I'm not sure—' she began.

But she was bundled into her coat, part of the flurry heading towards the door.

'I'll find some torches,' said Ivo.

'We should take a couple of predictions,' said Elizabeth. 'But don't take the whole bowl, Ivo, or they'll just blow away.'

Ivo grabbed a small handful, stuffed them into his pocket. 'Let's go.'

Outside, a cold wind swept across the lawn.

'This way.' Ivo strode off.

They followed him along the winding path. Ivo's torch picked out bracken unfurling among the old hazel coppices, and the gorse, dense and black. Along the path, ponies had cropped the grass short. Beyond the torchlight, the darkness waited.

The old chapel stood in a patch of moorland a few hundred yards to the north-east of the house. Built on a small patch of flat ground halfway down a steep-sided valley, it looked towards the meanders of the river. Dreamed up by some long-dead Fitzwilliam, the little chapel's proportions had been miniaturised. Despite its name, it was a folly rather than a church, crumbling to ruins now. Most of the roof had collapsed years ago, and the top of the little steeple had tumbled away. The spiral staircase that climbed the steeple was too narrow for an adult, and the door to the little nave only reached Maggie's shoulders. Blackthorn, spiky and impenetrable, had grown up in Sleeping Beauty banks around the small building, leaving only a narrow path through. Beyond the chapel, Maggie could remember the ground falling away sharply to the river, and its golden, peaty depths.

'I used to play in the old chapel as a child,' said Ivo, as they walked out along the narrow path. 'Then run down to the river for a swim.'

'It must have been wonderful growing up here,' said Maggie.

'It was,' he grinned, 'apart from the ghost.'

'The ghost?' she asked, before the memory loomed.

'You remember.'

'I do.'

A sideways smile. Then Finlay shouted something back over his shoulder and Ivo broke into a jog, catching up with him and Rory and breaking the spell.

Maggie found herself walking next to Elizabeth. 'I'm sorry,' said Maggie. 'About the not-working thing earlier.'

'Oh,' Elizabeth gestured. 'It doesn't matter. And you were right, after all, as it turns out.'

'Will you go back to work? Now you're...'

'Divorced? I don't know. Maybe. I don't even know what I'd do, nowadays. Your job's kept you up to date with everything, hasn't it? But I feel as if I'd go into cold water shock. All those millennials or Gen Z or whatever they all are. Wearing all our old clothes with such irony.'

'Combat trousers and butterfly hairclips?'

'Handkerchief tops and baguette bags? Exactly.'

'You'd be fine, honestly.' Maggie was watching Ivo laughing with Finlay and Rory. 'You'd pick it up in no time. It's weird seeing everyone, isn't it?'

Elizabeth nodded. 'Brings back all sorts of memories.'

'I hadn't thought about Mike Jansen for years, for example.' Maggie stopped to disentangle herself from a bramble wand that was tearing at her top. 'Poor Mike.'

'I had,' said Elizabeth unexpectedly. 'His twin sister showed up out of the blue a few months ago.'

'Really?' asked Maggie. 'How random. I didn't even know he had a twin sister.'

'It *was* random. She just pitched up at the house in Clapham one day.'

Maggie stopped in her tracks. 'Why on earth did she do that?'

'She just wanted to talk about Mike.' Elizabeth didn't seem to notice Maggie's abrupt halt. 'His death devastated her family, of course. I can't even imagine...'

'No,' Maggie shook her head, started walking again. 'Unbearable.'

In the darkness, she couldn't make out Elizabeth's expression.

'She told me she had taken off to Africa as soon as she'd graduated,' said Elizabeth. 'Kenya or somewhere like that. Just had to get out of the UK and go and do something completely different.'

'You can see why you'd want to,' said Maggie. 'When something like that happens.'

'Yes,' said Elizabeth. 'But now she was back and wanted to talk to anyone who had memories of Mike.' Elizabeth had picked up a stick and was swishing away fronds of bracken.

'I didn't know that you did.' Again, Maggie pictured Mike. Diffident, awkward, shying away from the crowds of raucous undergraduates. A sense of intelligence that was almost other-worldly.

'I didn't really. Mike and I volunteered at a homeless shelter together once, and that was about it. I think she was basically just working her way through the alumni list,' said Elizabeth. 'Poor girl. I'm surprised she didn't pitch up on your doorstep.'

'Maybe she didn't want the whole thing rehashed in the *Post*.' Maggie stumbled over a rabbit hole. 'People can be wary.'

'So horrendous, the whole thing. But it was quite interesting talking to her about it, if I'm honest. How it had affected her. How she remembered him. Apparently, Mike was a bit broken-hearted just before he died. He was really into some girl, who'd seemed keen and then gave him the brush-off. Helen was asking about her, but I just couldn't remember anything else about him, least of all who he'd fancied.'

'It's so strange, isn't it?' said Maggie. 'The way his story just stops on some muddy riverbank and that's just the end of it. None of us would have predicted that, would we? On our little pieces of paper.'

'I don't know,' said Elizabeth. 'I suppose statistically, it wasn't implausible that… oh, look, Maggie. We're there.'

24

Ollie, on Maggie: Underpaid journalist.

It was Finlay who lit the bonfire, crouching down with a practised efficiency. A small flame crackled along the newspaper and twigs, before roaring up through the piles of branches.

'I'm cold,' Elizabeth rubbed her hands together.

'You won't be,' Finlay promised, 'in a second.'

'You see,' said Ollie. 'I guessed pretty well for you, Maggie.'

'Did you just predict everyone's salary?' Maggie threw the piece of paper on the burgeoning fire and pulled a face at him. 'So tedious.'

'Well,' said Ollie, 'it's not a terrible way of working these things out. Figuring out where we'd all be, who we'd all be, what we'd be.'

'But it is,' Maggie insisted. 'It *is*.'

Finlay threw a big clump of ivy on the fire and the flames leaped up like a demon summoned from the earth. The raging flames lit the trees orange, and shadows danced on the crumbling walls of the old chapel.

'*The graces, my friend*,' Rory murmured, '*have abandoned the earth*.'

It was Jude who started to dance before the fire. Slowly at first, her arms reaching towards the sky.

'Lily!' She shouted, long, singing syllables, 'Liiiii – ly.'

In one hand, she held a bottle of vodka, taking occasional swigs. The others watched her dance and twirl, then Finlay caught her mood and started capering towards her. Jude handed him the bottle and he took a gulp.

'You mad girl,' he shouted.

'Our phoenix,' Jude tipped her head back, raging at the stars. 'Rising from the flames. Our beautiful girl.'

It was Ivo who started to clap, then Jude to sing. Not words, but a strange sort of lament. Finlay joined the clapping and slowly they all began to move. Self-consciously at first, then with more abandon.

The lament shaped into a chant – Lily, Lily, Lily – and the urgency spread.

Maggie found herself dancing around the flames; turning, shimmying, whirling. The years fell away. Ollie grabbed her hands, spinning her around and around. The chant grew. One moment, they were professionals, down for the weekend. The next, the mask had split. Ayda was spinning, leaping, a sprite in the forest; Ivo followed her, hurling himself into the air. The wilderness embraced them.

'LIIII – LY, LIIIII – LY!' The chant echoed among the trees. Defying life and its sorrows. Defying death and the years gone forever. Rory hurled another branch on the fire and sparks erupted into the air. Maggie pirouetted and sprang. Only Elizabeth watched them, uncertain.

When Jude took another swig of vodka, Elizabeth's voice cut through the howls. 'Don't you think you've had enough, Jude?' Without looking at her, Jude hurled the open bottle of vodka into the fire. There was a roar and the flames surged higher, tinged with blue.

'Jude!' Elizabeth squawked.

Ivo careened towards Maggie. In the blaze of the fire, he was a devil, face glistening, eyes wide. For a second, he threw his arms around her, hot from the dance, and then he was away again, colliding with Finlay, rolling him into some sort of hug. Until finally, they slowed, the tempo easing. The dance became gentler, more deliberate. One by one, they collapsed on the mossy ground next to the fire, exhausted. The centre of the bonfire was a mass of writhing scarlet.

'Anything can happen,' Jude muttered with satisfaction. She grabbed a bottle of red wine off Finlay and drank deeply.

'You crazy girl,' said Ivo.

'Lily and I would dance together for hours.' Jude gazed into the twisting heart of the fire, her voice sinking to a whisper. 'I need to know what happened to her. I need to know who killed her.'

25

Rory, on Elizabeth: Elizabeth will have lots of
gorgeous children with a very nice man.

Elizabeth read the words aloud. Then, without looking at Rory, she cast the piece of paper into the remains of the bonfire. It caught immediately, flaring brightly, then curling and crumbling to ash.

We took it for granted, thought Maggie. We took it all for granted. That most basic of predictions, unfulfilled.

'Well,' Elizabeth kept her voice light, somehow. 'We certainly tried.'

It was the only time Maggie had ever seen Elizabeth cry. At someone's wedding when Genet had turned up with a curve to her belly, glowing with joy. Elizabeth had joined in with the squeaks of excitement, of course, politely. But Maggie heard her murmur, *I've just got to…* Maggie had followed her towards the Ladies, but Elizabeth had dived off down a service corridor, bumping off walls, blinded by tears.

'Here,' Maggie had grabbed her, dragged her into a room. The hotel laundry, it turned out. Formica floors and neat piles of folded sheets, providing an inappropriate air of domesticity. Elizabeth held on to one of the shelves and leaned forward, arms rigid, eyes shut. Her whole body was stiff. A shiver started in her knees and spread. She made no effort to wipe away the tears that tracked down her cheeks.

When Elizabeth spoke, her voice was tight, controlled. 'I don't know,' she said, 'how to bear it.'

'I'm so sorry, Beth.'

'We've tried and tried,' Elizabeth spoke to the folded sheets. 'IUI, IVF, all the bloody initials. None of it works, *none* of it. Ollie and I… I don't think it will ever happen now. And none of it makes sense without it… nothing about my life makes *sense*.'

The words faded.

After a moment, Elizabeth straightened up. She stared at the top sheet, neatly folded and smudged with make-up, then she picked it up and hurled it with a shocking violence into the pile of dirty laundry. She pulled out her compact and began, briskly, to repair the tear stains.

'How are *you* though, Maggie?' Quick bursts of eye contact. 'I haven't seen you for *far* too long. Doesn't Amelia look *beautiful* today?'

Maggie thought about the hotel laundry when Elizabeth told her, mouth tight, 'Ollie's moving out.' But she didn't say anything because Elizabeth's eyes were dark with sadness and there were shadows beneath them.

'Sorry,' Rory murmured now, eyes on the bonfire.

'It's hardly your fault.' Elizabeth's laugh was almost a sob. 'We all just assumed, didn't we?'

Elizabeth had set out her timetable to Maggie while they were still at university, lolling in front of the fire in that shabby worker's cottage. Married at twenty-six, first baby at twenty-eight, second a couple of years later. 'Maybe a third, we'll see how we go. Not four though, that's just too many and you have to get one of those hideous people carriers.' All done and dusted well before the unimaginable thirty-five.

Elizabeth, the third of four daughters, with a son-hunting father. The clever one, in a family indifferent to intelligence. Her three sisters had made excellent marriages, stitched together with careful industry. There were flurries of nephews and nieces now, the grandparents delighted. Not carrying the family name, of course. But. Still. Lovely little things.

Once, when doorstepping an adulterous MP in Clapham, Maggie had popped to a nearby cafe for a two-minute sandwich. Elizabeth had been in the cafe with one of her nieces: blue eyes, blonde ringlets. And Maggie had known – just *known* – that Elizabeth was pretending that the little girl was her daughter. That Elizabeth was hoping that everyone in the cafe was assuming that she was the mother. Look at those two together: blonde, perfect, happy.

Maggie backed out of the sandwich shop, scuttled to the one next door.

In the end, Elizabeth had married Ollie at twenty-eight, not long after that announcement in *The Times*.

'I never realised,' Ayda sounded shattered. 'I'm so sorry, Elizabeth. And Ollie, of course.'

For a second, Maggie's gaze landed on Ollie. He was staring at the glow of the bonfire, eyes hooded. He looked very bleak, very sad. He couldn't look at Elizabeth, Maggie realised. Couldn't bear her sadness as well.

'It's odd, isn't it?' Elizabeth prodded the fire with a stick, sending up a shower of sparks. 'How almost none of us have children.'

A quiet exhalation from Rory.

'If they did, they probably wouldn't have made it along for this weekend,' Ivo tried to jolly things up. 'They'd be stuck at home, watching boxsets. My friends with kids never get a whole weekend away.'

His words fell into an awkward silence.

You're only forty, Maggie thought savagely. And a man. You've got *decades* yet.

Although he wasn't wrong about the boxsets. Maggie was used to losing friends to parenthood. Recognising the end as soon as it was announced with a cute little photograph on Facebook. "We're expecting," in bright bubble letters over a photograph of a scan, the husband pulling a shocked face, *nudge nudge*. Or a snapshot of a pair of Oxfords, a pair of stilettos and a tiny pair of cream booties. Quite often, the last time Maggie saw the mother-to-be was at the baby shower. Not a deliberate choice but an unavoidable reality. The exhaustion at first. And then later both sides envying the other's greener grass.

A flicker of flame was edging up a branch, devouring dried leaf by dried leaf.

'Only Finlay,' said Ollie. 'Finlay has a child.'

And he barely sees her, the words went unsaid. *Mia, that was her name,* Maggie remembered with an effort. And her mother was Hailey or Halley, and not a fan of Finlay's. 'We weren't in a relationship, exactly.' Finlay, at one of Rory's birthdays, with a schoolboy look that he was too old for. 'I never said we were exclusive.' Hailey or Halley and Mia lived somewhere near Tidworth. Not far from the Army base where Finlay had been billeted for a few months a few years ago.

'I see her as often as I can,' Finlay said defensively, prodding the bonfire. As the fire was dying down, the darkness was pressing closer.

'How old is Mia now?' Ayda asked, putting him on the spot deliberately.

'Seven,' but his eyes had flickered, the giveaway. He picked up another armful of dry wood and flung it roughly onto the fire.

'What a lovely age,' said Maggie tonelessly. Somewhere in the woods, an owl was calling to his mate.

'None of us make things, do we?' Ayda stretched out her legs. 'Nothing solid, I mean. Nothing you can *touch*. Maggie writes words that are obsolete within hours. Ivo moves money around. Ollie sells houses. Rory... talks a lot. I tinker around with deals, quibbling over commas and quarrelling over clauses, while someone half a mile away does their level best to undo whatever it is I am trying to achieve. And what will we all have to show for it in the end?'

'What would you have us do instead?' There was a sneer in Ollie's voice. 'Weaving? Pottery, maybe? A bit of light carpentry?'

Deep in the bonfire, a branch snapped in a shower of sparks.

'That's the twenty-first century for you,' said Jude.

'What do you actually do these days?' Ayda turned to Jude, half-curious, half-derisive. 'I've lost track.'

'I did a ski season last winter, actually, working as a chalet girl,' Jude said too brightly. 'Verbier. So much fun. Buggered up my Achilles, so I flew home early, but it was brilliant until then.'

'And now?'

'I'm working in a bar at the moment,' Jude met Ayda's eyes truculently. 'Near Highbury. It's very nice, actually. You should come by one day.'

There was the briefest of pauses.

'Which one?' Rory asked. 'I'll definitely pop by.'

And Jude smiled at him, shakily.

26

Ayda, on Jude: She'll still be depending on her
looks, and they will be fading.

'You bitch,' Jude spat, as Ivo finished reading the words. 'You absolute *bitch*.'

Jude was on her feet, the fury arcing through her. Finlay – always the first to sense a fight – straightened up from the bonfire and tried to put an arm around Jude that was half comfort, half restraint. But Jude shook him off, pacing towards Ayda.

'You fucking cow.' Jude's voice was low, feral. The smoke blurred the scene, but there was something in Jude's movement – a rage, an animal fury – that made Maggie shiver.

'Jude—' she began, but Jude dismissed her.

Silhouetted against the flames, Ayda's face was unreadable.

'You always had to put everyone down,' Jude hissed.

'Oh, chill out, Jude.' The drawl in Ayda's voice was exaggerated, the cadences calculated to drive Jude further to the brink.

'Fuck *you*, Ayda.'

Finlay took another step closer to Jude, put his arm out again. 'Jude, don't—' but Jude shoved his arm away.

Maggie mentally cursed Ivo for picking out that precise piece of paper at that exact moment. Jude had been raw from having to admit that she worked in a bar. Not that there was anything wrong with working in a bar – even in her head, Maggie was quick to add the disclaimer – but they all knew it was a long way from Jude's dreams.

'You know it's all bollocks, Jude,' Maggie said aloud, trying to keep her voice calm and sensible. 'Ignore it.'

'Yes, it's absolute crap,' Elizabeth chimed in. 'Total nonsense.'

Jude snatched a branch from the fire. One end was blazing and Jude whipped it in a wild circle, leaving a trail of smoke. Everyone went still. The only sound was the crackle of the flames. The burning torch was a brand, lethal.

'Jude—' whispered Maggie. 'Don't.'

In the darkness, all Maggie could see was the wild flaming torch, Ayda's eyes widened.

'No!' hissed Elizabeth. 'Jude!'

'Jude!' Maggie couldn't contain her scream. 'Stop!'

Ivo stepped forward, ignoring Jude and addressing Ayda. 'Come on, Ayds,' he said. 'That was a bit bloody harsh.' Ivo was trying to sound brisk, confident, thought Maggie. Giving both Ayda and Jude a way out.

Ayda looked around the circle, their faces lit up by the flames. The antagonism went out of her. She rocked her weight backwards, changed her tone.

'Okay, I didn't mean it,' Ayda said quietly. 'I'm sorry, Jude, it wasn't meant to—'

'It bloody was.' The flaming branch shook in Jude's hands. 'You always meant to, you fucking snob.'

Jude had never been close to Ayda or Elizabeth, thought Maggie, even though friendships formed so quickly at university. You could be friends forever after just one wild night out. Lily had been lifelong friends with Ayda, which meant that the friendships between Jude and Lily and Lily and Ayda linked the three of them like paper chains at Christmas. It meant Jude and Ayda were brought together often, but it had never been an easy match.

Jude had grown up in south London, the daughter of a single mother in a tower block in Peckham, back when Peckham was unlovable. There was a half-brother too, a decade older and occasional resident of HMP Brixton. But Jude herself had a chameleon quality, slipping like quicksilver into any situation. Her beauty, too, was a passport, and one she had flaunted frankly.

———

'Jude, I'm sorry—' There was a plaintive note in Ayda's voice now. A growing awareness that she might have pushed things too far.

'We don't all have Mummy and Daddy to fall back on,' Jude roared at Ayda. 'We can't just go home to the mansion and the safety net and the pretty, fucking pony.'

'And anyway,' Finlay interrupted. 'None of that matters any more. It's all irrelevant.'

Jude ignored him.

It still mattered.

Ayda had always had a capacity for sliding the knife in, Maggie thought. The quality was better hidden these days. Still there, though.

Now Maggie remembered that Ayda and Jude had been at loggerheads that evening in the Victorian cottage. All evening, Jude had been loud – her laugh bordering on hysteria – and then weepy. Both emotions irritated Ayda. She tolerated Lily's occasional dramatics because there were years of friendship and history there, but not in Jude, the new acquaintance.

Maggie remembered Ayda throwing herself on the sofa after the others left. Gone 4 a.m., sleep just up the stairs. 'I can't *stand* Jude Cox. She's so fucking irritating. Chippy bitch.'

Maggie, sleepy, not up for the fight. 'She's nice, honestly. You just need to get to know her.'

'You always were a bitch!' Jude was out of control now, screaming. The wine had clotted on her lips, the red hair tumbling over her eyes. 'Stuck-up little—'

Suddenly she was striding towards Ayda again, rage in every line.

'Steady on.' It was Rory who moved fastest this time, catching Jude in his arms so it looked as if he was hugging her, rather than stopping her. 'It's okay, Jude. It's okay.'

Jude was wailing in his arms, the anger spent, the tears unstoppable.

'Here.' Elizabeth stepped forward. 'Help me, Maggie.'

Elizabeth and Maggie almost carried Jude away from the little clearing, leaving the fading bonfire behind. They crossed the lawn and crunched over the gravel, supporting her between them.

'Which room is she in?' gasped Elizabeth, as they hauled Jude up the stairs.

Jude's eyes were closed now, her weight dead. They half-dragged her into the room next door to Elizabeth's, laying her out on the bed. Maggie stood back, looking down at the narrow figure. Jude was gaunt, almost emaciated. The skin on her arms was beginning to crepe, and she smelled of alcohol as if it was a tide rising inside her. It reminded Maggie of walking along a rocky beach in a gale once, the waves boiling, the spray erupting. The air was so permeated with salt that it tore at her nostrils. That was alcohol, for Jude.

Jude's forearms were striated with old wounds, the scars almost translucent as if they might split open any minute. Her forehead seemed more prominent than before, her hair thinner and drier. The auburn had a chemical tang these days.

'We should get a bucket or something,' Elizabeth said vaguely.

Maggie was tugging off Jude's shoes, trying to pull the duvet over her, although it was warm in the room.

'I'll sit with her for a while,' said Maggie.

'Fine.' Elizabeth shrugged. 'Suit yourself.'

After Elizabeth had gone, Maggie sat in the glow of the bedside lamp, flicking through her emails. It was almost a relief to escape the cascade of emotions.

Nothing interesting in the messages this time.

Spam from her favourite shoe shop.

Her hairdressers, suggesting she might want 10 per cent off a balayage, although she still wasn't quite sure what that was.

A quick email from Archie, the political editor at the *Post*, *You don't have a different mobile number for Ambrose Drummond, do you? The old one isn't working.*

Dross, she sighed. No one would notice if she didn't answer.

She sent the number to Archie, though. Easy: a few jabs of the phone screen. Remembering, for a moment, the brick-like phones they all carried at university, always having to delete texts so there was space for more messages to bleep in.

She heard the others return, clattering through the front door. They sounded as if they had bounced back from the scene between Ayda and

Jude. There were shouts of laughter and clips of sarcasm. Jude muttered in her sleep and Maggie turned to look at her. The row of earrings studding the lobe just looked painful now, cheap tat from a market stall. She thought of Elizabeth's elegant pearl earrings and Ayda's discreet diamonds, a thousand times more expensive, and turned away sharply from Jude's sleeping form.

She hadn't understood money at university. Not really. She knew they weren't all in exactly the same boat. Rory had his Golf GTI, Ayda had that Prada baguette under her arm. But they all moaned about being broke back then, buying own-brand food with a laugh and pre-loading before a night out, because a Smirnoff Ice was a whole £1.50 in the clubs.

And then at some point in their mid-twenties, some of them started buying flats. They were quite grotty flats, so she still didn't realise, not at first. Lily rented a room off Ayda, Maggie crashed in Elizabeth's box room for a few months. They were all still living together, so who cared? Then the market took off with a roar and suddenly the cottages in the cheap end of Queen's Park, the flats in the tatty bit of Bermondsey, they were worth almost a million, and she had left it too late. It was like watching a ship setting sail, thought Maggie, when you thought university and hard work, and doing the right thing were going to be your ticket. And then a watery chasm opened up and you realised that none of that had meant a thing. It had been bad luck in a way. She'd thought a few more years wouldn't matter much.

'It was when people's salaries started going up in fucking increments of mine that I started to think, hang on a second,' Jude had said to Maggie, once, on the edge of a picnic on Clapham Common. They must have been in their late twenties then.

'I know,' Maggie took another swig of Prosecco. 'I know exactly what you mean.'

At that point, Jude was renting a room in Dalston. Her landlord had just announced that he was cranking up the rent by £500 a month, overnight.

'I fucking gentrified that area,' Jude managed to laugh about it, just. 'And now I'm being booted out to Forest Gate. And just you watch: in a few years' time, I'll be moved on from there too. Another Tube zone, every year.'

'Tell me about it.'

'Have you seen Ayda's new flat? Daddy's bought her a chunk of some mansion block in Olympia. Ayda was banging on about how she hadn't realised how great underground car parks are and how handy it is for her BMW. I don't even have a fucking driving licence.'

Maggie had felt a moment of kinship as they watched Ayda stagger to her feet a few feet away, *thank you all so much for coming to my birthday drinks. And look! Even the sun's come out for me.*

Maggie herself had managed to buy a flat in Streatham, two years ago. Saving for years and she was taken aback by a hollow sadness on the day she moved in. It was only two steps from the tiny kitchen-diner-sitting room to a bedroom that was just big enough for a double bed. Another step took her to a bathroom that didn't quite fit a bath. And the thought: this might be it, forever.

It had taken so long. This little flat would have been perfect ten years ago, when it was a step to the next thing, whatever that was. But now every inch of the flat represented a different saving. The cheap mirrored wardrobes in the bedroom: that was waiting for hours for the night bus on the way back from Ayda's birthday party rather than jumping in a cab. The slightly wonky door to the bathroom that didn't quite close: that was saying no to Jessica Newton's hen weekend in Ibiza, and trawling through the photographs on Instagram later, #wishyouwerehere.

All those things she hadn't done for this low-ceilinged, modern flat with hollow walls and a juliet balcony overlooking a bus terminus.

Lucky though, of course. She wasn't even sure where Jude lived, now.

When Maggie turned back to the prostrate form in bed, she jumped. Jude was lying with her eyes open, staring straight at her, silent as a cat. Maggie didn't know how long she had been awake.

'Jude, are you okay?'

There was a long pause. Maggie watched Jude trawl for the words, her forehead slightly furrowed. A tear leaked out of the corner of one eye, drawing a smudge of mascara with it.

'Someone…'

The word faded away.

'Drink some water,' said Maggie. 'And try to get some sleep.'

There was another silence. A second tear trickled down Jude's face. Jude wiped it away, and tried again.

'Someone...' Jude whispered.

Maggie watched her, hoping she would go to sleep. She didn't want to get entangled with Jude's misery, not tonight. She wanted to be back downstairs, with the laughter and the shots. I looked forward to this weekend, she thought defiantly, and I don't get to look forward to much these days.

'Time to sleep, Jude,' Maggie went to switch off the bedside light.

'Wait.' Jude was trying to sit up. 'Someone...'

'I'm going back downstairs—'

'Someone killed Lily,' Jude's words came out in a rush.

There was a shout from downstairs, almost a scream, followed by a loud burst of laughter. Maggie felt a moment of instinctive dread and pushed it away, hard.

'Nobody killed Lily,' Maggie forced her voice to stay steady. 'Not this again. Go to sleep, Jude.'

But Jude's voice grew stronger. 'Lily was pushed, Maggie. Someone wanted her dead.'

Jude's eyes were sharp on Maggie's, watching for her reaction. She seemed quite sober, abruptly.

Maggie felt a prickle of fear again, and a sense of almost physical repulsion at Jude's words.

Someone wanted her dead.

Maggie straightened her back, forced herself more upright among the matching cushions.

'Lily must have slipped, Jude, or jumped. It was an utter tragedy but they haven't found any evidence that someone killed her.'

Don't be silly.

Maggie, I'm scared.

Maggie crushed the memory. The last thing she needed was to join Jude in her hysterics. And there was nothing... nothing...

'Jude,' she heard herself say. 'Go to sleep.'

'I spoke to Lily,' Jude was picking her words carefully, forcing herself not to slur. 'The night before she died. She was scared, so scared, but she wouldn't tell me why. She wouldn't tell me what it was, and then she hung up. I called her again and again, but she wouldn't answer.'

The wind moaned along the side of the old, old house, as if it were searching for a way in from the darkness.

'That doesn't mean—'

'Lily said something had happened. Something to do with the group going down to Wintercross. Something very bad.'

And Maggie felt that raw edge of fear again. That shiver in her spine.

'You're tired, Jude.' She didn't want to hear this, didn't want to be in this stuffy room with a sodden Jude.

'Lily knew something about one of the people here,' said Jude. 'I *know* it. She was really scared.'

'Jude, I'm sure—'

'You don't believe me.' Jude's eyes filled with drunken tears. 'I went to the police and they didn't believe me either. I could see it.' Jude gestured down at her pinched form. 'Because who would believe me, Maggie? Who would believe someone like me?'

'I'm sure,' Maggie heard her own voice, sensible, repressive, 'that the police checked everything out.'

'They didn't.' Jude slumped back against the pillows. 'They didn't.'

Maggie tried to pull the duvet up around Jude's shoulders.

'It could be any of them,' Jude sounded exhausted now. 'It could be any one of those bastards downstairs.' Her eyes flicked open for a second. 'It could be you, Maggie.'

'Sleep, Jude.'

'She didn't slip,' Jude wasn't crying now, the hysteria gone. 'Someone murdered her, Maggie. Someone murdered her and it was one of us.'

27

Lily, on Ivo: Still flirting with the world and his wife.

Everyone except Elizabeth was hungover the next morning.

Maggie was one of the first to stumble down to the kitchen just after ten, finding Rory and Finlay cooking eggs and bacon.

'It's kill or cure,' Finlay said cheerily. 'Hash browns, Maggie?'

The kitchen had been tidied overnight. Mrs Vereker must have let herself in while they were all still asleep, like the Tailor of Gloucester's mice.

'Poached?' Rory waved a spatula. 'Scrambled?'

'Fried, I think. And lots of toast, please.'

'We let the chickens out,' Finlay pointed to where some hens were scratching underneath a big cedar by the old stable block. 'We gathered the eggs and chewed on some straw. We're practically locals, Maggie, I tell you.'

Maggie looked out of the window. A topiaried peacock glowered back. Somewhere, a rooster crowed loudly.

Rory's phone rang. 'Hi, Link...' as he turned away. *The political editor of the* Sunday Times, thought Maggie. The news cycle never stopped now. Her own news editor expected her to start a day with *Today* and end with *Newsnight*, an unmanageable flood of information. She poured herself a coffee and rubbed her eyes. The toast sprang and made her jump. She listened idly to the radio, focusing in as the presenter read out the news bulletins. Ayda wandered in. Half an hour later, Jude appeared, unapologetic. But she made Ayda a cup of tea, which Ayda drank.

'What are we going to do today?' Elizabeth was freshly showered, cheeks glowing. The sun beamed down outside, promising one of the first truly hot days of the year. The air was still, a woodpecker busy nearby. A jay was screeching in the trees down by the tennis court.

Ayda looked up from her tea leaves. 'I reckon,' she grinned, 'that there is a sun lounger with my name on it somewhere near the pool.'

'Oh yes,' Maggie stretched luxuriously. 'That's exactly what I need.'

'We should go for a walk,' Elizabeth insisted. 'Up on the moor.' Elizabeth never went in the sun without smothering herself in factor fifty. Sunbathing was wasted on her. 'Or some of us could go for a ride?'

On Ivo's old hunter, Gulliver. Or the pony, Sweetie, comprehensively misnamed.

'Does Gulliver still bring you home when you drop the reins?' asked Rory. 'I remember you saying he could find his way back through any fog and rain after a day of hunting.'

'He does,' Ivo beamed. He had already been out for a run with Pagan, face glowing with health. 'He does.'

Jude disapproved of foxhunting. Elizabeth used to regard it as another sort of useful hunting ground.

'Come on,' Elizabeth persisted. 'Let's go for a ride.'

'You can,' Jude took another piece of toast. 'I'm not going anywhere.'

Jude glanced up and caught Maggie's eye. For a second, the rest of the kitchen disappeared.

Someone murdered her, Maggie.

Maggie turned away, telling herself she was looking for some jam in the pantry. Jude had been drunk last night, she told herself. Ludicrously so. But when she turned back to the table, Jude was still staring at her, cynicism in every line.

Someone murdered her, Maggie.

'Let's go down to the pool,' Maggie said loudly. 'Just for a bit.'

And it was one of us.

28

Maggie, on Rory: Well, we do have the pact…

'What pact?' Ayda pushed herself upright in her sun lounger, her eyes lighting up. 'What have you been hiding, you secretive witch?'

Maggie felt her face blush.

Thirty-two.

Unimaginable thirty-two.

She and Rory had agreed on it when they were slumped behind the garages at Ayda's house in Surrey. Both drunk, gone 5 o'clock in the morning, but still not quite ready for sleep. Ayda's twenty-first, and the Nassars had spared no expense. Rory had a crush on Lily back then. Had spent the evening watching her dance first with one boy, then another. Lily was just back from some holiday, her face deeply tanned, golden highlights in her long brown hair.

'I love her, Maggie May. I can't help it. I just love her.'

'You romantic, Rory. Don't worry, you'll get over her one day.'

'Can't you humour me just a bit? Pretend that she might suddenly realise and come bounding towards me in *Baywatch*-style slow motion…'

'Nope. You're not her type.'

Rory lit a cigarette – they all smoked back then – and squinted at Maggie through the haze. 'So brutal. How about you then?'

'Oh, you know. Still no one special.'

A lie, but she couldn't admit to Ivo, not even to Rory. It would sound ridiculous and she couldn't bear to be just one in the queue.

'We're so tragic, you and I.' Rory threw himself back on the tussocky grass. 'We'll both be single forever at this rate.'

And that's when they agreed, lying in the grimy grass behind the garages where Mr Nassar kept his carefully polished Aston Martin.

If we're still both single at thirty-two, we'll get married.

They'd crooked their little fingers, and promised.

Thirty-two: the age when they should give up all hope.

Rory had been her best male friend in those days, Maggie thought. It was sad that they had drifted apart after Genet died. After she was transferred to the lobby job a couple of years ago, Maggie had wondered whether bumping into each other regularly in the halls of Westminster might lead to a renewed friendship. But somehow the professional proximity had only pushed them further apart. She had hoped it wasn't because he couldn't relax around her, that he worried that she might betray old friendships for a few lines in her newspaper.

She wouldn't.

Well, not with Rory anyway.

But one day, she had caught sight of him hurrying through New Palace Yard on a cold November evening, and there had been such sorrow on his face, such total unhappiness that she had realised: the only way to survive the fog of grief after Genet died had been to bury himself in work. Rory had thrown himself into his job, spending hours battling on behalf of his constituents, days going through the minutiae of boring pieces of legislation. Work was a lifeline and Westminster could fill up all his hours and more.

He barely met up with his friends nowadays. Even Finlay moaned that he never saw him.

'Oh God,' Maggie forced a jaunty laugh and took a swig of coffee. 'I'd totally forgotten about all that!'

'Me too,' Rory cracked up. 'Bloody hell, that takes me back.'

Rory was married by the time they all began to turn thirty-two, blissful with Genet. Maggie had spent the evening of her thirty-second birthday in a bar with three of her girlfriends. Thirty-two, nothing much to celebrate. It was a fun evening though, she insisted to herself. Really great to catch up with buddies. And Ivo texted halfway through the evening, too.

Hope you're having fun, babe. She had read the message, made herself smile. Ordered another bottle of wine and forced herself not to wonder.

Now, of course, worrying about being thirty-two seemed insane.

But when she got home that evening, as she was hanging up her coat in the cheap wardrobe, she had found herself crouching down and slowly climbing into the darkest corner beneath the rack of clothes. With her fingertips, she edged the sliding doors closed. The hangers clicked together as she settled in the small space in the pitch-black dark. A stiletto she never wore any more bit into her thigh. She breathed out slowly as her eyes filled with tears. Rubbed them away with an angry harshness.

Later, she ran her hands along the back of the cupboard to make herself smile.

No lamppost here. No fauns. Not so much as a chunk of Turkish Delight.

There was nothing here at all.

'I can't believe it,' Ayda lay back on her sun lounger, laughing to herself. 'Can't believe you never told me about that.'

'It was years ago,' Maggie could feel the blush fading. 'And we didn't mean it anyway. Shut up, or I'll throw you in the pool.'

They were all lolling on the sun loungers, except for Elizabeth who was sitting on a sort of padded swing, pushing herself backwards and forwards with a toe. They had all had a good laugh at Finlay's tartan swimming trunks. 'The Adairs are Scottish-ish.' Finlay had taken the teasing in good humour. Now Maggie was getting too hot. She stood up and looked around blearily.

'Here.' Ivo helped her drag the sun lounger under two beech trees. Halfway up, the tree trunks had grown together, the bark closing unevenly over the graft.

'It's called inosculation.' Ivo followed Maggie's eyeline. 'When two trees grow together like that. They're called husband-and-wife trees.'

'I didn't know they could do that.'

'It's from the Latin for *kiss*.'

'They're beautiful.'

'It happens when the trees rub together in the wind,' Elizabeth said briskly. 'When the bark is scraped away. The injured trees fuse together in the end.'

Maggie lay back on the sun lounger and took another sip of wine.

'Do you remember?' Elizabeth began. 'Was it at that party that—'

'Oh, for God's sake,' Jude jumped to her feet. 'Why do we *always* have to talk about the past? All we do is hark back to this night out or that time Finlay got in a punch-up with some prop forward. Why can't we talk about now? The present? Because the way we're carrying on, any moment now we're going to be recalling that time in 2017 that Rory had a particularly good reminiscence about Lily losing her handbag in Toxic8 in 2003.'

'Alright, alright,' said Elizabeth mildly. 'What do you want to talk about anyway?'

'I want to know what happened to Lily!'

The name shattered the contentment.

Will it always be like this? Maggie wondered to herself. *Will this group always have a hollowness at its core now?*

'What do you want to know, for God's sake?' asked Elizabeth. 'I hadn't seen Lily for ages before she died.'

'Well, when was the last time you saw her?' Jude cocked her head.

'Probably not since the Newtons' wedding last summer, which was probably the last time most of us were together, wasn't it? Apart from the funeral, of course. There's nothing to know, Jude.'

'We all know you're upset about Lily's death, Jude,' said Ivo gently. 'It's unbearable, the whole thing. But the police spoke to everyone who was relevant and sometimes you just never know what happened or why.'

'There isn't an answer to everything,' Maggie agreed with Ivo again.

'When did you last speak to her, Ivo?' Jude asked.

Ivo blew out his cheeks, looking across the turquoise water. 'I honestly don't know, Jude. You know what my life is like. I spend so much time abroad. Same as Elizabeth, I suspect? At that wedding?'

But Jude's fury had burned out. Looking deflated, she wandered away from the group. The tension went with her. A sense of serenity drifted back. It was peaceful beside the swimming pool. Large cream umbrellas created patches of shade and high beech hedges stopped the worst of the Dartmoor winds. There was a small pool house close to the deep end with a well-stocked fridge. As the sun blazed down, Finlay went round again, filling everyone's glasses with rosé.

'Look.' Jude called Maggie over to the hedge.

Slightly unwillingly, Maggie got to her feet and walked across to her. It was a tiny baby bird, stretched out dead on the paving stones. Featherless, it was so young that its skin was translucent, its entrails a miniature anatomy lesson. A blackbird baby, maybe? Maggie didn't know much about birds.

'Poor little thing,' she murmured.

Finlay came up behind them, still holding the bottle of rosé. 'I could hear the magpies screeching down here earlier,' he said. 'Horrible birds. They attack the nests of other birds. They're so brave, the blackbird mums. Trying so hard to fight off something twice their size. I could hear their screams. This little one must have fallen out of its nest in the melee.'

'Grim,' Jude shuddered. They all peered at the little bird.

'I'll get rid of it.' Finlay nudged the tiny shape with his toe until it disappeared unceremoniously beneath the hedge.

'More wine please,' Ollie bellowed across at Finlay.

They wandered back.

'Time for a swim.' Ivo leaped to his feet. He dived in, sending up barely a splash.

'This is heaven,' Ayda took a photograph of her glass of rosé. 'You are so very lucky, Ivo.'

Elizabeth reached for another one of the scraps of paper.

29

Jude, on Lily: Whatever else, we WILL NOT
have turned into our bloody MOTHERS.

The corners of Jude's mouth lifted. 'Our bloody mothers,' she murmured.
'Our bloody, bloody mothers.'

'I remember that night,' murmured Rory.

'That night.' Jude's eyes were soft as she looked at Rory.

That night during their first term: Jude's mother, crying down the
phone. Incoherent. Drunk, maybe more. *I'm on my own, Jude, and I
can't stand it. I don't want to live like this... I don't want to be alive any
more...*

'She's going to do something stupid.' Jude, white-faced, trembling, all
the terrors flooding to the surface.

It had been past midnight when that phone call came in, so there
was no one like Elizabeth awake to suggest social services, or the
police, or a friend. Jude didn't believe in social services or the police
anyway. And her mother's friends were part of the problem. But Lily
understood. Lily knew exactly what it meant to have a mother who
cried about being dumped and cried about the gas bill and cried about
anything and everything. A mother who might, one day, float gently
off the edge.

'Parentifying', they'd call it now. But that word didn't exist back then,
or if it did, none of them had heard of it. Back then, most of them
still thought that at some point in your twenties – or possibly your

thirties – you were gifted all the answers. They didn't realise that you could hit forty and still not have a clue.

Back in those dingy student halls, Lily had understood Jude's panic at once. Both half-drunk, eyes mirroring those old childhood fears.

Lily *knew*.

'We need to get to Peckham,' Lily decided. 'You need to check up on her. Right now.'

'But how?' Jude curled in on herself. 'How do I get there? The trains…'

'Someone will drive us.' Lily, decisive. 'We need someone with a car.'

'You were so kind that night,' Jude said to Rory now. 'So calm. When we were both losing it.'

Maggie could imagine it. Rory, sound asleep. Jude and Lily at his door, hammering, hammered. Lily, the girl he adored.

Will you? *Please*.

Of course, he would.

He'd always been kind, Rory.

That night had bonded the three of them. Racing down the motorway, a stream of headlights flooding in the other direction. As they navigated across a dozing, empty London, Lily and Jude had discovered that they shared the same spark of humour, the same cool determination. The same fragilities too, most likely.

When they reached her, Jude's mother was asleep. Not overdosing. Not dead. They took themselves to McDonald's for breakfast, and it had turned into an adventure quite quickly. A shock for Rory though, Maggie guessed, to see how some people lived. The flat grimy and unloved, twelve flights up. The lift, broken and covered in graffiti, and not by Banksy either.

'Well.' Jude crumpled up the piece of paper. 'Lily never got the chance to turn into her mother.

30

Maggie, on Finlay: If he's still drinking this much, it will be getting out of hand.

'A *problem*?' Finlay took another gulp of rosé. '*Moi*?'

'Finlay's only just warming up.' Ollie filled up his glass. 'Chocks away, old boy.'

Maggie watched Rory's eyes land on Finlay for the briefest moment.

'This is the life.' Finlay took another swig and lolled back in the sun. 'The life.'

31

Maggie, on Ollie: We still won't have forgotten
you running across Great Court, stark naked.

A roar of laughter.

'We'll never forget that, mate.' Finlay. 'Never, ever, ever. It is scarred on our collective memory.'

'I know, I know.' Ollie rolled his eyes, enjoying the attention. 'Chisel it on my fucking tombstone. Christ.'

A one-night stand. Back then many of the student rooms didn't have an en suite. In the middle of the night, Ollie had gone to the loo and then stared – lost, befuddled – at a corridor of identical doors.

'You were so pissed, you decided to just sprint for your room.' Finlay loved this story. 'Belting across Great Court, stark bollock naked.'

Great Court, Trinity's ancient heart.

'Hurdling the flowerbeds.' Ivo shook his head. 'Skidding over the cobbles. What the porters must have thought…'

Rory hummed the *Chariots of Fire* theme tune.

'The poor girl never knew where I'd got to,' said Ollie. 'Must have thought I'd just legged it.'

'Lucky escape,' said Elizabeth.

32

> Lily, on Finlay: Will it still be a secret? And,
> God, I hope that you're here and you didn't get
> yourself killed in Afghanistan.

Maggie stared blankly at the scrap of paper.

'What did Lily mean by that?' She looked up at Finlay.

There was something Maggie didn't quite recognise in Finlay's face, but just as quickly, he was smiling again.

'Lily wrote what now?' Finlay raised an eyebrow, although Maggie knew he'd heard her perfectly well the first time.

'She was worried he would get himself killed in Afghanistan. We were all terrified of that,' said Rory. 'God, it's weird to think that war was only just starting then. Odd how for our generation, 9/11 was what bisected childhood and adulthood, really.'

'No,' Maggie interrupted him. 'I don't mean that bit.'

'What's that other bit?' Ayda craned to look over Maggie's shoulder. 'What's the secret, Finlay?'

'Yes,' Jude said pointedly. 'What was Lily talking about, Finlay?'

Ivo pulled himself out of the pool in one easy movement. They were all staring at Finlay now.

'I have absolutely no idea,' Finlay spread his arms wide. 'You know what Lily was like. Dotty.' But there was something forced about his voice, a hesitation that Maggie hadn't heard before.

'She wasn't dotty,' said Jude icily. 'She was unusually brilliant.'

'You know what I mean, Jude.'

'I don't, actually.'

'What does it say?' Ivo leaned forward, dripping water everywhere as he peered closely at the piece of paper. 'Go on, Finlay. What *is* the secret?'

'It must be a joke,' Rory said smoothly. 'It's just very sad that Lily isn't here to explain it.'

It might have been light-hearted, thought Maggie.

But.

'It doesn't sound like a joke,' said Jude. 'What do you think she meant Finlay?'

'I have no bloody idea, Jude.' There was tension in Finlay's shoulders.

'Maybe she thought you were gay,' Ollie jeered, reminding Maggie of how much had changed in the intervening years.

'Doubt it,' said Ayda. 'No one on the netball team was safe from Finlay's depredations.' She sat forward, pulling out some sparkly purple nail varnish to match her jewelled pumps. 'I didn't even have the time to have a sodding pedicure this week.'

'You must know,' Maggie's eyes were serious on Finlay's, 'what she meant.'

But Finlay was shrugging, dismissing it. 'Lily could be eccentric,' he said. 'You all know that.'

'But she obviously thought you would remember,' insisted Maggie. 'Even twenty years on. So it must have been something important.'

'A secret,' Elizabeth murmured. 'What sort of secret?'

'I think we're all keeping secrets,' Jude grabbed the bottle of rosé. 'We've all been keeping them for years.'

'Everyone has secrets,' Ollie looked up at her, squinting into the sun. 'Even you, Jude.'

But Jude refused to smile, refused to soften her gaze and let it become a joke. 'I think,' she said coldly, 'that Lily is dead because of a secret.' They were all staring at Jude now. She glowered back, her eyes moving from Finlay to Rory to Ivo, and back again.

'What do you mean?' asked Maggie. 'What do you mean by that?'

Jude's lips tightened.

'Oh, for heaven's sake, Jude.' Dismissively, Ayda began another layer of nail varnish. 'You really bring so much *joy* everywhere you go, don't you?'

Maggie persisted. 'What is it that you know, Jude?'

But Jude had fallen silent. She turned away from the group, looking up towards the wilderness of the moor.

'If you know something,' Maggie tried again, 'you really ought to...'

The silence curdled.

Dead because of a secret.

Dead.

33

Finlay, on Ivo: Will have made a stone cold
fortune out of his clever, clever maths.

Rory stood up and grabbed another piece of paper from the bowl. He
read the prediction aloud, their heads turning towards him. Ivo smiled
with just a hint of smugness and the mood lifted again.

'A stone cold fortune.' Ollie grinned approvingly. 'Well, you certainly
got that spot on, Finlay.'

The laughter pushed away Jude and her anger.

'How did you know he would chase another fortune?' asked Elizabeth.
'When he already had all this?'

'It was *because* of all this,' said Finlay. 'Some people just rest on Daddy's
laurels—'

'Or Great-great-great-granddaddy's laurels,' Ayda interjected.

'But other people...' Finlay thought about it. 'Other people have to
prove themselves a hundred times over. And Ivo was always one of those
people. You see it in the Army too, all the time. Ayda's the same. Daddy's
bought her the mansion flat but she's still at the office from dawn to dusk.'

For a moment, Ayda's face was a strange mix of pride and regret.

'How did you guess about Ivo back then though?' asked Elizabeth.

'I'm not sure...' Finlay's face cleared. 'You know what Ivo's like when
he's drunk? He suddenly gets an idea in his head, and just goes for it.'

Laughter. They all knew. For all the premature sophistication, after a
few drinks there would be a glimmer in Ivo's eye, an emerging wildness.

Ivo, clambering across the Trinity roofs as dawn broke, for a dare. Ivo, stealing one of the Trinity punts at midnight, and disappearing halfway to Grantchester. *Wise Monkey*, that had been the name of the punt. Later, Rory and Finlay had gone to the rescue in *Mad George*. They towed *Wise Monkey* home, Ivo sleeping peacefully in her flat bottom, tying her up between *Point Turn* and *Fury* before she was missed.

After Finals, Lily, Maggie and Jude had hired *Peace Sweet* for the day, drifting under the weeping willows, fingertips trailing in the water. This is *it*. This is when it all *begins*. At the May Ball, Maggie had fallen off *Lithium*, still clutching her Pimm's, her pink satin ball dress half-floating, half-drowning, crying with laughter.

Mile Island. Grace. Codon. Bear.

Fluffy. Harry Lime. Bronze.

The alumni magazine – always keen to keep in touch – informed her that a *Charles* had been launched, although the coronation of a former undergrad merited only a passing reference on page seven, somewhere after the most recent scientific breakthroughs. Trinity priorities, spelled out.

'Ivo hides that wilfulness most of the time,' Rory grinned. 'But when he's hammered…'

'Did you know?' Maggie asked suddenly. 'Had you already worked out the SummerX algorithm when we sat down to that dinner?' The SummerX algorithm, the foundation of all the millions. A trade secret, guarded as jealously as any maiden in her tower.

Ivo stared at the sky. 'I was starting to work on it,' he said. 'It was all starting to fall into place.' As the rest of them waved their hands to Justin Timberlake and Eminem and Christina Aguilera, he was doing the elegant mathematics that none of them would ever understand. And Ivo always understood the financial potential, while the other mathematicians gazed upon the Bogomolov conjecture with thrilled, bleared eyes.

Never quite enough for his father, maybe. But enough for anyone else.

'What are you up to in Boston anyway?' asked Elizabeth.

'Oh, I'm only there for twenty-four hours. Checking up on our real estate division.' The Americanism slipped easily off Ivo's tongue nowadays. Maggie imagined the towers climbing Jack and the Beanstalk high, carving out wealth from the sky.

'Where next?' Elizabeth pried further. 'After Boston?'

'Actually,' Ivo started to laugh, 'I'm off to Cushing, Oklahoma.'

'Cushing *where*?'

He was instinctively secretive about work, Ivo. Never spoke about it unless someone – usually Elizabeth – asked him. Unlike Ollie who would tell you at length about the Eaton Square duplex he was showing discreetly at the moment, because pads like that never hit the open market, you know?

'Cushing's all about tracking the oil market.' For once, Ivo decided to explain. 'Basically, the amount of oil the world is burning gives you a pretty good idea of how the world economy is functioning. Lots of oil usually means that the economy is booming. But most of the data on oil production comes from governments so it's slow' – a quick grin – 'and out of date.'

'So how do you get round that?' asked Elizabeth.

'There are massive oil storage facilities around the world, including in Cushing, Oklahoma, of all places,' said Ivo. 'We learned that the more oil being stored in Cushing, the lower the oil price, and vice versa. So, by tracking activity in Cushing, you can get a heads-up on what the oil price is going to do next.'

'What do you mean?' Elizabeth blinked.

'Cushing's a crazy place,' said Ivo, 'right in the middle of America. It just happens to be where lots of pipelines cross over, and so that's where they store oil. It's a little nothing town, surrounded by rows and rows of oil tanks. Huge ones, absolutely enormous.'

'How do you track how much oil's being stored there?'

'Well, there are some guys who just fly around all day in helicopters, firing infrared beams at each of these hundreds and hundreds of tanks to work out how much oil is being stored in each one. From that, they extrapolate how much oil there is in the whole of Cushing, and then they sell us that data before the official US government announcements. And there you go.'

'A few more million dollars to you,' said Finlay and Ivo inclined his head.

'So you're going all the way to Oklahoma to talk to some guys in some helicopters?'

'They've got some new masterplan,' another grin, 'that needs financing. I'm going out there to find out what it is they want to do.'

'Of course you are.' There was an eye roll in Elizabeth's voice.

Maggie wondered what it was like, endlessly circumnavigating the globe. Once or twice, she had found herself looking up the SummerX jet on one of the aeroplane tracker websites, idly watching N98CP blip from Cannes to Baku, from Nassau to Abidjan.

'I like seeing things.' The enthusiasm blazed in Ivo's eyes. 'I like talking to people and working out exactly what makes them tick. Deciding if they're full of shit or not.' A searing ambition not quite disguised by that opaque public school charm.

Once, Maggie had watched the blue dot of the plane sitting calmly in Rome-Fiumicino and imagined Ivo wandering the hot Roman streets. Was there a girl beside him? Laughing in the golden light, flowing silks blowing about her?

Perhaps.

Could he be lonely?

Surely not.

Maybe.

'When are you going to settle down, Ivo?' It was as if Finlay had read Maggie's mind.

'*It is a truth universally acknowledged...*' Ivo leaned back in his chair. 'One day, Fin. One day. Anyway, you're hardly one to talk.'

'But all this needs a chatelaine,' Finlay waved. 'Someone to open the church fête and hold soignée dinner parties.'

'Well, there might be more than one reason to spend twenty-four hours in Boston.'

A pang.

'When will you have enough?' Jude asked flatly. 'When will you think, right, I'm done, I'm going to go and loll in my French chateau or Swiss chalet or whatever.'

Ivo looked at her, serious for once.

'Never,' he said. 'Why would I?'

34

Maggie, on Jude: If we can survive Cyprus, we
can survive anything.

Jude defrosted. 'Christ, do you remember that holiday? And God, do
you remember those hangovers? They were *apocalyptic.*'

Lily and Jude and Maggie had gone to Cyprus at the end of the first
year, just for a week. Not for them the fortnight in Cap Ferrat (Ayda) or
climbing Kilimanjaro (Finlay) or a sprawling villa in Ibiza (Ivo).

'You're going to Ayia Napa?' Elizabeth had been horrified.

'Well, somewhere near there.'

'Is that even *safe*?'

'It's my first time,' Jude had admitted at the airport, eyes wide, brand-new
passport clutched to her chest. 'My first time abroad.'

'It'll be amazing,' said Lily. 'Just you wait.'

It had been magical. The cheapest flight – hopelessly delayed via an
unlikely connection through Istanbul – had landed just after dawn,
long before they could check into their hotel. Lily had bought a bottle
of cheap white wine and pleaded with an ice cream seller to let her
cool it in his freezer. He'd rolled his eyes and laughed and they'd drunk
it on the beach, eating nectarines and giggling, everything ahead of
them.

'Of course I remember that holiday,' said Maggie. Suncream that smelled of coconut oil and left them scarlet. Cocktails in alarming shades of pink and green. Dancing in the pastels of the dawn, the neon lights of the clubs bright against the cool of the sky. They had shared a room: three narrow single beds with threadbare white sheets, sleeping at unlikely times of the day.

'The Macarena!' said Jude.

'The YMCA! Saturday Night! We had all the moves back then.'

'We really did.'

'Do you remember the first apartment?'

'Oh *God*.'

After a long day on the beach, they had finally got around to checking into their scruffy little room. Lily, desperate to have a shower, had disappeared into the tiny bathroom. Then she screamed.

'It's the shower!' Lily, naked, her hair foaming with shampoo. 'The shower!'

'What's wrong?'

'The shower just gave me a massive electric shock! Jesus!'

They crowded into the bathroom, staring suspiciously at the shower unit. It dangled unpromisingly, wires trailing.

'We have to complain,' Jude insisted.

An hour later, the manager presented himself at the door to their room. Maggie opened it and for a second her brain couldn't process the scene. The man was short, greasy, wearing a grimy, stripy shirt. And he was holding his penis. A small penis, Maggie's brain concluded faintly. Not quite erect and unbelievably hairy.

'For fuck's sake!' Lily shrieked, coming up behind her. She slammed the door and they fell back onto one of the narrow beds, weeping with laughter.

'We're getting the fuck out of here.' Jude was hurling her possessions back into her suitcase. 'Men! *Men!*'

Too late, by then, to get another hotel room for the night. Instead, they found themselves back on the beach, huddled together for warmth. Jude unearthed a bottle of Archers from her bag and they drank it without lemonade, still giggling.

'This would never happen to Elizabeth Randall-Page,' said Jude, almost to herself, eyes on the stars. 'Off in fucking Cap Ferrat.'

Within seconds, it was a chant.

'This would never happen to Elizabeth.' Another gulp of Archers. 'This would *never* happen to Elizabeth.'

Later, Lily read her guidebook for something to do, flicking through the translations at the back.

'"Can we take it slowly, it's my first time?"' Lily was reading aloud. '"No thank you, I prefer to watch." God, I don't know *what* these Cypriots get up to.'

'They're talking about *dancing*, you fruitloop.' Jude took another swig from the bottle. 'The youth of today... I don't know.'

Jude was such fun in those days, thought Maggie with a hint of sadness. Those jokes, that wild sense of the ridiculous, the joy, the whip-lash of intelligence.

Jude was the first pupil from her school to get into Cambridge. Chaos all around, her eyes fixed on the goal. 'I'd do my homework with my head-phones on,' she told Maggie. They were sitting on the end of an old pier a few days later, feet dangling in the water. 'Blocking out everything else. Nothing else existed while I was working. Not my mother cracked off her head, not my brother giving me shit. Nothing – but *nothing* – was going to stop me getting to Cambridge.' Tiny fish shimmered around their feet. Jude threw in a scrap of her sandwich and watched them battle.

'Why Cambridge?'

'One of my teachers told me all about it when I was twelve. This beau-tiful place, all libraries and ivory towers. I thought it was something from a fairy tale. I'd never even heard of Trinity then. But I knew. I just *knew*.'

Jude had been tough, too. That night, four men pinned Lily to the bar. Lily was clinging to her smile, trying to make it a joke.

Let me go.

But they wouldn't. Hands slipping under the thin cotton dress, the circle tightening, not a joke, no.

Let me *go*.

Jude had turned and absorbed the situation in a second. She hadn't said anything, she'd barely moved. Instead she'd *hissed*. Eyes narrowed, teeth bared, ancient witchery all around. The men had vanished, scat-tered by that primitive male fear of a nameless female power.

'You okay?' Jude had inclined her head.

'I'm fine. Thank you.'

'Any time.'

'Cyprus.' Elizabeth shook her head.

'It was fun,' said Jude.

'Sure it was.' Ayda.

'But it was,' said Maggie. 'It really was.'

35

Rory, on Ollie: Teacher.

'Teacher?' Ollie laughed dismissively. 'I can *do*, mate. I don't need to teach.'

But there was a hollowness to Ollie's voice. A regret he couldn't quite hide.

'So many of our year got sucked in by Mammon,' said Rory. 'I just thought you would have made a great teacher instead. You were always brilliant with kids.'

A soft gasp from Elizabeth.

'Teaching would have meant something, right?' asked Ollie. 'That's what you're saying. A *purpose*. Instead of spending my whole life trying to inflate the value of Belgravia flats even further?'

'Sorry, Ollie. It wasn't meant to offend.'

'It doesn't,' Ollie took a big gulp of his drink. 'Don't worry, pal. It doesn't.'

Ollie rolled onto his stomach and the hours slipped away in a swirl of rosé and memories.

36

Ollie, on Ivo: Will have divided Wintercross
into flats and sold them off.

'What?' Ivo was startled out of his usual languor. 'I'd never do that.'

They were sitting in the courtyard, eating a late lunch. The food was simple and delicious. Tomato and mozzarella sliced together. Delicate slices of ham and a huge green salad. Mrs Vereker had brought in fresh bread from the village. The courtyard was beautiful, lavender and roses planted all around, protected from the wind by the wings of the house. Hollyhocks were an explosion of pinks and apricots and creams. Espalier apple trees were trained against the walls and swifts screamed overhead.

'I know you wouldn't sell off Wintercross,' Ollie agreed. 'I get it now.'

Even before Ollie became an estate agent, he had always appraised houses. Maggie remembered him pulling up outside her parents' house once – he'd offered her a lift to a party in the middle of the holidays, and she'd accepted before regretting it immediately – his eyes flicking over the neat lawn, dismissing it in a glance.

Ollie, on the other hand, had never invited any of them to his own parents' house. Years ago at work, Maggie had found herself searching – oh so casually – for a Steven and Deborah Radcliffe. Steve and Debs: she had only been allowed to meet them once. At graduation, when it couldn't possibly be avoided. There had been a sister at graduation too.

Danielle, but everyone calls me Dani. Sweet smile, worked in a shop, briefest possible reading at the wedding.

Steve Radcliffe ran a plumbing company, it turned out. Companies House led Maggie to a neat semi in Bromley. Google Maps guided her around a cul-de-sac, peering at semi-detached brick, privet hedges, an abandoned shopping trolley over on its side. There was a tall electricity pole at the mouth of the cul-de-sac, the wires fanning out to every home so that the pole looked oddly like a tall thin dog walker taking a pack of well-behaved houses for a stroll.

Zoopla opened the door to the other half of the semi, sold last year and the mirror image of the Radcliffes' home. Boxy rooms, laminate flooring, double-glazed front door. The estate agent's particulars gave a glimpse of number eleven's gardens: patio, green plastic garden furniture, Peter Rabbit rows of lettuces.

It looked nice, Maggie thought spitefully. Friendly.

The spite was because Rory had just signed off an email with a casual, *Are you going to the Radcliffes' later?* And Maggie had known at once that he must be talking about one of Elizabeth and Ollie's dinner parties that she was never invited to, because only couples with names like Allegra and Barty or Crispin and Daphne were invited to those, and Maggie failed on both counts.

Tied up this evening! she'd messaged back. *Have fun!*

And then she looked up Steve and Debs.

'I'd never turn this into *flats*,' Ivo looked around at Wintercross's high granite walls. 'Never.'

'You'd never get planning permission anyway,' Ollie said cheerfully. 'Not on somewhere like this.'

Wintercross was indeed spectacular. Years ago, Maggie had bumped into Ivo's father as she wandered alone in the garden early one morning. That must have been the first time she came down here. He had scowled at her for a second, and then filled the silence with a history lesson.

'Houses like this have been stitched together over centuries. They're a patchwork of history, really. That section's Regency, for example,' he waved at the ballroom wing. 'But the main house is much older. Tudor. And when we lifted the kitchen floor, we found medieval cobblestones.

There almost certainly would have been some sort of dwelling on this spot long before that.'

'It's an astonishing place.'

Mellowed slightly by her enthusiasm, Mr Fitzwilliam led her into the main house, pointing out stained glass windows, painted plaster ceilings, oak panelling. 'Nicholas Owen worked on this house,' he announced. 'The carpenter. Priest holes, you know?'

'Oh?' Maggie said uncertainly.

'Saint Nicholas Owen, I mean, of course.' Mr Fitzwilliam had a curious way of speaking, pruning sentences to a word or two, before allowing a flurry of words to burst forth. 'He was a Catholic. A Jesuit, in fact. He built priest holes in grand houses all over the country back in the sixteenth century. For the Catholic families who were trying to keep the old faith alive, you see. Hides for priests, secret passages for runaways. Only the owner of the house would know them all. Of course, that means that many of them are completely forgotten now. Consigned to oblivion if someone died without passing on the secret. My grandfather rediscovered one hiding place at Wintercross as a boy. It was almost impossible to spot.'

'How did he do it? Nicholas Owen, I mean.'

'Hidden trapdoors, false walls, false ceilings.' Mr Fitzwilliam rattled them off. 'Some caches were built into staircases. Others into fireplaces. There are seven different hiding places in Harvington Hall in Worcestershire, and those are only the ones that we know about. Their bluff hide, in particular, is remarkable.' They were walking up the oak staircase by then, Maggie's hand on the newel post, polished smooth by centuries of hands.

'Their bluff hide?'

'A hide within a hide within a hide. Under a false step on their grand staircase, there is the first hiding place. Filled with gold and jewels, maybe. You'd hope that your peasant soldier just pocketed the loot. But beyond that secret place, deeper in the house, would be the space for the men, for the priests, quivering in the dark.'

'It must have been terrifying.'

'The searchers would go round the house, tap-tapping on the floorboards, to see if one of them was hollow. They'd spend hours measuring the shape of the house, to see if the outside matched what lay within. At

Baddesley Clinton, the priest hole is hidden in an old privy. The priests climbed down and hid for hours, deep in shit, praying. Guilty as a rosary. That hide was one of Owen's, again.'

'What happened to him? To Nicholas Owen. Sainthood rarely points to a peaceful end.'

A bark of laughter. 'Quite. They caught him eventually. Not long after the Gunpowder Plot. Tortured him, racked him. A terrible death.' She sensed that he approved of the bygone agony, revelled in it almost. 'But he never gave away his companions. Never gave up his secrets.'

'How did they catch him?'

'Owen gave himself up. They'd hunted him down to Hindlip Hall, up in Worcestershire. A small group of rebels all hidden in different tiny spaces, only just big enough for a man. Imagine lying in the dark with barely any food or water, unable to even stretch out your legs for days on end. The footsteps coming closer, fading away, then coming back again. Slower this time. More thorough. *Tap, tap. Tap, tap.* It must have been unbearable. Owen surrendered, hoping that he would be enough, that by sacrificing himself, he would allow the others to escape.'

'Was he? Enough, I mean.'

'No. Henry Garnet, Owen's master, stayed hidden for another eight days. Eight days, with only water to drink. Imagine it. Imagine the *smell*. But eventually even he had to surrender. Garnet was also,' Mr Fitzwilliam briskly pre-empted the question, 'hung, drawn and quartered. Now where is that idle son of mine? He should be bloody up by now. Idiot boy.'

Always Mr Fitzwilliam. He never suggested that any of them should call him Hugh. He had done something unspecified in the City before retreating to Dartmoor. Maggie suspected that he thought she was named after Thatcher, and approved of that. She wasn't. She'd had a granny – a Frenchwoman who had brought an unprecedented glamour to the Fletcher family – called Marguerite.

Ivo was Mr Fitzwilliam's only son. Mrs Fitzwilliam was never mentioned by Ivo or his father. It was on a different visit that Maggie realised. She was wandering around the village churchyard, when she came across the stone beside a dark yew.

Verity Fitzwilliam, beloved wife and mother.
Requiescat in pace.

Maggie did the maths slowly. Ivo was eight when his mother died.

'Just going to the loo,' Maggie stood up. The sun burned down and for a second, she felt light-headed, unsteady. Then the world straightened out and she headed for the back door. In the kitchen, she found Mrs Vereker laying the long pine table for dinner. Mrs V was short, energetic, fiftyish. Her undyed hair was greying and she wore an embroidered blue tunic over black jeans.

'Hello,' she smiled at Maggie.

'All the food is absolutely delicious.' Maggie realised she sounded like Elizabeth. 'Thank you so much.'

'It's a pleasure,' she beamed, rounded tones.

'And what you've done with the house! It's stunning. So different from how it used to be.'

'Oh, thank you.' Another beam. 'Although it was the interior design company that did most of it. Amazing, they were.'

'I wish they'd do my flat.'

'Tell me about it.' The housekeeper prodded one of the high-tech ovens. 'Mind you, it's all a bit advanced for me. And the security system! It's always going off randomly. Drives my husband mad. State of the art, they said. I tell you… cameras everywhere.'

'I suppose it has to be locked up safely when Ivo's away.'

'Oh, absolutely.' Enthusiastic nodding. 'Some of the art and stuff is worth an absolute fortune. You couldn't leave a place like this to its own devices, even if we are just at the bottom of the drive.'

'It's a beautiful place.'

'I love it here,' Mrs Vereker said simply. She was stroking Pagan's face, the Labrador's tail wagging wildly. 'And you, you gorgeous boy.'

'Wasn't it awful about the body being found up on the moor?' said Maggie. 'We were talking about it last night.'

'Wasn't it just? Such a terrible thing.'

'Was she local?' she asked.

'No, not that I heard. There were police all over the place, though. They still seem to be hanging around, even now. And there were a few journalists! So nosy!'

Maggie decided not to reveal that she was also a journalist. 'Poor woman,' she said instead. 'It's so sad.'

'It is indeed. Now, do any of you need anything else?'

'It's all perfect,' said Maggie. 'Thank you.'

Afterwards, she strolled back out to the courtyard, enjoying the heat on her face. From a distance, the rest of them had an old school glamour. Elizabeth had tied back her hair with a Hermès scarf. Ivo was telling a story, gesticulating, cracking up at a memory. Ayda wore an emerald silk dress and huge sunglasses, immaculate as always. Jude was picking wild strawberries, popping them in her mouth.

Lily – the thought was in Maggie's head before she could stop it – would have loved it.

Maggie, I'm scared.

Despite the heat of the day, Maggie felt a shiver travel down her spine.

She shook the shiver away and plastered a smile on her face. Picked up a pink rosebud that had snapped off and tucked it behind her ear.

'What' – she walked towards them – 'have I missed?'

Elizabeth pulled out another prediction.

37

Ollie, on Elizabeth: I hope she'll be married to me.

When Elizabeth looked up, her eyes were sparkling with tears.

'But I was going out with Aubrey back then.'

Ollie was staring at his glass of white wine. 'I knew that, obviously.'

'But you still thought…'

Elizabeth was fiddling with a stem of lavender, pulling at the petals.

'Yes.' Ollie met her eyes squarely. 'It is what I hoped.'

'But…'

For a moment, they all sat there in silence.

They had to be *boys* back then, thought Maggie. She remembered Ollie bounding over to the sidelines after one of his rugby matches. Freezing fingers, sweating bodies, muddy knees, bruising cheekbones. Exhausted. Eyes shining though. A mob of players, a shockwave of noise and excitement and joy. Ollie and his rugby lads had made the same jokes at every meal for three years straight. They probably still made them now, in a curry house somewhere off Clapham High Street. Nicknames worn smooth with use. *Banter.*

But Ollie had loved Elizabeth as much as he was able. Awkward with words, he stumbled over his vows in that pretty, little church in Wiltshire near Elizabeth's parents' house, and pulled a face in the salvoes of pink and blue and yellow confetti hurled by Elizabeth's openly relieved sisters, Dani and a few carefully selected, overexcited aunts. There was a row of tiny, pastel bridesmaids and a string of terrible jokes during Ollie's speech. But also, a delight that he couldn't quite hide. Pride: my *wife*, *Mrs* Radcliffe.

A few years of dinner parties before it all began to slide away. The silence solidifying, calcifying.

'But that was what you thought then,' Elizabeth said slowly.

'Yes,' Ollie leaned forward, briskly poured a glass of wine. 'That is what I thought then.'

38

Ivo, on Finlay: Finlay will still be besotted with Jude.

'Ahhh, bless.' Ivo was holding the scrap of paper. 'How very sweet. Those were the days, indeed.'

Finlay flushed, eighteen again. Jude looked half-smug, half-flustered.

'It's all coming out now,' teased Ayda. 'All these missed romances.'

'They were definitely missed, were they?' asked Ivo. 'This' – a gesture at Jude and Finlay – 'never happened?'

'You know it didn't.' Finlay tried on chivalry like an ugly sister with a glass slipper. 'Much to my disappointment.'

'God, Maggie, do you remember we made that diagram once?' Ayda was laughing. 'Who snogged who snogged who? It took up a whole side of A3, just for our halls.'

'That was ages ago,' said Maggie. 'I've forgotten it all now.' She hadn't.

'Oh my God, I've just remembered that you snogged *Ollie*,' Ayda shrieked.

'That was in freshers' week,' Maggie rolled her eyes. 'Everyone hooked up with everyone else then. It doesn't count.'

'Freshers' flu,' said Ollie. 'I do remember that, thank you very much.'

Maggie still remembered that kiss, although not with any particular nostalgia. Unfamiliar lips, a tang of vodka Red Bull, neither particularly attracted to the other. It was relief rather than passion. *Someone here fancies me a bit, thank God.* In the middle of this morass of testosterone and uncertainty. Because at least you'd known where you stood at school.

Even if you were one of the geeks, you'd worked out where you were in the shifting sands of the school social order. But here, it was a kaleidoscope of, *that Elizabeth's a bit up herself, isn't she?* And *I saw that Ayda girl doing a line in the toilet,* and *oh my God, how hot is Ivo Fitzwilliam?* Status fluctuating every hour in the scramble for position. Because *this* was the start. This was the start of everything.

She remembered, too, the shock of being ordinary. Marguerite Fletcher, the star of her very unremarkable sixth-form college. Her teachers always so thrilled by this clever, clever girl who sat at the very front all the way through. Top of the class, brilliant A-levels, suddenly horrifyingly *average.* Mediocre, in a world where people gossiped in Latin and casually pushed at the very edges of science.

So, Ollie and Maggie had snogged in that club – what was it called again? It got rebranded regularly and the new name never stuck – and laughed about it afterwards. Not an unkind laughter, though. A sense of getting off the starting blocks together, even if they had no intention of completing the journey as one.

'Lily hooked up with Ivo at least once,' said Elizabeth, who had always known about Ollie and Maggie, and displayed an unflattering lack of jealousy. 'And, Ayda, I'm *sure* you went on a few dates with Finlay.'

'Everyone went on a few dates with Finlay. Doesn't count.'

The dalliances had melted away for the most part, floodwater efficiently drained. Only Ollie and Elizabeth had solidified into marriage and then shattered like ice.

'Besotted with Jude,' Ivo was smoothing out the piece of paper on the table. 'Besotted with Jude.'

Across the table, Maggie was looking at Ivo's writing. It was easy to identify each person's predictions. Elizabeth, with her pink paper, engraved fountain pen and italics that were so painstaking they were almost calligraphy. Ivo, too, had pulled a fountain pen out of his pocket that night. Navy-blue ink, the letters big and bold. Finlay had pressed down hard, almost puncturing the paper in places. Ayda had grabbed a biro, her writing precise and efficient. Maggie could remember searching for a pen and one of Elizabeth's notepads, and settling for a blunted pencil.

Now, Ivo was folding up the piece of paper, putting it neatly into his pocket.

'What are you up to these days, Finlay?' Maggie realised she didn't know.

'This and that,' he said. 'Maritime security, mainly.' A shrug. 'It suits me.'

Many ex-servicemen ended up on the huge cargo ships that surged across the oceans, from Singapore to Muscat, from Jeddah to Dalian. Three weeks on, three weeks off, very healthy salary. Didn't leave much time for Mia, obviously. The pirates – desperate Somalis mostly – were managed with a practised brutality. Maggie wondered – briefly – about what might have been between him and Jude. Jude might have dragged him out to festivals and concerts and plays. Offset the khaki with a few diamanté studs. And Jude? Jude might have been given some ballast, some equilibrium as she faced the storms.

Too late now.

All those choices, Maggie thought. All those chances. All those might-have-beens.

A game of consequences engraved in stone, when it wasn't a game at all, not really.

'God,' said Finlay, 'it all feels like it was a million years ago.'

'That's the thing about the one who got away,' said Elizabeth dreamily. 'They're the one you danced with on that beach in Bali. They're the one you climbed that mountain with in Sri Lanka. They shared that magical time when it was all ahead of you. You're in love with the memory of that time, not the person.'

Maggie turned sharply towards Jude. Framed by lavender and pink roses, Jude looked daisy-chain delicate, her eyes dark with sadness. She had taken all that adolescent adulation for granted, thought Maggie. Never considered that the boys might move on, find other lives, other loves, other trophies.

Then Jude jerked up her head. 'That's just clinging onto something that doesn't exist any more. There's no point,' she said, 'in being in love with the past.'

39

Ollie, on Lily: NHS doctor – penniless, basically.

'See.' Ollie was holding his prediction. 'It's pretty accurate, the salary stuff.'

It was only a few weeks before the dinner party that Lily had turned to Maggie at the end of a long afternoon in the library – Maggie trying to hammer out an essay on sexual violence and the cycle of revenge in *Titus Andronicus* – and murmured under her breath: 'I'm transferring.'

'What?' Maggie had whispered. 'Where?'

'I'm not leaving,' Lily said. 'But I am switching from Natural Sciences to Medicine.'

'*Medicine*? How? What?' Maggie was incredulous.

'They say it's okay,' said Lily. 'That I can swap over.'

Lily was very bright, Maggie thought. Personable, too. She imagined the fellows shrugging, *fine, whatever.*

'But won't it take years and years?'

'Yep,' Lily nodded. 'I'll have to start again from scratch, of course. Back to square one. But I really want to do it.'

'Won't it be – like – properly hard work?'

'Yes,' Lily was laughing.

'But why? I never thought you were interested in all that.'

There was a glimpse of something in Lily's eyes but then she was smiling again.

'It's just what I need to do.'

'Alright,' Maggie shook her head, making sense of it. 'Well, I'll miss the Haribo if you're stuck over in Addenbrooke's or wherever.'

'That won't be for ages.' Lily looked at her neat notes, then stuffed them carelessly into her backpack. 'And there will always be Haribo.'

'Lily was a great doctor,' Maggie said aloud. 'Incredibly dedicated.'

The pressure was constant. Lily, working for hour after hour whenever the hospital rota got mangled; which it always did. Maggie had barely seen her during the grinding misery of the pandemic. One desperate Sunday, a few weeks before she died, Lily turned up at Maggie's flat, crying over a premature baby, who had clung precariously to life for weeks, before finally, gently, letting go. Lily carried the parents through their grief and wept at Maggie's.

'She certainly worked bloody hard,' said Jude.

Maggie wondered if Jude had been happy about Lily's career change. Jude and Lily had been such good friends at university, when Lily was a slightly unenthusiastic NatSci. But then Lily veered off down a very different path, fulfilled and admired. They had stayed close, of course, but Lily had purpose, goals, ambitions. All the things that Jude's life lacked.

'Does this weekend have to be all about Lily?' There was an odd sort of resentment in Elizabeth's voice.

Maggie looked up, startled. 'She was our friend, Elizabeth. You know that.'

'We're sorry if that's inconvenient for you,' snapped Jude.

'That's not what I meant.' Elizabeth realised she had said the wrong thing. 'I suppose I was wondering if this is just how it will be now when we're all together? That we'll always be missing Lily.'

Lunch took the rest of the afternoon. They were wandering back towards the kitchen now, ignoring Elizabeth's demands that they trek across Dartmoor. Maggie deposited the remains of the salad in the compost bin and chucked some scraps of ham at an enthusiastic Pagan.

'But the forecast says the weather's rubbish tomorrow,' Elizabeth grumbled. 'It's our last chance for a proper walk.'

'You go on your route march if you must,' said Ayda. 'I'm having a gin and tonic.'

'But I'll miss out on the predictions if I go alone!' said Elizabeth.

'That is true.'

In the kitchen, Mrs Vereker had laid out dinner.

'There's a chicken and bacon pie if you can face another meal,' Ivo was reading a note. 'Just need to chuck it in the Aga for forty-five minutes or so. Let me know when.'

'I can do the vegetables,' said Elizabeth. 'But not for a few hours. I'm so full. It'll have to be a midnight feast or something.'

'Pudding's lemon tart,' said Ivo. 'Hers are amazing.'

Oh, to have a housekeeper, thought Maggie. The casual luxury.

They had gathered in the kitchen now. Maggie sat down at the long wooden table and reached into the Venetian glass bowl. Her eyes flickered over the piece of paper and she heard herself gasp.

'What?' Elizabeth said bossily. 'What is it, Maggie?'

Maggie's mind was simultaneously racing and blank. Everyone was staring at her now.

'Come on, Maggie,' Jude tried to grab the piece of paper. 'Get on with it.'

And there was nothing else to do.

40

Ivo, on Ayda: Ayda will finally have worked out
that Lily is her sister.

Silence. Maggie looked up to a battery of eyes.

'Her sister?' Maggie said. 'Her *sister*?'

Ayda was very pale, her mouth quivering. She turned on Ivo. 'You
bastard.'

She stood up and walked out of the kitchen. The door slammed and a
silence settled behind her.

'Ayda's sister?' Finlay was still trying to work it out. 'Lily and Ayda are
sisters? How? *What*?'

'But *Stella* was Lily's mother,' said Elizabeth. 'And Bassel and Fiona
Nassar…'

'Half-sister,' said Rory. 'That must be what Ivo meant.'

'Bassel Nassar was Lily's father?' Maggie asked.

They all looked at Ivo. He was sitting at the head of the table, his face
quite impassive.

'How…' said Elizabeth. 'I don't understand…'

'I think we all know the facts of life, Elizabeth,' said Finlay. 'By now.'

'Yes, but…'

'Trouble in paradise?' Jude's mouth curled. 'Maybe things weren't so
perfect at Casa Nassar, after all.'

'They were practically neighbours, weren't they?' Maggie remembered. 'The Nassars and the Blakes, they only lived a few houses apart.'

'But I thought they were all friends,' Elizabeth sounded outraged. 'That the Nassars were just helping Stella Blake because she was a bit... chaotic.'

'God,' said Ollie, 'when you think about it, they do look a bit similar, Lily and Ayda.'

There was a sense of injury in the air, almost childlike. It was a prim, adolescent response compared to how they would normally respond to gossip at this age. Maggie had a flashback to Wednesday's office gossip. *You heard about Griff? Banging that secretary from Greville Polignac in the conference room?*

But here, this, they were shocked.

'When did Ayda find out?' Rory asked. 'Her reaction just now: that wasn't shock. If it had come out of the blue, she would have questioned it. Denied it automatically. Having it announced to the room was a surprise, but she was angry more than anything else.'

'She didn't know at university,' Ivo agreed. 'I... worked that out.'

'Do you think Fiona Nassar knew?' asked Elizabeth.

Maggie thought about the elegant blonde bob, the neat pearl earrings. Espalier trained. Nothing in common with Stella Blake.

Well, one thing in common.

'I think women tend to know,' said Jude. 'Subconsciously, if nothing else.'

'I couldn't help it,' Maggie muttered. 'I didn't think fast enough.'

'It's not your fault,' said Rory. He turned to Ivo. 'Bit harsh, Fitz.'

'Yeah,' Ivo grimaced, almost apologetic. 'I'd forgotten about that one.'

Ivo had always had that capacity for sharpness though, Maggie thought. That hint of Machiavelli.

'All the Old Etonians I know are the same,' Rory had said to Maggie, once, not long after his first failed run at Parliament. 'Ruthless bastards, the lot of them. They're brilliant at seizing power and manipulation because that is just how the school works. They have to be elected to all the societies, everything that matters, so they learn to exploit everyone around them from the very start.'

'Oh,' Maggie had answered, only half-understanding what Ivo had been taught from the cradle. 'That certainly explains some of the politicians I've met.'

Ivo treated the rest of us like laboratory rats, she thought moodily now. Beagles in a cage, blinded rabbits. And a simultaneous thought: that was less leeway than she would have given him a few years back. She was almost proud of herself.

'How did you know?' Maggie turned to Ivo. 'Did you guess?'

'It was obvious,' he said.

And, of course, now that they all thought about it, it was. And it probably would have been back then to anyone whose brain was trained to think through all the possibilities. Anyone who wanted to see, could. A delicate probe, the gentlest of suggestions. But Ivo hadn't told Ayda then, thought Maggie, although he could have done, easily. Instead, he'd set up an *I knew all along* of brutal proportions.

'So, when did she find out?'

'I'm not sure,' Ivo shrugged. 'I never asked.'

'None of us see each other that often,' Ollie nodded.

Because you might not be able to guess from a glancing blow at a party. How are *you*? What are *you* up to these days?

These days.

'Shitty thing to do, Ivo.'

'I wrote it down twenty years ago, Rory.' Ivo was bored with Rory's disapproval. 'We were all arseholes twenty years ago.'

Were we? Maggie wondered.

'Yes, but you could have stopped it this weekend,' Rory was shaking his head, not letting it go. 'Chucked your prediction in the fire, and put something nice in instead.'

'Oh, but that wouldn't be right.' The words jerked out of Elizabeth at once. 'We have to read them all. We promised. Those are the rules, Rory.'

'Exactly,' Ivo said to Rory. 'The rules. And, anyway, I didn't remember.'

Maggie was watching Ivo's face closely, and couldn't tell. Couldn't tell if it had been an innocent mistake, or if he had known all along that a twenty-year-old bomb was waiting to explode in Ayda's face. A mine drifting in the sea, years after the armistice.

'You should go,' Maggie said now to Ivo. 'You should go to Ayda and apologise.'

Ivo sighed loudly, but he pushed himself upright and made for the kitchen door.

'Play nice while I'm gone, you lot.'

For a moment, they sat in silence.

'Lily and Ayda were half-sisters,' Elizabeth repeated. Then she paused, before saying aloud the words they were all thinking. 'Did Lily know?'

41

Jude, on Maggie: She'll still be obsessing over
Ivo Fitzwilliam.

Ayda and Ivo had come back into the kitchen together. Ayda's eyes were
slightly puffy but she was chatting easily with Ivo. I'm not talking about
it, her body language had telegraphed. Move on.

Now, Maggie felt her cheeks burn as Ayda read out the words. Ayda's
voice had a light bitchiness in it, and as she finished reading, she looked
up at Maggie with a sneer in her mouth.

'I'm *not*,' Maggie's voice had a squeak in it.

'Sorry, Maggie,' Jude was half-laughing. 'But you did have the most
almighty crush on Ivo.'

Maggie couldn't look at Ivo, the surge of humiliation overwhelming
her. For God's sake, she told herself. You're the deputy political editor of
a major national newspaper. Grow *up*.

'Well, I don't *now*,' she insisted.

'You're with what's-his-name,' said Elizabeth. 'Lucas.'

'Exactly,' said Maggie. 'Well, actually Lucas and I broke up a couple of
months ago.'

He'd been perfectly nice, Lucas. Worked for a think tank, enjoyed
running, took flowers when they went for Sunday lunch in the nice semi
in the suburbs.

But it was not enough.

Never enough.

Before that there was Elliot. Management consultant, cashmere jumpers, sideline in stand-up. Good-looking enough that there would be a gleam of jealousy in other women's eyes, occasionally.

But not enough.

Never enough.

'I liked Lucas,' Ayda mused. 'He was nice.'

'Lucas *was* nice,' Maggie said. 'Kind.'

Not enough.

'Well, Maggie,' Ivo was smiling, managing to not patronise her. 'I'm flattered.'

'Shut up.' She just about managed to laugh. 'Always so pleased with yourself, Fitz.'

She wondered briefly about who he was seeing now. She noted – pleased with herself again – that where once the thought would have been a stab with a red-hot poker, now it was a stub of the toe. Painful but bearable. Mostly. There had been several girlfriends for Ivo, of course, as well as Seraphine. Exquisitely beautiful, all of them, with an ethereal quality that made Maggie feel like a wildebeest, galumphing through the forest. None of them came from a nice semi, either.

She wondered if he would marry one of them eventually. Had even pondered if she would be able to sit through his wedding. Watch the bride float down the aisle, listen as they swore eternal love to each other under the rainbow sparkle of the stained glass windows. Not cry. Probably not. She would have to invent a prior engagement when the invitation arrived. The invitation would be embossed, of course, and Maggie would get out her own fountain pen, because she had one now.

Miss Marguerite Fletcher regrets that she will be unable to attend…

She might not even be invited, anyway.

42

Jude, on Ivo: He'll still be playing Cupid.

'Ha! Do you *remember* that weekend?' Ayda cracked up. 'Oh *God*.'

'What was that guy's name?' Elizabeth asked. 'Luke something... Luke...'

'Luke Russell.' Ayda winced. 'Bloody hell.'

Ayda had had a crush on one of Ivo's friends, Maggie remembered. Luke: tall, blond, charming. Ivo's school friend. Ayda had met him at some party in Oxford and returned to Trinity unusually starry-eyed. Ivo, entertained by Ayda's glow, had invited them down to Wintercross for a weekend. Ayda, Rory, Elizabeth, Lily and Maggie had arrived on the Friday night, Luke not due until the next day.

'What's the plan?' Ivo twirled Ayda in some complicated rock and roll move. 'We need a *plan*.'

He had always enjoyed a plan, Ivo.

In her first year, Maggie had found herself in the bathroom of one of the terrible clubs, applying lipstick and telling the beautiful girl at the next mirror how kind Ivo was, how genuinely, lovely, deep down.

People think he's just a charmer, because he's so... you know...

Another time, Ivo had told Aubyn or Aubrey – they'd been to prep school together, of course – that he wanted to marry someone exactly like Elizabeth one day. Maybe even Elizabeth herself if Aubrey didn't get his act together. *Better crack on, old boy.*

Then there was the night that Maggie had been walking home from a club with Lily and Elizabeth. Late – 3 a.m. maybe – and they stopped at the chip van the same way they always did. Elizabeth never got chips, of course. She just waited with them. Rory was just behind them in the queue, so he was next to Lily as they turned down the narrow lane that led back to Trinity, Elizabeth and Maggie ahead.

A scuffle. A scream. A bellow from Rory.

The crunch of fist on bone.

As Maggie whipped round, a figure – tall, solid, dark clothes, balaclava – shouldered past her, sending her reeling against a wall.

Lily was screaming. *He tried to grab my bag! Rory stopped him. Rory's hurt... help him! Oh God, is he okay... ?*

Rory was fine, of course. Bruised but triumphant, Lily clinging to his arm. The next day his black eye was a badge of honour.

Maggie had known though. Intuitively. Absolutely.

Tall, solid, that wild burst of energy.

Ivo.

Not that his masterplan had helped Rory, anyway. As soon as they got back to their rooms, Lily had insisted on ringing her most recent paramour. *You'll never guess what happened! And I dropped my chips! Oh, it would be amazing if you brought some over. I'm scared to be on my own.*

'We need a plan,' Ivo had said, as they gathered around the table that first night at Wintercross.

'Fine.' Ayda rolled her eyes. 'But what?'

'We could play spin the bottle,' said Maggie. 'Or you could go for a long walk on the moors and get lost together.'

'And hope Dartmoor Rescue bring a candlelit dinner with them?' asked Ayda. 'Hypothermia is famously erotic after all.'

'Gulliver could bolt with you?' Ivo suggested. 'Luke's an excellent rider. He could save the day.'

'I'd fall off,' said Ayda.

'I've thought of something,' said Ivo at last. 'I know what to do.'

'What?' Maggie, thrilled to be an accomplice.

'You'll see.'

It was at dinner that it began. Footsteps, crossing the floor upstairs.

Ayda, startled, looking around the table. 'Who was that? We're all here...'

'Nobody,' Ivo said airily. 'Just the old house creaking because it's blowing a gale outside.'

The wind was indeed howling. It whistled through the chimneys, lifted the curtains. Candles – the only light in the dining room – flickered.

'Are you sure?' asked Maggie. 'It sounded like—'

'Luke, are you going to the US this summer?' Ivo cut across her. 'I can't remember what you decided in the end.'

'Not sure yet. I want to go to Los Angeles, but my father's trying to drag us down to sodding Polzeath again.'

'Less Baywatch,' Lily rolled her eyes, 'more Braywatch.'

Elizabeth was looking at a small portrait in a corner: a beautiful woman with long black hair and ivory skin. It had been painted in the seventies, Maggie guessed, the woman smiling up from under her fringe. The artist had fun with the colours of the kaftan.

'She's gorgeous,' said Elizabeth.

'My mother,' said Ivo.

A hush. For a moment, Ivo's face was completely blank, the well of sadness opening up beneath him. Maggie wanted to reach out to him, to hug him close.

'You have the same eyes as her,' she said. Her words fell into an echoless grief. 'What happened to her?' Elizabeth's curiosity was sharp.

'A riding accident.' Ivo's voice was low.

'I'm sorry.' There was nothing else to say.

'Another drink?' Ivo smiled brightly.

They settled down in the drawing room after dinner. The fire was smoking.

'Bloody jackdaws.' Ivo poked it. 'Brandy, anyone?' They had all been drinking for hours by then, speakeasy fun. Maggie felt sleepy and content. She watched the smiling faces in the firelight and listened to the laughter. Ayda was lying in front of the hearth, stroking the dog. That

Labrador was Digby, nemesis of Catesby the cat. It was as Luke was telling a story about his new stepmother that they heard the scream. Luke stopped sharply.

'What was that?' Elizabeth's voice faltered.

'What?' Ivo lifted his head. 'I can't hear anything.'

'You must have heard it,' Ayda's eyes were wide. 'A scream.'

A pause. Silence. 'I can't hear anything?' Ivo shook his head. 'What were you saying, Luke?'

Then, just as Luke was laughing at his stepmother's rage when he was suspended from school right in the middle of Fashion Week, another scream echoed through the house. Closer now. Clearer.

'What was that?' snapped Rory.

Luke was looking around the room, counting heads. 'I thought I heard something too—'

'Oh.' Ivo's eyes gleamed. 'That will just be the ghost.'

'The ghost?' Even though she was sure this was part of Ivo's plan, Maggie felt a shudder down her neck. Instinctively, she and Lily drew closer together.

'Oh yes,' Ivo grinned down at Maggie. 'Once upon a time, a beautiful maid worked at Wintercross. Centuries ago. One of my ancestors took too much of an interest in her, and she ended up pregnant. You can imagine the shame. At midwinter, she walked out onto the moors, and lay down in the snow. They found her much later, white and cold. She still haunts the old house, pacing the attics night after night. If you listen closely during storms, you can hear her crying for her lost child.' Ivo stopped. They were all staring at him, hypnotised. Ivo's face was perfectly bland, and suddenly Maggie didn't know if this was part of his scheme, or not. The darkness seemed to stroke her face. A beautiful maid, who lay down in the snow.

'I don't believe in ghosts,' she said uncertainly.

'Sure,' Ivo shrugged. 'Nobody does until…'

'Have you seen her then?' Rory, swigging his glass of wine. 'Drifting along the corridors in her sheets?'

'I'm not sure,' Ivo mused. 'Once, when I was little – maybe four or five – I could have sworn that a woman in Victorian clothes came into my bedroom in the middle of the night. She crossed over to the fireplace, as if she was going to make it ready for the morning. I remember the sound of the hearth being swept, the clatter of the poker. It was all so vivid. Then I fell asleep again and when I woke up, she was gone. I didn't know if it was a dream. I told my mother, and she just looked very sad.'

'Ivo...' Maggie imagined the little boy going to his mother, a small hand tugging at her skirt.

Beloved wife and mother.

'My mother never said anything about a ghost, of course. Not to a little boy. It was my father who told me about the maid's disgrace,' said Ivo. 'Years later. He said that whenever she appears, death is never far behind.'

Footsteps, again, above. Elizabeth squealed.

'Come on!' Luke was on his feet. 'Let's go and see.'

They all surged towards the door, an explosion of bravado and giggles and shrieks. It was still dark in the hallway, the staircase lit only by the smouldering logs in the fireplace. Ivo waited. Maggie, seeing him hesitate, slowed too. She listened to the feet pounding up the staircase.

'You okay?' she asked.

'All good.'

'I like this plan. It's a good one.'

'What plan?' Ivo was all innocence. 'Honestly, Maggie, this house has always been weird.'

Maggie's mouth twitched. 'Sure, Ivo. What does Luke think about Ayda then? Does he fancy her?'

'Luke thinks Ayda likes me!' Ivo laughed at the ludicrousness of the idea.

Maggie managed to laugh too. 'Oh dear. Have you told him that's bonkers?'

'Yes!' Ivo rubbed his eyes. 'But Luke always was a bit of a thicko.'

Upstairs, they could hear the rest of them. There was an edge of hysteria in Elizabeth's laugh.

Maggie felt hazy, dreamy, excited.

'Kiss me,' she said suddenly. 'Then Luke will know there's nothing going on between you and Ayda.'

Ivo's eyes lighted on her face. 'Maggie...'

'Come on!' Maggie took another swig of her drink. 'Wait until we're upstairs, though.'

He was laughing, but his eyes were narrowed, gleaming.

'If you insist, Miss Fletcher.'

They cackled their way up the stairs, their laughter fading as they came across Elizabeth, shuddering.

'The footsteps…' she said. 'The footsteps…'

'What's the matter, Elizabeth?' Maggie was jerked out of her elation. 'What happened?'

There was a strange smell: the aftermath of fireworks, a hint of sulphur.

'What's that stink?' asked Ivo. He moved quickly to a light switch, clicking it down. Nothing. 'Bugger. There must be a power cut.'

A crash. The thud of footsteps was loud and shocking. They came from Ivo's room.

'What *is* that?' gasped Elizabeth. 'There isn't anyone in that room.'

Ayda, Luke and Rory burst out of another bedroom as the footsteps rattled away towards the other end of the house.

'What's going on?' Ayda was shuddering. 'I don't understand…'

A scream, sharp and piercing, from Mr Fitzwilliam's room.

'What the *fuck*?' said Luke.

Maggie was looking around. They were all in the corridor now. There couldn't be anyone in Mr Fitzwilliam's room. Even Ivo looked unnerved.

The smell of gunpowder grew stronger.

'Come on!' said Ivo. 'Let's go and see.'

'No fucking way!' said Lily.

Away from the fire, Maggie's eyes were adjusting to the dark. Moonlight glowed through the windows. 'Where are the torches?' she asked. 'There must be some somewhere.'

'They're under the kitchen sink,' said Ivo. They all imagined the long walk down through the darkness. 'Come on!' Ivo urged. 'Shit, what was that noise?'

'Okay.' Luke's eyes glimmered with challenge. 'Let's go and find out.'

There was a small boy's bluster in the air. Abruptly, Maggie could imagine the two of them, twelve or thirteen, behind the bike sheds.

Ivo's eyes lit up. 'How bad can it be?'

Luke and Ivo started down the corridor. Elizabeth squeaked. *Don't leave us.* And without thinking, Maggie was following them, just a few steps behind. The floorboards creaked beneath their feet. Maggie could hear Luke breathing, short excited breaths. Now they were at the big oak door that led into Mr Fitzwilliam's room. The clouds must have covered the moon, because the corridor turned abruptly darker. A second of hesitation, and Ivo had pushed the door open. The hinges groaned. Behind her, Maggie heard a gasp.

Luke and Ivo crept into the big bedroom, Maggie just behind them. The room was still, almost pitch black. Luke and Ivo stepped forward. It was a big room. Maggie could just make out the shapes of the windows but nothing else. The room was silent though. Still. Empty. After a few seconds, Maggie's heart rate began to slow.

'There's nothing here.' Luke sounded almost disappointed.

'We're just being idiots,' Maggie made her voice cheerful. 'Shall we go back to the others?'

Just then, the moon came out again. Maggie's eyes swept around the bedroom. Dark shadows that must be wardrobes. A four-poster... and a white shape hanging from the bed's crossbar. A cold draught swept across the room and the shape quivered and swung.

Maggie screamed. 'Ivo! What is—'

Ivo took two steps towards her and she found herself in his arms. For a moment, Maggie couldn't move, couldn't think, and then he was kissing her, his mouth hard against hers. And she was kissing him back, wrapping her arms around his neck. Her fear flowed away, the world shrinking to her and Ivo and a perfect sort of happiness.

This. *This.*

A heart-shaped moment.

A glimmer of candlelight in the hall. Elizabeth's and Ayda's voices were approaching fast. Maggie pulled away sharply. She looked up at the crossbar and at once the white shape was Mr Fitzwilliam's dressing gown, white and fluffy and innocent. Luke was looking across at the two of them, bemused.

'I didn't realise you two—'

'Oh, it's just...' Ivo made a careless gesture. 'Don't make a big deal about it in front of the rest of them.'

'Course not.'

Amidst their calm, Maggie was reeling. Words and thoughts were half-formed things that floated in the shadows of Mr Fitzwilliam's four-poster.

Ivo gave her a smile, half collaborator, half traitor.

Now the others were spilling through the door.

'What was it—'

'We heard—'

'Maggie screamed—'

The lights snapped on and Maggie was left blinking.

'Rory went to find the fuse box,' said Elizabeth. 'What happened?'

'It was nothing,' Ivo was saying. 'Just a creaky old house.'

And now it was, their fear blasted away by the bright electric glow. They were laughing again, mocking their own shrieks, their own nightmares.

Ayda's eyes were sharp on Maggie, knowing she had missed something.

'Come on,' said Ivo. 'Let's go back downstairs.'

He didn't look at Maggie as they all cavorted down the stairs, high on excitement, high on relief. Digby was jumping up hysterically. When Maggie reached the drawing room, Ivo poured her another drink, politely friendly, and never mentioned that kiss again.

Later, Ivo doled out pills, and Ayda snogged Luke to Faithless.

Not that it lasted. It never did.

43

Lily, on Rory: Rory will still be covering up for
his little brother.

The silence was broken by the fire crackling in the grate. A shower of
sparks and the burning logs shifting. It was getting dark outside now, the
colour draining from the day. Elizabeth was holding the small piece of
paper, turning wide eyes on Rory, who was standing beside the kitchen
counter.

'What?' She was almost fearful. 'What does that mean?'

Just for a second, there was a glint of something in Rory's eyes. Then
it was the politician's mask again: amiable, polite, as if someone – a voter,
maybe – was asking him for directions on a frosty London street.

'I have absolutely no idea,' he said smoothly. 'Chuck it over, Elizabeth.'

Maggie was watching Finlay. Finlay's eyes were on the piece of paper,
his face quite still. Holding the piece of paper between her index finger
and thumb as if it were grubby, Elizabeth passed it over the pine table
to Rory. Rory examined it, eyes cast down. Then he looked up, smiled.
'Funny old Lily,' he murmured. 'I miss her so much.' It was such a compas-
sionate smile that Maggie found herself smiling back at him with a sort
of relief. The mood lightened.

'Had you shagged someone you shouldn't have, Finlay?' Ollie, bawdy.

'Probably.' Finlay, rueful.

'Almost certainly.' Rory, the big brother.

They always fell back into their old roles, thought Maggie, all of them. Even if nowadays she was on chatting terms with the Prime Minister, the moment she was with this group, she reverted to being that slightly shy, slightly awkward teenager. Only Lily, really, had escaped her old role in the pack, and even then, not completely.

'Finlay,' Ollie said, 'was always getting into shit in those days.'

'Do you remember,' Ayda grinned, 'when Finlay hooked up with that girl – what the hell was her name? – and her boyfriend turned up for an unexpected romantic visit? Finlay ended up stuck in her bedroom with the boyfriend raging outside?'

'Rory had to get a ladder,' Ollie cackled, 'and rescue our Romeo from the rooftops.' He rolled the Rs.

Only Ivo was leaning back in his chair, his hands behind his head. 'Boys, boys, boys.' He stared first at Finlay, then at Rory. 'Whatever have you been up to?'

Finlay's head came round fast. 'Shut the fuck up, Ivo.'

There was a threat in his voice, a menace that jarred with the pretty surroundings of the kitchen.

'If you insist.' Ivo arched an eyebrow. 'If you insist.'

There had always been an edge of violence to Finlay, Maggie thought, long before he ever joined the Army. Over the years, she had written dozens of articles about PTSD in the Armed Forces: the violence brought home like the worst sort of souvenir. The hidden terrors boiling like acid and spilling into the pub, the sitting room, the bedroom.

'But look where they got us from in the first place.' This from a former corporal: broken teeth, skin yellow from years of vodka, but so self-aware that Maggie chided herself for her assumptions. 'The powers-that-be recruit the fighty ones from the shittest parts of the country, and then the do-gooders blame it on Afghan when we get home and batter our wives. Well, I'd probably have been battering my bird either way.' The broken teeth had gleamed and Maggie had felt a surge of something that was half-hate, half-pity.

If a fight kicked off in a club – pushing, shoving, *you starting something?* – it was always Finlay. Always, long before FOB Larka. She remembered an argument once, the hockey boys being rowdy, clumsy, irritating. Finlay grabbing a bottle by its neck – Bacardi Breezer, probably – and slamming it against the bar. Glass everywhere, the bottle a sudden jagged weapon. It had been such a smooth movement, so practised, that the hockey boys stilled, open-mouthed. You've done that before, Maggie thought. You've done that before.

And you'll do it again.

44

Ayda, on Ollie: Ollie will still be desperate to be
Ivo Fitzwilliam.

'Ouch,' said Ollie.

45

Jude, on Ollie: Ollie will still be playing his daft
drinking games.

The roar of laughter was a relief, Ayda's jab buried.

What was the boys' ludicrous drinking society called? For a second, Maggie couldn't remember. *The Lightning Bolts, that was it.* The initiation rite was something like drinking a bottle of Skittles vodka – or worse – through a sock – or worse – for breakfast. Nobody ever made it to lunch. The sister society was the Lightning Flashers.

'Thank God,' Maggie said, 'that Facebook hadn't been invented back then.'

'We dodged that bullet,' Rory gave her a real smile. 'Just.'

Finlay, Rory, Ollie, they had all been Bolt members. Ivo was invited to join as soon as he arrived, of course, but usually claimed a prior engagement for the actual dinners. Rory had always found himself too busy for the annual photograph: blazers, sepia, staring into the middle distance, a comms nightmare. Planning ahead, even then.

Ollie, the eternal rugger bugger, had adored it all, of course. It was that sense of *belonging*, Maggie thought. Connection without the tedious inconvenience of an actual conversation. Even now, she couldn't think of a single time that she had seen Ollie without some identifying item of clothing. After the football shirt was buried forever, he emerged in the union tie, a college scarf, the uni tennis shirt. Today, it was a battered rugby shirt: *Harry's Stag! Tallinn 2018! OI OI SAVELOY!*

'Thanks, Jude,' Ollie was saying now, completely unabashed, 'you've reminded me.' He lobbed a penny in her drink.

'Down it, down it.' The roar went up. Half smiling, Jude necked her glass of wine.

'And that reminds me,' Ivo grinned. 'Murder in the Dark.'

'No,' Maggie heard herself say. She spoke without thinking, instinctively. Wintercross in the dark. *No*.

'Come on.' A chorus. 'It'll be *fun*.'

'I'll get the cards,' Ivo jumped up. 'It's dark enough to play now. Rory, you go and make sure all the lights are off.'

'But I can't even remember the rules,' Maggie said weakly.

'Yes, you can,' Ivo was rifling through the pack. 'Ace is the murderer, King is the detective. We all spread out, and if you get a tap on your shoulder, you're dead. If someone comes across a corpse, they shout "murder" and we all come back down here. Hardly complicated. Even Finlay gets it.'

'I'd rather play Spin the Bottle,' Finlay grumbled.

'No chance,' said Ayda.

'And no cheating,' said Rory.

'How on earth,' asked Elizabeth, 'would someone cheat at Murder in the Dark?'

'I don't know,' Finlay waved his hands airily. 'Ivo's always been king of the gadgets. He's probably got infrared goggles lying about or something.'

'I do, actually.'

'See.'

'And the detective has to do a shot for every corpse,' said Ollie, 'unless they accurately identify the murderer, in which case he or she has to do them instead.'

'And doesn't every corpse have to do a shot?' asked Jude.

'Something like that,' Ollie agreed. 'Yes.'

'And after every round,' Elizabeth demanded, 'we'll read out another prediction.'

Ivo dealt out the cards.

'Aha.' Rory waved the King of Spades. 'It is I who is in charge of law and order in this licentious establishment.'

'Does the detective double as barman?' Jude held out her glass.

'Naturally, madam.'

'Right.' Ivo was at the door of the kitchen, hand on the switch. 'Off we all go.'

The room was plunged into darkness. The fire had burned down to glowing embers.

'Give us a couple of minutes, Sheriff.' Ivo held the kitchen door wide. 'Good luck, the rest of you.'

Maggie giggled nervously as she made her way through into the snug, running her hands over the backs of the armchairs to orientate herself. Jude bumped into her, spilling wine. There was the faintest glimmer from the moon outside.

'Are *you* the murderer?'

'It's Elizabeth, isn't it? She's looking very serious.'

'I *bet* it's Finlay. He's got that homicidal glint about him.'

A sudden urge to get away from the others overwhelmed Maggie. The clumsy shapes in the dark, the jags of raucous laughter. She needed a moment away from them all. But she had only a couple of seconds before the murderer began his hunt, and only a few minutes before Rory came after them all. The utility rooms? But they were a maze of boilers and freezers and lavatories and dog baskets and boot rooms, and she was always unnerved by the big cabinet, where Ivo kept his shotguns.

Maggie turned right, towards the entrance hall.

'An imperial staircase,' Mr Fitzwilliam had told her, pointing to the grand stairs that led up to a half landing before dividing. The two sets of ancient oak staircases then turned back on themselves until they met the gallery that overlooked the hall. The stairs creaked as Maggie climbed them, the banister cool beneath her fingers, the treads worn by centuries of feet. Four bedrooms led off the long gallery that ran right along the main section of the house. These bedrooms looked out over the front drive, and Maggie's was the furthest to the left as she came up the main staircase. Beyond that was the master bedroom, over the kitchen and snug.

Downstairs, Maggie could hear scuffles and laughter. Jude cackling, 'no, get *out*, Finlay, I'm in here.' Jude must be in the large cupboard under the stairs, the winter coats stretching back like Narnia. Wintercross was filled with odd spaces and hidey-holes, its medieval bones showing through.

'It was absolute murder putting in enough bathrooms for the twenty-first century,' Ivo had said once. 'We were practically besieged by English Heritage, trebuchets and all. And the bat people! Christ. A guerrilla army. Especially ironic when the entire place appears to be held together by guano alone.'

Maggie heard footsteps on the staircase behind her and fled down the corridor towards her room.

You're being *silly*, she told herself.

But there was a primitive urge to get to her bedroom, her space for this weekend, to get away from them all, just for a bit. She ran to the bedroom, closing the door quietly behind her.

Once she was safe in her room, she breathed out for a second, enjoying the privacy. She was used to living alone now. 'Crystallised into singledom,' someone had called it once, and the words had haunted her ever since. But she needed it, the empty quiet, the peace. She crossed the uneven floorboards, twisted by the centuries, and sat down on her bed, stroking the big linen pillows.

Footsteps. Coming down the passage.

Her throat tightened.

Hide.

Where?

It was that childish terror, half enjoyable. *Coming, ready or not…*

Under the bed? Ridiculous. In the tiny en suite bathroom? There was a linen cupboard in there, maybe that would do. Maggie hurried across, trying to move soundlessly over the creaky wooden floor. There. She yanked the cupboard open and folded herself under the shelves. But the door wouldn't shut, kept swinging open. She jammed her fingers into a knot in the wood and held it tight.

The door from the hallway opened, there was a hesitation on the threshold of the bedroom, then a floorboard squeaked. Shorn of sight, every sound echoed in Maggie's ears.

Footsteps, coming closer. Maggie's breath shortened, heart hammering.

Ridiculous, you're being ridiculous.

But someone *was* moving around in her bedroom.

They're looking for somewhere to hide too, she told herself. It's *normal*. Part of the game. You've known these people your entire adult life.

But she felt the fear snake up her spine, her hands beginning to shake. In the distance, far away, she could hear laughter, shouts. But in her bedroom, the steps were slow, cautious. Now they were closer to the bathroom door. Had someone followed her on purpose? Did they know she was here? Maggie held her breath, sure that the thud of her heart was loud enough to give her away.

Another step.

Another step.

And a scream from downstairs.

Maggie felt the air rush out of her lungs.

The scream dissolved into laughter: *Murder! Murder most foul! Forsooth!*

Maggie heard quick steps in her bedroom. A squeak, wood on wood. And silence.

Breathing out, Maggie let the cupboard door swing open.

She was the last one back to the brightly lit kitchen. Rory sat at the head of the table, notepad in one hand, imaginary spyglass in the other.

'Colonel Mustard in the library with the candlestick,' he was saying. 'Ah, Miss Fletcher. Suspiciously late back, I see. Any bloodstains on your hands? None whatsoever?'

Maggie laughed and slumped into her seat.

'Remember,' said Elizabeth, 'you can only lie if you're the murderer.'

'Elizabeth,' Rory turned to her. 'Where were you when the screaming began?'

'Who died?' asked Maggie.

'Ollie,' said Rory. 'Various prayers answered.'

Ollie was pouring himself a shot of vodka. 'Cheers, Rory!'

'I went towards the ballroom,' said Elizabeth. 'And hid in the cloakroom next to that.'

'Didn't want to be killed, did you? Sensible, most sensible.' Rory twizzled a non-existent moustache.

'And you, Jude,' Rory turned on her. 'I believe I heard some kerfuffle in the hall. My beloved brother, trying to get in the cupboard, perhaps?'

'Indeed,' Jude was Lady Bracknell for one word. 'I told Finlay to hop it.'

'Which suggests Finlay was not the murderer,' Rory said thoughtfully. 'Because he would have simply killed you in the cupboard.'

'I suppose so,' said Jude.

'So that leaves Ivo, Ayda and Maggie,' Rory said. 'If we trust Elizabeth's word, which I don't. Ayda, where did you get to?'

'I went into the library,' said Ayda. 'Caught up on my reading.'

'And you, Ivo?'

'I saw Ivo going into the drawing room,' Finlay interrupted.

'Shh,' Ivo was laughing.

'The drawing room where the still-warm body of Mr Oliver Radcliffe was discovered a few minutes later?' Rory asked, frantically twirling his moustache.

'Indeed,' cried Finlay.

They were all giggling now, slightly hysterical.

'In that case,' Rory declaimed, 'I declare the killer to be Mr Ivo Fitzwilliam, a noted murderer.'

Ivo held his hands up. 'Alright, alright! You bunch of idiots.'

Ollie passed him a shot of vodka and Ivo drank it in one, closing his eyes against the kick of the alcohol.

'You read the next prediction,' Elizabeth passed him the glass bowl. And Ivo was still laughing as he grabbed one. Laughing until he read it, that was, and then his laughter stopped.

46

Ayda, on Lily: Lily will always be the other woman.

'Meow,' said Finlay.

'Well,' said Ayda, 'she was.'

'But you two were friends,' Maggie protested. 'Old friends. And the other woman thing only happened once.'

'Or twice,' said Ayda.

A snapshot of a memory, faded at the edges. Meeting Lily for a run, Maggie a few minutes early. Professor Norton and Lily springing apart. Professor Norton: well over fifty and definitely married. Revolting to Maggie's eyes.

'What?' Afterwards, Lily was defiant. 'It's not as if his wife's ever going to find out.'

'But, Lily...' Maggie, mired in adolescent morality. 'It's... wrong.'

'Why?' Brisk.

'It's adultery,' even as she said the word, Maggie knew it sounded ridiculous.

'Do you know,' Lily mused, 'when I was young, I thought adultery was just what adults *did*? Adult-ery.'

'But Professor Norton shouldn't. He's taking advantage of you.'

'Of me? Maggie, do you actually read any of these books you're set? I'm hardly Lolita.'

Although Maggie did read the books, actually. And she couldn't remember things turning out particularly well for Madame Bovary, Hester Prynne or Anna Karenina.

'Look at Thérèse Raquin, Lily.'

'Maggie,' Lily was laughing. 'That's not real life!'

'He'll hurt you.'

'I'm already hurt,' Lily made it a joke. 'It's too late.'

Maggie had never told the others about Professor Norton. No Governor Bellingham, she. Although perhaps they had known all along. She never asked after Professor Norton and Lily never told. They stayed friends despite, not because.

'I'm sure I'd have been burned for a witch a few centuries ago,' Lily said once.

'We all would have been,' said Ayda. 'Apart from Elizabeth, maybe. Crispy, crispy. I'd chuck Jude on the flames myself.'

Maggie had spoken to the police after Lily's death. 'She had a… complicated love life,' one of the police officers declared, fidgeting with his phone. One of the other officers made a click of disapproval and Maggie knew exactly what he was thinking. Anna Karenina, safely under her train. It wasn't anything especially wild either, Maggie thought defensively. A few Tinder dates, the odd party. It was just that these officers believed women Lily's age should be married off, pinned down.

'Where were you?' one of the officers asked, too casually. 'On the day Ms Blake died?'

'Westminster,' Maggie replied. 'I work in the House of Commons. I'm a journalist, my newspaper has an office there. I was there all day. There are electronic passes to get in and out.'

'Sure.'

The police hadn't turned anything up about Lily's death. Not enough to prove she'd jumped, not enough to swear she hadn't.

Maggie, I'm scared.

The health editor at the *Post* had written an article on the pressure on junior doctors: the long hours, the chaotic funding. It was illustrated by an old photograph of Lily, ravishing in her scrubs. Maggie had read the article carefully. It sounded right.

'I suppose if Stella Blake had an affair…' Finlay spoke hesitantly, stopping as Ayda whipped around.

'Lily had her Daddy issues, alright,' sighed Ivo. 'We all knew that.'

'She didn't just go for father figures,' said Elizabeth, 'either.'

Do not speak ill of the dead. Although, at the same time, you can't libel them either, as every journalist knows.

'Did Lily know?' Maggie asked Ayda cautiously. 'Did she know your father was… also hers?'

'I don't want to talk about it,' Ayda's eyes blazed. And then, because she couldn't resist it, she spat out the words. 'She was just like her mother, that girl. Exactly the bloody same.'

'Right,' Elizabeth cleared her throat, reached for the cards. 'Next round.'

They all concentrated on the cards as Elizabeth doled them out. This time, Maggie was ready. As Ivo waved around the King of Spades, Maggie clutched the Seven of Hearts close to her chest.

As soon as they were all out of the kitchen, Maggie headed up the backstairs, making for Ayda's room, the one next door to hers. The wood panelling in this room was ancient. In the daylight, the panels were a dark burnished gold. Tonight, the room was lit only by a faint moon, the four-poster bed a menacing shadow. To Maggie's left, there was a huge fireplace. She crossed the room and kneeled down next to it, her fingers feeling for the wainscoting on the left of the vast chimney breast. The oak panels were edged by carved roses, beautiful shapes blackened by age. Maggie pressed first one rose and then another.

Downstairs, she could hear Ivo's voice. 'Come on, Pagan, time to hunt them down.' The dog was barking enthusiastically, bewildered by the revelry of the night. She hadn't heard anyone coming up the imperial staircase, but the backstairs didn't creak in the same way. Someone might be creeping up, even now. She pushed another wooden rose hard, stubbing her fingers.

Nothing.

The nerves rose again, that thread of fear winding around her heart.

She pushed another rose and a rumble made her jump. A panel slid back, revealing a pit of darkness behind. A priest hole, one of Wintercross's secrets. A cramped chamber where a man might hide, just. Maggie shifted forward, crouching down. She could fit, she remembered. It was tight though. She manoeuvred carefully, Mr Fitzwilliam's instructions echoing in her head.

By your left hand, you'll feel a sort of knob. Push that.

And she did, hearing the rumble again as the panel slipped back into place.

In the priest hole, the darkness was complete. Maggie lay in silence, feeling like an animal in a burrow. Imagine hiding here, she thought, as the Queen's men hunted. Determined, indefatigable, tearing the place apart. Imagine lying here, praying to the same God as theirs as – just the other side of the narrow wooden panels – the hunters went over the building inch by inch by inch.

Unable to trust even a silence, because even stillness might be a trap: waiting, watchful, deadly.

But – desperately, paradoxically – they would pray that the searchers wouldn't tire of their hunt. That they wouldn't lose patience and surround the house with a row of jeering watchers. That they wouldn't strike the match.

Because the old oak would burn, raging flames against the deep blue of the evening sky. And then the decision would be forced. Stay and die, or flee and pray.

Secret places seared away.

A trial by fire, a horror.

'These are the breathing holes,' Mr Fitzwilliam had pointed out prosaically. 'Ingenious, aren't they?' Embedded in the wooden roses, so they were almost invisible.

In the darkness, Maggie could just about make out the shouts from downstairs, and the laughter, and the sound of someone running up the stairs. Or down? The dust was making her nose tickle. She lifted her hand to rub it, forgetting for a moment the narrowness of the space. Her hand bumped against the top of the chamber, and at once she was in a coffin, the old oak terrifyingly close to her face. There were only a few inches of air above her. What if the old mechanism failed? What if she was stuck in here, trapped and forgotten forever?

Scrabbling, scraping. Desperate, dying.

Don't be silly, she told herself. *You can hear them, so they would hear you if you screamed and screamed.*

But it was a relief when she heard someone shout, 'murder!' and the babble of laughter rose up again. Maggie pressed the knob and without hesitation the panel slid open. Elizabethan technology, still running smooth. She wriggled out and standing upright was a reprieve, her joints easing back into place, her muscles stretching out. Imagine the days. The weeks. Limbs seizing up, stomach cramping with hunger. Maybe the old martyrs enjoyed it. Maybe they thought their God would smile down on their agony, and glorify them as they were torn into quarters, guts spooling like ribbons.

Maggie hurried out of the room, taking the narrow stairs back down to the snug.

By the time she reached the kitchen, Jude was already drinking a large glass of vodka.

'I didn't bloody see you,' Jude was laughing between gulps.

'Hopeless,' Ivo grinned back at her. 'You were right under my nose when you killed him.'

'Rory needs to do a shot too,' said Finlay. 'Imagine being killed by Jude. The shame of it all.'

Jude was pulling a face at him as she reached for a piece of paper, and as she read it, her face froze.

47

Ollie, on Jude: Will have spent everything she
ever earned on drugs.

'Wow,' said Jude. 'Thank you so much, Ollie.'

There had been drugs at university, Maggie remembered, and the
intake had ticked up when they moved to London in their twenties.
MDMA for the raves in east London, coke for house parties, weed up
on Hampstead Heath in the glow of a sunny evening. Ketamine for
the people who were starting to spin out of control. Crack and you
disappeared.

She wondered who was still at it. She hadn't for years now. Couldn't
face the hangover, and was too busy saving for a juliet balcony. In their
twenties, it was done openly. Ostentatiously, almost. Here, it might be
going on in a discreet bathroom, she wasn't sure. No one would do it in
front of Rory, of course, because he had to be able to say, *I had no idea.*

Even if he had every idea.

Finlay? Maybe. Ollie? Maybe. Elizabeth, never.

Ayda? A lot, back then. She used to bring it up from London. Maggie
had boggled once at a weighing machine that ran to several decimal
places, casually pulled out from under her bed. *Ayda! No! Oh, Maggie,
chill out.* A world away from today's glossy partner at Throwleigh Pearce
in the shiny Liverpool Street citadel. Lawyers were end users only.

But today. Ivo? Yes. Lily, yes, very occasionally, back then.

Jude. All the time.

Coke, Maggie guessed, was on the menu this evening. Jude was jittery, eyes glassy, her jaw working too hard.

'I don't,' Jude said defensively. Then, 'I don't do that much.'

'Sure,' said Ollie, and Maggie couldn't quite decipher the tone of voice. Neither could Jude from the toss of her head.

'You think I buggered up my life, don't you?' Jude raised her chin. Her eyes were full of tears, Maggie noticed. 'That I had it all and fucked it up?'

'No, we don't,' Maggie said. 'And you haven't.'

'Don't patronise me, Maggie,' Jude snapped.

'I'm not.'

'It's okay,' Jude said. 'I know I haven't made bloody partner or set up my own megacorporation or whatever. But I'm happy.' Maggie caught Ayda rolling her eyes. 'And anyway,' Jude added pointedly, 'it's not like I'm the only one who likes a party.'

Maggie knew that some of them went to wilder parties, the parties she had never gone to. Killing Kittens and Crossbreed and Klub Verboten.

Ivo and Finlay, Maggie guessed.

Ayda, on occasion.

There were the dark stags, too. A polite outing for the father-in-law and the bride's brother, maybe, to a strip club in Soho. And then, quietly, a smaller gang would fly to Prague or Berlin or Las Vegas. Whatever happened on those weekends was never mentioned again.

Jude sat, eyes burning as she stared at one face, then another. Elizabeth brushed over the awkward silence by dealing out the cards.

'Do you want to play or not?' Elizabeth asked Jude, and Jude picked up her card sulkily.

Maggie looked at hers. The Seven of Hearts, again.

'Ooh,' said Ayda. 'I'm the detective.'

This time, Maggie veered past the staircase. She wanted to stay downstairs, close to the others, even if they killed her. Beyond the staircase was the ballroom, a beautiful Regency space. But then she spotted Jude ahead of her, weaving slightly. She couldn't face Jude and the hysterics that were likely to turn into spitting rage any second. Instead, she turned towards the two big drawing rooms that ran together to the left of the front door.

A movement to her right, and she jumped.

'It's only me,' Rory whispered.

'Oh… are you—'

'No. You?'

'No,' she breathed a laugh. There was a creak out in the hallway. 'Quick,' she whispered. 'Hide.'

In the far corner of the two rooms, there was a heavy oak door. Maggie yanked it open to reveal a narrow spiral staircase winding down.

'The cellars?' asked Rory.

'I guess so. I've never been down there.'

They squeezed on to the top step together, laughing silently. Maggie pulled the oak door closed behind them, leaving only a crack of light.

'Honestly,' Rory stood on her toe. 'Thank God, the Chief Whip can't see me now.'

'Shh,' she whispered. 'Someone's coming.'

It was Elizabeth, pacing silently.

'I can just see her as Chief Whip,' Rory whispered in Maggie's ear.

'Do you think she's the murderer?'

'Might be.'

As Elizabeth made her way through the two rooms, the moonlight caught her face. She looked very sad, thought Maggie, quite unlike her usual façade. But Maggie's thoughts were pushed to one side by Rory shoving his fist into his mouth, trying to muffle his own laughter.

'Let's get down the stairs,' he murmured. 'Quickly.'

Moving as quietly as possible, quelling her own giggles, Maggie edged her way down the narrow staircase. The steps were narrow and it was too low to stand up straight.

'Damn,' she said. There was a door across the bottom of the staircase. Bright steel, new.

'Get down,' Rory muttered. 'She's coming.'

They pressed themselves against the metal door, just out of sight of the doorway. Maggie shook with suppressed laughter.

Even in the dark, she could tell that Rory was smiling.

It was odd to be squashed against Rory in the darkness. His body was solid, the muscles dense. His shape was familiar and unfamiliar all at once, and she was acutely aware of how long it had been since she was this close to anyone. A flashback to the tussocky grass behind Mr

Nassar's garage, cigarette smoke drifting in the light of the dawn. That sleepy flirtation, *marry me if…* flattering, in its own way.

'Sorry,' she tried to move away, her cheeks flushing in the dark.

'Don't mind me.'

Above their heads, the oak door opened. Maggie clapped her hands over her mouth, pushing down the nervous laughter. For a second, her fingers entangled with Rory's and she jerked them away. Rory was flattened against the metal door, trying to keep out of Elizabeth's line of sight. Maggie imagined her peering down, listening intently. They stood in the dark, perfectly still. Elizabeth must be looking at the grimy bricks, wondering if there was any point in covering herself in dust. Not Elizabeth's style, dirt. Then there was the sound of the oak door closing, the creak of Elizabeth's footsteps moving away.

'Phew.' They relaxed against the damp bricks. It felt companionable, thought Maggie. The awkwardness that had built up between them for months had broken down.

'I miss you,' Rory said into the darkness.

'I—' For a moment, Maggie couldn't think what to say. 'I'm always around, Rory.'

'I know. And I know I've been crap.'

'After Genet…' She felt him flinch at the name. 'Sorry.'

'Don't be sorry. And after this whole business with Lily—'

Above them, someone started to scream.

48

Lily, on Jude: Dearest Jude, I hope you will
have survived all this, my darling girl. You are
golden. Always, always remember that.

It was Jude screaming. By the time Rory and Maggie reached her in the
ballroom, she was hysterical, crouched down, her back against the wall.

Finlay was standing next to her, looking shifty.

'I didn't...' he was saying. 'I didn't do anything.'

'What happened?' Rory snapped.

'She was in the false wall in that little room next to the ballroom,'
Finlay sounded pleading. 'I saw her slide open the panel and climb in. I
thought it would be a good place to...'

Jude was howling, her words indecipherable. She started banging the
back of her head against the wall. She must have sprinted to the ballroom, Maggie guessed, desperate for space. Above their heads, great
chandeliers glistered in the moonlight.

'What happened?' Elizabeth appeared. 'Jude! Are you—'

Jude's wails redoubled.

'It's alright, Jude,' Maggie kneeled down beside her. 'You're okay.
You're safe.'

'I didn't do anything.' There was a desperation in Finlay's voice. 'I'm
sorry, Jude. I never meant to scare you...'

Ivo and Ollie appeared, Ayda a few paces behind them. Again, Maggie
caught Ayda's eye roll. *Jude, always such a drama queen.*

'What the fuck's happened, Finlay?' Ivo's voice was icy. He switched on the lights, leaving them all blinking.

'Nothing,' Finlay insisted. He was almost tearful. 'I was the murderer, and I couldn't find anyone because you'd all bloody hidden. Then I saw Jude climbing into the false wall, and I thought...'

'You fucking idiot,' said Ivo. 'You know... you know how she gets.'

A silence, flickering glances.

'So you only tapped her on the shoulder?' said Rory.

'Yes!' It was a near shout. 'Jude, tell them, for God's sake–'

Finlay was holding the Ace of Spades, waving it defensively.

'Jude—' Ayda, leaning against the doorframe. 'Come on.'

For a moment, Jude's sobs eased. 'It wasn't Finlay's fault,' she managed. 'He just surprised me, that's all.' The tension eased at once. Jude started crying again, but the hysteria was passing.

Maggie stood up. 'Guys, give us a moment, can you? It's too hectic for her, all of you crowding around like this.'

Ivo hesitated. 'Are you sure? I could—'

'It's fine.' Maggie made a pushing-away gesture. 'She needs space.'

'Of course.'

They crowded out, making for the kitchen. Finlay pushed Rory, who shoved him back, the physicality or brotherhood boosted by relief. Even before the double doors closed, the rest of them were back to laughing, joshing. Jude waited until their voices had faded into the distance.

'I'm not crazy,' she said.

'I know,' said Maggie. She sat down next to Jude, and they both stared up at the chandeliers.

'They used to draw all over these floors,' Jude said dully. Her mascara had run, leaving Pierrot tear stains.

'What?' Maggie turned, bewildered.

'In chalk,' Jude waved carelessly. 'For the balls, for the dances, they drew all sorts of... fripperies all over the floors. Nymphs and mermaids, centaurs and satyrs. Arabesques. The moon, the stars, the planets, the comets.'

'I didn't know that.' *Jude,* she thought, *the autodidact with the fierce, wasted intelligence.*

'If a ball was held for a specific event,' Jude went on, 'an artist might spend days drawing something appropriate. Flowers for an engagement. Foxhounds and horses for a hunt ball. If both the bride and groom had coats of arms, they might be combined.'

'It must have been spectacular.'

'Practical too, of course,' Jude rubbed away at the mascara. 'The chalk stopped the dancers sliding about in their slippers.'

'I never knew.'

'Well, why would you? It was ephemeral. Magical for just a few hours, before it was all danced to dust. Beauty, forgotten.'

'After reading all that Austen, I should have known.'

Jude shrugged. 'They could hardly put it on Insta.'

'I know that, thanks, Jude.'

'It was designed to be a memory,' said Jude. 'Conceived for destruction. And one day, the curtains and the memories fade.'

Jude pulled out a packet of cigarettes, stared defiantly at the chandeliers and lit up. Smoke spiralled towards the high Regency windows.

'Come on,' Maggie hauled her up and pulled her towards the doors that led out to the garden. Jude allowed herself to be towed.

'I'm not crazy,' Jude said again. There was an urgency in her voice, and an unfamiliar determination.

Maggie, the journalist, let the silence take hold.

'I'm *not*.'

'What happened then?' Maggie asked. 'What's this all about?'

'Nothing.'

A stone balustrade marked the edge of the terrace, with a small drop away to the lawn. Jude leaned against the balustrade, putting all her weight on her stomach.

'Come on, Jude. I'll never tell anyone. Journalists are surprisingly good at keeping secrets.'

'Only because you know the value of them.'

'Sure.'

'Fine, Maggie.' Sarcasm. 'Something bad happened, Maggie.'

'I know that, Jude.'

Jude's eyes flicked towards her. She pushed herself away from the balustrade, turning to face Maggie. 'You know what?'

'Nothing,' Maggie said hastily. 'I just remember how you were when you arrived at university. You were different then. And one day, you changed.'

Freshers' week, that carnival of the new. Maggie had felt as if she was sloughing off her school uniform. She dyed her hair blonde like at least four other people that week. Jude had sparkled back then, joyous, clever, silly.

And then.

'What happened?' Maggie asked again.

'Oh, come on, Maggie,' Jude was impatient, trying to blot away the tears with anger. 'I'm sure you can guess.'

Maggie thought about the hair sliced away. The shape of Jude's skull, suddenly shockingly visible. Half defiant, half vulnerable. A plea for help designed to unnerve. And Maggie guessed, because deep down she must have known all along.

She kept her voice steady, imperturbable, so that it almost wasn't a question. 'Did someone hurt you, Jude?'

A long pause. Jude was scraping pieces of lichen off the balustrade, gouging her fingernails along the unyielding stone.

'Did someone rape you, Jude?'

Rape. Jude tossed her head at the word. That word. One syllable. Nothing.

'Why did you never ask me before, Maggie?'

'I hadn't been a journalist for almost two decades before.'

'Just ask the question?' Jude's mouth curled. 'Steer into the pain?'

'Something like that.'

'And do you find it helps? Any of it? Peeling the truth like an onion. Or does it just lead to a whole lot of tears?'

'I don't know.'

Their eyes had acclimatised to the darkness again. The stars were so bright they might almost be touched.

'Then, yes,' Jude said slowly. 'I suppose so. Yes.'

They sat together, looking out over the gloom of the garden.

'I'm sorry,' said Maggie, after a pause.

'Me too.' Flippant.

'I wish I had known.'

'It happened to lots of girls,' Jude jutted her chin, 'back then.'

Maggie met her eyes. 'Oh, Jude, I am so sorry. So sorry that this happened to you. I wish… I wish I had been able to help. I'm so very sorry that someone hurt you.'

'It was different then.' Jude was holding herself very upright, the garden dark behind her. 'A different world.'

A world when boys still really thought that 'no' might turn to 'yes', if you asked enough times. And sometimes Maggie said 'no' when she meant 'yes', because of Anna Karenina and Thérèse Raquin and Hester Prynne, so you could almost understand the confusion. But also, not. The boys – were they still boys then? No. No, they weren't – groped without thinking. Although who knew if it was any better now? With the porn and the revenge and the endlessness of it all.

'A Maggie sandwich,' Finlay would bawl, trapping her between him and Ollie on the dance floor of one of the terrible clubs.

Four men circling Lily in Ayia Napa, hyenas drawing closer.

And it was normal. Or normalised, anyway. Didn't mean anything. Much.

There were darker whispers still, of course. Warnings, really. So-and-so after that party, when she was so pissed she could hardly stand.

Him.

Watch him.

So they watched.

She'd never heard anything about Jude though. Never put the pieces together, as Jude fell apart. Because, of course, now it all made sense. Jude, a blaze of wit and ambition in the first year, fading to anger and turmoil and sadness.

Crazy bitch.

'It's funny, isn't it?' Jude kept her voice analytical, dispassionate. 'How we were all there at exactly the same time, doing exactly the same thing, and the boys and the girls had completely different experiences. Lived completely different lives, really.'

'Who?' Maggie asked. 'Who was he?' For a second, she thought Jude might tell her. But then she looked away, stubbed out her cigarette.

'You,' Jude said, 'never knew him.'

Jude stood up, conversation over. Maggie couldn't tell if she was lying or not.

'Let's talk more,' said Maggie.

'Let's not.'

'Jude… you've got all these suspicions. This conviction that something happened to Lily. But you won't tell me what you think you know.'

But it was too late.

'Danced to dust,' Jude was walking away across the ballroom. 'We were all danced to dust.'

49

Ivo, on Lily: Will have gone for Plan B and be
married to Finlay.

Finlay actually blushed.

'Oh, Christ, sorry, Finlay.' Ivo started to laugh. 'That one's a bit harsh on multiple levels.' He stood up and chucked the piece of paper in the fire.

'Plan B,' Finlay shook his head. 'Well, I suppose I was, really. And that was why we never worked out.'

'You could have done...' Maggie was abruptly back in her Streatham flat, Lily folded into the sofa, sad. 'Maybe. If things had been different.'

They had always been close, Lily and Finlay. Best friends, really, as time went on. Rory's crush on Lily had precluded any romance, so instead a proper friendship had blossomed. After university, just before Finlay joined the Army, they had travelled around Thailand together. There were months of golden beaches and hammocks and fire juggling. Maggie had flown out for a week of pad thai and kiteboarding and weed, and at the end of it all, Finlay had gone off to Sandhurst with a suspiciously short haircut.

'I suppose Finlay was my back-up plan.' Years later, Lily had been staring blindly at the juliet balcony. 'I think, on some level, I knew that all along. I was his *best friend*. But there was always an undertone of something else between us too.'

'I know. I saw.'

'We *flirted.*'

'Yes.'

'Finlay used me to keep his girlfriends on their toes.' Lily, acid bitter. 'I can see that in hindsight. Because no one can criticise a guy for being best friends with a *girl*, can they? It just shows how cool they are, how in touch with their feelings they are. And I liked it, if I'm absolutely honest. It felt as if I was *special* to him. Until, of course, I wasn't.'

In the end, it had been brief. No more than a few dates, really.

'He never even deleted Tinder,' Lily howled, almost laughing now. 'The notifications would pop up while we were having dinner! What an arsehole. Why the hell did I think he would be any different with me?'

'He's desperately insecure,' said Maggie, who was going through a phase of reading self-care books. 'He always was. He'd use you to keep his girlfriends on edge and then he used the whole of sodding Tinder to keep you on your toes.'

'Wanker. Fucked-up wanker.'

'And you never even really fancied him,' Maggie reminded her. 'Not really.'

'I *know*,' Lily raged. 'But I suppose with everyone else settling down all of a sudden… I always thought that he was genuinely kind underneath it all. And that with me, it would be different. I thought that we suited each other, in some deep and meaningful way.'

'He *can* be a good friend.'

'If you think every aspect of his life is truly fascinating and you're happy to listen to hours of stories starring Finlay, then, yes, fill your boots. But, Jesus… I used to wonder why we never saw a single ex of his ever again. Well, now I know. Scorched bloody earth.'

'But you guys will be okay around each other, won't you? The friendship group…'

'*Friendship group.* God, I hate that phrase. Of course, I'll be fine. I just need to vent a bit.'

'Okay.'

'What does a friendship group even mean, anyway?' Lily asked querulously. 'It's just a cluster of rivalries and allegiances and feuds and regrets.'

'Maybe it was mixing up male and female friendships that made everything so complicated,' said Maggie. 'Maybe when the men were sitting monosyllabically in the pubs and the women were knitting at home, it was all more straightforward.'

'Maybe.'

It had left Lily sad, though. The loss of Finlay as a friend had wounded her, for all her defiance. Plan B failed and she was left casting around, unsure all of a sudden.

Maggie looked at Finlay now. She had never really thought about the Lily debacle from his perspective. Finlay, who was attracted to the vulnerable girls. The insecure ones. And then he would keep them on edge, winding them tighter and tighter. Flirting with Lily and Tinder and the girl at the bus stop, and then wondering, *why are all women such bloody nutters?*

Finlay's own insecurities, thought Maggie, ran deep.

His mother, icily intelligent, had stopped working after getting married. She had been a woman who needed to work, who burned with frustration. Forcing her gym-twisted body to run miles every morning. Driving her sons from rugby to Scouts to football to violin lessons, all with an acid sweetness. Welcoming her husband home with a smile. Energetic, potent, *what might have been*. She made Maggie think of a tiger pacing to and fro at the zoo, bored and vicious. Maggie could imagine her eviscerating an eight-year-old Rory, a six-year-old Finlay. Humiliating them with a gleam in her eye.

She attended every rugby match her boys played, turned up for every cricket match. Snarling on the sidelines. By graduation, she was curdling. The energy warping into something else. 'I always wanted a daughter,' she had stared at Maggie with an old hunger. 'But Patrick said two children was enough. I *always* wanted a daughter.'

And Maggie wondered if it would have made any difference whatsoever.

50

Finlay, on Ollie: Still trying to keep up with the Joneses.

'Ouch,' said Ollie again. 'Thank you, Finlay.'

'I didn't mean it.' Finlay looked abashed. 'You know I didn't mean it.'

But Ollie looked tired. Bruised. Elizabeth was looking away.

'You did mean it.' Ollie looked straight at Finlay. 'You lot always mocked me. You mocked me for wanting what you took for granted.'

Elizabeth's head jerked, her eyes sharpening on Ollie.

'We didn't—' Finlay began.

'You did.'

If Rory or Ivo made a joke back then, Ollie often repeated the exact same words with twice the volume and half the subtlety. Then he would laugh loudly, hopefully.

'Guys! Guys!' Maggie could see it again. Ollie, running to catch up with Rory, Finlay and Ivo, down an alley, late at night, the light pooling beneath the streetlights. They must have been off to a club somewhere; Ollie was always trying to catch up. Rory and Finlay had been sent to the local private school with the smart uniforms and silly hats and the iron self-confidence. Ivo always had the glory of Wintercross like a wall behind him. Ollie only had Debs and Steve, and never realised that was fortunate.

'I'm sorry,' said Finlay, so quietly that Maggie almost missed it. 'I'm really sorry, Ollie.'

'It's okay,' said Ollie. 'It was all a long time ago.'

51

Maggie, on Ayda: Ayda will never have children.

Maggie felt her face flame.

'Maggie!' Just for a second, there was a sharp look of pain on Ayda's face. 'Why the hell did you write that?'

The kitchen fell silent.

I'm a turncoat, Maggie thought. A traitor. Apostate, almost.

The memory of writing those words was so faint that she wasn't even sure it was real.

'I'm sorry,' Maggie said. 'I'm really sorry, Ayda. I didn't mean it.'

'You must have done.'

'Well, I don't know why.'

'Well.' Ayda was tossing her hair back, dismissing the hurt. 'Bit harsh, Maggie, but whatever.' There was another silence. Finlay began topping up people's glasses. Maggie stared at the fire in the old hearth, as if she might find an answer there.

Ayda bent down to stroke Pagan, her face hidden. Then she straightened up. 'I'm just popping out for a quick ciggie.' Wine glass in one hand, cigarette in the other, Ayda headed towards the double doors that led towards the high moor. Maggie hesitated for a moment, the glances flickering around the table, and then followed her out.

Beyond the kitchen door, there was a herb garden hemmed in by pleached hornbeams. The box hedges were clipped low and the air was filled with mint and rosemary, sage and thyme. A statue of some ancient nymph peered round coyly. *There's rue for you, and here's some for me,* thought Maggie.

'I'm sorry, Ayda,' she said again.

Ayda was sitting on a stone bench close to the nymph. As Maggie drew close, she realised Ayda was crying. Maggie had never seen Ayda cry before, not once. The first crack in the dam, a sense of things falling apart.

'I didn't,' Ayda didn't bother looking round as Maggie sat down, 'expect to be here, you know? Not by now. Not like this.'

'I don't think any of us did,' said Maggie. 'Not really.'

She thought back to Ayda, nineteen-year-old Ayda. She had arrived from boarding school – *yes, Cheltenham Ladies', I had* such *a fab time* – a whirl of highlights and tea lights and Marlboro Lights. As Maggie looked out over the herb garden, she remembered her confusion during those first few days. They all seemed to *know* each other, these girls. It was as if everyone had been issued with a special guidebook along with the reading list, but she'd missed hers somehow, and only learned about Sir Gawain and Beowulf, who turned out to be surprisingly irrelevant here.

'Oh, *yes!*' one blonde would shriek, 'do you know Cazzy Astley?'

'Of *course!*' someone else would scream back. 'She was in the year above me. And if you were at Calne, you *must* have known Ophelia Capell?'

'God, yes, do you remember that time she…'

On and on it went.

So it had taken a while for Maggie and Ayda to become friends. Not that long, though. Time stretched and sprawled, so that by the end of the first term, it felt as if they had all known each other forever. And would know each other forever and ever and ever, obviously.

A few days before the Christmas holidays, Elizabeth and Ayda had sidled up to Maggie.

'We're thinking about houses next year.'

'People are getting organised already? We'll only get rubbish rooms if we stay in college.'

And Maggie had felt a shock and a surge of joy, as she realised they meant *her. Sharing.*

'I'd love to,' she had babbled. Even now, she could still remember that happiness: acceptance. One of *them*. A future as thrilling as the presents under a Christmas tree, wrapped up in tinsel and hope.

Elizabeth and Ayda played lacrosse together. That was how the two of them had become friends. Because having lacrosse and Cazzy Astley in common was more than enough for friendship. They were all the same, those girls, back then. It was only later that the varnish cracked and warped and revealed what lay beneath.

Lacrosse looked absolutely terrifying to Maggie, especially when Elizabeth was playing.

'You've *never* played lacrosse?' Elizabeth could barely process the idea.

It had been the same at Elizabeth's twenty-first, when Maggie had no idea how to join in at a ceilidh. 'I thought you just meant you weren't very *good*,' Elizabeth again. 'Not that you'd never actually done it.'

'But I *said* I'd never done it, Elizabeth. Those were my *precise* words.'

There had been boyfriends along the way for Ayda, too.

'But none that lasted,' Ayda sighed now. 'Not for long.'

Maggie and Ayda had dissected it so often over bottles of rosé in Soho.

'People blame my career,' Ayda had gestured widely with a glass, only a few weeks before. 'But they're getting it the wrong way round. I'm at work because I'm not with someone, not vice versa.'

'I know,' groaned Maggie. 'I *know*.'

'Or is it chicken and egg?' Ayda topped up their wine glasses. 'A vicious circle?'

'Don't talk to me about eggs. Do you think I should get mine frozen? But it costs a bloody fortune and what if they turn to mush when I defrost them at forty-seven? Or fifty-seven? What then? I've probably left it too late anyway.'

'Give me a clear target,' said Ayda, 'and I can achieve almost anything. GCSEs, A-Levels, degree, traineeship, partnership.' She ticked them off her fingers. 'I've billed more hours than anyone else on my team for three years straight. Work is somewhere to hide. It's something I can actually do.'

Ayda had explained the billing system at her law firm to Maggie. Six-minute slots, the clock ticking away on her screen all day long. 2,000 hours last year, every minute accounted for. They had to be, at £800 an hour.

'I hit every single target except this one,' Maggie took another swig of Whispering Angel. 'But what if it's the only one that really matters in the end?'

'Because eventually,' Ayda rubbed her temples, 'even I have to admit that in every single one of these romantic disasters, the common denominator is *me*.' Her phone buzzed. *Rose J*, the screen read. 'Stop *bothering* me, Rose,' Ayda snarled, clearing the call. She caught Maggie's mildly disapproving eye. 'Useless PA won't allow me one sodding evening off. Now where were we?'

'Common denominators,' said Maggie. 'We're overeducated, that's the problem. Another bottle?'

Because one between two wasn't enough.

'It doesn't seem to be Elizabeth's problem, or any of those girls.' Ayda's voice was bitter. 'And yes. Why the hell not?'

Rose J rang again, and again. Ayda cleared it with a jab.

Ayda and Elizabeth had begun drifting apart even before Elizabeth became Mrs Radcliffe. Elizabeth was unbearably smug at that time, Maggie acknowledged, flourishing that emerald-cut diamond as if it held the future. Relieved, probably. For Ayda, it was acid in the wound.

'I wish I had a PA,' Maggie slurred later.

'You don't. They pity me, the PA squad. The huns with their hubbies and their holibobs.' Ayda Eliza Doolittled the consonants. 'They pity *me*.'

'When did you find out?' Maggie stroked the manicured box hedge. 'About your father and...'

At the other end of the bench, she sensed Ayda stiffen and then shrug.

'He told me himself,' said Ayda. 'Not long ago. When he got cancer. When he knew he was dying. He didn't want to take the secret to the grave, I suppose. Because it won't be long now.'

'Does your mother know?'

'I don't think so,' said Ayda. 'I think she may have suspected different women at different times. But Stella Blake,' Ayda was pleased about it, 'wasn't anything special.'

Although she must have been, Maggie had thought to herself. That Surrey street was expensive, and Stella Blake hadn't bought it on her own. She had been kept close, for years.

'And Lily knew?' Maggie asked.

Ayda went still. 'Yes,' she said. 'I think Daddy told her about the same time he told me.'

Daddy. The word faded into the darkness.

'I'm sorry, Ayda. It must have been… difficult.' A thought struck Maggie. 'Your father didn't come to Lily's funeral, did he?'

'No,' said Ayda. 'They were away on that cruise. I don't know whether it was booked before or after Lily died.'

'And your mother booked it?'

'Probably.' Ayda took a sip of her drink. 'The irony is that for years, I put my parents' relationship on a pedestal. I couldn't find anyone to match up to what they had. And all along… and at the same time, in hindsight, it's so bloody obvious,' said Ayda. 'I didn't even feel especially surprised when he told me.'

'Yes. And then Lily died.'

'My half-sister,' said Ayda simply. 'My half-sister died.'

They sat in silence. Maggie could make out the skyline of Dartmoor in front of them, the bulk of the moor just darker than the sky beyond.

'How did you know?' Ayda asked abruptly. 'How did you know all the way back then that I wouldn't have children?'

'You could still—'

But Ayda waved away the words. 'We won't, Maggie.' This *we* was a slap, a casual exclusion from all that. 'How did you know?' Ayda asked again.

'I don't know…' But Maggie found that she did. 'You were spiky, Ayda. Too sharp. I'd watch boys try and flirt with you and you'd almost smack them away.'

It had been shyness, Maggie realised now. Insecurity, again. Dancing for a father whose attention was endlessly elsewhere.

Ayda blew out a long stream of smoke and the wind swept it away.

'I know,' she said, 'that you didn't have the easiest time either.'

'Oh…' Maggie curled her legs up on the bench, shrinking away. 'I don't know about that.'

It had never been possible to explain to Ayda about Maggie's father and his drinking.

Mostly, he was alright. He was a *good* father. Even now, the protest was automatic. Mowing the lawn, cleaning the car, fixing the fence.

Except.

Except sometimes.

At a party, Maggie and her mother and her sister – Rachel, five years younger, departed for New Zealand as soon as she turned eighteen – might count his drinks, getting quieter and quieter. Chicks in a nest with a sparrowhawk overhead. Or the front door might crash open, late at night, angry footsteps. When work was going badly, he would sit in the front room, a silence growing up around him like Sleeping Beauty's forest. Until Maggie and Rachel and her mother were communicating in glances and the smallest of gestures.

A wave towards the fridge: *Dinner?*

A nod: *Yes, please.*

Another wave: *Scrambled eggs?*

Yes, please.

Bedtime?

Yes. Please.

Because at any moment, the silence might explode into a million pieces.

Maggie had tried to explain, once or twice. But the silence formed around her instead. She had watched Ayda try and make sense of it, when all Ayda knew was Surrey and ponies and county netball. Ayda had never even come close to understanding.

Maybe she'd understand now. Come close.

Too late.

Ayda stubbed out her cigarette, grinding it into the ground. It was turning colder, the wind starting to blow in from the north.

'If the wind changes,' said Maggie, for something to say, 'your face will stay like that. That's what my mother used to say.'

'I wish mine would bloody stay like this,' said Ayda. 'I need to book in for some more sodding Botox.' Laughter was a relief. Ayda touched the triangles of immobility on her forehead, her cheeks.

'You never know when life will sort of *fix*, do you?' said Maggie. 'When it's all going to set like jelly. You think you have it all ahead of you, and suddenly, you don't.'

'I know.'

'Do you think the die was already cast all the way back then?' asked Maggie. 'That everything was already setting by the time we sat down for that dinner?'

'Yes,' said Ayda. 'I'm starting to believe that it was.' She stood up and walked back towards the house. 'Time for the next prediction.'

52

Ivo, on Ollie: Will be cheating on his wife.

Elizabeth's hand shook as she poured herself a glass of wine. 'Thanks for that, Ivo.'

'You really were on fire that night, weren't you, Ivo?' said Rory. 'Was there anyone you didn't stitch-up?'

'I didn't know that Ollie would marry *Elizabeth*,' Ivo protested. 'It was just an *observation*.'

And he had been right anyway, thought Maggie. Ollie was always exactly the sort of man who would end up cheating. The wife's praise, taken for granted, and never quite enough. Elizabeth was still on her pedestal when they married. Pretty, blonde, the right sort of school: everything that mattered to Ollie. Even so, time wore away the delight; waves gnawing the foot of a cliff. But when Maggie looked across at Ollie, he looked stunned. Shocked to his very core, as if it had never occurred to him that Elizabeth had guessed.

'You knew?' He was looking straight at Elizabeth. 'You *knew*?'

There was absolute contempt in Elizabeth's eyes as she looked at him. 'Of course I knew,' she spat. 'What sort of an idiot do you think I am?'

'Oh God, Elizabeth… I'm… I'm so sorry.'

Elizabeth stared at him, and then spoke purposefully, every syllable vicious. 'I never should have married you, Oliver Craig Radcliffe.'

Ollie twined his fingers together, almost in prayer. 'I am truly sorry.'

'It's too late, Ollie. Far, far too late.'

'But you never said anything about…'

'What would have been the point?' Elizabeth dismissed him.

'You never told Ollie that you knew he had cheated?' Ayda was openly fascinated. 'Just chucked him without a word?'

Elizabeth didn't even bother to nod.

'How?' Ollie stammered. 'How did you know?'

Elizabeth pulled a disgusted face, as if the sordid details were beneath her, then shrugged. 'That's none of your business, Ollie.'

'Who was it?' Ayda, agog, asked the question no one else would.

'It's none of your business either,' Elizabeth dismissed her. 'Thanks,' she turned on Ivo. 'Thank you very much for that.'

'I'd forgotten!' Ivo held up his hands in apology. 'I'd completely forgotten.'

'It's fine,' said Elizabeth. 'Anyone sensible could have seen what Ollie was. God, I wish I had.' She snatched up the playing cards and glowered around the table. 'Who,' she asked icily, 'wants to play again?'

The King of Spades grimaced up at Maggie. 'It's me,' she said reluctantly. 'I'm the detective.'

'Excellent,' said Ivo. 'You can put that investigative genius to full use.'

He was lightening the mood on purpose, Maggie thought, but she smiled back all the same. 'By the way,' she said. 'What's in that little room at the bottom of the stairs in the drawing room? Rory and I were exploring.'

'It's a panic room!' Ivo rolled his eyes. 'The security company insisted. I thought it was ludicrous.'

'A whole room just for panicking,' said Jude morosely. 'I could use one of those.'

'It's not—'

'I *know*, Elizabeth.'

'Give us a few minutes to escape,' Rory said to Maggie. 'And then come at us.'

Maggie sat at the head of the table as she watched them make their way out of the kitchen. They were quieter now. The fun of the evening had drained away. She heard the ancient floorboards creak as they made their way out into the main house. There were the muffled sounds of someone climbing the little stairs. A gurgle of laughter as someone – Finlay, she guessed – bumped into someone else. Jude's footsteps were a stumble now. Veering to and fro, careening off walls.

The house grew silent. Maggie watched the fire glow.

Another minute.

Now.

She stood up.

Without the others, the house echoed. Maggie walked through the snug and along the passage that led back to the main hall. The house was silent. She glanced into the dining room, with the library beyond. Nothing. Crossed the hall to the two big drawing rooms. Empty. Where? Back to the small staircase that led up from the snug, the narrow steps built for invisible hands. She had heard someone creaking their way up here, she was sure of it. She didn't stop at the first floor, but kept going for the warren of rooms that had been the attics. Still nothing. Maggie imagined eyes peering out of the shadows. Mocking her, maybe. *Daft old Maggie, hasn't got a clue.*

Upstairs, she felt her way along a corridor. It was much darker up here, the moon peering through narrow windows, the rooms nipped to odd shapes by the roofs. The doors to these smaller bedrooms had been left open carelessly. Was this Rory's room? Or Ollie's? She tripped over a jumble of muddy walking boots. Finlay: those must belong to him. She startled as she bumped into something that started creaking. Smooth hair beneath her fingers, the jingle of a bridle. A rocking horse, retired to dusty pastures. Still, there was no one. Not a muffled giggle. Not a sly whisper.

This is where the servants would have slept once, she thought. The kitchen maids and the scullery maids, who woke before dawn. *A beautiful maid, who lay down in the snow.*

No. Don't think of her.

No.

There's no one up here, she told herself firmly. Time to go back down those narrow stairs. Time to leave these crooked bedrooms behind.

She wondered if the murderer was wandering around too. Avoiding her, Policeman Plod. They were taking their time, whoever they were.

She was just about to make her way down the backstairs, when she heard a noise from below.

'Who's that?' Her voice sounded wavery, so she tried to make it a joke. 'You can't escape the boys in blue!'

A scuffle. A ragged gasp. A scream ripping through the dark.

Maggie raced down the stairs. At the first floor, she paused, disorientated. Another scream. Coming from her own bedroom. Maggie leaped to the door. She couldn't make out anything. There was another scream, desperate. Maggie slapped on the light. For a second, she was dazzled. The room seemed to be empty. Then the curtains breathed and Maggie realised the French windows out to the balcony were open. Another scream and Maggie was running, shouting. Sprinting to the balcony and reaching down.

Jude was clinging onto the old iron railings. Kicking and scrabbling, fingers clutching, her eyes a blaze of terror. Hanging on, but only just. Kicking at thin air as she struggled and battled, and slipped a bit further: fifty feet down to rough Dartmoor granite, a fall she would never survive.

'Jude!' Maggie screamed. '*Jude!*'

She leaned over the railings and grabbed Jude's wrists. Yelled. 'Help, everyone! We need help!'

Jude was sliding, her fingers losing their grip. Maggie wrapped her hands around the narrow wrists and tried with all her strength to heave her up. But Jude – tiny ballerina Jude – was too heavy. Maggie felt her jaw clench, her veins pop. Jude was screaming. Begging.

'You'll be okay,' Maggie shouted. 'Someone will come. Any second… just hold on, Jude. Hold on.'

'Help me, Maggie!'

Jude's grasp transferred to Maggie's wrists and Maggie felt gravity snatch up at her. All at once, she was sliding, her feet slithering on the balcony floor. Inch by inch, slipping further and further. Now her stomach was scraping the iron railings, her centre of gravity shifting further and further forward. The railings were old, rusty, creaking ominously. Maggie felt a desperate urge to twist out of Jude's grasp. To let go, to save herself.

'Jude!' she shouted. 'Jude, I can't…'

Any second, she would be pulled too far. Her pathetic grip on Wintercross would be jerked away and they would both be falling through the darkness. Two small figures – soft flesh, red blood, pathetic

– down to the unyielding granite. Teeth shattered, bones splintered, meat spattered. *No.*

'Please, Maggie.' Tears on Jude's cheeks. '*Please.*'

'It's okay, Jude,' Maggie managed through gritted teeth. 'It will be alright.'

And it was just as she thought she couldn't hold on a second more – that the sinews and tendons were tearing, that the pain was too much – that Rory and Ayda burst through the French windows.

For a split-second, they just stood there, bewildered. It was Finlay who pushed past the two of them, running forward with the speed of someone who knew all about disaster. He grabbed Jude's arm. 'Rory, grab her. Quickly.'

In seconds, they had heaved Jude back up and onto the balcony, dragging her unceremoniously over the railings. Jude fell to the floor, Maggie collapsing beside her.

'What happened?'

'Oh my *God…*'

'*Jude—*'

They were all there now, crowding out to the balcony. They stumbled back into the room; Ayda collapsing into a peach silk armchair, Elizabeth folding to the floor, putting her hands over her eyes. Ivo and Rory picked up Jude and lowered her carefully onto the bed. The tendons in Jude's neck were standing out as she fought for air, and she was shaking so hard that the bedclothes rustled.

'Jude,' Maggie cried out. 'What on earth happened?'

'It's okay, Jude,' Rory stroked Jude's hair. 'It's alright.'

The tears were leaking out of Jude's eyes, soaking into the linen pillows.

'What happened?' Maggie said again.

Jude was beyond speech. Maggie caught a glimmer in Ayda's eyes: *what a drama queen.* But Ayda hadn't been there. She hadn't felt the void open up beneath them. Ayda hadn't thought she was about to die.

'Here.' Finlay reappeared with a bottle of brandy. He poured Jude a large measure and she steadied slightly. She sat up and gulped at the brandy.

'What on earth were you doing?' asked Elizabeth.

Jude stared across the beautiful room. A stern Fitzwilliam with a ruff of blackened oils glowered back.

'I…' Jude stalled. Finlay poured her another dash of brandy. 'I needed a cigarette and I remembered that balcony, so I thought I would pop out while the game was going on. Then I was looking at the moon, leaning against the railings,' she quavered. 'It was so pretty that I just thought… I was leaning right out to see if I could see the moonlight on the river.'

'Oh, *Jude*,' Ollie rolled his eyes, 'you idiot. You could have been killed.'

'You really could have been,' Elizabeth chimed in. 'You have *got* to be a bit more careful, Jude.'

'Thank you, Maggie,' Jude looked across at her. 'And you, Finlay and Rory. I don't know how to… it was stupid of me.'

'Any time,' Maggie managed a smile. She pushed away the thought of her feet scraping at nothing, of two figures tumbling through the air. Relief flickered around the room. Maggie caught Rory breathing out heavily and taking a swig of her drink, the headlines almost visible in his eyes. *MP linked to suspicious death. Police raid Devon mansion.* Not what he needed. Not right now. Ivo, too, looked relieved that the police would not be turning up at Wintercross. Investors, Maggie guessed, didn't like that sort of thing.

'I must get that balcony sorted,' said Ivo. 'It's a bloody death trap.'

'She's alright,' Finlay's bounce was returning. 'Jude, you muppet. Let's all go back downstairs and have a drink.'

The mood lifted. They began crowding towards the door, shoving the moment into the past. Behind them, Jude sat up, made as if to stand and then sat down again sharply. She was still trembling, Maggie noticed: not alright. Not at all. Maggie hung back, letting the clutter of people thread their way downstairs.

'Are you okay, Jude?' she asked.

Jude's eyes met hers mutely. She shook her head.

Maggie waited until the chatter had faded away.

'What's the matter?'

Jude's eyes were huge in her face, her hand quivering as she pushed back the mass of red hair.

'I…'

'What is it?' Maggie asked again. 'It's okay, Jude. You can tell me.'

Jude looked up at the old wooden beams. She folded her arms around herself, looked up at Maggie, bit her thumbnail.

'Someone…' Jude said quietly. 'Someone tried to kill me.'

53

Ivo, on Jude: Will have drunk herself to death.

'What?' said Maggie. 'Jude, that's impossible. No one would…'

'It's not impossible.' Jude burst into tears again. 'Somebody pushed me.'

'What?' Maggie felt her brain move slowly, stickily. Too much adrenaline and alcohol and emotion. 'How? *What*?'

'Someone came up behind me,' Jude cried, 'as I was leaning against the railings. I really was looking up at the moon, Maggie, that part was true. It was so beautiful that I… But then someone shoved me really hard. And I fell… I only just managed to grab the railings.'

'Jude.' Maggie looked down at Jude. At the wild eyes, the tear stains. 'Jude, no one would have…'

'They did.' Defiance came into Jude's eyes, followed by anger at Maggie's disbelief. 'I promise you, Maggie. Whoever it was ran off.'

'But I was on the backstairs,' said Maggie. 'I would have seen them running off.'

'Would you? It was pitch black, Maggie. And I was screaming my head off. That's what you would have been thinking about.'

Maggie replayed the memory. Could there have been someone there? Standing in the shadows, watching her race past? Maybe. The memory dipped and swayed.

'But none of us would do anything like that,' she said, pushing away the tendrils of fear. 'That's…'

For a moment, Maggie was out in the night again, hearing those footsteps, slithering down Lion's Rock, peering into the darkness, the scent of roses all around.

'It *happened*, Maggie,' Jude insisted. 'I know it.'

'Jude...'

'And it was one of the people here tonight, Maggie.'

Maggie breathed out a long sigh. 'You might have just slipped, Jude. These old windows, the stairs... you heard Ivo. The whole place is a death trap, really.'

'Maggie,' Jude gestured wildly. 'Why won't you listen to me? I felt someone *shove* me.'

'But you didn't see anything? See who it was?'

'No,' Jude snapped. 'I was looking up at the moon. I didn't hear them coming up behind me.'

They both looked out of the windows. The moon glimmered, almost full, calmly magnificent. Maggie stood up and pulled the curtains closed. She didn't want to believe Jude's story, she admitted to herself. She wanted to go back to the fun and the excitement, and not be stuck upstairs with Jude and her endless melodrama for the second night in a row. She thought of Jude earlier: hysterical over Finlay's accidental clumsiness. Could Jude have imagined someone pushing her? Could she be making it up for some mad reason?

A small voice, somewhere, said: yes.

'You think I'm crazy, don't you?' Jude said quietly, resentfully.

'No, Jude. Of course I don't.' Automatic.

'You *do*.'

'Fine,' Maggie made herself sound brisk, prosaic. 'I don't know what happened tonight. But if you really think that someone tried to kill you, we ought to call the police.'

At the mention of the police, Jude curled in on herself. 'No.' A childish note in her voice. 'I don't want to call the police.'

'But, Jude,' Maggie felt a surge of frustration, 'what do you want then?'

Jude was tangling her fingers together. 'No police.'

'We must, Jude. If someone really—'

'No.' It was almost a shout.

'Why not, Jude? What else are we going to do?'

'I went to the police before,' Jude's eyes overflowed again. 'And they didn't do a single thing. They were fucking useless. Made me feel like a complete idiot.'

'When?' Before she finished the word, Maggie kicked herself.

'After I was raped,' Jude said flatly. 'It wasn't entirely the police's fault, admittedly. It took me a whole week to get up the nerve to go to them. And by then there wasn't any...' Jude hesitated for a second. 'There wasn't any physical evidence.'

'I'm sorry, Jude.' Maggie sat down beside her on the bed. 'I really am.'

'And, of course,' Jude's fists clenched, 'I was hammered when that happened too. Completely fucking out of it. And I know what you're thinking, Maggie. That I'm too pissed to be sure about what happened just now, as well.'

They sat in silence, side by side.

'What do you want to do then?' Maggie said in the end. 'I'll do whatever you want. Call the police. Call a taxi. Whatever you think is best.'

'I don't know,' said Jude, her words a surge of frustration. 'I don't bloody know.'

'I'm not even sure what the police would be able to do,' Maggie said cautiously. 'Everyone's fingerprints would be everywhere in this room. On the door handle, the balcony, everywhere.'

Her eyes ran over the pale peach roses, the bunch of sweet peas, the tiny birds skipping amongst the wild roses. A bright blue Moleskine notepad sat on the dressing table. Attempted murder was impossible.

'I know,' Jude's voice broke slightly. 'The police would just think I'm a psycho all over again. I went to them after Lily died, and they treated me like a moron then, too.'

'Do you want to leave? I can call us a taxi, we can find a hotel somewhere nearby.'

Although I don't want to go, Maggie thought to herself. Because this might only have happened in Jude's head. And we'll never get this time again. Not all of us, at Wintercross. Who knows when we'll all be together again? If ever.

Jude was shaking her head. 'No, Maggie. I need to know.'

'Need to know what?' Although Maggie already knew the answer.

'Someone,' Jude's voice was stronger now. 'Someone killed Lily. It was the same person who attacked me just now.'

'You can't know that.'

Jude ignored her. 'It must be, I'm sure of it. And I have to know who it is.'

'Jude...'

'This ends now,' said Jude. 'All this. Drugs and all.'

Jude looked at the balloon glass of brandy on the bedside table: Finlay's cure-all. She stood with a degree of ceremony and picked it up, holding the cut crystal up against the glow of the bedside light and stared deep into the golden depths.

'Enough,' said Jude. 'Enough.'

She walked through to the en suite. Maggie heard the liquid splashing into the sink, the mundane sound of the taps running.

'I've been running for years,' Jude came back into the bedroom. 'For so much of my life. But no more, Maggie. That's it. I'm staying.'

'I'm really proud of you, Jude.' Maggie wondered what was coming next. 'I'm so—'

'I have to know what happened to Lily. And I need to know who just tried to kill me.'

'But,' Maggie didn't want to ask the question, 'who would do something like that?'

Jude shrugged, raised her chin. 'Someone did.'

'Why?'

'Because they know,' said Jude. 'They know I'm getting close to working out who killed Lily.'

54

Lily, on Ollie: It's too late to rebel now, pal. Still wearing your chinos and your blue sweaters and your Trinity scarf.

Ollie looked down at his chinos and his walking boots, and just about managed to laugh. 'Good old Lily.' He pulled his college scarf tighter around his neck.

Saturday morning had dawned, windy and brilliant. 'We *must* go for a walk,' Elizabeth had insisted, and it was easier to agree than not. Even Jude pulled on wellies resignedly. A winding path led past the old chapel. They peered down at the little blunted steeple. The bonfire had branded the grass. The path was lined with bold pink stands of rosebay willowherb and the wishy-washy flowers of the blackberries. Far in the distance, Maggie could hear the roar of a tractor as a farmer raced to get the hay in. Then they were through a gate, and up in the wilderness of the high moor. Skylarks skimmed the purple heather and stone walls criss-crossed the fading gold of the moor grass. Pagan jumped carefully over bright yellow gorse, the sheep bustling away as he approached. Elizabeth, of course, had remembered to take a selection of predictions. With an odd dread, Maggie had watched her pick a handful from the bowl, paper secrets to be ripped apart.

'Too late to rebel now,' Ollie said again. He opened his fingers and let the scrap of paper whisk away over the heather.

'You shouldn't litter,' Elizabeth scolded.

Ollie grumbled to himself and slowed his pace. Maggie, at the rear of the group, found herself matching his step.

'I *did* rebel,' Ollie muttered. 'We were all pretty wild in those days, weren't we?'

Maggie smiled. 'Oh yes, Ollie. Crazy.'

'I *was*,' he insisted.

'What, because you went to Torture Garden once and Berghain twice?'

'Shut up.'

Pagan bounded up to them. He had found a sheep skull somewhere and was crunching delightedly. A few wisps of wool still clung to the bone.

'Yuk,' said Maggie.

'It was so easy for that lot to rebel,' Ollie gestured at the others. 'Take a year out to do ayahuasca halfway up the Amazon, or go and get stoned on a beach in Thailand or whatever it was. That's the whole point of having a safety net, right? We had to choose, you and I. Because whenever they trekked back from the Himalayas, all the opportunities were just waiting for them. And they could try again and again, as if they were at a coconut shy. If they hit the target just once, they're a genius. You and I, we were lucky to have one shot.'

They were passing a small group of sheep. The lambs were almost as big as their mothers already. They lost their skippy charm so soon.

'We were lucky,' Maggie agreed. 'How are Steve and Debs anyway?'

His head came round sharply. 'They're fine.'

'Great.'

And of course, Maggie thought, Steve and Debs were fine. Because nowadays, a semi in Bromley was nudging half a million while Ollie's own dreams had got smaller and smaller. Nobody ever caught up with their parents, let alone overtook them. Even the bankers had expected Knightsbridge and ended up in Clapham.

They walked on in silence for a while. Maggie could hear the seed pods of the gorse popping in the warmth. She stepped over a stag beetle crawling inelegantly over the path. Then Ollie kicked at a heather root.

'Is Jude okay?'

The genuine concern in his voice made Maggie soften. 'I don't know,' she said. 'You know how Jude...'

'She always was a bit woo-woo,' said Ollie.

'Something like that.'

'I was talking about her at uni just the other day, actually.'

'How come?'

'Well, actually, it came up the other night,' said Ollie. 'That Mike Jansen guy. His sister came to see me.'

'What?' Maggie felt a lurch of surprise. 'Mike Jansen's twin came to see you?'

'How did you know she was his twin?'

'Because she went to see Elizabeth too,' said Maggie. 'His sister's been talking to lots of people in our year at uni, apparently, trying to process Mike dying all those years ago. The poor woman.'

'Yes.' Ollie nodded. 'Elizabeth gave her my address; that's how she found me. Helen, that's the sister's name.' After the divorce, Ollie had moved into a flatshare in Stockwell. One mile, a different world.

'Elizabeth said she'd just come back from Africa?' asked Maggie.

'She's been abroad ever since we left university,' said Ollie. 'She went off to work in some refugee camp as soon as she'd graduated. Kakuma, I think she said the camp was called.'

Ahead of them, the others were skirting a bog, the cotton grass bobbing its warning.

'That's where people end up after escaping south Sudan,' Maggie said bleakly. 'Thousands and thousands of them. I suppose she just buried herself in helping other people for years.'

'One way of dealing with it all, I guess.'

'So why were you talking about Jude with Mike Jansen's sister?' Maggie reminded him.

'Oh, only because we all hung out one night not long before he died. Me, Ayda, Ivo. The usual crowd.'

'Not me.' Maggie made it a joke.

'Ivo knew him a bit, because they were doing maths together. I think they even had the same supervisor at some point.'

Supervisions, the Cambridge system where one or two students spent an hour a week being grilled by one of the world's experts in their subject. Not an entirely relaxing experience, Maggie remembered, especially when you were relying on the *Lett's* version of *Macbeth*.

'So what did you tell this Helen person?'

'Only that Mike had a bit of a crush on Jude before he died,' said Ollie.

'Did he?' asked Maggie. 'How did you know that?'

'Mike was doing maths,' said Ollie, 'and I was doing Economics, and that meant we had some lectures in common. We used to chat a bit, every so often.'

'I didn't know that.'

'Well, you did English Literature, didn't you? Barely went to any lectures at all, from what I remember. Slacker.'

'Mm-hm.'

'So, yeah, Mike was into Jude.'

'Lots of people were into Jude,' Maggie said meditatively.

A shrug. 'Sure.'

'Was Jude into Mike?'

'Don't think so.' Ollie yawned. 'Poor Mike. Not much in the way of social skills, from what I remember, although he was a good mathematician. I told Helen that he hung out with us a few times, not long before he died. He was so fucking desperate, though, not that I told his sister that. Trying so hard to impress Jude. We were in Finlay's room one night, and Mike was trying to do a handstand, of all bloody things. Hopeless. Jude was off her face anyway.'

'Was she flirting with Mike?'

'You know she always could flirt with a post box.'

An alarm, somewhere at the back of Maggie's mind. A sense of quiet foreboding.

'What happened that night?' she asked casually. 'What happened between Mike and Jude?'

'Haven't a clue,' Ollie said cheerfully. 'I passed out cold on the sofa.'

55

Jude, on Finlay: I hope your kindness won't
have caught up on you.

Maggie and Ollie caught up with the rest of them as they paused at one
of the old stone clapper bridges. Ayda was peering closely at the slab of
granite balanced on a solid stone stanchion, running her fingers over the
ancient shape.

'Aw, Jude,' Ayda looked up as Ivo read out the prediction. 'That one's
quite cute.'

There was an expression on Jude's face that Maggie couldn't quite
interpret.

'Finlay was always a sweetheart under the nonsense,' Jude said.
'Although admittedly, there was quite a lot of nonsense.'

Lily, crying on the sofa.

'Stop it,' said Finlay. 'You'll make me blush.'

Rory was wandering towards a stone circle that stood not far from
the clapper bridge. Rough-hewn standing stones, their history lost
to the wind. The tallest pillar was three feet taller than Rory, lichen-
camouflaged, eternal.

'It's beautiful, isn't it?' Ivo put a hand on one of the pillars.

'Yes. You love it up here, don't you?' said Rory. 'Despite the accident.'

'Yes,' said Ivo quietly. 'I've always loved it up here. It's always been… a
part of me somehow. Even when I'm on the other side of the world, I feel
as if I could close my eyes and be here.'

The eternal rocks beneath, thought Maggie.

'Despite the accident?' asked Elizabeth, all inquisitive.

'The riding accident.' A short pause, a swallow. 'My mother.'

'Oh God,' Elizabeth looked stricken. 'I'm so sorry.'

For a moment, the wind whispered between the stones. Then Ivo shook his head, pushing away the memories. He bent down to look closer at a notch on one of the chunks of granite.

'I wonder,' Rory wondered, in cheerier tones, 'who placed these here? Some Neanderthal?'

'My father,' Ivo laughed to himself, 'always insisted that he and some mates put it up after a massive night in 1972.'

Seagulls were screaming overhead, dancing with the wind.

'Why are there seagulls here?' asked Jude. 'Not out to sea somewhere? We're miles from the coast.'

'They come inland when a storm is brewing,' said Ivo. 'When it's going to be wild along the shoreline. They start arriving a few hours before. They *know*.'

The wind roared around them, the rage of the Atlantic in the air. Dartmoor, where it could go from glorious sunshine, to rain, to howling gales and back to sunshine in the space of an hour.

Beyond the stone circle, three rows of smaller stones pointed to the east. 'But they're off kilter,' said Elizabeth. 'I read somewhere that they were placed here so long ago that the earth has shifted on its axis since.'

'I guess they really were off their tits in 1972,' said Finlay.

Jude was touching the tallest stone in the circle, moving her fingers to her mouth.

'You can sense something from them, can't you?' Jude asked. 'An aura. You feel safe around them somehow.'

A short pause. 'Something like that,' said Ivo kindly.

'It is interesting though, isn't it?' Rory had a tendency to lecture. 'The way in which virtually all civilisations created these monuments, and the rituals to go with them. To celebrate birth, to mark adolescence, to honour unions, to commemorate death. Those rites of passage repeat over and over, all around the world, in virtually every religion. I wonder which moment in life these stones saluted?'

'Nowadays, we have baby showers,' said Jude idly. 'Sweet sixteen proms. Matching tattoos.'

'And tutus at Leatherhead crematorium,' said Maggie quietly.

'Tutus and tattoos,' said Jude. 'That sounds like a band that might play in my crappy pub.'

'Instead of prayer,' Rory was laughing now, 'we have meditation or yoga or tai chi. Confession somehow alchemised into therapy.'

'And instead of fasting,' said Ayda, 'we have the 5:2 diet. Insta, not icons, and somewhere along the line, we dumped forty days in the wilderness for sponsored marathons and climbing K2.'

'Today, we bow down before the Kardashians.' Rory was smiling now. 'And for churches, we have—'

'Clubs,' said Finlay. 'Our own sort of ecstasy. There are still plenty of martyrs kicking about, of course. Strapped into their suicide vests: tick tock, tick tock.'

'No marriage for me,' sighed Ayda. 'No handfasting.'

'One day,' Ivo grinned. 'One day.'

'There isn't a ceremony for the onset of middle age,' said Elizabeth, 'is there?'

'Oh God,' said Ayda. 'Is that where we are now?'

'They didn't need a ceremony for middle age,' Finlay said cheerfully. 'You'd almost certainly have been dead by now, Elizabeth.'

'Charming. What would the ceremony be, anyway?' Elizabeth stretched her arms up towards the sky. 'Ritualised hair implants? The ceremony of the first HRT prescription? The solemn presentation of the key to the bright red Porsche?'

They began to walk up a rise towards a jagged tor. 'That's Kes Tor.' Finlay, naturally, had some map on his watch.

Dartmoor ponies – dark brown, sandy noses, suspicious eyes – watched them pass. A foal startled and raced to his mother's side, springing over the bracken in a flurry of delicate legs. The mare hurried to position herself between the foal and the intruders, busy with disapproval. Maggie let herself drift until she was beside Jude. She sensed Jude was glancing her way, waiting for Maggie to say something. In silent agreement, their pace slowed. The others pulled ahead, laughing, gossiping.

'What?' Jude snapped eventually.

Maggie turned towards her. 'It was Mike Jansen, wasn't it? Mike Jansen who raped you?'

A long sigh, almost a moan. Jude watched the foal canter away, bucking gleefully in the bright sunlight. 'Yes.' Jude's face was tight, half-angry. 'Yes, alright, it was. Well done, Maggie. Excellent investigative skills. Gold star for you.'

'I didn't mean that…'

'I know you didn't.'

'Jude, you should—'

'Should what? What exactly can I do about it now?'

'You could tell someone.' It sounded lame. 'Talk to someone about it, at least.'

'Oh, Maggie. *Maggie*. You're such an innocent. Besides, what does any of it matter now, anyway?'

'It matters.'

'Water under the bridge. Nothing to be done, move on.'

'Have you?'

'Mike's dead.' Jude let the word blow away with the wind. 'He *died*, Maggie.'

'But that didn't fix you.'

'No. I suppose not.' They watched the seagulls wheel overhead. 'I didn't kill Mike,' Jude said. 'If that's what you're thinking.'

'I wasn't.' Maggie spoke too hastily. Guiltily.

'You were.' Jude turned towards Maggie and met her eyes squarely.

'You'd told the police about the rape, though.' Maggie moved the conversation back to facts.

'I'd told them a week too late. Makes it very difficult to get a prosecution, apparently. Impossible, really. And we'd all been partying the night it happened: Finlay, Ivo, Ollie, Ayda, everyone. I was off my head. We all were. You know what would have happened if it had ever got to court.'

'I do know.' She'd covered enough rape trials.

'How did you guess?' Jude asked a few minutes later. 'About Mike.'

'Ollie told me. Well, he didn't tell me that you'd been raped, but he said that Mike had a crush on you. And that not long before Mike died, you'd all been partying together. So I just guessed.'

Jude had a small lump of granite in her hands, was turning it over and over.

'That was always the problem, really,' she said. 'They'd all seen me hammered and messing about with Mike. So they couldn't have lied about that in court. Someone would have slipped up. It was just... true.'

'Did the police ask you about it when he was killed?' asked Maggie. 'The fact that you'd reported Mike for rape and a few weeks later, he ends up dead.'

'They did.' For a moment, Jude looked sly. 'But I was in London the night he died. I was in Fabric, trying to forget.'

'They checked that out?'

'Yes.' All at once, there was an expression on Jude's face that Maggie couldn't interpret. Half fear, half something else. 'I was in Fabric with Lily. Lily was my alibi.'

56

Ayda, on Ivo: We'll still be watching sunsets together.

For a second, Maggie felt winded. *Sunsets. Together.*

She read Ayda's neat handwriting again, looked up and caught the briefest of glances between Ivo and Ayda. Recognition, that's what that was. A quiet acknowledgement of affection and secrecy and history.

Reciprocated.

'What,' Maggie was still hoping that she had misunderstood, 'does that mean?'

Ayda was too dismissive. 'Oh, nothing much. Ivo and I just chat, every so often, at sunset.'

'What do you mean, you chat?' Maggie knew she sounded possessive, ridiculous.

A shrug. 'It's nothing, Maggie. It just started years ago, right the way back when we were at university. Sometimes we'd go and hang out on the common in the evening. Take a few drinks, watch the sun go down, whatever. Later, we got in the habit of calling each other around that time of day. Chatting as we watched the sun setting.'

A surge of jealousy, a heart burning.

'I didn't know that.' Maggie managed to ram down the envy, cram it into a little box somewhere near her liver, an oubliette. 'I hadn't realised you did that together. You... you never mentioned it.'

Her eyes met Ayda's. *Did you? What happened during those long, slow nights down by the river?* Ayda looked away, fixing her eyes on the horizon and closing Maggie out.

'I love sunsets,' said Jude dreamily. 'And dawns, when you've been dancing all night.'

'That's the only good thing about my job,' Ayda said blithely. 'I get to see a lot of dawns.'

'To each their own is beautiful.'

A key change in the light. The moor was darkening almost imperceptibly. Clouds were gathering to the west, a curtain of rain drifting across the moor.

'Look,' Maggie plastered on a grin and pointed. 'Those seagulls were right.'

'We should head back to Wintercross,' Elizabeth was brisk. 'We don't want to be caught in that.'

They turned. 'I hadn't realised how far we'd come,' Jude, worried, looking at the rolling moorlands ahead. 'It'll take us ages to get back.'

'It won't take us that long,' Ivo said confidently. 'Don't worry.'

Rory was prodding his iPhone. 'It's about an hour back to Wintercross from here.'

'Funny, isn't it?' said Ayda, 'How the youth of today will never know what it feels like to be lost. They'll always be a neat blue dot on their screen, no matter where they go.'

'God, yes.' As she always did, Elizabeth took up the conversational baton, moving on swiftly from any awkwardness. 'I found an A to Z when I was cleaning out a cupboard the other day. A tiny one that I used to take everywhere with me. It felt like an archaeological relic. I wonder what it does to your brain, never knowing how it feels to be lost? Never having that feeling of looking around and just not knowing where you are.'

'Do you remember going backpacking?' asked Finlay. 'Weeks on end without getting in touch with anyone until you found some dodgy little internet cafe. Our poor parents. Now you see the kids on the beaches, nose down to their phones.'

'Never feeling lost,' said Ayda. 'Never feeling alone.'

'You can,' Jude said flatly, 'feel very sodding lost, even when you're holding a bloody iPhone.'

Maggie trudged along silently. Every so often, she glanced back. The curtain of rain was blowing closer. She saw that Ayda was manoeuvring closer to her and braced herself.

'Don't be cross,' Ayda said softly.

'I'm not cross.' A pause. 'Did you, then?'

Ayda lit a cigarette. 'Once or twice. It didn't mean anything, Maggie.'

'You could... you could have told me.'

'I could have told you.'

'You're one of my best friends, Ayda. All those times we've talked about literally *everything*. I feel... stupid not knowing.' Left out, she almost said.

'Don't be daft. It was never anything serious. And I knew you'd...'

'And you still call each other at sunset?'

'Only once in a very blue moon,' said Ayda. 'It really isn't a big deal. Not least because most of the time, Ivo's in a completely different country and our sunsets are hours apart. But very occasionally, if I'm up on the roof of Throwleigh Pearce having a fag, I'll give him a buzz.'

'Six minutes,' Ayda had said once. 'I can get up on that roof, have a ciggie and be back at my desk in six minutes.'

'Time-wise,' Maggie had worked it out, 'every cigarette costs you eighty quid.'

'*Fuck.* Don't.'

A shadow raced across the moor. The clouds had caught up with them, blotting out the sun. It was abruptly colder.

'I just wish you'd told me,' Maggie could hear the whine in her voice.

'There really wasn't anything to tell. I enjoy chatting with Ivo every so often, that's all.' They all did. 'We talked the night before we all came down here, actually. I was up on that godforsaken roof and he was sitting on Lion's Rock. We got into the habit again during the pandemic. It's like that bit in *When Harry Met Sally* when they're watching Casablanca at the same time, just that our thing is to chat as we watch the sun go down.' *Our thing*, another pang. Ayda stopped, as if realising she had been insensitive. A quick change of subject. 'He was up on that rock the night that Lily died.'

'Did the police ask you what you were doing that evening?'

'That's how I remember. I guess they asked a lot of people where they were when she went under that tube. Poor Lily. Poor, poor Lily.'

'I was in Parliament,' said Maggie. 'Which at least was nice and easy to prove.'

Although hacks sometimes borrowed each other's passes to scoot out and grab a coffee, so it wasn't a perfect system.

'Useful alibi.'

'Did Mike Jansen's sister come and see you?' Maggie asked suddenly.

'Helen?' Ayda nodded. 'Yes, she did.'

'What did she ask you?'

'Just if I'd known Mike. Any little anecdote, that sort of thing.'

'Did you?'

'Nope,' Ayda lobbed a stick for Pagan. 'He wasn't the most anecdotey guy, was he? I don't think I'd remember him at all if he hadn't died. Admittedly, that was quite a memorable thing to do.'

'Unforgettable.'

'He was so young, wasn't he? Only now do you look back and realise how pathetically, tragically young he was to die. We were *such* babies back then. And God, isn't that a depressing thought? We're not *so* young to die now. Back then we'd have been *so* young to die or to get an Olympic gold medal or to win an Oscar. Now, we're too old for gold medals and not particularly surprised by death.'

'Did you love him?' Maggie asked. 'Ivo.'

'We all did,' Ayda was flippant. 'You know what Ivo was like.'

'No, but—'

'Course not, Maggie. It wasn't like that.'

'But we did,' Maggie said flatly. 'We all did.'

57

Rory, on Lily: I hope I'll have found the nerve
to tell her how much I love her.

Catcalls.

It was raining now. Hard, cold drops that soaked through Maggie's coat in moments. An icy wind ripped June apart.

'Rory.' Ayda was laughing as she looked up from the shred of paper. 'You old *romantic*.'

Rory was laughing and blushing. 'I was *crazy* about her back then. Lily, gorgeous Lily.' He was walking at the head of the group, turning round to laugh at his youth with them.

'But then you fell in love with Genet,' said Ayda.

Rory's face softened. 'I did.'

'How did you meet Genet exactly?' Elizabeth asked. 'I never knew.'

The wind blasted harder. Rory was fiddling with a sprig of heather. 'Heather for luck, isn't that what they say?' He held it up. 'God, it seems so long ago now. I was a thrusting young spad. That ghastly combination of ambition and earnestness. Genet came to Parliament for a meeting with my minister. A violence against women campaign. We thought we should give them ten minutes, cut it to eight maybe. And she just… saw through me. I couldn't be this *Thick of It* prat, because she knew it was all nonsense.'

'So you dragged her off to the Red Lion for a swift half?'

'No!' Another laugh. 'It took me months to convince her to go out for even one drink and I certainly wasn't going to waste that on the Red Lion. I made a picnic and I took her to Green Park. That was the best I could manage back then.'

They were nearly back at the standing stones now.

'Not a bad effort though,' said Jude. 'Champagne? Strawberries?'

'All that. Well, I was never going to get another chance, was I?'

'Then what?' Ivo, intrigued.

'Then I asked her to marry me.'

They came to a standstill, the rain pattering around them.

'Just like that?' Elizabeth asked. 'In the middle of a picnic in Green Park on your first date?'

'Just like that. A couple of glasses of champagne in.'

'What did you say to her?' Finlay, who already knew.

'Oh.' Rory fidgeted with the heather.

'Go on.' Jude insisted.

'I told her…' Rory paused, then went on. 'I told her what my father had told me about love and relationships. That some marriages are like two Shire horses harnessed together. Side by side, going through life, always pulling in the same direction, and that works perfectly well. And others are like bamboo frames, holding up sweet peas. Without the bamboo, the sweet peas collapse to the ground. And that also works, as long as you're both happy, as long as it's what you both want.'

'Some people actually like being bamboo poles,' said Elizabeth.

'Exactly. Because being a bamboo pole on your own is a bit dull, anyway.'

'But?'

'He also said that sometimes it's like two rivers meeting,' said Rory. 'And within seconds, it seems as if you were always together, and you can never be separated. Commingled. I told Genet that is how I felt about her.'

A silence. '*Two* glasses in?' asked Ollie.

Laughter. 'Two glasses in.'

'And she *agreed*?' Ayda, incredulous.

'She did.'

Maggie remembered that wedding. Genet, cackling, switching to flats as soon as they left the church. Then dancing and dancing, her dress bustled up. Someone handed round sparklers as the night drew to an end, and Rory and Genet ran out to the car in a starburst of glitzing, glinting, glittering magic. She wondered, briefly, how Mr Adair had seen his own marriage. Less Shire horses or bamboo poles. More of a gauntlet run, probably.

'How are you now?' she asked Rory. 'About it all?'

'I—' Rory started.

'Now?' Finlay's voice was halfway to a jeer. 'Well, there's a certain type of woman to whom a tragic widower is absolute catnip. And then there are others who are irresistibly and inexplicably drawn to MPs. And if you combine those two elements… well. Our Rory here spends quite a lot of his time fending off ravening females.'

'It's not like that,' Rory protested.

'It bloody is. I've seen them in action. Piranhas.'

'You're just jealous, little brother.'

'Yup.'

'Have you been out with any of these huntresses?' asked Ivo, amused.

'I've been on a few dates,' said Rory deprecatingly. 'It's been almost seven years since Genet died, after all.'

'Really?' said Ollie, as if Rory might have miscalculated.

'But how are you?' Maggie persisted.

'I'm fine,' said Rory. 'Honestly. There will always be sadness, always. But Genet wanted joy for everyone, and she wouldn't have wanted less for me.'

'You don't need to explain yourself,' said Ivo.

'I know. I *know*. Just for years, whenever I thought about anyone like that, it would just take me straight back…'

'Rory…'

Rory stood in silence. He reached out to the tallest stone, running his fingers over the roughnesses, the imperfections. They all stood in silence, a congregation. Mourners, Maggie thought. And it was the right place for this strange confessional.

'Genet lashed out at me in the middle of the night.' The words came suddenly, and Maggie couldn't make out if it was rain or tears on Rory's face. 'I was fast asleep, totally out cold. But she must have been desperate. Panicking. I woke up and I didn't know where I was for a moment. Then this massive surge of excitement. The babies! She must be in labour! It's *happening.* But then she made a sound. No words, just a sort of sob. I switched on the light and I realised… I realised. And that panic, when it's just you and everything depends on you getting everything right, and if you make one tiny mistake, everything will be smashed beyond repair, forever. And all you know is that you don't know enough.

'I froze for a second. It was just the total horror of it. And then I was on the phone, begging the ambulance to come as quick as it could. Come now. *Now.* But Genet was struggling to breathe. I remember the tendons in her neck sticking out. She was losing consciousness and I was begging her. Genet, stay with me. Stay with me, please. *Please.* And then it was just this frenzy of paramedics and blue flickering lights and her fingers going limp and I knew. I *knew.*'

'Rory.' It was Finlay who hugged him, an echo of childhood. They stood there for a long time, the wind blowing colder and colder. A wake, a sort of vigil.

'Come on,' said Ivo in the end, and slowly they began walking towards Wintercross again. One by one, plodding along the peaty path in silence. Rain dripped down the back of Maggie's neck. She watched Rory trudging along. When the path widened, she found herself next to Jude and Elizabeth.

'It slightly puts one's own love life into perspective, doesn't it?' muttered Jude. 'Rory and Genet being that in love.'

'It does,' Maggie felt bleak. Elizabeth said nothing. She had turned her face away from them, unreadable. They were in the cloud now, the mist swirling around them.

'Do you think I'll ever find love like that?' asked Jude. 'That head-over-heels, across-a-crowded-room love? Although it would never be like that for us now anyway, would it? In their twenties, Genet and Rory could just leap in, all innocent optimism. But everyone our age has so much *baggage.*'

Ahead of them, the mood was lightening. Ivo, Rory and Finlay were walking in a row. Maggie couldn't hear what they were saying but she heard a roar of laughter, saw Finlay shoving Rory so that he splashed into a boggy patch.

Ayda was still holding the scrap of paper with Rory's prediction on it. 'Did you ever get together in the end?' she called out to him. 'You and Lily?'

'Nope,' Rory sighed ostentatiously. He turned back to the path, concentrating on climbing over some slippery rocks.

Lily, Maggie thought, would have been happier with this brother. Not Finlay, and his playful cruelties.

'You were about the only one,' snapped Elizabeth.

'What do you mean?' Maggie asked. There was an awkward silence, and again Maggie had the sense of being the only one who didn't know. Left out, even though she wasn't sure she wanted in. But she was fed up now, and enough of a journalist to let the silence spread like spilled ink.

It was Elizabeth who cracked. 'Lily,' she said, icy as the wind, 'was a silly little slut.'

'Ollie?' Maggie asked. 'Lily hooked up with *Ollie*?'

Ollie's face was burning. Again, that look at Elizabeth: you *knew*? 'I'm sorry.' The wind whipped his words away. 'Really sorry.'

'But why would Lily sleep with *Ollie*?' The words were out of Maggie's mouth before she could stop them.

'Thank you, Maggie.' Even in his humiliation, Ollie managed a wry glance.

'I've never,' Elizabeth spat, 'bothered to enquire.'

'How did you guess then?' Ayda had moved quickly through shock to curiosity. 'How did you find out?'

'Oh, I don't know… Rory told me, I suppose.'

'I what?' Rory half-turned.

'Not in so many words,' said Elizabeth.

'In how many words then?' asked Ayda.

Elizabeth began to speak. Slowly at first, the words gradually forming into a torrent. 'Rory texted me one day saying it was funny bumping into Ollie. He'd been out canvassing for the Bermondsey Central by-election, and he'd spotted Ollie. They'd had a nice chat and said we should all have dinner soon.'

'The Bermondsey Central by-election?' asked Maggie. She had covered that last autumn, shadowing various would-be MPs round south-east London. They looked like teenagers now, the aspirant MPs. 'But why would it mean anything that Ollie was in Bermondsey?'

Elizabeth looked at her witheringly. 'Ollie works for the Sloane Square branch of Feversham and Cecil. He'd never do a viewing in *Bermondsey*.'

'Right.'

'And it just started me thinking for some reason,' said Elizabeth. 'Because Ollie didn't mention being in Bermondsey at all. I brought it up that evening, saying we should go to that antiques place in Maltby Street, but he just started talking about the lunch he'd had with one of his clients at the Botanist. And I just *knew*.'

They were all agog, including Ollie. It must be very odd, thought Maggie, to watch the post-mortem of your own marriage. Like being awake for brain surgery.

'So then what?'

'Oh, it was easy,' Elizabeth's lip curled. 'I put one of those tracking apps on his iPad. He never noticed, of course. And then I just sat and watched. I watched as he came out of the Tube at Bermondsey. I watched as the blue dot blipped its way up Tooley Street. And then I watched it stop.'

They all knew that address. They'd all been to the housewarming a few years back.

It's only a short walk to the hospital. So convenient. And it's such a buzzy area. Lily, with a broad grin on her face.

Great place to buy, Lily. It'll zoom up in value. Ollie, of course.

Have you been to White Cube yet? Jude.

Maggie had spent hours on the roof terrace there, surrounded by the plant pots that Lily never remembered to water. The flat was in one of the big modern blocks, with the London Bridge train lines far, far below. Maggie would stare down at the rows of steel tracks. They were a scar in London's cyborg skin, a gash down to the screech of metal-on-metal. She and Lily would sit and watch the sun set. Rosé clinking with ice, the Shard a broken tooth lit to gold.

She'd never wondered: how is the junior doctor affording *this*? Because it might have been just about doable, but Lily had never struck her as a careful saver, a careful planner. And now she thought: *Mr Nassar. Affectionate, guilty, secret.*

'Then what happened?' Ayda, with roadkill fascination. 'After you'd worked out it was Lily.'

'Nothing much. I'd watch the little dot rove about. Sometimes they would be in the flat. Sometimes in a bar down the road. I thought about sending two glasses of champagne across to them with a note – *All my love, Elizabeth*, in some barmaid's handwriting – because a friend of mine did that to her husband once and I thought it had a certain *je ne sais quoi*.' A bitter smile. Maggie imagined the Clapham witch wives, heads together, plotting. 'But I thought it would be too… humiliating.'

'So?'

The rain was getting harder now. Elizabeth, the only one dressed for the weather, adjusted her hat. 'So I changed the locks.' So simple. Ollie, trotting up the front steps one day. Ollie, pulling out his keys. Impatience, irritation, confusion.

Icy shock.

'How did you and Lily get together, Ollie?' Ayda should have been a journalist, thought Maggie. Always asking the question when no one else had the nerve.

'Oh…' Ollie pushed away the question.

'No,' Elizabeth barked. 'I would like to know, actually.'

Ollie groaned. 'I don't—'

'Come on.' Elizabeth should have been a schoolmistress circa Laura Ingalls Wilder, thought Maggie, ruler at the ready.

'If you must know…' Ollie looked around for salvation. 'It was here.'

'*Here*?' Elizabeth looked across at the standing stones, bewildered.

'Not *here*, here. At Wintercross. We came down here last summer, when you were off at that spa weekend with Tory and Cazzy. I told you I was coming down here.'

'You did.'

'And Lily… it turned out that Lily was here for that weekend too.'

'You *knew*?' Elizabeth turned on Ivo.

'No!' Hands up.

'Ivo had no idea,' Ollie said miserably. 'It was late. We were all hammered. Ivo had gone off to bed.'

And Ollie and Lily were left lolling around the firepit in the courtyard? Or curled up cosily in the snug? Maggie could see the same questions crossing Elizabeth's face. Ayda was mercifully silent for once.

'Lily was unhappy,' said Ollie. 'I didn't know about the fuck-up with Finlay, but it can't have been long after that. She was a bit blue, a bit down about things.'

And Ollie, Maggie thought, house-trained by Elizabeth, was cast in a new light.

'Lily was a bit blue,' Elizabeth said crushingly. 'A bit bloody blue.'

Ollie's face contorted. Maggie could just imagine it. The excitement of being at Wintercross, the innate glamour of the occasion. That sense of licentious freedom, because isn't this what the upper classes do anyway? And somewhere, too, there would have been that growing awareness blistering at the back of Ollie's mind: when they first came to Wintercross all those years ago, it was *maybe someday*. Now it was *never, no chance*.

Ollie summoned some honesty from somewhere. 'We hadn't been happy for months, Elizabeth. You know that. For years, even. Did you really want to spend the rest of our lives rattling around Clapham, wearing the same chinos, with fluffy towels and everything matching? We... we stopped working long ago.'

The wind howled around them. Maggie began to shiver.

'Did Lily want children with you?' There was a savagery in Elizabeth's eyes that Maggie had never seen before.

'What? I don't—'

'She didn't,' Jude interrupted flatly.

'How do you know?' Elizabeth snapped.

'Lily never wanted children,' said Jude. 'I don't either, for the record. Lily might have been wanting to settle down in some way – hence the mess with Finlay – but it wasn't because she wanted kids. We spoke about it many times.'

Maggie could see from Elizabeth's face that this thought was incomprehensible. 'Everyone—' Elizabeth began.

'No,' said Jude. '*Not* everyone. Women without children get treated like failures, but that's only because most people can't begin to process the idea that a lot of women simply don't want a posse of ankle-biters. Lily wanted to live her own life on her own terms. She wanted freedom and independence and the ability to change her mind if she felt like it. She wanted to be able to spend the weekend dancing in Ibiza or the afternoon kite-surfing at Camber Sands. And some days, she just wanted to lie around on the sofa eating chocolate and watching *Bridgerton*.' Elizabeth was shaking her head, repudiating the idea. 'Lily knew she wasn't getting everything right,' Jude went on. 'But she was living on her own terms. She didn't want to shape her life around some mewling brat. I'd happily have been a *father*. But fuck the mothering crap.' Jude came to a halt, chin defiant. Maggie's gaze flicked from Jude to Elizabeth and back again.

Elizabeth wrapped her scarf tighter around her neck.

'I'm sorry, Elizabeth,' said Ollie again. 'I'm so very sorry.'

'Not that any of it matters now, I suppose.' Elizabeth's voice was steel. She turned away from the group, staring through the rolling mists towards Wintercross. There was a burning rage in her face, a spitting, uncontrollable fury. For a second, she was Boadicea, gazing down upon her enemies. Revenge personified. 'It doesn't matter at all now that Lily's dead.'

58

Finlay, on Maggie: Maggie will still be buried in work.

As soon as they were back at Wintercross, Maggie raced up the stairs to her bedroom and slammed the door behind her. She needed to think. She needed to know. There was the dressing table and the hydrangea blue notepad. Still in her wet clothes, Maggie sat down and grabbed a pencil.

Lily, strong bold letters, *is dead. Jude was attacked.*

Hating herself, she wrote down seven names. Elizabeth. Rory. Ivo. Finlay. Ollie. Jude. Ayda. *Possible motives*, underlined.

Impossible, she told herself. This is *preposterous*.

This *is* possible.

Why? Maggie asked herself. Why would any of these people have killed Lily?

Think.

I can't.

You can.

One thing you can do is journalism.

The only thing, perhaps.

So be a journalist. Start with the obvious thoughts and work your way through.

Maggie began to scribble.

Elizabeth: Lily and Ollie had an affair. Elizabeth found out not long before Lily was killed (if she really was killed? We still can't be 100% sure.) Elizabeth was definitely angry enough to do almost anything.

This is *absurd*. But already Maggie felt calmer for writing things down. She always did.

Ollie: Ollie didn't know that Elizabeth already knew about the affair. So if Lily threatened to tell Elizabeth – for whatever reason – might Ollie have panicked? But why would Lily tell Elizabeth? Lily was always secretive.

Maggie sucked the end of the pencil and turned back to Elizabeth.

Could Elizabeth have thought that Lily might have Ollie's child? Might the thought that Lily could get pregnant with Ollie have driven Elizabeth over the edge?

A knock at the door. 'Hello?'
Jude, clingy and nervous. She had insisted on sharing Maggie's bed last night, then twitched and turned all night.
'I'll be down in a second,' Maggie shouted. 'I'm just having a bath, Jude.'
Back to the notepad.
A wince at the next name.

Ayda: Discovering that Lily was her half-sister must have been horrendous for Ayda. What does Mr Nassar's will say? (Impossible to find out until he dies.) Was he planning to leave a chunk of money to Lily? Had he already given her a deposit for the Bermondsey flat? Does Mrs Nassar know? If not, Ayda would want to protect her mother from finding out about her husband's illegitimate child. Is it possible that Fiona Nassar might only have found out about Lily from Mr Nassar's will? Surely not. As he approached the end of his life, might he have decided he had to build some sort of relationship with Lily? Could Ayda have found that an unbearable thought?

Disloyalty was a prickle of acid. For a second, Maggie stared out of the window. The oaks had been frost-burned back in the spring, autumn-rusted in the height of summer.

Finlay:

Maggie stopped. There was no reason for Finlay to kill Lily.
No reason at all.
Think.

Finlay suffers from PTSD. He is unpredictable, impulsive, very capable of violence. By the time Lily died, she and Finlay were back on speaking terms but I don't think they would ever have gone back to being proper friends again. There was too much anger for that. But they weren't at war with each other (NB As far as I know. I don't know what happened in the last few days before she died.) There was no reason for them to be interacting around that time, but who knows?

Maggie was writing slowly, unwillingly.

Rory: Rory was in love with Lily at university. BUT he then moved on with Genet and was very happy with Genet for years. Could something have happened fairly recently between Lily and Rory? And then it went disastrously wrong? Seems unlikely given that Lily had a fling with Rory's brother last year. Could Rory have been angry about that? Doubtful. Could Rory have been involved in some scandal – something that threatened him as an MP?

A thought struck her. Back to Finlay.

What did Lily mean when she wrote: Will it still be a secret? *about Finlay? Or when she said that Rory will still be covering up for his little brother. Why did Rory think Finlay might be in jail? What happened between the three of them?*

Back to Rory.

Would Rory kill to protect his little brother?

Written out in black and white, it made her wince. Maggie heaved out a long sigh. Her shoulders were protesting at her position at the dressing table.

Jude:

Maggie sat back in the delicate chair for a moment, then forced herself forward again.

Jude can be manic, drinks too much, takes too many drugs and is very angry with the world. She and Lily were very close – stayed friends through thick and thin. But could Jude lose her temper and do something mad? Maybe. I don't know. When did Jude come back from Verbier? Was she even in the country when Lily died? And would she have been wearing some sort of cast after her accident? Difficult to make a run for it wearing that. Surely someone would have spotted her?

Another hesitation.

Lily was Jude's alibi for the night that Mike died. What if Lily had lied about Jude being in London? And what if she was about to tell the truth for some reason?

Maggie caught a glimpse of herself in the mirror. She looked tired, puffy. Two nights of heavy drinking had deepened the creases around her eyes.

Ivo:

There was no reason for Ivo to kill Lily, either. Ivo operated in a different world from the rest of them now. An international whirl, while the rest of them plodded around London.

Could Lily have been a threat to SummerX in some way? Hard to see how, as a junior doctor, but…

Maggie stood up, walked to the bathroom. Turned on the taps to make the lie to Jude true.

Jude, she thought. *Why would one of them attack Jude?* A new page.

NB Anyone might attack Jude if they murdered Lily and thought Jude was getting close to working it out.

Elizabeth: No obvious motive.
Rory: No obvious motive.
Finlay: No obvious motive.
Ivo: No obvious motive.
Ayda: Never liked Jude.
Ollie: No obvious motive.

Not an especially helpful list. Another thought.

Jude. Could Jude have faked the fall out of the window? Very dangerous way of doing it, but she enjoys risk. And she loves drama. But why not tell everyone what happened straight away? Why only tell me?
Or could Jude have tried to kill herself and changed her mind at the last minute?

Maggie could hear footsteps outside the room, and the sound of Ayda mocking Ivo.

One last thought.

Helen Jansen has visited Elizabeth, Ollie and Ayda. Is there any reason why she is asking about a twenty-year-old murder now? Has Helen Jansen found out something important?

The bath was almost full, the room an expensive cloud of orange blossom. Maggie closed the notepad and pushed it away.

59

Lily, on Elizabeth: I hope we'll still be adventuring
down tin mines and up mountains.

'Oh.' Elizabeth sat with the piece of paper drooping in her hand. 'Oh.'

After baths and showers, they had all gathered slowly in the kitchen. Ivo mixed drinks as they appeared one by one. Maggie asked for a Bloody Mary and then sat staring at the stick of celery and the speckles of pepper, still half-queasy.

'Oh, Elizabeth...' Maggie couldn't find the words.

'I *liked* Lily,' said Elizabeth. 'That's why the Ollie thing hurt so much. I know we weren't close. Not like she was with you, Maggie. Or Jude. Or Ayda, even. But still.'

'Unhappy people,' Ivo said slowly, 'do stupid things.'

Even Elizabeth smiled as Ollie raised his hands and dropped them sharply, face wry.

'Lily had probably just found out that Mr Nassar was her father,' said Maggie tentatively. 'And that meant that Stella had been lying to Lily for her whole life. The thing with Finlay... it undermined Lily's confidence even more, just when she was at her most vulnerable. She did something stupid, Elizabeth. Awful. And it had horrible consequences for you. But I don't think she would have done it if she had been thinking straight.'

'I know,' said Elizabeth. 'I *know*, but...'

'Tin mines?' asked Ayda. 'Mountains? What was she going on about?'

'Mountains must have been that uni ski trip,' said Elizabeth. 'Do you remember? That Christmas holiday not that long before the predictions dinner party.'

Maggie remembered: fondues and Aperol Spritz and the thickest hot chocolate. Night clubs with names like the Blue Night and Chez Michel, dark and sweaty, glittery and fun. And Ivo, of course, searing down the mountain in perfect parallels, while Maggie fumbled about on the nursery slopes.

'That was a brilliant trip,' she said wistfully.

'Lily and I got lost one day,' said Elizabeth. 'We thought we knew a shortcut from one run to another, but suddenly we were stuck in this massive pine forest and we had no idea where we were. I was starting to have a – well, you know – a bit of a meltdown. But Lily just made it funny. We had to walk miles through deep snow and it was getting darker and darker. But Lily kept singing these ridiculous songs. And finally, we got to some road, some back road in the middle of nowhere, and she managed to charm some French nuns – of all people – into driving us back to the resort.'

They could all imagine it. Lily chivvying Elizabeth along, making her giggle as the icy Alpine winds blew about them.

'And tin mines?' asked Rory.

'You were there,' Elizabeth turned to Maggie. 'That day.'

They had all been down to Wintercross for Ivo's twenty-first, just a few weeks before Elizabeth's dinner party. Dozens of them, camping chaotically in tents, in the drawing rooms, in the ballroom. Mr Fitzwilliam had issued ground rules and then firmly retreated to his library.

On the second afternoon, Elizabeth insisted that Maggie and Lily climb down to the river for a swim. They peered at the old chapel and sauntered through new bracken and fading bluebells. The beeches were bright in their spring gowns. It had been Lily who spotted the gap in the bank, the ferns unfurling all around. A deeper shadow, an unexpected caesura. 'Look.'

The three of them moved closer. There was a trickle of water, stubs of granite, thick green moss muffling everything. Maggie felt a shudder, fairy-tale superstitions swirling.

'What is it? A cave?'

They peered through the curtain of ferns. Behind the greenery, the gap was wider than Maggie had realised. A tunnel, maybe six-foot high. The walls were granite, stained here and there with patches of rusty red or khaki green. In the deep distance, lost in the darkness, they could hear the slow drip of water. Man-made, it was clear at once, the top shaped into a rough arch. Inside, the water was maybe a foot deep, pooling deeper here and there before trickling out in a narrow stream that wound its way through the trees and down to the river. Someone had created makeshift stepping stones by dumping lumps of rock into the water.

'It must be one of the old tin mines,' Elizabeth whispered. 'I've read about them. They're all over the place on this side of Dartmoor. Lustleigh and Hennock, Chagford and Moretonhampstead.'

Lily pulled out her lighter, a Zippo, and clicked it on. 'Bloody hell.' The tunnel stretched out in front of them. Maggie couldn't make out the end. It writhed away until its darkness was complete. 'Come on,' Lily was bright with excitement. 'Let's see where it goes!'

'Don't be ridiculous,' squawked Elizabeth. 'You could get killed in there.'

'We won't go far,' urged Lily. 'Just explore a bit. Don't be such a wuss, Elizabeth.'

Maggie was surprised by how unnerved she was by the tunnel, how threatened. It was the stillness, this strange silence right in the heart of Dartmoor. The quiet was only interrupted by the seep and trickle of water. Maggie imagined all the old tunnels burrowing under the moor, long seams of hollowness. Unknown from above, these dark, forgotten secrets.

'Imagine the miners,' murmured Elizabeth, 'trekking up here from those tiny little villages. Through the rain and the wind, all the way out along those rough old tracks. They must have walked miles every day before they even started working.'

Maggie glanced around. With the green whisper of the trees, and the peat gold babble of the river, and the slow warmth of the sun, the old mining ghosts seemed impossible. But they had been here. Abruptly, Maggie could imagine the smudge of a fire, the clanging jar of metal on rock. That steely, brutal cold.

'It was impossible to dig straight down into the ground on Dartmoor back in the eighteenth century,' Elizabeth spoke authoritatively. 'The shafts would have filled with water immediately.' The ground beneath Elizabeth's feet squelched as she shifted her weight, the earth permanently saturated here. 'But because Dartmoor is full of these steep-sided valleys, they could come in horizontally. Creating built-in drainage as they went, basically. A bit primitive, but functional.'

Maggie touched the granite beside the opening. It was chillingly cold, utterly unyielding.

'How on earth,' Lily asked, 'did they get through this stuff?'

'God knows,' said Elizabeth.

'Desperation,' said Maggie.

'Come on!' Lily's eyes glittered. 'We've got to see where it goes.'

'Lily...' But Elizabeth's doubts were shoved away as Lily took a few steps into the tunnel.

Maggie felt a surge of dread and excitement, of fear and fascination.

'Come on, Maggie. Where's your sense of adventure?' Lily's eyes were sharp as she glanced back. They started slowly, hopping from stepping stone to stepping stone, the roof of the tunnel only a couple of inches above their heads. On her third leap, Lily missed her footing and splashed into the water, giggling. 'Christ, it's cold.'

Ten yards in, Maggie looked back. From here, the green of the trees was framed by the ferns, shafts of sunlight glinting off the trickle of water.

'Lily—'

'Don't be lame, Maggie.'

Maggie felt the challenge bite deeper. 'Get on with it then.'

Lily led the way, the flicker of her lighter flame shining in the darkness. Elizabeth followed, then Maggie. At first, Maggie could make out patches of lichen on the damp walls, spot the hammer scars on the granite, but gradually the circle of light narrowed. Step by step, they made their way deeper into the mine.

'There are abandoned villages on Dartmoor.' Elizabeth's voice was higher than usual. 'You can see them here and there; just the walls left now, with everything else crumbled away. Imagine walking away from your village. Leaving behind everything you know.'

'They were refugees,' said Maggie. 'Nineteenth-century refugees.' Here and there, the tunnel widened out, before constricting again until it was only just wider than Maggie's shoulders.

'I wonder how long it takes for houses to disintegrate like that?' Lily was concentrating on her steps now. 'Fall to ruin.'

'I suppose once the roof collapses, it all goes quite fast—' Elizabeth slipped and fell hard against the side of the tunnel. 'Bugger.'

'You okay?' Lily pulled her back onto a stepping stone. Elizabeth was rubbing a scraped knee.

'Fine. Don't you think we've gone far enough, Lily?'

Maggie looked round and realised the circle of light behind them had disappeared. They must have come around a corner. Their whole world was glistening granite walls, the distant trickle of water, the darkness closing in. It felt oppressive, menacing. 'Do you think there are bats in here?' Maggie said without thinking.

'Oh *God*,' moaned Elizabeth. 'Right, I've had enough. Let's go back.'

Lily paused on her stone and turned back towards them. She raised the lighter. 'Okay. Hang on. I just want to see...'

She shut off the Zippo. Total blackness.

'Lily!' A shriek from Elizabeth.

Maggie felt detached, almost as if she were floating. It was as if her brain refused to believe that such darkness could exist. She swayed on her stepping stone and put out her hand to where she remembered the granite wall. Nothing. Maggie felt a sort of dizziness: her mind trying to fit together the known and the unknown and coming up short. A flood of panic.

No.

Reach further.

What if there's nothing there? What if...

She forced herself to stretch out into the blackness, to reach until she was almost losing her balance, and at last her fingers touched the slippery cool of the wall.

'Put the lighter back on, Lily,' she said into the dark.

'Isn't it amazing?' Lily's voice. 'All this was right under our feet and we never even realised?'

'Lily!' Elizabeth's voice was taut. 'Please.'

'You're scaring us, Lily,' Maggie said calmly. 'Put the lighter back on.'

'Okay, okay,' said Lily. 'I just wanted to see.' A fumble. A yelp of pain. A splash. '*Shit.*'

'Lily!' Elizabeth, almost a scream. 'What happened?'

'I… I dropped the lighter,' Lily admitted.

'Oh, for fuck's sake.' Elizabeth didn't swear often. 'Where is it?'

A splash as Lily bent down, feeling around in the water for the lighter. Maggie could hear Elizabeth breathing faster and faster.

'I can't…' After a few more seconds of fumbling, Lily's voice was half-apologetic, half-scared. 'I can't find it.'

The empty air seemed to press down on Maggie's head. Her eardrums pounded as if she was deep underwater. She pressed harder against the granite wall, desperate for some solidity in this strange, shifting blindness.

'Lily,' Elizabeth's hand reached out to Maggie and grabbed her arm. 'Find it.'

More splashing sounds, faster now. Lily was panicking. Maggie stepped off her stone, feeling the bitterly cold water filling her shoes, rising up to her knees.

'Maggie!' An edge of hysteria in Elizabeth's voice. 'What are you *doing*?'

'I'm going to try and help Lily find the lighter,' said Maggie tightly.

'It had heated up so much.' Lily sounded penitent. 'It burned me. Took me by surprise.'

'You fucking *idiot*,' Elizabeth said into the darkness.

Maggie was feeling around under water. The bottom of the tunnel was rough gravel, larger chunks of stone scattered here and there.

The water was pooled here, not seeping helpfully, not babbling towards safety. Everywhere, all around, there was the ooze, the slow trickle of water.

Elizabeth bent down too, yelping at the cold of the water. 'It has to be here,' she was muttering to herself. 'It *has* to be.'

'We'll find it,' said Maggie, not believing it.

It was so dark that Maggie couldn't tell if her eyes were open or closed. She thought of the Dartmoor hillside high above the mine, thousands and thousands of tons of granite and earth, balanced just above her head. This mine has been here for centuries, she told herself. Of course it won't close up right at this moment. These walls are solid. Of course the roof won't start to crack and crumble. Of course. But her mind was filled with the rumble, the roar, the chunks of rock starting to fall away. The chaos in the darkness. The fear, the terror.

Trapped.

It would be unnoticeable from above.

Nobody would know where they were. They would just be three girls who disappeared one beautiful Dartmoor day.

Maggie forced her hands to feel across the rocks, scraping them backwards and forwards in the icy water. Her fingers were catching on sharp stone edges, hurting now. She was getting colder, soaked through, not sure if she would be able to feel the difference between steel and granite any more. Beside her, she could hear Elizabeth and Lily splashing louder, getting more desperate.

'Would it even work after being underwater for so long?' asked Elizabeth.

There was a long silence.

'I don't know,' said Lily. 'Oh *fuck.*'

Maggie heard Lily stand up sharply. Or was it Elizabeth? She felt disorientated, panicked. In the darkness, nothing was real. Maggie reached out and grabbed Elizabeth's hand and then felt for Lily's.

'We're here,' Maggie said firmly. 'We're together. We're going to be okay.'

'Maggie—'

'It's going to be alright, Lily.'

'But Maggie... Maggie, I don't know which way we came in.'

Sound roared in Maggie's ear. The dizziness overwhelmed her for a moment, the darkness crushing down.

This way or that?

'Oh my God,' breathed Elizabeth. 'Which way is out?'

Searching in the darkness, they had moved around each other, bumping into each other, nudging one another aside. Now Maggie could feel her brain reeling, fighting to re-establish the certainties. 'We must...' Maggie tried to remember how she had moved while searching the cold, cold water. 'We must have...'

Her voice faded into the darkness.

'Fucking hell!' Elizabeth screamed. 'Which fucking way did we come?'

Maggie thought of the tunnels leading blindly into the hillside. Were there offshoots? Did tunnels branch off? How long might they wander aimlessly down here? They were in summer clothes, already soaked through.

'We'll be okay,' she said again. 'We didn't come that far. We'll be alright.'

'We won't,' shouted Elizabeth. 'There could be shafts dropping down, we could brain ourselves, break our legs—'

'Elizabeth,' Maggie cut in, 'we have to try. We can't stay here bawling at each other.'

She heard Elizabeth take a deep breath, battling for calm.

'Which direction do we all think we came from?' asked Lily. 'Let's start with that.'

Maggie tried, but it was like being caught in a roaring breaker at the beach, the waves knocking her under again and again. All sense of direction was swept away. Theseus and Ariadne and a ball of yarn in a labyrinth.

'I think it was this way,' said Elizabeth suddenly. She had stepped away slightly, still gripping Maggie's sleeve with one hand.

'Why?' Maggie and Lily chimed together.

'When Lily stopped, I was standing on a wider piece of rock,' said Elizabeth. 'Then I came forward to where you're standing now. It's this way, I think. We need to go out this way.'

'Are you sure?' Lily's voice was tight.

'No,' said Elizabeth bluntly, 'I'm fucking not. To be quite honest with you, Lily, I'm touching one piece of freezing granite that feels a lot like all the other bits of freezing granite, in total fucking darkness. But it's fifty:fifty and I've got nothing else to go on.'

A sound that was almost a laugh from Lily.

'I'll go first,' said Maggie. 'We don't want to split up, but if I walk a bit that way, I may be able to see light.'

'Or not,' said Elizabeth.

'Well, let's see.'

Maggie edged past Elizabeth and put her hand against the right side of the tunnel.

'Keep talking to me,' she said over her shoulder. 'I need to hear your voices.'

It was Lily who talked. Always Lily who talked. So funny and so impulsive, her voice reaching bravely down the tunnel behind Maggie. A long, complicated story about Ollie and a traffic cone and a rather bewildered parrot. Maggie made her way slowly along the tunnel, one hand on the wall, moving cautiously. She was too wet to care about keeping to the stepping stones any more, and couldn't risk slipping off, snapping an ankle. As the story culminated with Ollie and the traffic cone and the parrot falling into the river next to King's, Maggie stared ahead. Was that the faintest gleam of light, reflecting on the water?

'Maggie?' Elizabeth called down the passage. 'Can you see anything?'

'I think…' Maggie said carefully. 'I think that I can.'

They erupted through the ferns, laughing with delight.

'We're alive!' Lily threw herself to the ground, rolling around in ecstasy.

'Light!' Elizabeth raised both arms to the sky. 'Fresh air!'

'Jesus.' Maggie leaned against a beech. 'Jesus fucking Christ.'

The euphoria of survival bubbled.

'Lily,' Elizabeth was laughing, 'you absolute sodding *idiot.*'

'I know,' Lily admitted. 'I'm sorry. That wasn't my best decision.'

'Nope.' Maggie lay back on the grass, looking up at the green mosaic of leaves. 'But we made it.'

'And we know a lot more about mining on Dartmoor now,' said Lily.

'I never wanted to know that much about mining on bloody Dartmoor,' said Elizabeth. 'Never ever again.'

'Nope,' Lily agreed. She lay back too. 'But at least we know now. At least we know.'

'Blimey,' Ivo looked shocked when Elizabeth finished telling her tale. 'I had no idea.'

'You were all playing rounders out on the lawn when we got back,' said Maggie. 'There was a nail-biting finish to the game.'

Someone had handed them glasses of wine as they joined the cheering mob. Their clothes had dried in the warm spring sunshine, and the story stayed untold.

'We just forgot about it,' Elizabeth nodded. 'More or less.'

'It wasn't a big deal,' Maggie lied.

'Have you been down those tunnels?' Rory asked.

'Years ago.' Ivo nodded. 'Of course. With some friends from the village, when we were fourteen, fifteen. We knew every inch of the moor back then. Those mines scared us shitless, quite frankly. Some of them are absolutely lethal. If that's the same one, it goes back almost half a mile.'

'Especially,' Finlay was laughing, 'if you head off without so much as a torch. You raving loons.'

'I know,' Maggie shook her head. 'I dreamed about tunnels for years after that.'

'But it sounds like you saved the day?' said Ivo. 'Leading the way out? Left to their own devices, Elizabeth and Lily would still be down there.'

'Don't.' Elizabeth shuddered. 'If we'd gone the wrong way... it's just one decision, isn't it?'

'Yes,' said Maggie quietly. 'Just one decision.'

60

Finlay, on Lily: Lily will be a poet, and she will be broken.

'What?' Maggie looked up from the prediction. 'Why did you say that, Finlay?'

'I'm not sure.' Finlay looked surprised at his own insight. 'I suppose she always seemed slightly... unmoored. Even before we... I loved Lily, you know I did. And I wish it had worked out between us, but she was... tricky.'

'We're all tricky,' said Maggie.

'I know. But when we were seeing each other, or sort of seeing each other, or whatever the hell it was, she was so tense. She couldn't just be herself. She was spiky, snappy. It was difficult. She never told me about Bassel Nassar being her father, though. It all makes more sense now.'

'Stella Blake lied to Lily,' said Maggie. 'She told her that her father was a violinist from San Diego, and that he was over in the UK on tour with some orchestra when they met.' San Diego was conveniently distant, Maggie realised now, and the violinist had been noticeably short on relatives. A couple of years ago, she had tracked him down at Lily's request. Dark curly hair, curving mouth, death certificate.

'He died when I was three years old?' Lily had asked, a wobble in her mouth.

'I'm afraid so, Lils. Look.'

'Oh.' A lost future in a syllable.

'I'm so sorry, Lily.'

'I don't think my mother knows that he's dead,' Lily said, a few minutes later. 'I won't tell her, I don't think. It'd just upset her and there isn't… there isn't any point.'

Although now, of course, Maggie wondered whether Stella Blake had carefully selected this long-dead violinist, knowing he was eternally unfindable. For the first time, Maggie wondered now if Lily had only learned the violin so that she might play alongside her father one day. If she had spent all those years rattling through the scales because one day, maybe he might be real. A duet with a father who was only ever a lie. Another thought struck her for the first time. Whether after the violinist had disappeared into the ether, Lily had thought some more. Thought some more, and applied the thumbscrews to Stella, and finally, finally learned the truth. She wondered if it was the shredding of the violinist that set Lily on the hunt for Bassel Nassar.

'Lily was insecure,' Maggie said slowly. 'There wasn't any – well – ballast, was there? No self-esteem. If someone did or said something cruel, or just a little bit mean even, it cut her to the quick. She'd put the worst possible interpretation on things, catastrophise.'

'It was why her relationships always went wrong,' said Ayda. 'On some level, she was always assuming the worst. That they'd hurt her in the end. That she didn't deserve love.'

'Maybe that's just what happened in the end,' said Finlay. 'Maybe she just broke.'

'Maybe,' said Maggie. *Maybe.* She stirred her Bloody Mary, the flecks of pepper disappearing. She took a gulp, eyes watering at the Tabasco.

Among the silver-framed photographs above the fireplace sat a picture of Ivo's mother. She was riding a big bay hunter across Dartmoor, enchanting in a beautifully-tailored jacket. Foxhounds cavorted around her.

'Maybe we all broke,' Ivo said suddenly.

They turned towards him, startled. For once, Ivo seemed to shrink away from their stares, turning to fiddle with the coffee machine.

'What do you mean?' Maggie asked.

'Oh, I don't know.' He kept fiddling with the coffee machine.

'Ivo?' Ayda asked.

'It's just…' A gesture of frustration. 'None of us seem especially happy, do we?'

The silence rolled around the room.

'We're not *unhappy*…' Elizabeth's voice faded away.

Ivo turned towards them. 'It just feels as if all of us who made these predictions…' He looked back to the coffee machine.

'What do you mean, Ivo?' Ayda again. They were all wrong-footed, caught off guard by his change in mood. Ivo, so very charming, so amiable, suddenly so melancholy.

'The forbidden arts, they used to call them in the Renaissance,' Ivo told the coffee machine. 'Hydromancy, aeromancy, geomancy, and so on. The making of predictions – fortune-telling, soothsaying, clairvoyance – has always been regarded as dubious. Taboo. Because it is not down to us mere mortals to try and know the future; that privilege is reserved for a higher power. *A man also or woman that hath a familiar spirit, or that is a wizard, shall surely be put to death: they shall stone them with stones: their blood shall be upon them,*' he recited. 'That's the Bible giving fortune-telling a firm no. Islam and Judaism are equally disapproving. So maybe…'

'Maybe what, Ivo?' Elizabeth sounded disapproving.

'Maybe we cursed ourselves with our own predictions.' Ivo had turned round again, facing the stares. There was a strange expression on his face. Half-mocking, half-serious.

'A curse,' Jude murmured.

Their blood shall be upon them.

'All around the world for millennia,' Ivo was talking faster now, as if he was trying to explain before he could be interrupted, 'humanity has cobbled together ways of trying to read the future. There's astrology, of course. Or palmistry. Crystal balls. Tarot. Those are just the ones we recognise, standard-issue circus acts. But there were dozens of others, too. Nephomancy, reading the clouds. Ceromancy, watching molten wax cool and solidify. Lithomancy, reading gemstones. Naeviology, looking at scars or moles. Scapulimancy, divination from the cracks in the burned shoulder blade of an animal. Alectryomancy' – a half-smile, skewed – 'watching a rooster peck at grain.' Ivo had always been able to create a spell with words. It was hypnotic, thought Maggie.

'Cleromancy, the casting of lots,' Rory was nodding now. 'Haruspicy, the examination of the liver of a sacrifice. We pin down the future because we are scared of it. The great unknown.'

'And the one thing they all have in common,' Ivo went on. 'The one thing that unites these pathetic efforts to scratch at the edges of the future, is that they are regarded as dangerous, forbidden, verboten.'

Cursed. Maggie heard the word whisper around the room.

'You're hardly cursed, Ivo.' Ollie, trying to make it all a joke. 'The jet, the houses, the girls.'

A glimpse of something in Ivo's eyes. 'But are any of us really happy? Truly?' His eyes moved from Jude to Elizabeth to Ollie. Maggie flinched as his gaze turned on her. 'Lily fell under a train,' Ivo said. 'And we all know that it's perfectly plausible that she was unhappy enough to jump. How did this *happen*? How did we all end up here? *Us*?'

'Maybe by trying to predict the future,' Jude was nodding, 'we called down the anger of the gods.'

Ayda's mouth tightened at Jude's theatrical tones, but there was a flicker of recognition among the others.

'Perhaps.'

'But aren't *you* happy?' Elizabeth asked Ivo.

'I'm starting to realise,' he said carefully, 'that maybe there is a difference between fun and happiness.'

Ivo looked uncharacteristically vulnerable, the blue eyes veiled. *Old friends*, Maggie thought with a rush of pleasure. *We are old friends.*

'Reunions like this are always odd,' Maggie said quietly. 'We were twenty-ish when we wrote these words twenty years ago. And there's a background awareness all the way through this weekend that there aren't that many blocks of twenty years in a life. Twenty, forty, sixty. Eighty if we're lucky.'

'Three score and ten,' Rory agreed.

'That's a part of it,' Ivo nodded. 'It's weapons-grade nostalgia. Because what do we all have to show for the last twenty years, really?'

'But, Ivo,' Maggie said without thinking, 'you've got *everything*.' It broke the spell. Ivo's eyes sharpened. Maggie felt as if she had stumbled, clumsily, and misjudged the moment.

Ivo turned back to the coffee machine. 'Cappuccino anyone?' his voice was brisk. 'Latte?'

'Surely you've made a fortune out of predicting the future anyway?' Finlay was back to sarcasm. 'With your algorithms absorbing everything and spitting out the buy and sell orders? Algorithmancy, you should really call your fund.'

'Besides, it rather depends on who's making the prediction, doesn't it?' said Jude acidly. 'If you're a man making a prediction, you're a shaman, a prophet. If you're a woman, you're a witch. Cassandra.'

'Divine inspiration,' Elizabeth added, 'gets a free pass.'

'Something like that.' Ivo was clattering the coffee machine now, making the milk froth up, sprinkling chocolate powder. Normality returned in a cloud of cinnamon.

'What shall we do now?' Ollie yawned, looking at the rain hammering against the windows.

'Monopoly.' Ivo disappeared towards the snug. They could hear him opening and closing cupboards. 'Scrabble, chess, backgammon, take your pick.'

Ayda groaned. 'You always win sodding Monopoly and it goes on forever.'

They doled out the gaudy paper money all the same, and rolled the dice, and sat and drank and chatted. It was almost like being back at university, thought Maggie. When time was endless, and a conversation about the merits of brown sauce over tomato ketchup could go on for actual days. Before time was sliced into six-minute slots, allocated weeks in advance. The day faded slowly. Despite the clouds, there was a hard bright light, the June day refusing to go peacefully. Rory won Monopoly, the silver top hat triumphant.

'White nights,' Ivo said, glancing out of the window. 'Have you ever been to St Petersburg at this time of year? When the sun never sets?'

'Nope.'

They were all drinking fast, Ivo topping up their glasses. 'Right,' he said. 'Time for the next prediction.'

61

Ayda, on Finlay: You know what you did. And
your temper will have destroyed you.

Finlay looked straight at Ayda.

'Fuck you,' Finlay said simply, in the end. 'Fuck you, Ayda.'

He stood up and walked out.

'What?' Maggie sat up sharply. 'What just happened?'

Ayda's eyes were burning, hot coals that might set fire to the room.

'What the hell was that all about?' asked Ollie.

'Nothing,' Ivo said firmly. 'Just Finlay Finlay-ing.'

'But why?' Maggie had the sharp sense that half the people in the room knew exactly what was going on. 'And what did Ayda mean by her prediction anyway?' She looked around. '"You know what you did. Your temper will have destroyed you." Finlay... what did he do?'

'Finlay has just drunk too much.' Rory chucked the prediction onto the fire. 'Take no notice of him, Maggie. Time for a round of Scrabble, anyone?'

'Wait a minute, Rory.'

'Maggie—'

'Finlay must have seriously lost his temper about something all the way back then,' Maggie said slowly. 'And Ayda evidently knows about it. What was it, Rory?'

'Time to choose your letters,' Rory shook the Scrabble bag at her. 'Come on.'

Maggie ignored the bag. 'Lily referred to something similar in her prediction about Finlay, too, didn't she? "Will it still be a secret?" And she also said something about Rory still covering up for his little brother. So what's going on, Rory?'

'Maggie.' It was almost a plea. 'Leave it.'

But it was like picking at a scab, impossible to stop. There was an electricity in the room now, a sense of the inevitable.

'Ayda,' Maggie turned on her, 'you know too.'

'I don't remember, Maggie.'

Maggie stared at her. Ayda stared back, face bland.

'You do,' said Maggie.

'I don't.'

'I can't think of anything Finlay had done *then*,' said Maggie. 'Not at the time of that dinner party. Since then – well – we all know what he's got up to.' Finlay had been discharged from the Army for fighting. Not a regular punch-up either, Maggie guessed, because the Army still swept such things under the carpet. This must have left a man in hospital, lucky to be alive. Breathing through tubes, for all she knew.

'We need to start cooking dinner,' said Ivo. 'Tomahawk steak, anyone?'

'I bloody love—' Ollie, delighted.

Maggie scorned the change of subject. She felt as if something important was within her grasp at last. 'Something happened,' she said carefully. 'And it wasn't long before that dinner party.' Maggie stared around the room. There was a gathering curiosity on Elizabeth's face, too: she didn't know either.

But Ivo... Ivo, Maggie saw abruptly, had known all along.

Rory was chucking Monopoly pieces in the box now, making too much noise, a rattle of desperation about him. Maggie switched her gaze to Jude. Small random muscles were quivering in Jude's face. In her eyelid, her lower lip, the hollow of a cheek. As Maggie's eyes fell on her, Jude ducked away, the tears overflowing.

'Jude,' Maggie realised. 'Jude, you know *too*.'

'Stop it, Maggie.'

'But what *happened*, Jude?'

'Maggie!' It was Ivo, stamping his authority. 'Not now.'

'If not now, when?' Maggie snapped. 'What the hell happened?'

Silence. The door to the snug opened. Finlay, calm again. 'Sorry about that, Ayda. Where were we?'

He came to a sharp halt as he realised.

'What the hell did you *do*, Finlay?' Maggie's eyes met his.

'I—' Finlay was lost. 'I don't know what—'

It was Jude who crumbled. 'They were trying to *help*, Maggie.'

'Shut up, Jude.' Rory spoke with a sudden violence. 'Just stop talking.'

A strange calm descended over Maggie. A moment of knowledge, of purest clarity.

'Mike Jansen,' she said quietly. 'The attack on Mike Jansen.'

'No—'

'Mike died.'

'Maggie—'

'Mike was *murdered*.'

'Stop it—'

'Finlay. Oh my God, Finlay. You killed him. You killed *Mike*.'

'We didn't!' Finlay was shaking his head, big frantic movements. 'Maggie, we didn't!'

'*We*?' Maggie turned on Rory. 'You? *You* were there?'

'I—'

'We didn't kill Mike,' Finlay's voice was pleading. 'I hit him, yes.' A hiss of air from Rory. 'Maybe I hit him more than once. And I shouldn't have... I never should have... But I didn't *kill* him, Maggie.'

'You didn't...' Maggie was looking at Rory. 'It wasn't *you*—'

'I never touched Mike,' Rory sat down abruptly, still clutching the Monopoly dog. 'I swear I never touched him.'

'But you were there? You were out on the common that night?'

'It was only because I didn't want Finlay to go alone—'

'Because you knew what Finlay would do,' Maggie finished his sentence. 'You know what Finlay is, Rory. And the moment you let him anywhere near Mike—'

'Mike raped Jude,' Finlay's control snapped. 'He roofied her or something like that. She was completely out of it that night, and then he...'

Roofies, Rohypnol, rape.

Jude was shivering, an aspen in the wind. 'Mike put something in my drink,' Jude whispered. 'I was almost unconscious. I've never...'

'Jude…'

'I know you all think I'm a pisshead,' said Jude.

'I don't—'

'But this was completely different, Maggie. I remember how I felt so clearly. I *know* that Mike drugged me.'

'Did you get tested?'

'No… but it was *different*, Maggie. Nothing like that has ever happened to me before or since. It was awful. All the colour faded away in the room until I could only see in black and white and everything was fizzing like an old television. I couldn't speak, I couldn't get anyone to understand how I was feeling. I just had this huge urge to get out of Finlay's room – I *had* to get out of there – and… and it was Mike who led me out.'

'I never should have let you go,' Finlay's eyes glistened.

Jude. Jude, the girl he'd loved.

'I remember looking up at the ceiling as I left Finlay's room,' Jude murmured. 'And I saw that it was coming down towards me. Just sloping down, for some weird reason. I couldn't work out why, couldn't think at all. And a second later I had walked straight off the top of the staircase. I hadn't even realised I was in a stairwell. Mike had to help me stand up again.'

'It was my fault,' said Finlay. 'I should have realised.'

'It wasn't your fault,' Jude said fiercely. 'It was Mike's fault. Everything that happened was Mike's fucking fault.'

'I—'

'I woke up in Mike's room the next morning,' Jude's face distorted at the memory. 'Only a few hours later. He was smiling at me, all gooey-eyed. Disgusting.' Jude looked sick. 'He'd actually made me a cup of coffee. Everything was blurry, curling around the edges. I just got up and left. I didn't know what else to do.'

'You should have told me,' said Maggie.

'What would you have done though? I rang Lily. It was only 6 a.m. and she was still up. Completely out of it though, just saying, "*come to Finlay's room. Come to Finlay's room, Jude,*" over and over. So I did, in the end. I didn't know what else to do. Ayda and Ivo were still up. So were Finlay and Lily. Ollie had crashed out.'

'God, Jude.' Ollie was looking appalled. 'I had no idea. I'm so sorry.'

'We all just sat there,' said Jude. 'I was crying and crying. Ayda and Ivo kept telling me that I should go to the police, but I wouldn't. I couldn't. Not then.'

'Jude.' Maggie reached across, put a hand on her shoulder.

'I ended up going to the police a week later, like I told you.'

'But you all could have said that Jude was drugged,' Maggie looked around at them. 'The police could have made a case out of that, surely? If you'd all seen her in that state?'

'How could we have said that we knew she was drugged and that we also let Mike take her away by herself?' asked Ivo.

'We were all off our tits,' Ayda summarised. 'None of us could swear that she'd been given Rohypnol or whatever because we just didn't realise.'

'Like that girl Katia,' Maggie said. 'The one you and Finlay picked out of the flowerbeds in Great Court. She reckoned she'd been roofied too, didn't she? It was just luck that you and Finlay were there, not some creep.'

'Just luck,' said Ayda quietly. 'Just luck.'

'I didn't look that different,' Jude laughed drily, 'to how I am normally. It was just that inside my head everything was black and white and fizzing.'

'So the police told you they weren't going to do anything?'

'The whole investigation was over in a few days. I was back in Finlay's room after I found out, and I couldn't stop crying.'

'Ivo was spitting tacks over the police refusing to do anything,' Ayda said. 'He was saying he would get his father to call the Chief Constable, all that sort of thing.'

'He was great. But Mike was being such a *creep*,' said Jude. 'He wouldn't leave me alone.'

'So what happened?'

'Nothing happened straight away,' said Finlay. 'But… eventually, I found out that Mike walked home from the maths facility after he'd finished there late at night. Sometimes a few of them would have a quick drink at the pub next door and then walk back to college. Very late, sometimes. And one night, I just waited for him. Rory was with me. He was trying to convince me to go back to our rooms. "Stop it, Finlay. Leave it. Don't do this." But just then, Mike appeared.'

Maggie could imagine the eruption of rage. The punches raining down. The pounding, the pulverising, the explosion of pain. 'You beat him up,' she said.

'Yes, but I *only* beat him up,' Finlay insisted. 'Rory stopped me, pulled me away. Dragged me. I was so *angry*. I was so angry at what Mike had done. But I never meant to kill. *Never*. And he wasn't in the river when we left him. I promise you, Maggie. I'd never...'

'The autopsy showed that he drowned,' said Rory. 'That was what killed him. He didn't die of his injuries. There was water in his lungs.'

'Was Mike conscious when you left him?'

A long silence. 'No. Not really.' Finlay said.

'So he could have come around after you left? Stumbled into the river? Concussed, in pain, terrified.'

Another silence. An admission. 'Yes.'

Maggie pictured it, scrabbling against that muddy bank. Cold, clogged with weeds, slipping, slipping. Can't reach, can't grab, can't... the panic, the terror, the shouts turning into bubbles, the bubbles into silence. Getting weaker, struggles fading and then nothing. Nothing at all. A shape drifting away under the dark, dark water.

'Ivo saved us that night,' Finlay said flatly. 'Me and Rory. He saw the state we were in when we got back to our rooms. He got rid of our clothes somehow, fixed everything, came up with an alibi for us. I don't know what we would have done.'

Ivo, quick and ruthless, contra mundum.

'Did you know Mike was dead by then?' Maggie asked. 'When you got back to your rooms?'

'No.' Finlay's face was white. 'We had no idea. I heard a whisper of it over lunch. Just a rumour it was, then. I felt... I felt as if I was dissolving right there in the dining rooms. The terror. The absolute horror of it.'

'I remember,' said Maggie. The ripple of fear around the room. *Mike. Mike Jansen. Dead.* A feeling of being right at the top of the rollercoaster, about to roar into the unknown.

'Ivo came to my room that afternoon,' Ollie recalled wonderingly. 'Said that Finlay had been drink-driving the night before and had had a crash. Just a fender-bender, nothing serious, but still. I had to tell anyone who asked that we'd all been together all night.'

'Ollie!' Maggie was contemptuous. 'For fuck's sake!'

'What?' Ollie looked wounded. 'The police were obviously going to be asking questions about that whole night, and Ivo said it was important that they didn't rumble Finlay on top of everything else.' Ollie would have been flattered to be asked for help, Maggie knew. Thrilled. Part of Ivo's gang.

'Then what?' she asked.

'Then we just kept our heads down,' Ayda cut in. 'Lily and Jude had been down in London that night.'

'Not a coincidence,' said Maggie.

'Nope.'

'Ollie, Ivo, Finlay and Rory swore blind they'd been together,' said Ayda. 'We all promised never to tell anyone what happened. We promised.'

They promised.

'We made a vow,' Rory said solemnly. 'None of us ever said a word about it to anyone. Until tonight.' He turned on Ayda. 'Why the fuck did you write down that prediction, Ayda?'

'I'm sorry.' Ayda looked genuinely contrite. 'It must have just felt like twenty years was so far away that it basically didn't count. I completely forgot that I had written it down.'

'Idiot.'

'The police,' Maggie interrupted, 'never got anywhere near working out what'd happened to Mike, did they?'

'To be honest, I'm not convinced the police tried as hard as they might have to get to the bottom of it all,' said Ayda. 'They knew what had happened to Jude.'

'They didn't bother to work out what happened with the rape,' Ivo said. 'And they certainly didn't bother to work out what had happened to the rapist.'

Maggie felt battered, exhausted. Rory was looking straight at her 'What are you going to do, Maggie?'

'I don't know,' she answered. 'I don't know yet.'

It would finish Rory's career, they all knew that. He should have reported Finlay and condemned his brother. Murder. Manslaughter, at the very least. Maggie wasn't sure about the legalities of Rory's own position, but she suspected they weren't good.

They were all staring at her. *Now you know.* Even in the middle of all the confusion, the uncertainty, Maggie had a sense of finally knowing their secrets. Of finally being at the core.

'I don't know,' Maggie repeated. 'I'll have to think.'

Ollie and Elizabeth, too, were looking dazed.

We all need to agree, thought Maggie. We'll all need to decide if we will keep this secret forever. Or not.

'It was justice,' said Ivo. 'Mike... he got what he deserved.'

'Mike would have got ten years in jail?' Elizabeth raised an eyebrow. 'Maybe? And he would have served half of it? He'd have been out fifteen years ago, Ivo. You know that perfectly well.'

Jude stood up. 'He fucked up my whole life, Elizabeth. I don't know if I'll ever get over what he did to me.'

'I know,' Elizabeth said quietly. 'And I am sorry, Jude, truly. But—'

'But what?'

Elizabeth was standing by the fire, the flames crackling behind her.

'Mike's sister came to my house,' Elizabeth said slowly. 'Helen Jansen. She's the same age as us, but she looks a decade older. Her face looks as if it had been soaked in grief. Drowned in sorrow. It's as if every single part of her has been saturated in sadness for all these years. And she still has all these questions. Questions that will never be answered unless...' Her voice trailed away.

'Helen Jansen came to see me too,' Finlay, confessing. 'A few months ago now.'

'She came to see *you*?' Maggie's head spun around. 'She went to see Ollie too.'

'Did she? I didn't even know who she was until she was in my flat,' said Finlay. 'When she told me, I thought my heart might stop altogether.'

'Christ, Finlay.'

'I don't know how she even knew to come and see me. I wasn't even in the same year as Mike.'

A brief silence. 'I may have told Helen that you knew Mike a bit,' Ollie admitted cautiously. 'Only because of that night we were all in your room. It was practically the only time I ever spent any time with Mike, so I thought I might as well mention it, seeing as she was desperate for any information at all. It was something to say, really. I just thought that Jude and Mike had been flirting a bit. I had no *idea*.' Ollie stopped, horrified. 'Helen Jansen asked me for your address, Finlay, and I didn't have any reason not to give it.'

'Of course not,' Finlay said. 'It was totally fair enough, Ollie. You weren't to know.'

'I certainly bloody wasn't. What did you tell her about that night?'

'I didn't tell her anything,' Finlay had shrunk in on himself. 'I didn't know what to do, or say, or anything. I was just in a panic.' Confronted by his sins two decades later. Maggie almost felt sorry for him. Almost, not quite. 'Helen kept asking me what Mike's friends were like.' Finlay scraped his hands back through his hair. 'Who had he hung out with? Who was this Jude character?'

'She asked about *me*?' Jude winced.

'She asked for your address. I told her you were doing a ski season and that I couldn't remember which resort you were in. Which was true anyway.' He glanced towards the door as if Helen Jansen might be standing there.

'Thank God,' Jude said with feeling. 'Thank God she didn't track me down.'

'She really wanted to know where you were though,' said Finlay. 'She had all these questions, kept asking and asking. I just burbled on about how much everyone had liked Mike and how he'd been such a good mate. Bullshit, of course. But I just wanted her to go and I couldn't very well throw her out.'

'Did she guess that you were a bit rattled?'

'She must have done. I was shaking, talking too fast. I think that's why she kept asking me more and more questions. Seeing if I would crack.'

'How did you get rid of her in the end?' Ivo asked.

Finlay winced at the memory. 'I told her that Lily was Jude's best friend. I thought Lily might know what to say to her, especially if I warned her Helen was on her way. I told Helen Jansen that if she wanted to find Jude, she had to go and see Lily first.'

'Can you track down Helen Jansen?' Jude asked, as she trailed Maggie up the imperial staircase. 'See what she's up to now?'

'I can certainly give it a try.'

'It would be easy enough to find Mike's parents, wouldn't it? Their names must be in the cuttings from back when he died.' Jude knew how newspapers worked, after years of knowing Maggie.

'Mike's parents live in West Malling.' The memory floated to the surface. 'In Kent. Or they did when we were at university, anyway.'

'You never forget anything, Maggie.'

'I'll check my email too, just in case Helen Jansen tried to get in touch with me, and I missed it somehow.'

They had reached Maggie's room. She picked up her laptop and logged into her emails. There were thousands of unread messages in Maggie's inbox. If someone had emailed her in the middle of the Budget, she would never have spotted it for a hundred emails from PRs insisting that their client had something especially fascinating to say about junior ISA thresholds or NHS spending or fiscal drag.

'I suppose Helen might have emailed Rory and Ivo too,' said Jude, 'and just not been able to get through to them.'

'Yup.'

Maggie, Ivo and Rory were probably the hardest to contact on a personal basis. Parliament security was strict these days, and none of Rory's staff would dream of handing out his home address. Ivo ricocheted around the world so fast that Helen Jansen would have been lucky to find him at his Chelsea townhouse, with its gouged out mega-basement complete with gym and swimming pool – unused – and staff quarters. The *Post*, too, would never reveal Maggie's address to an unknown caller.

'Ivo's PA can be a right cow, too,' said Jude. 'She would hardly put some random through.'

'She is a dragon,' Maggie agreed. 'A very well-paid one. I can't see an obvious email from Helen.' Maggie's fingers were pattering over her keyboard now, checking the databases. 'She's not on Facebook or Snapchat, or anything like that. And I can't see an address for a Helen Jansen of the right age on the electoral roll. Although if she's spent years in Kenya, she might not show up on our systems anyway.'

'Okay. So we know that Helen Jansen spoke to Elizabeth first, then Ollie,' Jude ticked them off on her fingers. 'Ollie sent her in the direction of Finlay who panicked and hot-potatoed her to Lily. Then where did she get to?'

'Ayda mentioned that Helen spoke to her too,' said Maggie. 'While we were out on the moor earlier. But I'm not sure when that visit was in the sequence of events.'

'What the hell did Lily tell Helen?' wondered Jude. 'God, I wish we knew.'

'And how long after Lily spoke to Helen,' Maggie asked slowly, 'did Lily fall under that train?'

In the circumstances, it felt odd to be getting ready for dinner. Inappropriate. But nevertheless, Maggie found herself stripping off her Saturday afternoon clothes and looking through the outfits she'd hung up in the creaky old wardrobe. She chose a black dress in the end. Not sure if she was mourning the loss of Rory and Finlay, or lamenting something else. If she was willingly plunging into a lifetime of secrecy, of wondering: *who knows, what if, when will?*

'What does Helen Jansen know?' Maggie murmured to herself. 'What did she find out?'

It was easy to track down Antony and Rosemary Jansen, still living in West Malling. Google Streetview showed a pretty brick cottage, with a fanlight over the front door and a neatly pruned cherry tree flowering in the front garden. Would Antony and Rosemary Jansen actually be happier for knowing the truth? Maggie wondered to herself. Because Mike's death was a grief of the deepest, cruellest nature, but an agony this ageing couple had learned to live with. A sorrow they had survived. Because no matter how agonising Mike's death had been, they still planted lavender along the garden path, and trained wisteria up the fence and had found a way to live somehow.

So would the truth help them in any way? Maggie pondered.

Mike wouldn't be a sweet boy any more.

Not a brilliant mathematician, wrong place, wrong time.

No.

It would be your son: the rapist. Your son: he got what he deserved.

It was tempting to tell herself that they would prefer silence, that they would choose blindness over that.

And maybe it was true.

But I *tell* the story, Maggie said to herself. I tell the story without fear or favour.

Finlay, in jail. Rory, destroyed.

Maggie put on the black dress slowly. Because there was another thought, too. Another thought buried right at the back of her mind that was fighting to emerge.

If I tell, they will cast me out.

Maggie tried to shove the knowledge away. To ram it down into that little box somewhere by her liver.

If you betray them, they will never, ever forgive you.

No more Wintercross, even though this was the first time she had visited in years.

No more Rory, and an affection that might be repaired even now.

All those friendships, lost forever. Ayda, Ivo, all of them.

Over a *mistake*. A silly mistake.

Maggie took another swig of her drink. Gin and tonic. A strong one. What had she meant to do? Oh yes. Check her emails. See if there was any reference to a Helen Jansen in them.

Maggie grabbed her laptop. 'Helen Jansen', typed clumsily. Nothing.

That didn't mean Helen had never emailed though. It just meant that the exact phrase wasn't coming up anywhere in Maggie's vast inbox. She had no idea what email address Helen might have used.

'Helen' and 'Jansen'. Hundreds of emails.

Sigh.

Maggie fiddled around for a while, trying to narrow down the selection.

Through the gin and tonic, it wasn't straightforward. There turned out to be dozens of Helens in her acquaintance, a special adviser called Roland Jansen, a PR company called Jansen&Fox, some government building on Jansen Street. Maggie grumbled and clicked and deleted.

The email from Arthur kept popping up first in the search options.

'Go away!' she said, clicking crossly.

'What?' Jude, out of the shower in a glow of orange blossom.

'Nothing. Just this bloody email keeps coming up when I'm looking for an email from Helen Jansen.'

'Why?'

'I don't know.' Without thinking, Maggie opened the email and skimmed it.

Skimmed it and came to a grinding, shocked halt. 'Oh my God,' she murmured.

'What?' Jude crossed the room.

'Nothing.' Maggie shook her head automatically, shutting the email. 'Don't be daft.'

Maggie didn't try to stop Jude clicking on the email again. Jude scrolled down through the cuttings sent through from the *Post*'s database. Then there was a sharp intake of breath, and a whisper.

'Oh fuck, Maggie. Fucking, fucking hell.'

Because there it was. *Aid worker dies in Dartmoor tragedy. Helen-Ann Jansen, 39, found close to Devon tourist hotspot Barras Tor.*

62

Finlay, on Rory: Still a bossy git. Still looking out for me.

Jude and Maggie had sat staring at the laptop. The room was so silent that Maggie heard one of the pale peach roses collapsing in a sigh of petals.

'Helen Jansen is dead?' Jude asked, as if she couldn't quite believe it. 'Dead?'

Maggie shook herself, clicking on the laptop again. 'It might be another Helen Jansen. Although it does look as if she's the right age. And, oh God, look at this bit. From the *Okehampton Times*, not long before they found her body. "*Tony Jansen, Helen's father, appealed for information about her disappearance. 'Helen-Ann had lived such an extraordinary life, helping hundreds, probably thousands, of people in the Kakuma refugee camp year after year. It is impossible for us to imagine life without her. Please, if anyone knows anything at all, please tell us.*" It must be the same Helen, Jude. Ollie said that Helen Jansen talked about travelling out to Kakuma after leaving university.'

'I can't believe it.'

Maggie was searching again. She found an appeal for information on the charity's website. *Helen-Ann Jansen, a much-loved member of our team, went missing shortly after returning to England after a long stint in Kenya. Helen's parents are keen to hear from her. Please contact us...*

There was a photograph, too, on the charity's website. Helen, holding a small child, the backdrop a clutter of tarpaulins and dust. Maggie stared at the picture. Helen had pale auburn hair, freckles on her nose, echoes of Mike. Her eyes were sombre, her mouth unused to smiling. She must have been pretty once, before years of sun and terrible sadness.

'Do they think it was an accident? Or suicide?' asked Jude. 'Christ, she was found in the middle of nowhere.'

'It's not clear from the article.' From years of pulling together articles without much certainty around the facts, Maggie recognised ambiguity. 'We never put in much detail about suicides anyway. Press code.'

'"*No foul play suspected*",' read Jude. 'I always assume that's a euphemism for topping yourself.'

'It usually is.'

'And you're meant to be going to the inquest next week.'

'Yes.'

'And there weren't any witnesses?'

'Apparently not,' said Maggie, still reading. 'Helen was found in March this year. She was up there by herself. Her car was found near a reservoir. Bloody hell, they don't even know when exactly she died. She went missing and was found a few days later. She'd been dead for several days by the time they found her. They could tell that much.'

'Poor girl.'

'It doesn't look as if the police have done much really.'

'"*The area is known for raves*",' Jude read over her shoulder. 'Which means that people go missing every so often, off their tits on MDMA, and the police search is pretty fucking cursory.'

'She was last seen on the twenty-sixth of February this year,' Maggie murmured. 'It'll be an open verdict, when they reckon it's suicide but can't be sure about intent.'

'The back end of February isn't the most hospitable time to be up on Dartmoor. And I doubt there were any sodding raves then.' Jude stood up. She walked across to a little armchair next to the fireplace and threw herself down in it. 'What the hell is going on, Maggie?'

'I don't know.'

'Lily falls under a train,' said Jude. 'Helen Jansen dies somewhere out on Dartmoor. I almost get shoved out of a window.'

Three's a crowd.

'We don't know that it's not—'

'Coincidence? *Please*, Maggie.'

'Well, we don't.'

'Maggie! You're so sodding desperate to believe that it's all hunky-dory and we're all such fabulous friends that you're not looking at the most basic facts,' said Jude. 'What's it going to bloody take? Being slung off the battlements yourself?'

'Okay,' said Maggie unwillingly. 'There probably is some connection.'

'Why would Helen Jansen have been up near Barras Tor?' asked Jude. As she spoke, Jude was searching on her phone. 'Barras Tor is only a few miles from here, look. Although I think "tourist hotspot" must have been a bit of journalistic licence; it's in the middle of nowhere.'

'I have no idea. Her car was found out on some track.'

'She may have come down to Devon to try and get hold of Ivo,' Jude narrowed her eyes.

'I'm sure—'

'*Maggie.*' Jude carried on. 'If Helen had been determined enough about tracking him down, someone would eventually have told her about this place. We all knew about it at university, and quite a few other people in our year visited at some time or another.'

'I know.' Ivo's twenty-first: an explosion of champagne and fireworks and the bruising realisation that all his school friends were a million times more glamorous than his university crowd would ever be.

'I'm sure Helen could have found it some other way, too,' said Jude. 'This place isn't exactly a state secret.'

Mr Fitzwilliam, Maggie knew, had been a director in several companies. He had listed Wintercross as his address on Companies House, so the information was unquestionably in the public domain.

'Why would she have parked on the other side of the moor then?' As she spoke to Jude, Maggie was searching one of the flight databases. Quietly, surreptitiously, trawling back to February. Ivo's private jet had flown to Stuttgart three days before Helen Jansen had gone missing. The day after she went missing, it flew on to Athens and then headed back to Devon two days later. Ivo had been out of the country when she disappeared. A quiet sigh of relief.

'I don't know why she would be parked by that reservoir,' admitted Jude.

Then Maggie realised.

'Helen Jansen went missing just a couple of days before Lily died,' she said.

'You're fucking kidding.'

'Helen disappeared near the end of February. Lily died at the very beginning of March.'

'Oh God,' Jude murmured. 'Oh no.'

'Helen was still missing when Lily died.'

'And Helen disappeared on the doorstep of Wintercross?'

Hating herself, Maggie checked again. N98CP flew to Germany before the time Helen disappeared and was back in Exeter when Lily died. That was exactly where Ayda had said Ivo had been that evening. Sitting on the top of Lion's Rock as the sun went down over Dartmoor. Wrapped up warmly, enjoying the brief apricity of the sun. Probably with a gin and tonic and some delicious pistachios.

'Ayda said that Ivo was in Devon when Lily died in London,' she told Jude, knowing she sounded defensive. 'So he can't have killed her,' she explained quickly.

'That's not proof,' said Jude firmly. 'Where a bloody jet is parked up at the relevant time.'

'I know,' said Maggie. 'I *know*.'

Wincing, she clicked back to the tab showing the West Malling cottage. That image had been taken last summer, she realised. She wondered how it looked now. Were they still clipping the lavender? Training the wisteria?

To lose one child: unbearable.

To lose two…

'The poor Jansens,' she murmured. 'The poor, poor parents.'

'The Jansens deserve to know what happened to Mike,' said Jude. 'And they deserve to know that someone almost certainly murdered Helen.'

'They do,' Maggie agreed quietly. She was about to say something else when she was startled by a gasp from Jude. 'What is it?'

'I've just realised,' said Jude. '*Lily* was my alibi. If we tell the Jansens the whole story, they'll probably push to have Mike's case reopened. And if it comes to that, there's nothing left to link the boys to his death. But Lily… my alibi disappeared the day that Lily died.'

'Guys?' Maggie jumped as Ivo's voice echoed up the backstairs. 'Are you coming? The food's almost ready. And it's time to read another prediction.'

63

Maggie, on Lily: Lily is dead.

Ivo's grin disappeared.

'What?' asked Maggie. '*What?*'

They were all in the kitchen now. The tomahawk steak, a vast chunk of bloody flesh, was sizzling in the oven.

'Lily is dead,' Ivo read out again.

'But I didn't…' said Maggie. 'I didn't write that.'

'Maggie,' Ivo shrugged. 'That's your handwriting.'

'Give it here.'

Maggie grabbed the paper out of his hand.

It was written in the same pencil as all her other predictions. It was the same slightly stiff paper. Definitely her own handwriting, too. Hurried, slightly cramped.

Lily is dead.

'Sounds a little bit odd, Maggie.' Rory was hesitant. 'What were you…'

'Of course it isn't odd. And I didn't write that.' Maggie stared at the Venetian bowl. 'Anyone could have put that prediction in the bowl at some point over the weekend.'

'In your handwriting?' asked Elizabeth. 'Maybe you were just pissed off with Lily for some reason, all those years ago?'

'I wasn't!' said Maggie.

'Well, what do you think you wrote about Lily then?'

'I don't know,' said Maggie. 'I can't remember.' Recalling the memory of that prediction was like trying to reach for a bubble. It sailed out of her grasp, iridescent, bursting as she snatched.

'How can you be sure what you wrote then?' Ayda said flippantly. 'Sounds a bit like you had it in for Lily.'

'I didn't,' said Maggie. She felt oddly close to tears. She put the piece of paper down on the table, pushed it away from her.

'Oh, for heaven's sake,' Ayda snatched up the scrap, balled it, lobbed it in the fire. 'It doesn't matter, Maggie.' But it did matter. Maggie felt their eyes on her with just that hint of a doubt. That tinge of suspicion.

'How did you know though?' Of course, Ollie wouldn't let it drop. 'That Lily would be dead by now.'

'It was just a joke, Ollie,' said Ayda. 'Not that you have much of a grasp of such things, admittedly.'

'Anything could have happened to any of us, quite frankly,' said Rory, 'Finlay in Afghanistan. Health scares. Car crashes. Anything. We've been lucky.'

'Apart from Lily,' said Elizabeth.

'Well… of course.'

Maggie was listening to the evening being tugged gently back in the right direction, when she realised. 'Back in a second,' she said, and she sensed the others glancing at each other as she headed out of the room.

Up the backstairs, two steps at a time. Over to her bed with a bound. Upending the pillows, nothing there. Maggie's glance swept around the room. Maybe it was over on the dressing table? No. Kicked under the bed by mistake? No.

There was nothing there. Nothing, nothing, nothing.

The blue notepad was gone.

'I don't understand,' Jude whispered. 'What do you mean your notepad's gone missing?'

The two of them were in the dining room, setting the table.

'The tomahawk deserves the dining room.' Ollie had insisted, so they were all to-ing and fro-ing with plates and forks and steak knives.

'Let's go to the ballroom,' Maggie muttered back to Jude. 'We can talk better in there.'

They waited for a pause between Rory carrying salt and pepper and Elizabeth bearing a complicated flower arrangement and then slipped away.

'You wrote down your suspicions about who killed Lily?' Jude rolled her eyes. 'Christ, Maggie. What the hell were you thinking?'

'I always think better when I'm writing by hand.'

'I *know*,' said Jude. 'And so does everyone else. We've all seen you scribbling away for decades.'

'Okay, Jude. I know. It's just a habit.'

'Christ. So who did you decide had done it, then?'

'I don't know.' Maggie made a wild gesture with her hands. 'I just wrote down possible motivations. Some thoughts.'

'*Maggie*. Jesus. Okay. Who was the most *motivated* then?'

Maggie blew out her cheeks. 'Elizabeth, maybe? If she thought that Lily was planning to get knocked up by Ollie? Even though we now know that Lily wasn't. Or Ayda obviously had a strong motive to try and protect her mother from finding out that Lily was Mr Nassar's daughter.'

'Great,' said Jude. 'Just brilliant.'

'And at the top of it all, I wrote "*Lily is dead*." I often do that, just setting out the issue and seeing what it sparks.'

'So someone came in and took the notepad? While you were off somewhere else?'

'I suppose they must have done.' Maggie paused.

'Any idea when?'

'It must have been this afternoon,' she said. 'I only wrote it this afternoon. The notepad was just sitting there on the dressing table.'

'Okay.'

'Thinking about it,' Maggie said cautiously. 'I'm not sure if it was on the dressing table when we arrived on Thursday. It might have only appeared while we were playing Murder in the Dark last night.'

'What do you mean?'

Maggie thought back to arriving in her bedroom, admiring the peach roses, the bunch of sweet peas, the tiny birds hopping on the wallpaper. There was no notepad in that memory, she was sure of it. 'In the first round, I hid in my en suite bathroom, and while I was in there, I heard someone coming into my bedroom. I remember that the floorboards creaked.'

'So what?' Jude answered her own question. 'You think that maybe someone read your predictions and worked out what pen and paper you'd used and decided to give you a similar pencil and notepad while we were all playing Murder in the Dark? God, that's quite devious. I suppose they thought that at the very least, they might get a heads-up on what you were thinking.'

'I'm sure it wasn't there before the game of Murder in the Dark,' Maggie racked her brain again. 'It was just… there when I needed it.'

'Right,' said Jude. 'Okay.'

'The notepad left on the dressing table was Moleskine,' said Maggie. 'And it's possible that I scribbled on a Moleskine notepad belonging to Elizabeth that night at university. Although I didn't know what Moleskine was back then, or how expensive they were.'

'How much do these notepads cost?'

'Forty quid?'

'Forty quid!'

'Yup.'

'So they may have been trying to set you up, with an expensive note-pad and some pencils?' said Jude. 'Or perhaps they were just trying to work out what you were thinking?'

'Yes.'

There was a fire in Jude's eyes, a light that Maggie hadn't seen for years. For a second, Maggie was back at freshers' week, meeting a bright, sparky girl and being drawn instantly to her style, to her charisma. She had almost forgotten that Jude. Another sharp pang for the long-lost years.

'Who was where during that first game of Murder in the Dark?' Jude asked.

'God, I can't remember.' Maggie dropped her head into her hands, trying to squeeze out the memory. 'Rory was the detective, I think. Yes. And Ollie was killed by Ivo in the drawing room. Ayda was in the library.'

'Finlay and I were messing about in the cupboard under the stairs,' said Jude. 'Then he told Rory that he saw Ivo going into the drawing room. I think I saw Ayda coming out of the library after Ollie started shouting his head off about being dead.'

'Elizabeth said something about going to the ballroom,' remembered Maggie. 'And it was a long game, Jude. I suppose that anyone could have zoomed up and down to my room. And, really, it could have been put in there at any time, not necessarily during the first round of Murder in the Dark. It's just when I happened to be in the linen cupboard and heard footsteps.'

'The first round would have been the earliest opportunity,' Jude insisted. 'If someone was determined enough, they could just have gone for it.'

'The paper wouldn't have been forensically the same as the rest of my predictions anyway,' said Maggie. 'Would it?'

'Wouldn't have thought so. Anyway, Ayda chucked the prediction in the fire, didn't she?' said Jude. 'So bang goes any evidence.'

'Yes.'

'It may be a coincidence that it was Ayda who burned that prediction. And, then again, it may not.'

'Ayda wouldn't…'

'Everyone has to be a suspect now, Maggie. What else did you write down, in this ritzy little notepad?'

Maggie tried to remember. 'Nothing particularly odd,' she said. 'Nothing that wasn't already fairly obvious.' She bit her thumbnail suddenly.

'What is it?' asked Jude.

'I may have written down the fact that Helen Jansen had visited Ollie and Elizabeth and Ayda,' Maggie said slowly. 'And I may have put in a sentence or two, wondering what exactly Helen Jansen might know.'

Jude winced. 'Bugger,' she said into the silence. 'Our murderer will know that if you started trying to find Helen, you'd very quickly run into… well, a bit of a brick wall. And that would make you even more suspicious.'

'Yup.'

'Damn it.' A quizzical look. 'What did you say about me, by the way?'

A wry smile. 'That you might have been in Verbier when Lily fell anyway.'

'I was. What else?'

'Just that you're a bit nuts and you love a bit of drama.'

'Fair enough.' Jude sobered up. 'You could be in proper danger, Maggie. If you've written something that panics the murderer.'

A shudder ran down Maggie's back. 'I think we should leave, Jude. I can call a taxi. We could be in Exeter within an hour.'

'I'm not going,' Jude looked stubborn. 'We need to find out what's happened.'

'We could go to whoever's investigating Helen's death,' said Maggie. 'Tell them they need to dig a bit harder.'

'Oh yes.' Heavy sarcasm. 'Because the police have done such a stellar job so far.'

'Jude, this is really serious.'

'Maggie, for the first time in *years*, I feel truly alive,' Jude's eyes were filled with purpose. 'I'm not leaving without getting to the bottom of whatever the hell happened.'

'Jude—'

'There's no fucking point in carrying on the way I am, Maggie.' Jude was suddenly serious. 'My life… it's just a bloody mess. I have to know what's going on. I *need* to. You go if you want to. I'm staying.'

'You know I can't leave without you.'

'Fine. So that's decided then.' A brisk change of subject. 'It's Rory and Finlay now, isn't it? The people you'd put as most likely to have killed Helen and Lily?'

Maggie moaned. 'I suppose so. Yes.'

'If Finlay and Rory thought they were about to be busted for murder,' said Jude thoughtfully, 'Finlay would definitely shove someone off a Dartmoor tor. Rory can be a ruthless fucker too.'

They sat in silence. It was still raining outside, the hard grey light fading at last.

'There is something that you haven't thought of,' said Maggie.

'What?'

'What if they're trying to set me up?' Maggie's voice was apprehensive. 'What if they're going to make it look as if I killed Helen and Lily?'

'What do you mean, Maggie?'

'I don't know. I just… why put that prediction in the bowl? *Who* put that prediction in the bowl?'

Jude considered it. 'I have no idea. They could just be messing with your head?'

'But I don't understand—'

'Jude!' There was a shout in the distance. 'Maggie! Where are you? The steak is ready!'

64

Rory, on Maggie: Maggie will only just be
working out how to be happy, but that's okay.

Rory's prediction took Maggie by surprise.

'What do you mean by that?'

The ribs of beef stuck up between them, still bloody. Elizabeth had
lit dozens of candles, and the light was flickering over the silver, the
crystal, the flowers. The air was hot, heavy with the smell of wax. Rory
scrunched up his face, thinking. He had always done that, Maggie
thought, but he must have mostly broken the habit in recent years. It
was not a photogenic look for a hopeful backbencher, although it was
quite endearing.

'I don't know,' he said. 'I suppose I thought you would be coming into
your own round about now. And you are.'

'Why?' She managed to laugh. 'Because I was so awkward back then?
So spectacularly gawky?'

'You weren't.' There was a genuine surprise in his voice. 'But I do
think you were still surprised to find yourself at Cambridge. And I knew
it would take you a long time to realise that it was exactly where you
belonged.'

'Twenty odd years?' she asked. 'You had me down as a fast learner then.'

'You've never seen yourself the way the rest of us have,' Rory said, eyes
solemn. 'You don't *see* yourself, Maggie.'

Maggie caught a glimpse of herself in the gilt mirror opposite. Dark hair twisted up, eyes soft, for once. The candlelight was flattering.

'I see myself perfectly well, Rory.'

'You don't,' Jude chimed in. 'You don't realise, but you've made it, Maggie. You're *there*.'

'Where?'

'*There*.'

'I don't feel *there*.' Maggie threw herself back in the chair, aware it was the gesture of a grumpy teenager.

'Well, you should.'

Maggie raised an eyebrow. But there was a warmth in her chest that she hadn't felt before. A new sense of fulfilment.

For a second, Rory and Maggie smiled at each other. Then the thought hit her again. The shouts, the anger, the flaring violence. The cold of the river. And a body drifting away into an endless darkness. Maggie jerked her gaze away.

'I'll go and grab some more wine,' she said. She stood up sharply.

'There's loads in the kitchen,' said Ivo. 'I can go if—'

'It's fine,' she said. 'I'll get it.'

It was cooler in the kitchen. Calmer. Banished from the dining room, Pagan wagged his tail as Maggie walked in but didn't get up from his basket. Maggie sat down beside him and patted his nose. She leaned her head back against the chill of the wall, enjoying the moment of peace. The dog's basket was next to the door that led out to the herb garden. They had all been dumping their shoes as they walked in and out during the weekend. Someone – Elizabeth, doubtlessly – had lined them up in neat pairs.

Maggie gazed idly at the row of shoes. Finlay's walking boots: rugged and muddy. They looked incongruous next to a pair of Tod's moccasins, which must be Elizabeth's. Then Maggie's own Havaianas, bright pink and turquoise. Boat shoes: Ollie's. Red espadrilles were next. Tiny, with a wedge heel. She had seen Jude wearing those. Then Ayda's purple, jewelled ballet pumps, with a small peep toe.

Purple, jewelled ballet pumps.

Maggie stopped stroking the dog's ears.

Purple, jewelled ballet pumps.

Ayda had been wearing them down by the swimming pool on Friday morning. She had been painting her toenails and complaining about not having the time to get a pedicure.

Purple, jewelled ballet pumps.

Maggie sat up sharply. She reached for her phone, tapping in a website address.

The site was slow to load. *Come on.*

Maggie jumped to her feet with frustration, chewing at her thumbnail.

Any moment.

There.

OH MY GAWD WE WENT TO THE TOWER OF LONDON AND A WOMAN FELL IN FRONT OF THE TRAIN RIGHT IN FRONT OF ME SO SO SAD<3<3

Maggie pressed play.

Three teenage girls, smiling for the camera. Cropped tops, flat stomachs, pink hair. A sudden movement to the left, that familiar melee of screams. Shapes, silhouetted by two bright lights. The camera fell away.

To the briefest glimpse of a purple, jewelled ballet pump.

Then the phone landed in a close-up of a patch of dirty platform. There were a few seconds of grimy darkness and then another blurring swirl as the phone was picked up. A young face wet with tears, make-up smudged.

The screen went black.

'Are you coming?' Maggie looked up to find Elizabeth standing next to her. 'We want to read another prediction.'

Maggie hid her phone screen hastily. 'Could you ask Jude to meet me upstairs? I feel as if I've got a migraine coming on and I remember Jude saying she had some great pills.'

'Don't think I'd trust any pill of Jude's,' Elizabeth grumbled. But she disappeared towards the dining room. Maggie took a quick snap of the purple ballet pumps with her phone. Then she hurried up the back stairs.

'Are you feeling okay?' Jude came into Maggie's bedroom. 'I've got some bog-standard paracetamol, but I'm not sure—' Jude jumped as Maggie shoved the door closed behind her. 'What the hell, Maggie?'

'Look.' Maggie found that she couldn't say any more. She sat down on the bed and watched as Jude pressed play.

'Maggie… I don't want to.' Jude recoiled.

'Oh God. Sorry, Jude. I've watched it so many times. You don't *see* anything.'

'Yes, but… still.'

'Fine.' Maggie grabbed the phone, fast forwarding the video to the moment just before the phone was dropped, pausing the footage at exactly the right point. 'There.' The briefest glimpse of a ballet pump and a slender ankle. Then Maggie scrolled through to her photograph of Ayda's shoes neatly lined up by the back door. 'And there.'

'Ayda?' Jude looked stunned. 'Ayda was there when Lily fell under the train? It's *Ayda*?'

'I don't know.' Maggie clenched her phone with frustration. 'I mean, it's certainly not proof, is it?'

'But they are the same shoe,' Jude peered closer at a slender brown ankle, a cropped black trouser leg. 'For sure. Although they may be LK Bennett or Kurt Geiger, or whoever else sells a billion pairs of the same shoe. Fuck.'

'I photographed the label inside too. I don't recognise it, but I'm sure…' she broke off. 'Why would Ayda… *Ayda*?'

Without speaking, they both sat down on the bed. Jude shook her head, looking unusually sympathetic.

'Maybe it was just that finding out that Lily was her sister completely devastated Ayda?' Jude said. 'We all know that Ayda had been the centre of her parents' universe for her entire life and then all of a sudden, out of the blue… We don't know what her father was up to, either. He may even have told Fiona Nassar. He may have… we just don't know.'

'And maybe Ayda…' Maggie said slowly. 'Ayda, in a fit of rage.' Fiona Nassar flashed through her mind. Not a cool reserve, no. An icy rage, studded with pearls.

'It is possible,' said Jude. 'Or as possible as any of us doing it. You know I've never… well, we've never been exactly bosom buddies, Ayda and I.'

'No.'

'But still. Shit.'

Maggie's glass of wine was on the bedside table. Maggie picked it up and gulped it down.

'But why on earth would Ayda kill *Helen*?' asked Maggie. 'What on earth does Helen have to do with any of this?' Maggie visualised Helen's face. The pale auburn hair. That sun-battered skin. Not another of Bassel Nassar's children. Not that, at least.

Jude opened her mouth to speak and then closed it again. 'I have no idea,' she said in the end. 'It doesn't make sense.'

'Finlay killing Helen makes a horrible sort of sense,' said Maggie. 'If Helen had worked out that he had killed Mike. And Ayda killing Lily makes a sort of sense too. Grimly enough.' A bubble of laughter almost escaped her, the blackest of humour frothing up. 'But not two different friends killing two different people within days of each other, completely by chance. It doesn't make any sense at all.'

Jude was also fighting down the edge of hysteria. 'We're not that insane,' she insisted. 'Surely. There must be some other connection between Helen and Ayda. There has to be.'

They pondered it. 'I just have no idea,' said Maggie in the end. 'Fiona Nassar might have been Rosemary Jansen's sister. Bassel Nassar could have been business partners with Tony Jansen. It could be almost anything.'

Maggie's hysteria was bubbling up again, the wine churning unhappily in her stomach.

'If it is something completely random,' Jude agreed, 'it might take ages to work it out.'

'We're not even sure if anyone did kill Helen,' said Maggie. 'The police obviously didn't think it was murder, so whatever happened out there...' A thought struck Maggie. Her laughter died. 'Ayda...' she began, then stopped.

'What?' asked Jude. Then, when Maggie didn't speak, she said with more urgency. 'What is it, Maggie?'

'I was out with Ayda a few weeks ago,' Maggie stalled. 'In a bar in Soho.'

'Get on with it, Maggie.'

'We were getting hammered. It had been a crappy few days for both of us and we ended up getting through a lot of rosé.'

'And?'

'A call came in,' Maggie said slowly. 'I saw it flash up on her screen, just for a second or two. It was from a Rose J. Ayda cleared the call straight away. Said it was her new PA. Bitched about her a bit. I never thought…'

'Rose J.' Jude sat down heavily on the bed. 'Rosemary Jansen? Why on earth would Rosemary Jansen be calling Ayda?'

'Mrs Jansen must have contacted Ayda before too,' said Maggie. 'Otherwise, how else would Ayda have her number saved in her phone?'

'Yes.'

'Ayda told me that Helen Jansen came to visit her,' said Maggie. 'But she was very vague about it. She also told me that she could barely remember anything about Mike either. And I know that's a lie now. Ayda knew all about the rape. She hadn't forgotten a single bloody thing about Mike.'

'Ayda was lying,' said Jude. 'She was lying all along.'

'It means that there is a link between Lily's and Helen's deaths,' said Maggie.

'Ayda.' The excitement leached out of Jude's voice. 'Ayda is the link.'

'Does that mean,' Maggie didn't want to say it aloud, didn't want to make it real, 'that Ayda killed Helen and Lily?'

Footsteps along the gallery. A voice, echoing. They froze.

'Jude! Maggie!' It was Ayda. 'Come on! We're all waiting for you!'

65

Ayda, on Elizabeth: She will be realising she
could have done so much more with her life.

Elizabeth winced.

Across the dining table, Maggie saw a gleam in Ayda's eyes that she
had never noticed before. Cruelty. A cat, toying with her prey. Ayda
had known that prediction was coming, Maggie saw. Had known
that Elizabeth would be wounded, bitterly hurt.

Ayda had known.

Maybe she remembered writing it down all those years ago. But
Maggie was certain now that Ayda had read the predictions in advance.
That she had crept to the Venetian bowl at some point over the weekend,
and picked out the scraps of paper while the rest of them were laughing
in some other room. Irrationally, Maggie felt annoyed that Ayda had
cheated, reading the predictions before the rest of them.

We promised.

Lily is dead.

Ayda, she thought. *It's Ayda.*

Ayda – sleeping in the bedroom next door to Maggie – could so easily
have explained wandering through the wrong door in the darkness. She
had the perfect opportunity to slip the notepad onto Maggie's dressing table.

It's Ayda.

For the first few moments, Maggie hadn't been able to believe it.

'Why the hell would Ayda?' Maggie had whispered as Ayda's footsteps disappeared back down the staircase.

We're coming… The headache pills are working brilliantly… I'll be down in a tick… Pour us a drink, Ayda.

'She did it.' Jude's face was hard, unforgiving. Any sympathy had evaporated. 'And now we need to prove it.'

'Let's just go to the police,' Maggie pleaded again.

'And show them what, exactly? A blurry photograph of a ballet pump at the scene of a suicide? It's not enough, Maggie.'

'Maybe the police would be able to place her on the platform? Phone data, that sort of thing.'

'Maybe. But that still wouldn't be enough. We need to connect her to Helen Jansen's death, too. Properly, I mean. Not just a rejected call from a Rose J that you saw once, maybe, possibly, weeks ago. Ayda's a lawyer, for God's sake. We're going to need proper proof.'

'But how?'

'I don't know,' said Jude. 'I don't know *yet*.'

Jude had headed for the stairs, pursuing Ayda back down to the dining room. A moment later, Maggie – unwillingly – had followed her.

There were tears in Elizabeth's eyes as she looked across the table now. 'There's no need to be such a bitch, Ayda.'

Ayda tossed her head. 'I'm not.'

'Yes, you are,' Jude said flatly, 'and you always were.'

The mood shifted sharply. Ayda turned to Jude but Elizabeth was quicker.

'You think that just because you've made partner in some bloody law firm,' Elizabeth flared, 'you can treat me and Jude, and Maggie even, like failures. But we're not, Ayda. We've all made mistakes along the way, sure. But we're all decent human beings, unlike you.'

'Oh, Elizabeth, stop being so melodramatic,' Ayda sighed.

The four men sat silently, eyes down, staying safe below the parapet.

'We're not failures,' said Jude. 'And this weekend… it's made me realise a few things.'

'Like what exactly, Jude?' Ayda sounded bored.

'That friendships change,' said Jude, 'and some of them break.'

'Oh, for heaven's sake, Jude.'

Finlay was turning a silver knife over and over but Rory was watching Jude intently. Ivo's gaze was switching between Jude and Ayda.

'We're all frozen in time by this friendship group,' Jude gestured. 'But that didn't mean we were proper friends, not all of us.'

'Jude—' Even now, Maggie felt a desperate urge to hold the fragile threads of their lives together.

Jude had picked up a glass and was studying a candle through the red of the wine.

'We know that marriage isn't for life any more.' Jude put the glass down carefully. 'So why do we expect friendship to accommodate all the same changes? We worked out that *Titanic* and *Romeo and Juliet* were basically bollocks, and that the world wasn't going to give us meet-cutes and hourly orgasms. But we never spotted that *Thelma and Louise* and *Friends* were bullshit too.'

'How very cheery you are,' said Ayda. 'And not remotely bitter.'

'We've all gone through life using each other as touchstones,' said Jude, ignoring her. 'Dancers on a stage who know their position by glimpsing each other in their peripheral vision. If you're there, I should be three steps to the left. If he's there, I should be two paces downstage. We're starlings, flying through the air, a whole murmuration darting as one.'

'We shape each other,' said Maggie.

'More like bloody bonsai each other. I've had enough of it. I'm not a fucking starling. I don't want to be compared to Ivo's annual profits or Rory's promotions or Ollie's sales figures any more.'

'Fine,' said Ayda. 'Off you trot to your posse of alkies in Chingford or wherever it is you actually live now. No one will miss you, Jude.'

'They will.' Maggie found that she was on her feet, meeting Ayda's eyes defiantly. 'And we won't let you go, Jude.'

Ayda started to say something and stopped.

'We won't let you go.' Quietly, Elizabeth echoed Maggie. 'Stay, Jude. Please.'

Rory was turning his wine glass round and round so that the cut crystal edges sent shards of light around the room. 'Surely, Jude,' he said softly, 'it is these friendships that have survived life – and everything that it has thrown at us – that are the most important of all?'

'Of course they are,' said Ivo. The men were able to join the conversation now it had shifted to generic relationships. 'We're the ones who *know* each other. Who were there at the very start, before we all learned how to be other people.'

'We know,' Rory murmured, 'each other's secrets.'

'It's not enough,' Jude said flatly. 'We're too different now. A friendship based on a secret isn't a bond; it's a shackle.'

She stroked Pagan, who was hoovering round the edges of the table.

'My grandmother,' Elizabeth said thoughtfully, 'travelled out to South Africa just after World War II. She was twenty-one, newly married. She settled out there, but every single week, she wrote a letter to her best friend back in England. Forty years they wrote to each other, hundreds and hundreds of letters. Childbirth, debt, illness. Married life, basically. When she was widowed, my grandmother came back to England and moved home to the village. And she and her best friend had nothing in common. They didn't even *like* each other. People change, Ivo. We've all changed.'

'They should have swapped their letters back,' Ollie had obviously heard this anecdote before. 'It would have been like writing a diary without meaning to. Handy, really.'

'We're not Betty and June living two doors down from each other for an entire lifetime, you mean?' said Maggie cautiously. 'We go off and do a million different things, and what are the chances that everything stays aligned?'

'But what alternative is there?' asked Ivo soberly. 'Dumping your old friends and making new ones? A fresh selection from the spring/summer cruise collection? You forget that there's something special about childhood friends and childhood sweethearts. We mock adolescent love. Dismiss it as a crush. When actually, the way you love when you're seventeen years old, when you haven't yet learned to be careful with your heart, that's the most overwhelming emotion you'll ever feel. It's the same with friendship. I look at my friends' children, the way they are *best best best friends* and every minute of every day revolves around each other. You never get that intensity again.'

'You never get that amount of time again,' Rory said drily.

'You can't just start over,' said Ivo. 'It just doesn't work like that.'

'But otherwise you're trapped,' said Jude. 'You're stuck with being whoever you were at eighteen forever. Hardening too quickly in the mould. You wouldn't know it, Ivo, but I'm getting my life together these days. I'm… I'm changing. And yet, six hours with you lot, and I'm back to where I started in a hundred different ways. From the moment I walk in, I'm a basket case.'

'But we *need* each other,' Ivo insisted. 'We're the keepers of each other's history. No one else remembers.' He sounded impassioned, almost pleading. Maggie was watching him, wondering if he was speaking about them or his school friends. Those golden boys who all seemed to be called Arlo or Milo or Ludo. Although perhaps Ivo, orphaned Ivo, had fewer memory keepers than most.

'I'm sure you can hire someone to follow you around whispering in your ear as you step from your limo to your private jet,' said Jude smartly. '*Memento mori, memento mori*,' she hissed. 'You don't need us, Ivo.'

Remember you are mortal.

Remember you must die.

'I think I prefer being that eighteen-year-old version of me anyway,' said Ollie slightly sadly. 'I'd choose your memories of me over someone who met me for the first time when I was a thirty-nine-year-old estate agent, starting to lose his hair.'

'You preferred the earlier series.' The corners of Maggie's mouth rose. 'The original characters. Now we've jumped the shark.'

'The thing is that if you do move on,' said Finlay, 'you have to admit that friendship is basically only ever a matter of geographical convenience.'

'Your parents' friends' kids. The guys you play football with on Saturday mornings,' Maggie added. 'Your NCT mates.'

'Not,' said Elizabeth pertly, 'that I'll ever have those.'

'Friendship matters,' Ivo insisted. 'It does.'

A glimmer of a smile from Jude. 'You old romantic, Ivo.'

'To the friendships that really last,' Ivo was on his feet. 'To the very best sort of friendships.'

66

Ollie, on Ayda: I do know when you're patron-
ising me, you know? And you'd better bloody
have stopped by now.

Ayda's eyes widened as Ollie's prediction was read out, but she managed to force down the words.

The conversation moved on. Maggie sensed Jude on her left, tense and watchful, a storm rising. The candles were burning down now, red wax pooling on the table. On her right, Rory was filling airtime with a visit to Africa... 'really fascinating to see the work of grassroots indigenous groups around Lake Turkana.'

Jude took a breath.

'Lake Turkana,' Maggie spoke before Jude could, 'that's quite near the Kakuma refugee camp, isn't it?'

Rory turned towards her politely. 'Yes, a couple of hundred kilometres, I guess?'

'I suppose I've been thinking about Kakuma,' Maggie dropped her voice as the conversation babbled on around them, 'because of Helen Jansen working there for so long. Have you ever visited the camp?'

'No,' Rory shook his head. 'I'd like to though. It's meant to be—'

'Did Helen Jansen visit you?' Maggie interrupted him, low and forceful. 'Did she ever come to ask you about Mike's death?'

A pause.

'No.' Rory also spoke quietly.

'Did she ever try to get in touch with you?'

Another pause, the seconds ticking past, and a slow nod. 'Helen got in touch through my parliamentary email. I… I fobbed her off. Panicked, I suppose. Got my researcher to reply, saying very sorry but I could only respond to constituents' issues.'

'Because Finlay warned you she was investigating Mike's death?'

'Yes. I know it was shit of me, Maggie, but I just couldn't face her. I know what you're thinking. God, I know. If I could undo that night, I'd do anything. *Anything.* I've spent *years* obsessing over it. The number of times I've wished that I'd dragged Finlay away. That I'd called the police before Mike came down that path. It's been… it's been a shadow over my entire life.'

'Did you ever tell Genet about Mike?'

'No.' Rory looked ashamed. 'It was the only thing I never told her. The only thing I should have told her, really. There were so many times I nearly blurted out the whole thing… but I just couldn't find the words. And it wasn't only because I couldn't face the look in her eye. That horror as she realised what I really was. It was the thought that she would be tainted with the knowledge too. Contaminated, like me. That unless I handed myself in to the police, she would have to carry this nightmare through the whole rest of her life, too.' He realised what he was saying. 'Sorry, Maggie. I never meant you to… if Finlay hadn't flipped out like that… Bloody Ayda and her prediction.'

'You never thought to just get it over with, go to the police?'

'Jesus, a million times! But it wasn't me who would have… it was always Finlay who could have gone to jail for the rest of his life.'

'Yes.'

'It's been this *curtain*, Maggie. Like one of those fire safety curtains at the theatre, except I'm frozen on this side and everyone else is on the other. All my life, ever since that moment out in the darkness by the river. When Genet died, it honestly felt like as if it was my punishment. And I was glad – so glad – that she never knew the truth about me.'

'So you've only ever spoken about it with Finlay?'

'Yes, and that was only a couple of times, and not properly even then. I always thought that was why he went off to Afghanistan. The only place…' The only place to channel that murderous rage, thought Maggie. 'The only place that he could try and undo what he did. I know it's nothing – *nothing* – compared to what happened to Mike, of course. To what his parents have gone through… to what his sister…'

'When did Helen Jansen get in touch with you?'

Rory didn't seem to notice the change in subject. 'A few months ago. At the beginning of the year? I can't remember.'

'And she never tried again?'

'No.' Rory looked haunted. 'But every event I go to, every single constituency surgery, I'm convinced she'll turn up. Just before we came down here, Finlay and I went to the local county show in Somerset – you know the sort of thing, lots of cows and freakishly fluffy sheep and welly wanging – and I was looking for her everywhere. It's like expecting Banquo at every rubber chicken lunch. It's the same for Finlay. A whole lifetime of looking over your shoulder.'

Maggie was staring at Rory, trying to work out if he was lying or not. Helen's death had only briefly been reported, but if you knew her name… Although maybe Rory didn't even dare google her and risk leaving those electronic traces in his blackened history.

'So you've never met her?'

'No. Has she tried to get hold of you?' Rory's eyes were wide, unsuspecting. Probably. 'Helen?'

'I don't think so,' said Maggie. 'I don't know why she hasn't.'

'Maybe she wants to get to the bottom of things without the press getting involved,' said Rory. A thought struck him. 'Maybe she'll come to you when she's worked it all out? So you can write up the story?'

'Maybe. Rory, can you ask Ivo if Helen Jansen got in touch with him?'

Rory gave her a searching stare. 'What, right now?'

'Yes.'

'Why though? Why don't you ask him?'

'It's important.'

For a moment, Maggie thought he would refuse. But again, there was that odd sense of power as Rory leaned back in his chair and called out: 'Ivo, has Mike Jansen's sister ever come to visit you? Or tried to? She seems to be doing the rounds as far as we can make out.'

'Not,' Ivo was pouring wine, 'as far as I am aware. But…'

I have people to deal with that sort of hassle, he didn't need to say.

'How about you, Ayda?' Maggie turned towards her. 'How did Helen get in touch with you?'

'How?' Ayda raised her eyebrows and then realised the whole table was waiting for her response. 'She waited for me outside the Throwleigh Pearce offices one evening, actually.'

'When was that?'

'Does it matter?' Impatient. 'I don't know. A few months ago?' Irritable.

'I'm just trying to get to the bottom of when Helen went where,' said Maggie evenly. 'Elizabeth, I think she started off by visiting you at the house in Clapham.'

Elizabeth, baffled but trying. 'I suppose so.'

'So when was that exactly?'

'Gosh, I don't know.' Elizabeth thought about it. 'She came to see me on a Wednesday morning, I think, because I was just coming home from pilates. She was waiting for me on the doorstep. Gave me a bit of a fright, actually. You know how it is, living on your own.'

'Then what?'

'Well, once I realised who she was, I invited her in. We went down to the kitchen. She was freezing cold, I remember. Had obviously been waiting quite a long time. I made her a cup of tea.' The frown on Elizabeth's face cleared. 'It must have been the Wednesday after Valentine's Day, because one of my friends had sent me some chocolates – such a sweet thought, even though I basically never eat chocolate – and I got them out for Helen.'

'Okay.' Maggie pulled out one of her work pads, made a note.

'Hey.' It was Finlay. 'What are you up to, Maggie?'

'It's important, Finlay,' she said, and Rory silenced him with a gesture.

'Ollie,' said Maggie. 'I think she went to see you next?'

Ollie had anticipated her question, swiping at his phone. 'She came to see me on a Thursday,' he said. 'She also waited for me outside my house. Well, flat. I remember thinking it was lucky for her that she hadn't come the next day, because I was off skiing for a week and she'd have had a bloody long wait.'

'When did you go skiing?'

'Eighteenth of Feb,' Ollie waved his phone calendar at her.

'So she visited you on the seventeenth? The day after she went to see Elizabeth.'

'I guess so.'

'And you gave her Finlay's address?'

'Yes. Sorry about that, mate.'

'It doesn't matter—'

'When did Helen visit you?' Maggie asked Finlay.

'I don't know.' His words came too fast.

'Try.'

'I honestly don't know,' Finlay insisted. 'I'm not like Elizabeth doing yoga at the same bloody time every week, or writing everything down like you, Maggie. Helen came to my flat out of the blue and I have no idea when that was.'

'You'd have messaged Rory about it,' Maggie said tonelessly. 'Scroll back through your messages. Go to the beginning of March and then read backwards from there.'

'I—' Finlay looked around the ring of silent faces. 'Okay.'

Finlay began scrolling back. Maggie watched him.

There weren't any new worries in Finlay's face, she thought. He had admitted what he'd done and he wasn't expecting any fresh horrors.

'She came to see me on the twentieth of February,' Finlay said after a few minutes. 'I didn't mention Helen by name in the text, just in case. But I asked Rory to meet me for a quick drink that evening and I told him then. I sent that message there the day she came to my house. Almost as soon as I closed the door behind her, actually.'

Rory was nodding. 'I remember that drink,' he said. 'Hardly likely to forget it. And I remember that Helen emailed me the very next day.'

'But she didn't get through to you?' Maggie clarified.

'No.'

'I wonder why Helen starting investigating then?' said Elizabeth. 'Why did she come back from Kenya?'

'It was twenty years,' said Maggie bleakly. 'Twenty years since Mike died. I imagine it's quite an anniversary for that family.'

'Oh God,' said Elizabeth. 'Of course.'

Maggie turned to Ayda. 'When did Helen visit you at Throwleigh Pearce?'

'I don't remember.'

'Try,' said Maggie. 'Try harder, Ayda.'

Something flickered in Ayda's eyes. 'I told you that I don't know, Maggie. Helen Jansen waited for me outside the office, so there wasn't anything scheduled in my calendar. I just don't know.'

'You didn't message anyone about it?'

'No,' Ayda was confident. 'You're the person I would have told, Maggie, and I didn't.'

It was pointed.

'Were you heading off somewhere? Was it dark? Did she delay you meeting someone else, maybe? Think, Ayda. Please.'

'Why does it matter?' asked Ivo. 'Why is it so important?'

Maggie didn't answer him directly. 'I think that Helen probably went to visit Lily sometime after she saw Finlay. Finlay had told Helen that Jude and Mike had had some sort of flirtation' – a hiss from Jude – 'shortly before Mike died. Finlay had also told Helen that Lily and Jude were best friends. Given that Jude was abroad and unavailable, I reckon that Lily would have been very interesting to Helen. If you look at the pattern, Helen was moving fairly quickly from one person to the next, not wasting much time. I'd guess that Helen would have spoken to Lily as soon as possible after the twentieth of February.'

'While I was still in Verbier,' said Jude quietly. 'Thank God.'

'She may have spent time looking for you,' said Maggie. 'But I think it's more likely that Helen went to see Lily as soon as possible. And I'm guessing it's possible that she went to see Ayda around the same time.'

'We don't know that,' Ayda insisted. 'I said that I didn't know when she came to see me.'

'Up until then,' Maggie looked squarely at Ayda, 'Helen seems to go wherever the last person suggested. Elizabeth suggested Ollie, for example, so Helen went off to see him. Ollie gave her Finlay's address, and she was at his place three days later. Finlay suggested Lily, so I'm assuming that is where she went next. And maybe,' Maggie paused deliberately, 'Lily suggested Helen talk to you, Ayda.'

'There's quite a few suppositions there.' Ayda, lawyer's tones.

'Sure.'

'And I don't see,' Elizabeth spoke very precisely, 'why it matters so much, Maggie. Helen wanted to find out as much as possible about her brother's death, and to be honest, that's not an unreasonable thing.'

'I know,' Maggie said slowly.

'So why—'

'Helen Jansen died sometime after February the twenty-sixth,' Maggie said flatly, 'That was the last day she was seen alive.'

Maggie's gaze darted from Finlay to Ayda, from Ollie to Ivo. They all looked stunned. Ayda's face was twitching slightly, her eyes two pools of darkness.

'Helen Jansen is dead?' Finlay was horrified. 'What?'

'How?' asked Elizabeth. 'What? How did she die?'

'She was found a few miles from here,' said Maggie. 'The body that was found near Barras Tor. That's Helen Jansen.'

'Jesus fucking Christ,' Finlay murmured. 'What the fuck?'

'Helen Jansen died on Dartmoor?' Elizabeth's eyes were wide with horror. 'Mike's twin sister died *here*?'

'Yes,' said Maggie. 'I'm going to her inquest on Monday.'

'You're going to her inquest…'

'What happened to her?' Ollie asked urgently. 'If they found her near a tor, did she fall?'

'I'm not sure,' said Maggie. 'It's not clear from the notes. She'd been up there a long time before they found her. But I can't think of any reason why she would have been hiking on the moor in late February. So I think it's suicide or murder.'

Suicide. Murder. The words crushed the room.

'She's dead?' Elizabeth couldn't believe it. 'Helen Jansen is *dead*?'

'Yes.'

'But it could have been an accident?' Elizabeth sounded as if she was pleading. 'She might have – I don't know – just decided to clear her head with a walk on Dartmoor. And then got lost. We all know what it's like up there. The weather changes so quickly.'

'Sure,' Maggie nodded. 'It just seems odd that she was knocking on all our doors and then she disappears on Dartmoor, just a few miles from here.'

'It wasn't anything to do with me.' Finlay was panicking. 'I swear I had no idea.'

Rory's eyes were bleak, contemplating the catastrophe. 'When did you say she died?'

'She was last seen on the twenty-sixth of February.'

Rory dropped his head into his hands, rubbed his eyes hard. 'The twenty-sixth… that was only a few days before Lily died.'

'Yes. Lily died at the very beginning of March,' Maggie looked from face to face, deliberately slow. 'They probably died within a couple of days of each other.'

67

Ollie, on Rory: I'll be embarrassed when this
is read out, but you're a good guy. I hope I'm
more like you in twenty years' time!

'Jesus.' A hiss from Ivo.

'So you see,' Maggie fixed her eyes on Ayda's face, 'it really is very important that you remember when you saw Helen Jansen.'

'I don't like what you're trying to imply, Maggie.'

'What do you think I'm implying, Ayda?'

Ayda, the lawyer, fell silent.

'Maggie thinks that Helen found out something that got her killed,' said Elizabeth guardedly. 'And that whatever it was, it was either Lily or Ayda who told her about it.'

'This is ridiculous,' Ayda stood up. 'How dare you? How dare any of you?'

'What did you say to Helen?' Elizabeth asked Ayda. 'What did she ask you about?'

'I don't remember.' Crisp. 'It was a very brief conversation.'

'Who had Helen spoken to when she came to you?' Ollie was leaning forward tensely. 'That'll give us some idea of the timeline. Had she spoken to Lily by the time she came to you?'

Ayda glared at him. 'I don't remember.' And now they could all see that she was lying.

'Ayda...' There was despair in Elizabeth's voice. 'Ayda, what did you *do*?'

'If Helen Jansen was getting close to working out who murdered her brother,' Ayda's voice was rising, 'Rory and Finlay had every reason to kill her. We all know that.'

'I think this conversation should end.' Ivo, very firm. 'This is my house and I am not prepared to have accusations thrown around like this while you are all my guests.'

'Oh, for God's sake.' Jude turned on him. 'You're not some feudal seigneur, Ivo. You don't get to tell us how to behave.'

'I do while you're in this house, Jude. Helen Jansen's behaviour strikes me as obsessive and – at the very least – slightly unstable. She was obviously still profoundly sad about her brother's death, which is natural. That makes it perfectly plausible that she committed suicide.'

'In a geographically inconvenient location for you,' snapped Jude.

Ivo stared at her. For a second, Maggie thought of a hawk hovering high above the moor, watching every tiny movement on the ground. Riding the winds, a stillness in the storm.

But then Ivo's face split into a grin. 'Come on, Jude. You can't be serious. You can't think that I shoved some random woman off Barras Tor? When I wasn't even in the country when she disappeared?' His words broke the tension. There was a collective exhale. 'This is all getting a bit ridiculous,' said Ivo. 'Time for pudding, I think.'

'We need to know where people were around the time that Helen disappeared and the day that Lily died too.' Jude was whispering to Maggie in the kitchen. They had carried the remains of dinner back to the long scrubbed table.

'Helen was last seen on a Saturday,' said Maggie. 'Lily died the following Wednesday.'

'Ollie said he was away skiing for a week, didn't he?' said Jude. 'So he would have been back the day that Helen disappeared.'

Ivo came up behind them. 'What are you two whispering about?'

'We were just wondering about people's alibis for when Helen and Lily died.' Jude refused to apologise. 'Where were you, as a matter of fact?'

'Oh, Jude.' Ivo shook his head. He pulled out his phone. 'If the two of you are going to have hysterics about it all. Let's see… what were the dates again?'

'Helen disappeared on the twenty-sixth of February,' said Maggie. 'Lily died on the second of March.'

'Okay, I flew to Germany on the Wednesday before Helen disappeared. I then flew on to Athens before coming back to the UK on the Tuesday. There are dozens of witnesses who will put me in Germany and Greece, and obviously I used my passport to get through various airports. I was down here on Wednesday when Lily died. I remember that.'

That was exactly what N98CP's flightpath suggested, thought Maggie. 'Would anyone have seen you here that Wednesday?' she asked.

'I don't know,' Ivo shrugged. 'Mrs Vereker would have been around, I imagine. But she doesn't come to the house unless I specifically ask her when I'm staying. This weekend, for example, I asked her to tidy up after meals and so on, and then she did a quick clean while we were up on the moor.'

'But usually she stays away when you're here?'

'Not in an antisocial way,' Ivo protested. 'We get on perfectly well. But if I've got a… guest or something, she knows not to come up unless I ask. It suits us both. She gets most of the day off, I get proper downtime.'

'And what were you doing while you were here?'

'I can't really remember. I've got a study set up next to my bedroom, and if I had work to do, I would have been in there most of the day. And if I wasn't in there, I was probably up on the moor with Gulliver and Pagan.' Ivo was patting the dog's ears, squashing his jowls. 'I'm sure I'd have logged into the SummerX systems at some point, and that would show up my location. I was making calls, on and off. They would prove I was down here, anyway. I wasn't busy pushing Lily under a train, if that's what you're asking.'

'Someone pushed me,' Jude said abruptly.

'I'm sorry?' Ivo was still messing about with Pagan's ears.

'Yesterday evening, when I was looking at the moon,' said Jude. 'When I nearly fell off the balcony outside Maggie's bedroom. Somebody pushed me.'

'What?'

'I didn't slip.' Jude made each word slow and precise. 'It wasn't an accident.'

'Jude, I…' Ivo paused. 'Why didn't you say something? That's—'

'Because none of you would have believed me,' said Jude. 'You all think I'm some sort of hysteric—'

'I don't! But what you're saying—'

'I'm saying that there is a murderer running around this house, Ivo, and you still think it's all a fucking joke.'

'I don't! Who do you… what do you…' For once, Ivo looked bewildered. 'Who do you think it is?'

A glance between Jude and Maggie. Maggie held up her hands, repudiating the thought, suddenly unable to say the name aloud.

'Ayda,' Jude said quietly. 'We think that it's Ayda.'

'Ayda?' Ivo looked stunned. 'But that's insane. Why on earth would *Ayda* do something like that?' He was getting angry now. 'Ayda is one of your oldest friends, Maggie. How the hell could you even—'

Maggie didn't know where to begin. In the face of Ivo's outrage, her suspicions melted away.

'We think that Ayda killed Helen and Lily—' Jude began.

'Both of them? What? Why would she? This is utter madness, Jude.'

'We have evidence.' Jude insisted.

'It wasn't Ayda,' Ivo said firmly. 'I know it wasn't Ayda. Ayda was on the phone to me at the moment that Lily died.'

68

Ayda, on Maggie: She'll still be hopelessly
jealous of Lily.

They were back in the dining room. Over the mess of meringues and
strawberries and cream, Ayda looked at Maggie with a new gleam of
triumph in her eyes. Maggie dropped the piece of paper as if it had
stung her.

'What do you mean?' asked Maggie. 'I was never jealous of Lily.'

Maggie and Jude had stayed in the kitchen for as long as possible, discussing possibilities in tense whispers. Pagan stayed at their feet, hoping for
more dropped beef. Elizabeth popped in and out, tidying frantically, as
if polishing the draining board for long enough might fix everything.
Ollie wandered in, watched Elizabeth scrubbing at a baking tin with a
dried-on anger and wandered out again. Eventually Ivo reappeared and
herded them back to the dining room, doling out chocolates and coffee.
Gradually, he hauled the evening back to a state of polite decorum.

Rory had analysed the chances of the Chancellor being sacked for
a poorly-received Budget and Ollie had given a lengthy monologue
about trying to sell a house in Belgravia, 'where both the bloody neighbours were digging out their basements simultaneously. You know,
those iceberg houses with their underground bowling alleys and their
climate-controlled fur closets and their God knows what else. Diggers
from dawn to dusk.'

Now Maggie stared at the piece of paper. 'I was never jealous of Lily,' she said again.

'Yes, you were,' insisted Ayda. 'I remember. Lily had hooked up with Ivo a few months before that dinner party, and you hated that.'

Maggie's cheeks burned. 'I wasn't jealous of Lily. That's bullshit.'

Maggie had picked up the prediction again and was folding the piece of paper into smaller and smaller squares, embarrassed and furious.

'Of course it's bullshit, Maggie,' Ivo said smoothly. 'Although it goes to show, doesn't it, that things taken out of context can be rather misleading?'

'What do you mean? What are you talking about?' Maggie asked. Ivo stared back at her, his eyes opaque.

'Just that we don't want to read too much into small things. Into things that might just be a misunderstanding.'

'Spell it out, Ivo.'

'Well, you may have noticed,' Ivo gestured around the room, 'that there are security cameras all over this house. For the paintings, because the insurers are very picky about that sort of thing. There's a camera just outside your room, in fact, Maggie, keeping an eye on the little Watteau hanging there. The camera is pretty tight on the painting, and there's no sound of course, but it picks up anyone going in and out of your room. While you guys were sorting out pudding just now, I checked the time period when Jude said she was attacked on your balcony.'

'Jude was *attacked*?' asked Elizabeth. '*What*?'

Ivo dismissed Elizabeth with a wave. 'You can see Jude going into Maggie's bedroom,' he said, 'but then there is… well… nothing. Nothing, that is, until Maggie enters the bedroom. A few seconds later Rory and Ayda rush in, then Finlay, and so on.'

'What do you mean?' asked Maggie.

'The only person in Maggie's bedroom when Jude fell,' Ivo was smiling, somehow making it sound like small talk, 'was you, Maggie.'

Across the table, Maggie saw Jude's eyes widen. 'I didn't make it up,' Jude said firmly. 'Someone pushed me.' A split-second of hesitation. 'And it wasn't Maggie.'

'Of course that's what you think,' said Ivo. 'But in the panic and the rush, anything might have happened. That balcony is north-facing, lethally slippery.'

'I don't understand what happened—' Elizabeth started again.

'You were absolutely wasted, Jude,' Ayda said bluntly, 'more to the point.'

Jude's mouth opened and then closed again. 'It wasn't…'

'I'm just saying that we have to be careful about leaping to conclusions,' Ivo paused, looking up at the ancient beams, letting the mood change. 'Wintercross is mysterious. It always has been.'

'That's not—'

'Strange things have always happened at Wintercross,' Ayda said thoughtfully. 'Things no one has ever been able to explain.'

A beautiful maid, who lay down in the snow.

'Two women are dead,' Jude cut through his musings. 'I could very easily have been killed, Ivo.'

'But I thought you just *tripped*, Jude.' Elizabeth sounded distressed.

'Both Helen and Lily may have been suicides,' said Ivo, brisker now, ignoring Elizabeth, 'or accidents. We have no way of knowing what either of them were thinking. And, of course, there is another possibility.'

'What is it?' Jude asked resentfully.

'We don't know what exactly Lily may have said to Mike Jansen's sister,' said Ivo. 'What if Helen did or said something to infuriate Lily? What if it was *Lily* who pushed Helen off some tor?'

'Lily?' said Maggie. 'Why on earth would she do that? And how?'

'God knows,' said Ivo. 'But who knows what Helen had uncovered by then? Lily's parentage? Lily's affair with Ollie? And if Lily did kill Helen in a moment of madness for whatever reason, her conscience might have overwhelmed her in the aftermath. Maybe,' Ivo paused, his gaze sweeping the room, 'Lily murdered Helen… and then killed herself.'

There was a long silence.

'I don't know if…' Jude's voice trailed away.

'Time for another prediction?' Ivo suggested.

69

Ivo, on Rory: Rory will turn into his father, as
we all will in the end.

'Some of us,' Elizabeth was forcing herself to smile, 'will turn into our
mothers, actually.'

'Of course,' said Ivo. 'Of course.'

'Both your fathers were so charming,' said Elizabeth. 'I always enjoyed
chatting to Mr Fitzwilliam whenever we were down here.'

Next to her, Maggie sensed Rory shift in his seat, very slightly.

'We're out of brandy.' Ivo held the bottle up to the light. 'Give me a
moment.'

Maggie waited until he had left the room.

'You didn't think that Mr Fitzwilliam was charming?' she asked Rory
in an aside.

'Of course I did.'

'No, you didn't.'

'I thought that he was perfectly nice,' Rory stonewalled.

Maggie peered closely at him. 'I can tell, Rory.'

The Adairs and the Fitzwilliams had been friends in some distant way.
Perhaps the fathers had been to university together? Rory and Ivo had
worked it out in the first week at Trinity. One of those conversations.

Oh, you went to—

Yes, of course.

Fantastic! How are… ?

'Hugh Fitzwilliam was very thoughtful at the start of my career,' Rory insisted. 'He put me in touch with a lot of people, helped me as much as he could. He saved me from years of photocopying.'

'Sure. But.'

'But nothing.'

'*Rory*.'

'He was also a ruthless businessman,' Rory shrugged. 'Lots of people are, though.'

'In what way was he ruthless?'

'Oh, I don't know.'

'Yes, you do.'

'Well, there was the way he behaved with the Shorehams, for example.'

'Who were the Shorehams?'

Rory contemplated his wine glass for a few moments and then decided to tell her.

'Conrad Shoreham was a few years above Hugh Fitzwilliam at school. Heir to a baronetcy.' Maggie could tell that Rory had been told this story on several occasions. 'Conrad made Hugh's life a misery for years. You know what those schools were like back then. *Lord of the Flies* in a tailcoat.'

'Yes.'

'So Hugh loathed Conrad Shoreham,' said Rory.

'Okay.'

'Years pass. The Shorehams had two main income streams, okay? A steel factory and some land in Oxfordshire which was ripe for development.'

'Okay.'

'So first, Hugh Fitzwilliam goes into steel imports specifically to screw over their factory.'

'Right.'

'And the next thing, he'd bought the land next to theirs in Oxfordshire and turned it into a massive landfill site.'

'Huh.'

'Basically, Hugh dedicated *years* of his life to fucking over Conrad Shoreham,' said Rory. 'When Shoreham House was finally sold off, Hugh Fitzwilliam's holding company bought it and turned it into a hotel.'

'I had no idea.'

'Hugh was always very low profile,' said Rory. 'And I suppose his heyday was long before you started in journalism. So how would you know?'

'But I thought your parents liked the Fitzwilliams.'

'They did. They still do. It's funny, that sort of ruthlessness, if you tell the story right.'

'Is it?' Maggie shook her head.

'Hugh could be charming when he wanted to be, it's just that he didn't always want to be.'

'He must have been devastated when Ivo's mother died.'

'I'm not sure it was a terribly happy marriage,' said Rory hesitantly. Rory didn't mind discussing Hugh Fitzwilliam's business activities, Maggie diagnosed, but he felt he was sliding into gossip now. She stayed quiet, waiting for him to fill the silence. After a moment, Rory went on unwillingly. 'Ginny couldn't have any more children after Ivo. And then there were rumours she had a fling with the hunt master.'

Maggie could almost hear the envy echoing down the generations. Rory's father, she guessed, had been more than a little jealous of the Fitzwilliam glamour.

'Do not speak ill of the dead,' Maggie rolled her eyes. 'But I suppose that only applies to dead men.'

Rory started, then stalled.

'Chuck down the wine!' Finlay shouted to him.

After Rory had passed the wine, he sat in silence, fiddling with a teaspoon.

'Go on, Rory,' Maggie urged. 'Please. This is important. I need to understand.'

Trust me, she wanted to say, but worried that it might only remind him that he couldn't, not really.

Rory exhaled. 'There were whispers that she died because of the affair.'

'What do you mean?' That shiver again.

'She'd been out hunting all day,' said Rory. 'By the time the hunt finished, everyone else had gone home and it was just her and the huntsman right over on the other side of the moor. They were out there for ages and then she decided to ride home. Said she knew the moor like the back of her hand and it would be fine. But it got dark, started snowing. By the time Hugh Fitzwilliam realised she was missing, it was too late.'

'Oh God, that's awful.'

'It must have been horrendous.'

'Poor Ivo. Little *boy*.'

Maggie realised that Elizabeth was listening to their conversation. She turned towards her.

'More coffee?' Elizabeth leapt to her feet. Maggie found herself following Elizabeth towards the kitchen, carrying a couple of empty bottles.

'I'll get the mugs out,' Maggie said. She was looking through the cupboards when she heard Elizabeth dissolve into tears. 'What is it, Beth?'

She moved towards Elizabeth and thought – briefly – about hugging her.

'It's everything, isn't it?' Elizabeth looked at her. 'What the hell happened to Jude out on that balcony? And this whole thing with Finlay and Rory, for God's sake. They *killed* Mike, and we're all pretending it doesn't change a thing. Just carrying on with our silly parlour games and drinking Ivo's cellar dry. But it does change things, doesn't it?'

Maggie stared at the mugs. 'Of course it does, Elizabeth. Of course. I suppose… I suppose I just can't get my head around any of it. Not here. Maybe we're all just pretending things are still normal, and giving ourselves one last weekend before it all…'

'I *know*,' Elizabeth's eyes overflowed again. 'But how can they act so normally? And how can they have kept all this a secret for such a long time?'

'I suppose it has been their normality for years and years.'

'But how did we not realise? That they were carrying this huge secret with them all the way along?'

'I don't know,' said Maggie miserably. 'I'm replaying so many things in my head. So many times that…'

They didn't trust us, she thought. And there was a surge of affection, too, for Elizabeth, uncompromising, honest Elizabeth, who held everyone to her own standards and was constantly disappointed.

'Me too,' said Elizabeth. 'Do you remember when we were all up on the common after Finals? That huge picnic. Everyone was there, the whole year group. Were the six of them looking across at the river the whole time? Thinking, *oh, that's where Rory and Finlay*… it makes everything a lie.'

'Ayda knew,' said Maggie. 'Jude knew. Lily knew. They all knew. And they never said.'

'It's down to us.' Elizabeth looked at her. 'Ollie won't do anything about it. You know what he's like. It's you and me, Maggie. We have to tell the truth.'

'Yes.' Maggie felt her stomach clench. 'I suppose we must.'

'You will come with me?' asked Elizabeth. 'Won't you, Maggie?'

'I—'

'Mike… he was a nice person,' said Elizabeth. 'I remember volunteering in that homeless shelter with him. He was kind to people. Thoughtful. Shy, of course, and very naïve. But he was helping those people in that shelter, despite being so very awkward. He was finding ways to make their lives better. It wasn't instinctive for him, and he knew it too, but he wanted to be kind.'

'Just because he helped out in a homeless shelter once or twice doesn't mean he wasn't a rapist,' hissed Maggie. 'That's not how it works.'

'But it doesn't make sense, Maggie. None of it.'

'Mike raped Jude, Elizabeth. It's that simple. Jude never consented to having sex with him and that's the end of it. He wasn't a nice person.'

'We only have Jude's word for that.'

'And you don't believe her?' Maggie's anger flared up. 'I don't believe *you*, Elizabeth.'

'Maggie—'

'What? Is Jude a bit too much of a flawed victim for you, Elizabeth? Not wearing the right clothes, was she? Not tucked up in bed by midnight waiting for Prince Charming?'

'Stop it, Maggie. I'm just saying… you didn't know Mike, and you didn't meet his sister either. They both… I don't understand what happened, that's all. And, either way, it wasn't up to Finlay and Rory to dispense justice. Finlay lost his temper and murdered Mike, and Rory helped him cover it up. It's that simple.'

Maggie crashed the mugs together on a tray, the fight seeping away. 'I know, Elizabeth. I do know.'

It was very late. Now and again, the moon glinted through the clouds as they raced low over the moor. It was that shallow summer darkness, so fleeting.

They left the dining room in a clutter of wine-stained glasses and candle stubs, and drifted away in smaller groups. Jude had ferreted out some chalk from somewhere and was sketching silvery flowers on the ballroom floor. Rory and Finlay were playing billiards in a room off the library, Ayda keeping a haphazard score. Maggie found herself in the snug with Ivo and Ollie. Ivo was lying on a sheepskin rug in front of the fire. He had the poker in his hand and was sending showers of sparks up the chimney. Maggie watched him, silhouetted against the blaze. Ollie was almost asleep in one of the big armchairs.

'Why?' Maggie was almost speaking to herself. 'Why did Helen come down here? How did she end up at Barras Tor?'

'I don't know,' Ivo yawned. 'I've been wondering about that. Maybe she thought I was down here and was planning to come and visit me?'

'If anyone sent her down here, it must have been Lily or Ayda,' said Maggie.

'It could have been almost anyone,' said Ivo. 'Wasn't Helen going round everyone in our year? Any number of people might have given her Wintercross's address. For all I know, someone else from our year lives in the next village along from wherever she left her car. Helen might have come down to bang on the door of someone completely unconnected to us.'

'I suppose so.' Maggie hesitated. 'You were saying that you and Ayda were talking on the phone when Lily was killed?'

'Yup,' Ivo lay on the rug, prodding idly at the fire. 'Ayda told you about the sunset thing, didn't she? Every so often, we give each other a call and watch the sun go down. Just a silly habit.'

'Ayda told me.' Pushing away the pang.

'She was up on the roof of Throwleigh Pearce that night,' said Ivo. 'She was annoyed about some guy not calling. Noah, I think his name was? She'd met him on Bumble or something.'

'I think I remember a Noah.'

A sharp snore from Ollie and they both laughed.

'We were chatting for ages,' said Ivo. 'I was sitting up on Lion's Rock because there's phone reception up there. I got bloody cold after the sun went down, mind you. Came back into the house.'

'What time were you speaking?'

Ivo rolled over, so that he was looking straight at her. 'I'd have to look it up in my phone records again, Maggie. But it was for about an hour from 5.30 to 6.30. I was talking to Ayda, Maggie. I promise. It wasn't her.'

'I know that Lily died during rush hour,' said Maggie. 'The platform was rammed.'

'Yes. But if someone pushed Lily, it wasn't Ayda,' Ivo repeated gently. 'It just wasn't.'

'I…'

'Why do you think it was her, anyway?'

'It sounds stupid saying it aloud,' said Maggie. 'But I've seen some mobile phone footage from the platform. A few seconds before and after Lily fell. And in the chaos, as the phone is dropped, you can just make out a couple of frames of a purple shoe.'

'And?'

'I'd swear it was the same shoes that Ayda was wearing on Friday morning. They're by the back door right now.'

Ivo was fiddling with the sheepskin rug. He wasn't laughing at her, Maggie thought with relief.

'Anything else?'

'I think Helen Jansen's mother rang Ayda,' said Maggie. 'We were out in Soho one night when Ayda's phone went. I saw that it was someone listed in her contacts as Rose J. Ayda just cleared the call and said it was her PA.'

'But?'

'Helen Jansen's mother is called Rosemary,' said Maggie. 'Rose J. And the other thing is that I've met Ayda's PA several times. Ayda spends so much time at work that Lucy has become quite a good mate of hers. Ayda calls Lucy her "work wife" and I'm sure she would have mentioned if Lucy had left Throwleigh Pearce and someone else had joined. I suppose I could check, but…'

'When was this? The Rose J phone call?'

'April. I went back through my messages and worked it out. Ayda and I met at Ducksoup and then went on to a new bar just around the corner. That's where we were when Rose called. It was a few weeks after both Helen and Lily died.'

'Maybe it's just that this Lucy woman was off sick and Rose J was covering for her?' Ivo looked up at Maggie. 'I know you need to solve all the mysteries, Maggie, as if life is a series of sudokus, but I really don't think—'

'I know. I *know*.' Maggie shook her head.

'Why would Helen and Mike's mother be calling Ayda anyway?'

'I don't know. Do you often meet up at sunset too?' The words were abrupt. She hadn't meant to ask. 'Ayda said you did.'

'Sometimes,' he nodded. 'Bold Tendencies, or Primrose Hill with a bottle of wine. Or that place near the Tate Modern. Wherever there's a view, really. Sometimes the night takes off and things get a bit wild, and sometimes we just have a quick gossip and go in different directions. You know that moment, just after the sun has set? When the colours seem to get deeper, even more spectacular? That moment. I love that moment. And it was so beautiful down here the night Lily died. Miraculous.'

Tears burned Maggie's eyes. 'I miss her,' she said. 'I miss Lily so much.'

'We all miss her,' said Ivo. 'She was a glorious person.'

'Sorry,' Maggie rubbed away the tears. 'It's been quite a weekend.'

'Hasn't it?'

'This thing with Finlay and Rory...'

'I know.' Ivo paused. 'I wish you had known about it all back then, Maggie. I wish we had told you. I think you would have made us do things differently.'

'For Rory,' Maggie said slowly. 'It would all be in the past by now. A youthful mistake. But if it comes out now...'

'It'll destroy everything,' said Ivo.

'Even Finlay. It would be history. He'd never have got twenty years in jail.'

'Yes, but then again, spending most of your twenties in jail...'

'I know. And for Jude, it's unbearable, the whole thing. It's screwed up so much of Jude's life.'

'Does Jude want you to go to the police?'

'I don't know. I don't think so. Not about the rape anyway. What's the point now? You can hardly prosecute a dead man.'

'Poor Jude.'

'Fucking, fucking Mike. I was going through the cuttings of his death earlier. Everyone banging on about how nice he was. What a brilliant mathematician. They have no idea.'

'Yes.'

'I wonder if he ever attacked anyone else,' said Maggie. 'No one else said anything after he died, did they?'

'Do not speak ill of the dead,' said Ivo. 'I guess.'

'I suppose so. He just came across as such a shy, harmless type. "Naïve", Elizabeth called him. You wouldn't even have thought he knew what Rohypnol was. I can't believe that he...'

'I know,' said Ivo. 'I think that's why we let Jude go home with him that evening. He just seemed so completely innocuous. I wish...'

'Bastard,' Maggie stared into the depths of the fire. 'Fucking arsehole.'

'He got,' Ivo rolled over again, 'what he deserved.'

'What do you think I should do?' Maggie asked him.

'Well, you know what I think,' said Ivo. 'I've been covering it all up for twenty years, and there is a reason for that.'

'Yes.'

'But maybe that was what cursed us, after all. Maybe this secret that we've all dragged with us, every step of the way. Maybe that was the real curse.'

'You don't mean—'

'Our very own life sentences.'

'Ivo...'

Ivo flopped onto his back, looking away from her. After a few seconds, she realised that he was staring at a portrait of his father hanging in the corner of the room.

'He would definitely not have approved,' Ivo spoke quietly. 'But he didn't approve of much anyway.'

'I never realised he was quite such a ruthless businessman. Rory told me a bit.'

'You don't hold onto all this,' Ivo gestured widely, 'without being fairly tough.'

'I suppose not. I'm so sorry about your mother, too. Rory was telling me about her over dinner.'

For a moment, Ivo's eyes were dark. 'It's odd, isn't it? Back then, you were just expected to get on with it. Nowadays, it would be therapy and hugs and mandalas all over the shop. But back then...'

'I'm so sorry.'

A spatter of rain rattled the windows.

'I was in the nursery with my nanny when my father walked in,' Ivo said slowly. 'It was late in the afternoon by then. He asked the nanny where my mother was, wanted to know if they were free for drinks with the Trelawneys or something utterly irrelevant like that. It was only then that I saw how dark it was. "She hasn't come home yet," said the nanny. I saw this glance go between them. *She hasn't come home yet.*' Ivo stared up at the ceiling. 'And just then, it started to snow. A blizzard, really. This was all long before' – a cynical half-laugh – 'we knew what the weather would be doing hour by hour.'

'Oh God.'

'My father went out searching for her. The whole village went out. The police, the rangers, everyone. And then all of a sudden, her horse came trotting into the stable yard, sweating, exhausted, and that was when we knew. I still remember the empty stirrups, the tired horse looking round for his supper.' For a moment, Ivo looked eight years old again, a little boy waiting for a mother who would never come home.

'Oh, Ivo. It must have been terrible for you. And for your father.' Abruptly, she remembered the hunt master. Her expression must have changed.

'Rory told you about that too?' A mocking shrug. 'You pair of old gossips.'

'No, I—' Maggie flushed.

'Maggie. It doesn't matter any more. None of it does.'

'Of course it does, Ivo.'

Their eyes locked.

'Is your glass empty?' It was another quick change of mood. In one movement, Ivo had sat up, grabbed the bottle and pushed himself until he was sitting next to her on the sofa. He poured out more wine and they both sat there in the golden glow of the fire. Ollie was fast asleep now. Maggie could hear his breathing and feel the warmth of Ivo's arm just a few inches from hers.

'I wish you'd known about Mike Jansen, Maggie.' Ivo's words were so quiet that she almost missed them. Maggie turned towards him and found that he was already facing her. 'I wish we had told you,' he said again.

'Would it have made any difference?'

'I think so. Somehow.'

'I think I'm glad I didn't know.' She wasn't sure if that was true.

'I wish…' But this time, he didn't say what he wished. He just sat there, staring at her face. The silence wrapped itself around them like a fur coat, soft and heavy. 'Maggie.' Ivo put his hand to her face, running his fingers along her cheekbone.

Maggie couldn't move, couldn't breathe. *Is this real?*

'Maggie!' It was Jude, crashing into the room. 'I've been looking everywhere for you. Come and see.'

70

Lily, on Maggie: Maggie will be understanding
her own beauty at last.

The ballroom was a flurry of chalk flowers and stars and angels underfoot.

'This weekend was meant to be *fun*,' Jude had insisted, shepherd-
ing them all down the corridor. 'Come on. We've only got a few more
hours left.'

A determined Cinderella, clutching her enchanted silks about her.

So they danced, pushing away the demons just for a little while longer.

Beneath the frolics, the tension of sex. Perhaps it had always been that
way in this grandest of rooms. The briefest of glances. A smile just for
her. Fingers touching so lightly that Maggie wondered if it was only her
imagination. But she had never dared imagine this. Jude was fiddling
with her phone, giggling to herself. 'A waltz,' she announced, the music
tinny and distorted. 'Take your partners, ladies and gentlemen.'

Ivo bowed deeply to Maggie.

He knew how to dance, always had. But this time: his hand on her
waist, her hand in his. He was half smiling and there was something else
in his eyes, as they swirled and whirled. They were all dancing now. Ayda
and Finlay, laughing: one-two-three, one-two-three. Ollie and Elizabeth,
with the ingrained steps of their first dance. Rory whirled Jude in wild,
pirouetting circles. The music changed from a tango to the Charleston,
from a samba to drum and bass. Jude looked down with delight as the
ghostly flowers blurred beneath her foxtrot.

'Come with me, Maggie.' The words were so quiet that Maggie almost missed them. But she felt herself follow Ivo as if in a dream. The chaos of music disappeared behind them, the heavy doors shutting away the jitterbug.

Ivo kissed her at the foot of the staircase, pushing her back against the newel post. They stood there, bodies pressed together. And Maggie was glad the post was solid against her back, because otherwise everything might have dissolved into light and magic and joy. She opened her eyes once, so that she could see his face: so close. So that she could remember this moment, this instant right here, forever, in case it was all she ever had. She touched his face, his hair, his shoulders, and pulled him closer, hungry. He stopped then, looked down at her. That flickering smile again and she felt his hand on hers.

'Come.' He led her up the stairs, kissing her on every tread.

Along the gallery, past her bedroom door. Not in there, not tonight, no. Here.

His bedroom door was Bluebeard's ancient oak. He kissed her in the doorway and she had a sense that he was letting her decide. This way or that. You can choose the ordinary, the normal, the cheap mirrored wardrobes and the juliet balcony.

Or this way, and everything changes.

She never hesitated.

His bed was huge. Four-poster, the red curtains tied back. He pushed her back and followed her down and kissed her until she felt as if she belonged to him, and him to her, and it was all already decided.

The sky was brightening, she realised hazily, a few moments later. Hours, still, until dawn, but already – far, far to the east – the horizon was lighter against the black of the hills. Such beauty, Maggie thought dreamily as he kissed her again and again. The earth spinning through the starry skies. The sun blazing with the brilliance of a new day, a new life, a new world.

Far to the east…

Ivo pulled back for a second and looked down at her with such delight that Maggie felt a surge of ecstasy overwhelm her. He kissed her, deeper and deeper, just the cotton of his shirt and her thin black dress between them. Maggie could feel his chest solid against hers. She wrapped herself around him, pulling him closer.

Far to the east…

His hand was grinding against the silky black material.

'Ivo.' Maggie heard herself moan.

His legs were pushing hers apart now. She felt as if she was dissolving, flowing, earth and air and fire and water.

Far to the east… Maggie tried to push the thought away.

Ivo's hand was on her leg now, edging her dress up her thigh. She kissed him harder, pulling his face close to hers.

Far to the east…

The east…

Stop it.

No.

She had to know.

He was tugging down her neckline now, his breath warm against her skin.

'Ivo,' Maggie said, and her voice was a shock in the old room.

'Maggie.' A moan.

'Ivo.' Her words were loud in her ears, jarring. 'I can't stop thinking about you and Ayda.'

He looked up, startled. 'Maggie…'

He kissed her again, pushing away the words. For a moment, she kissed him back, letting the world drift away again.

The east…

'Ivo… wait a minute.'

Maggie put a hand on his chest and pushed him away very slightly. He was taken aback, but then stroked her cheek.

'Maggie…' Another kiss. 'Come on.'

'No. Sorry. I can't help it, Ivo.'

'Okay… I…' He let himself slide off her, still close, propping his forehead on his hand. 'What do you want to know?'

'How long since… ?'

'Since Ayda and I last hooked up? God, I don't know. Years. Nothing's happened between us since uni, I don't think?'

'But you still talk?' It was her interviewing voice and she hated it. Wanted desperately to go back to the warm kisses and the burn of excitement. 'You still have this thing of talking at sunset?'

'Every so often, yes.'

'And you watched the sun set the night that Lily died?'

'Yes, Maggie.' Getting impatient. 'That glow in the night sky just after the sun goes down. That exact moment. It was stunning that evening.'

'That exact moment. You watched it together, talking to each other when it happened? At 5.30 p.m., or whatever time the sun sets in early March?'

'Yes!'

'Okay.'

'Are we done now?' He was laughing down at her, sliding his body until he was covering hers again. His mouth was on her, his lips drifting down to her throat. That quiver of excitement was starting to ripple through her body again. 'Ayda doesn't mean anything to me. Not like that, anyway. She's just an old friend.'

Far to the east…

Their blood shall be upon them…

Maggie sat up. 'What is it?' Ivo wasn't worried. His hands reached out for her again, tugging her back down towards him.

'I've got to… I just need to grab something from my room.'

'Maggie!' He was laughing up at her. 'For God's sake.'

'I won't be a…' Maggie slipped out of the bed and tugged her dress up and down and back into some sort of shape. 'I won't be a moment.'

Ivo sighed. Laid back on the bed. 'Hurry up then.'

Maggie ran across the floor. Only a few steps down the passage and there was her bedroom door, ajar. Maggie shoved it closed behind her and raced across the bedroom floor. Hurried with a speed that pushed away the passion, the lust, the romance.

Because this was a thought she couldn't push away any more.

This was a thought that was filling up her mind until she thought she might scream.

A thought that…

She seized her laptop, tapping quickly. *There.* Maggie grabbed her phone, found Jude's number and began to type.

Ayda and Ivo both told me that they watched the sunset together. That they were talking on the phone at the exact moment that the sun went down. They both said that Ayda was on the roof of Throwleigh Pearce and Ivo was down here.

A deep breath. It was as if she was watching a mirror falling through the air. Tumbling, sparkling, down and down and down. Shuddering, Maggie checked the weather at the beginning of March. It had rained for weeks on either side of the day Lily died, snow and sleet too, but it had cleared briefly on that Wednesday evening. Bright skies over both Wintercross and London: there had indeed been a sunset to watch.

A pause. No response from Jude.

Maybe Jude had abandoned her phone in the ballroom, still blaring tinny Beyoncé.

Maggie turned to that footage, one more time. Pink hair, flat stomachs, bright orange digital numbers on the platform sign: 17:38.

Lily had died as the sun set over London.

But...

Maggie reached for her phone again, the despair cold against her skin.

> Jude, Ayda is lying about watching the sun set that evening. They can't have watched it while they were chatting to each other.

A sense of a moment that could never be undone.

> London is 200 miles to the east of Wintercross. In London, the sun sets ten minutes earlier than it does on Dartmoor. Ayda is lying.

The mirror hit the ground, smashed into a thousand pieces. Unfixable, destroyed, forever.

> Ivo...

Maggie wrote slowly.

> is lying too.

71

Rory, on Ivo: The gilt will be wearing off.

'I'm so hammered!' Jude was cackling on the threshold of Maggie's bedroom. 'Come on, Maggie. Let's go and do a few shots and then we can draw some more bee-yoo-tiful flowers.' Jude waved a bottle of tequila and swayed wildly.

'Jude.' Maggie's heart sank. 'Oh, *Jude*.'

'It's barely worth going to bed now, Maggie! Let's go and dance around Lion's Rock as the sun rises over Wintercross.'

'Jude, you haven't—' Maggie jumped as Jude slammed the door shut behind her.

'What?' Jude's whisper was fierce in the gloom. 'What the fuck is going on, Maggie?'

'Jude… wait. You're not pissed?'

'Of course I'm not. Jesus, Maggie, there's at least one murderer running round this house, I'm hardly going to help them out. But at the same time, it's not unhelpful for them all to think that I'm smashed.'

'No, no, you're right. Sorry.'

'So what the hell are you going on about in these text messages? All this stuff about different sunsets?'

'"Look, love, what envious streaks, Do lace the severing clouds in yonder east", Maggie recited tonelessly. 'The sun rises in the east, and it sets in the west.'

'I'm aware. Get to the point.'

'But London is a couple of hundred miles to the east of Devon,' said Maggie. 'So the sun rises about ten minutes earlier there. It's the curve of the Earth.' Maggie gestured hopelessly. 'They can't have watched it set simultaneously, sharing the moment while chatting on the phone in the way they claim. They're lying.'

'Okay,' Jude rubbed her eyes. 'Although I suppose they could say that they were both on the phone as the sun set.'

'That's not how they phrased it though. They said they watched the exact moment of the sun setting together.'

Jude absorbed the thought. 'So why the fuck is Ivo Fitzwilliam giving Ayda an alibi? Why is he bullshitting for her?'

'I don't know,' said Maggie. 'It could just be that Ayda needed his help. They're old friends, like we all are. If she asked him to cover for her, he probably would.'

'Like he's been covering for Rory and Finlay all these years?'

'Yes, exactly like that.'

'But to kill *Lily*? This isn't just some punch-up that got out of hand, Maggie.'

'I know. I can't imagine...' Another thought hit Maggie and she breathed out sharply.

Jude looked up. 'What is it?'

'I've only just realised,' Maggie said miserably, 'that Ayda and Ivo can't have agreed to all this retrospectively.'

'Why?' Jude answered her own question. 'Because he had to be on the phone call before anything happened. For Ayda's alibi to work, they needed to have records of a phone conversation that stretched from before Lily died until a decent time after.'

'It had to have been premeditated then,' Maggie felt the prickle of tears in her eyes. 'Ivo had to know what Ayda was planning in advance. They planned together for Ayda to murder Lily. *Lily.*'

'Yes.' Jude was brutal. 'Ayda must have gone up to the roof of Throwleigh Pearce, started the phone call, left the phone on the office roof and followed Lily down onto the Tube platform. Then she pushed Lily,' Jude's voice stalled briefly, 'and got back to the call.'

'Ivo just kept the line open,' said Maggie. 'Ayda must have found a way off the Throwleigh Pearce roof that isn't covered by CCTV cameras. She's spent enough time up there over the years to work that out.'

'Down a fire escape?' asked Jude. 'Or maybe she just nicked a friend's pass to buzz herself in and out of the building. Who'd notice their pass missing for an hour or so?'

'Lily fell under the train at Tower Hill Tube station,' Maggie was thinking aloud. 'She usually works at Guy's, but she'd been seconded to the Royal London in Whitechapel for a bit. She was heading there for a shift.'

The District Line scraping and screeching eastwards, sparks flying from steely train wheels.

'Yes,' Jude was nodding. 'Lily always walked up to Tower Hill from her flat, because it was quicker walking over the bridge rather than messing around with a change at London Bridge.'

'It was a beautiful day, too,' said Maggie sadly. '"Only time I get any fresh air". She said that a lot.'

'I knew that she was working in Whitechapel,' said Jude. 'And you did.'

'Anyone could have found out,' said Maggie. 'Anyone could have found out, and anyone could have waited for her on the District Line platform. We all have our routines and that was hers.'

'It's not far from Throwleigh Pearce to Tower Hill, is it?'

'No,' Maggie said bleakly. 'Throwleigh Pearce is in Liverpool Street and that's just a few minutes' walk away. One stop on the Circle Line. Ayda could easily have started the call to Ivo, headed to Tower Hill, hung about for a few minutes and hurried back within an hour.'

'Lily was always punctual for work,' said Jude. 'Ayda could be pretty sure what time she would reach Tower Hill. And you know what it's like on train platforms in the rush hour. People stand right on the edge. It wouldn't take much. A nudge, really.'

'Yes.'

'Would the police be able to track Ayda's movements?'

'Well, she left her phone on the roof,' said Maggie, 'so obviously they wouldn't be able to track that. I don't know how long CCTV is stored for. Presumably if she used her own card to tap into the stations, there would be a record of that somewhere. But if she was careful enough to leave her phone on the roof of Throwleigh Pearce, and nick someone else's security pass, then I'm pretty sure she won't have left much of an electronic footprint.'

Ayda, the lawyer, whose pretty smile disguised a most ruthless intelligence.

'People leave things on their desks all the time,' Jude was nodding. 'Especially somewhere like Throwleigh Pearce where they basically live at their desks, from what I can make out.'

'Yes. If someone was in a four-hour meeting or something.'

'Can we prove it?' Jude asked. 'That it was Ayda who killed Lily?'

'I don't care any more,' said Maggie. 'We need to get out of here, Jude. I've had enough. I can't…'

The rain was hammering against her bedroom window, a cold draught sweeping across the floor.

'If Ayda and Ivo repeat this nonsense about sunsets,' said Jude, 'then maybe we can nail them. We don't know if they've made statements to the police about it. Affidavits, whatever.'

'They could spin it,' said Maggie. 'Say that of course they knew there was a delay between the London and Devon sunsets; they just weren't clear about it in the statements. They'll have regular phone calls between them at those times. They'll be able to prove there is a pattern. I *know* Ayda.'

'Why the hell did Ivo get involved?' Jude wondered aloud. 'What's in it for him?'

'Maybe it's just the same thing as Rory and Finlay. He knew that Ayda was in trouble and offered to help.'

'Yes, but *Lily*.'

'Or maybe,' Maggie admitted, 'it's just that Ivo just likes knowing. Knowing where the bodies are buried. Which strings are available to be pulled.'

'He can be a manipulative fucker.' Jude nodded and Maggie felt a pang. 'Always was.'

'But what about Helen?' Maggie asked. 'We still haven't worked out what happened to her?'

'Christ,' Jude rubbed her face.

'Helen disappeared on a Saturday.' Maggie worked it out slowly. 'It's the one day of the week when Ayda might well not be in the office. If Helen turned up on Ayda's front doorstep, maybe Ayda told her they both needed to speak to Ivo together? But Ivo wasn't in Devon so that doesn't really work. He was in Stuttgart or Athens or somewhere like that, wasn't he?'

'Even if he was abroad, Ayda could have used Ivo as bait to get Helen down here. Dartmoor is a better place to dispose of a body than west London,' Jude said bleakly.

'Maybe.'

'Could they have driven down together? In Ayda's car?'

'Helen's car was found near Barras Tor,' Maggie remembered. 'Maybe Ayda got Helen to drive her down?'

'Wouldn't Ayda's DNA and fingerprints be all over the car in that case? The police would have checked for fingerprints, wouldn't they, when they found her body?'

'I don't know. They could have driven in convoy. Oh, who bloody knows? There are so many unknowns.'

'Okay.' Jude sounded decisive. Focused, in a way Maggie hadn't seen her for years. 'Let's say that Helen goes to Lily and finds out something that makes her decide she needs to go back to Ayda and confront her again. She does that on the Saturday morning.'

'And whatever it was that Helen had discovered,' Maggie continued the thought, 'it was enough for Ayda to convince Helen to come down to Dartmoor.'

'Or Helen ordered Ayda to take her down to Dartmoor,' said Jude. 'Or Helen drove down to speak to Ivo on her own, not knowing that he was in Germany or Greece or wherever, and Ayda never left London. It's impossible, Maggie. There's too much guesswork. We need more.'

'We need the police,' said Maggie.

'If there aren't fingerprints in Helen's car and if we can't work out what the hell Lily said to Helen, Ayda will get away with it, Maggie. You know that.' Jude blinked at Maggie with a moment of realisation. 'And is that what you actually want, deep down?'

'No,' Maggie insisted. 'It's not. But how do we actually get any proof?'

A knock on the door and they both jumped.

'Maggie?' It was Ivo. Jude raised an eyebrow.

'I'll be there in a second, Ivo,' Maggie called out. There was a pause and then the footsteps receded.

'What,' Jude narrowed her eyes, 'the fuck is going on, Maggie?'

'Nothing.' Too hasty. 'Nothing serious.'

'*Maggie!*' Jude hissed. 'He's *playing* you.'

Maggie felt a jolt of pain, then forced herself to smile. 'Just because someone kisses me, it doesn't mean there has to be something else going on.'

'I *know*. But, Jesus…'

'What do we do then?' Maggie asked. 'I think we should get the fuck out of here, but—'

'We need to catch them talking about it,' said Jude. 'Ayda and Ivo. We need to rattle them so badly that they panic.'

'Neither of them are the panicking type,' said Maggie. 'And' – the realisation hit her – 'and I've already told Ivo about a lot of our half-arsed evidence. Ayda's shoe. Rose J calling Ayda's phone.'

Jude looked frustrated. 'Fine. None of those things tie-in Ivo, anyway. They just damage Ayda, and I bet he'd cheerfully chuck Ayda under a bus if necessary. We need to shock him into realising his neck's on the line too.'

'It'll have to be the sunset thing,' said Maggie. 'But how do we record them talking?'

'You've done undercover stuff, haven't you?'

'Only a little bit. But the equipment's not part of my weekend-in-the-country packing. Maybe we could leave one of our phones set to record? But I'm not sure the sound quality would be great. And unless we hid it – in which case you definitely wouldn't be able to hear much – they'd probably spot an iPhone recording. What is it, Jude?'

Jude was looking shifty. 'There's a secret passage,' she admitted. 'Mr Fitzwilliam showed it to me years ago.'

Wintercross. Wintercross, and its layers of secrets.

'What? A passage where?' asked Maggie. 'I know about the hide in Ayda's room but I didn't know about a passage.'

'There are four big bedrooms along the front of the house,' Jude gestured. 'You're in here, then Ayda, then Elizabeth. I'm at the far end, in what used to be Ivo's room before he moved into the master bedroom. There's a secret passage that runs most of the way along the front of the house.'

'Where?' Maggie spun towards the window. 'How?'

'You access it from my room,' said Jude. 'Mr Fitzwilliam showed me how to get in once. It's set into the front wall and it runs along below the window sills, through Elizabeth's room, through Ayda's room, all the way to here. The Borrowers would love this place.'

'Here?' Maggie stood up, walked towards the window with its deep, cushioned seat.

'I don't think you can access it from this room,' said Jude. 'I don't know if you ever could. But look here.'

They crouched down together. Close to the floor, the oak had been carved into elaborate roses, blackened by age. Maggie peered closer. In the flourishes of the ornate design, two small holes were almost invisible.

'Spyholes,' Maggie murmured. She ran her fingers over the carefully disguised apertures. 'Jude, you haven't…'

'No! I've only peeked in the passage once since we got down this weekend, and that was for old times' sake, not Rasputin-style enterprises. It's pretty cosy in there, quite frankly. I didn't bother coming all the way along. Ye olde medieval types were less fussed about headspace, evidently.'

Maggie remembered that night all those years ago. Luke Russell, and a whiff of sulphur, and the screams echoing oddly around the house.

A beautiful maid, who lay down in the snow.

'You mean there are spyholes into Ayda's room as well?'

'Yup. This place is a voyeur's paradise.'

'So what's the plan?' asked Maggie. 'You go downstairs and tell everyone that Ivo and Ayda are lying about the sunset and hope they come up to Ayda's room for a crisis summit?'

'Yes,' said Jude. 'I'll record that first conversation on my phone – just whack it in my pocket and hope for the best – and then you hide in the secret passage and film whatever they say to each other when they come upstairs.'

'*If* they come upstairs.'

'Well, they're not going to go and have a quiet chat outside.' Jude waved at the wind and rain buffeting the window.

'But what if they go back to Ivo's room instead of Ayda's?'

'You go back to Ivo's room now,' Jude decided. 'Then they can't go there. You go in there now and then I'll come and tell him that I need to speak to him downstairs straight away. While we're downstairs, you go into my room and sneak along the secret passage. You get in by pressing hard on the third wooden rose on the left.'

'Right.' Maggie rubbed at her face. 'Right. But Jude, he may know you're in here right now. There's that security camera pointing at the painting outside this room. I'll have to say you're upset about something but that you wouldn't tell me what it is. Then a couple of minutes later, you hammer on the door and demand to speak to him downstairs.'

'Okay. We need to make sure that none of the security cameras catch you leaving his bedroom to get to my room. He may be able to access the feeds on his phone. The security system seems to be pretty sophisticated.'

Maggie almost laughed, 'I'll avoid going near the Watteau.'

'Right,' said Jude. 'Let's go.'

'For God's sake, just go downstairs, Jude,' Maggie put loud irritation into her voice. 'Either tell me what the problem is or go. I'm knackered.'

They were hovering on the threshold to Maggie's room, just a few feet from Ivo's bedroom.

'Come *on*, Maggie,' Jude whined loudly. 'Come and have another drink. You're so bloody boring these days.'

Maggie yawned ostentatiously. 'Bye, Jude.'

'Maggieeee.'

'Goodnight.' Maggie shut her bedroom door firmly.

Jude grumbled loudly all the way down the corridor.

Maggie waited a couple of beats and then stepped across to Ivo's room.

The room lay in darkness, with just a hint of the light from the faraway dawn. Ivo had kicked off his shoes and was lying on the bed, flat on his back.

'You're back.' Warmth in his voice.

'Sorry.' A hint of a giggle. 'I got caught by Jude.'

'Christ, what does she want now?'

'I don't know. Wouldn't bloody tell me, after all that.' Maggie was walking towards the four-poster bed. She felt self-conscious, suddenly, faintly ridiculous. Ivo sprang to his feet.

'Come here.'

His mouth crushed into hers. 'Ivo...'

He spun her around. Pushed her back slowly until she reached one of the four-poster's uprights, the oak hard against her back. Then he took her hands in hers, and pushed them up until she could feel the cool polished wood against her fingers. A moment later his hands were all over her, tugging up the hemline of her dress, dragging the neckline down. He was kissing her mouth, her throat, edging down.

A bang on the door.

Maggie jumped, no need for acting. 'Who the hell?'

'Ivo! I need to speak to you!'

'That's Jude.' Maggie stopped kissing him.

'Ignore her,' said Ivo. 'She's pissed. You know what she's like. Mad.' He kissed her again, his hands tangling in her hair.

Another thump on the ancient oak. 'Right now, Ivo. It's important.'

'Fuck *off*, Jude,' Ivo shouted back. 'We're busy.'

'I'm not messing about, Ivo,' Jude yelled back. 'I need to speak to you right this minute. Come downstairs.'

'For fuck's sake,' Ivo muttered into Maggie's hair. 'She's bloody nuts. Not now!' He bawled.

'No!'

'You'd better go,' Maggie pretended to suppress a giggle. 'She won't bugger off until she's had her way. You know what she's like. And it is slightly spoiling the mood.'

For a moment, he rested his head against her cheek. 'Fucking *Jude*.'

'Come on, Ivo!' Jude bawled.

'What is it? Just shout whatever it is through the fucking door, Jude. You don't seem to have any problem doing that.'

'I need to speak to you and Ayda,' Jude said firmly. 'Both of you, downstairs. Right now.'

Maggie felt a tautness ripple through Ivo's body.

'You might as well go and see what she has to say,' she murmured. 'I'll wait here.'

Ivo pulled back slightly. She looked up at him. At the tangled dark hair and the blue eyes, solemn, grey in the dark. 'Don't go anywhere,' he murmured. 'Stay right here.'

'I promise.'

She listened to his footsteps receding down the corridor, and the surge of pain was such that she almost called him back.

Fragments of mirror, no light to reflect.

She sat up on the bed and bit her fingernails hard.

Maggie made herself wait for two minutes, the seconds creeping past slowly, before inching her way across the bedroom floor. She knew that the door to Ivo's room creaked, but there was no other way out. Maggie swallowed hard and pushed. She could say she had lent Jude a book, or that she needed another headache pill, or anything. But still her knees wobbled as she crept down the corridor.

There was the Watteau.

Feeling ludicrous, Maggie dropped to her knees and crawled under the camera's beam. Past Ayda's door. Maggie paused and clicked on the light in Ayda's bedroom so she would be able to see into the room from the passage. Past Elizabeth's door. Again, she switched on the light. Now she was at the top of the second of the double staircases and Maggie could hear Jude was on the attack. She could make out voices, not words. Elizabeth, confused, fraught. Rory, trying to pacify. Ayda and Ivo, furious and defensive. They were all in the drawing room.

Jude had helpfully left her bedroom door open. Maggie crept in and pushed the door almost shut behind her. This room was directly above the drawing room. Maggie crept across the floorboards, wincing at every creak. She might not have long. They could all storm out at any moment. Maggie reached the corner of the room and crouched down next to the oak panelling that covered the whole wall.

Third wooden rose on the left.

Maggie found it, pushed it. Nothing. She pushed harder.

For a moment, there was no movement at all. Then there was the faintest of sighs. The house, giving up her secrets. A quiet rumble as a panel slipped back, the sound of brick on brick making Maggie recoil. Then the passage opened.

Inside the secret corridor, there was a velvety darkness. Maggie could only tell there was an empty space beyond the opening by reaching out and touching nothing. She reached for her phone, clicking on the torch. It was less a passage than a tunnel, she decided. It dropped about two feet below the floorboards and rose two feet above. There was no possibility of standing up straight, she would have to crawl along somehow. In the narrow beam of light, the passage looked even less appealing. It was very narrow; its stony walls thick with dusty spider webs. Maggie could see where Jude had climbed in at some point in the last couple of days, but the spiders had returned already, busily mending their lace. It wouldn't be far to Elizabeth's room, Maggie told herself. Just a few yards, and then she would see the light shining through the spyholes down into the passage.

I don't want to.

You must.

Maggie took a breath and squeezed through the opening. Spider webs veiled her face.

For a second, she froze. Sulphur and screams and a beautiful maid, who lay down in the snow. It felt as if it was the house's memory, not hers.

A shudder of superstition.

Their blood shall be upon them.

Ignore it.

Maggie felt around the opening to Jude's room. There must be some mechanism for closing the panel behind her, surely. But she couldn't feel anything. She would have to climb in and hope that no one looked into Jude's room and saw the dark gap in the polished oak.

Come on.

Moving carefully, Maggie began to make her way along the tunnel. Odd edges of stone jutted out, catching at her dress as she squirmed along. Spider webs shrouded her face and hair. Hunched down, she failed to notice a heavy wooden beam and banged her head hard.

Cursing, she glanced up and saw them.

Two narrow beams of light, cutting through the gloom.

This must be Elizabeth's room. Maggie peered in. For a second, she was blinded by the light. Then she made out a pale blue cashmere cardigan folded neatly on an armchair; polished shoes lined up precisely under the bed. Yes, this was Elizabeth's room, alright. The spyholes were easy to see through, perfectly positioned for her eyes. Maggie felt as if she were wearing the house as a veil. Or had become a stagehand peering out from the wings.

Come on.

Maggie clambered.

It felt like a long way to Ayda's room. Maggie crawled along, bruising her knees and elbows, trying to stay as silent as possible. She imagined those old, scared souls, crouching in the dark. Listening to the shouts and curses below, waiting patiently for a death as painful as anyone could devise. Or maybe they had crept along this passage searching for clues of dissidence, of malice. Of apostasy, that spiritual death beyond agony.

Was she hiding or was she searching?

She must be nearly there now. Surely. Her arms and legs were beginning to ache.

Maggie sat back on her heels and switched off the torch.

Perfect darkness for a second.

And then she saw it: two spears of light, motes of dust glinting.

There.

Maggie edged forward.

Clothes chucked over an armchair, a laptop charging on the bedside table. It was Ayda's room. Maggie huddled down in the darkness. The sounds from downstairs were muffled and it was almost comforting, after the last few days, to hide away in the darkness, far from the chaos. She could imagine the scene downstairs. Jude, the consummate actress, drawing out the fight, giving Maggie long enough to scurry to her position. Ensuring that Elizabeth knew, that Rory knew, that the secret was ripped apart like a paper bag.

Ayda and Ivo: plotting to kill Lily.

Ayda and Ivo: plotting to kill their friend.

Maggie imagined Ayda, the ground slipping away beneath her feet. What would she do?

Maybe someone – Elizabeth, most probably – would call the police at last. Would watch gravely as the blue lights flickered up the long Wintercross drive and stand guard as they parked before the huge oak door.

No.

She knew them all. Ayda and Ivo would never surrender. They would find a way to quell Elizabeth's anger and to retreat, regroup, rearm.

They would find a way.

Maggie waited.

Only a few minutes must have passed before Maggie heard feet pound up the staircase. The bedroom door was flung open and Ayda raced in, slamming the door shut behind her. Ayda looked like a hunted rabbit. She stood for a second, panting, her eyes flickering around the room as she searched for an escape.

Maggie felt something close to pity.

But not.

With tiny movements, Maggie pressed record on her phone and turned the blank eye of the camera to the right spyhole. Then she leaned forward and put her right eye to the other opening. Ayda took a couple of steps forward. She put one hand to her throat, then joined both hands in what almost looked like a prayer before pressing her fingers hard against her mouth.

The door flew open and Ivo surged in. Maggie gasped. He looked like a stranger. There was a vicious twist to his face, all the charm and civility seared away. He looked distorted, contorted, almost deformed by fury.

'Jesus fucking Christ, Ayda.'

Even through the spyhole, Maggie could see that Ayda's whole body was shaking.

'I never...' Ayda was muttering. 'I never thought.'

'How many people have you told about this stupid alibi?' Ivo spat. 'Maggie, Jude, Rory... the police? Jesus, they all know, Ayda.'

'They won't tell,' Ayda shook her head, trying to convince herself. 'Rory, Finlay, they all have too much to lose.'

'You stupid *bitch*.'

Maggie watched Ayda cringe. The words seemed impossible coming from Ivo, unbearable.

But then Ayda straightened her shoulders. 'Don't you dare talk to me like that,' she spat. 'I can take you down with me, Ivo, and you fucking know it.'

'You fucking idiot,' Ivo's voice was harsh with rage. 'You stupid *cunt*.'

Maggie felt as if she had been punched.

The fight went out of Ayda. She turned and crumpled on the bed, a fallen puppet. Ivo watched her, his expression like ice. He would kill Ayda without hesitation if it solved this crisis, Maggie realised. Stub her out like a cigarette. This man – this stranger – could do anything.

'They still don't know.' Ayda whispered so quietly that Maggie knew the iPhone would never pick it up. 'None of them know about...' Slowly Ayda pushed herself upright until she was sitting up on the bed. She turned away from Ivo, elbows on knees, chin on her hands, locking him out. 'They still don't know,' she said, slightly louder.

Whatever she meant, it was enough to drag Ivo back from the brink. He took a ragged breath. 'And they never will, Ayda.'

'You don't know that, Ivo.' Ayda intertwined her fingers, pressing them hard against her mouth again. 'Jude… Maggie…'

Ivo was forcing down the rage now, Maggie saw. Pulling the shreds of charm into a threadbare coat. Maggie could see him making the calculations. There was no possibility of disposing of Ayda like trash: not here, not now. She needed to be brought back onside.

'It'll be okay, Ayda,' he said, calmer now. 'We'll think of something. I promise.'

Maggie shifted her gaze to Ayda and flinched. That expression. That expression, so familiar. Love, helpless love. Even now, all along, she loved Ivo.

'But what do we *do*?' Ayda pleaded. She had turned back towards Ivo. 'Elizabeth. We don't have anything on her. Or Ollie.'

'Ollie won't…' The cool confidence was returning to Ivo's face now. 'Leave Ollie to me.'

'What about Maggie, though?'

'Maggie won't say a word,' said Ivo, and Maggie felt a sharp pain somewhere near her heart. 'She wouldn't.'

'And what about Elizabeth?' Ayda said again.

Ivo made a gesture that was almost flippant. 'This weekend was always going to be a bloody nightmare, Ayda. You knew that. But it has to be—'

'Beyond all reasonable doubt,' murmured Ayda. 'It has to be beyond all reasonable doubt.'

And Maggie understood with another slash of pain why they were all here this weekend. Because they all had to be tainted by suspicion. Rory and Finlay's attack exposed. Elizabeth baited into revealing Ollie's affair. Jude: drunk, mad. Maggie herself, jealous of Lily, past threats emerging, fleeing round the garden. Perhaps she had been meant to race into the kitchen, hysterical at shadows? They were all stained. All blighted. No jury would ever be able to say with confidence: it was *her*. It was *him*.

And if Jude really had fallen out of the window, Maggie realised with a wave of horror, the footage from the security camera would have shown Maggie and Maggie alone following Jude into the bedroom within seconds of her falling. Jude, the only person to be asking questions about Lily's death. Jude, yet another convenient suicide. Leaving Maggie the only suspect if anyone ever bothered asking questions. Maggie, Elizabeth, all of them, were just collateral damage, planned in advance.

'This weekend,' said Ivo, 'it was a calculated risk. Bloody Elizabeth was going on and on about it. And we needed to know…'

They had needed to know who knew what, Maggie realised. Lab rats crammed in a cage, together. Because Lily… Lily had known too much.

Ayda was staring into the fireplace now. Only a few feet away, so that Maggie felt as if she might almost reach out and touch her. 'I won't survive a court case,' Ayda's face was wet with tears. 'It would destroy me. It would destroy everything, Ivo.'

Ayda wasn't looking at Ivo's face. She couldn't see his eyes, cold, ruthless slits behind her. Maggie shuddered. But Ivo's words were gentle. 'You'll be okay,' he murmured. 'SummerX will always need top IP lawyers. We'll get through this, Ayda.'

'Don't you understand?' Ayda whipped round with a snarl. 'At the very least, I would be struck off. You'll get away with it all, because you always bloody do, but I… I could lose everything.'

'It's all so far in the past,' Ivo had his hands on Ayda's shoulders now, pulling her towards him until she collapsed back on his chest. 'There's no proof, no evidence.'

'I can't,' Ayda was saying. 'I just can't.'

'Don't panic,' Ivo was hugging her now, wrapping those strong arms around her shivering body. 'That's the worst thing we could do. We have to keep going. This weekend was always going to be difficult, but we're nearly there now.'

'And they all know,' Ayda murmurs. 'They all know so much.'

'But they don't know enough.'

All at once, Maggie was imagining Ollie getting a text message last summer. *Fancy a weekend down in Wintercross?*

Cancelling everything, because they always did for Wintercross.

Then when Ollie arrived, he found Lily here too.

Sad Lily. Broken Lily.

So convenient. A calculated temptation. And a marriage, so casually destroyed.

A *motive*.

How long? She wondered. How *long* have they been planning this?

There were pins and needles in her left foot. Without thinking, Maggie shifted her weight. It must have been the tiniest sound but Ivo's eyes swept across the room and landed on the spyholes.

Maggie shoved herself away from the twin openings, a choke of fear in her throat.

Ayda sensed the new tension in Ivo's body. 'What is it?'

Maggie threw herself to the right, burying her phone beneath her, praying that no blue glow would give her away. 'I thought I heard something.'

'What?' Maggie heard Ayda ask again. 'What is it?'

Footsteps crossed the room. The spears of light disappeared. 'I don't fucking know.' Ivo's voice was just inches away. 'I think there's someone in there.'

72

Rory, on Ayda: Still ruthless.

Maggie imagined those blue eyes pressed to the spyholes. Peering, suspicious, the rage rising again. A curse and she heard Ivo spin away and march towards the bedroom door.

Maggie gasped in horror. The panel would be open in Jude's bedroom. It would be blatant, incontrovertible proof that someone had crawled into the passageway. It would take only moments to work out there was just one person missing. Only moments for Ivo to realise that Maggie – his useful idiot Maggie – was spinning out of his control. And there was no possible way to scramble back into Jude's room and out before Ivo reached the panel. He would be at the opening within seconds.

'Who's there?' Ayda had heard Maggie's gasp. The beams of light disappeared again as Ayda crouched down, peering through the spyholes. 'Who the fuck is there?'

Maggie jerked away from the spyholes, her mind a blur of terror. She couldn't go back to Jude's room. Maybe Jude was wrong, maybe there was some way out from her room as well. It was the only possible option. Maggie forced her way down the narrow passage, smashing into beams, jags of stone. There must be… there had to be. She crunched into a solid wall and looked up dazed.

Two more beams of light to her left. Maggie put her eyes to the openings. Pale peach roses, sweet peas, birds skipping amongst the wild roses: her room. It was another world, just the other side of the unyielding oak.

Maggie hammered at the panels but they never even creaked. Ancient wood, hardened by centuries: immovable. A lever, a knob. There *must* be something. Anything that would set the old wooden panels sliding back.

Nothing.

A slight give in a panel. A tiny indentation. *Anything.*

No.

But Nicholas Owen, and all his ancient devilry. There *had* to be something.

Maggie tried to remember the location of the hide in Ayda's room, relative to where she was now. Maybe they linked up, maybe they… but it was hopeless. That hide was the other side of the chimney breast, far away from where she crouched now. She ran her fingers over the solid oak again.

Nothing. Nothing. *Nothing.*

A sob of frustration. Anger, burning up. To be defeated like this, crouching in the dark.

She thought she heard a sound from the direction of Jude's room and the anger melted into fear. Maggie cowered against the solid wall to her right.

The hide within the hide within the hide.

Mr Fitzwilliam's words came back to her like some lost spell.

They built priest holes within priest holes, she remembered, so that the searchers congratulated themselves on finding that first hidden space and turned away to hunt for the next mystery.

They didn't search for the secret within the secret.

Maybe.

Maybe.

But Ivo would know this house better than anyone.

Maggie imagined Mr Fitzwilliam passing down his secrets, one by one, determined that Ivo's birthright should survive. An inheritance of secrets and memories. Intangible wisdom. A fortune, so easily lost.

Only the owner of the house would know…

The hide within the hide…

A façade that didn't match what lay so deep beneath.

A sound came down the passageway, from far away.

Someone was coming.

There was the screech of brick on brick. The oak panel in Jude's room must have rolled back into place. She could feel a desperate panic at the idea of being trapped in the passage. Claustrophobia like a fist pressing against her throat.

I have to… I must…

But only a cold silence came down the passage. Ivo must have closed up the gap, trapping her like a rat.

Maybe Ivo thought there was only one way out.

Maybe Ivo *knew* there was only one way out.

Perhaps he had gone downstairs, all charm again, while that ruthless brain worked out a plan. Jude: the thought flashed into Maggie's head. Jude, wild brave, Jude, whom Ivo needed to silence more than anything. She had to get to Jude. She had to protect Jude. They had to escape together. But she was stuck, a small brown mouse peeking out from behind the skirting boards.

There had to be a way out.

My grandfather rediscovered one hiding place at Wintercross.

Maggie forced herself to think slowly. Knowledge had been lost, once, at least. And found again.

The hide within the hide.

There had to be a way.

Maggie ran her fingers over the wall to her right, pushing at stones, tugging and prodding, tapping at any bump or bulge.

Nothing.

What was below her?

The library.

A moment of realisation. That attack on Jude. Someone emerging silently from a secret passage and shoving her off the balcony. Someone ruthless, determined. Someone murderous. Ivo, later, calmly checking the security camera. Knowing what he would find. *The only person in Maggie's bedroom when Jude fell was you, Maggie.*

There *had* to be a way from this passage into her bedroom. Although Ivo, with all that Fitzwilliam arrogance, had decided she wouldn't find it. Had calculated that he still had time to think, to plot. Even with his back against the wall, he knew – *knew* – that he would come through. That he always did. That he could never be defeated by a couple of girls. He would deal with Jude first, then Maggie, coolly certain.

Maggie ran her hands around the spyholes again and rammed her fingers into any crevice she could find. Her fingernails were beginning to tear now, the desperation raw. Where were the rest of them? Maybe she should shout? But she didn't know if Ayda and Ivo had found some way of getting the rest of them out of the house. *Maggie! She's missing! We have to search for her.* She imagined them all searching futilely down by the swimming pool, sprinting around the gardens.

Until she escaped this passage, she was on her own.

Think.

The library. Downstairs.

Maggie turned her attention to the floorboards beneath her hands and knees. They were rough, unsanded. The bare bones of the house, unadorned.

Maggie ran her fingers over the splintery, sharp boards. Her fingertips were bloody now.

Nothing.

Maggie pressed down, squeezing her fingers into any cracks, any knots in the wood.

Nothing.

There had to be something…

There *had* to be.

Maggie pressed down harder, running her hands back and forward over the boards. She could feel two metal shapes jutting out from the wall, partly embedded in the floorboards. Maggie shifted position, tried again. They were rock solid. She moved again, until she was jammed up against the right wall. Still nothing. Tried again. But it was impossible to move them. She pushed harder, until her fingers bent back. Nothing. Maybe if she put her entire weight on them? She swivelled and squirmed until she was standing on the two metal shapes.

Nothing.

Again, her fingers ran over the walls, testing every bump, every dip.

No.

She bent down, running her fingers over the floorboards.

And almost couldn't believe it when a knot in the wood sank away beneath her fingers and the boards beneath her slipped sideways, disappearing smoothly under the rest of the floor. It was her own weight, Maggie worked out, combined with pushing the knot that had revealed a narrow shaft running down the front wall of Wintercross. These walls, deep enough to bury all the secrets. Maggie pointed her torch down the hole. It was only around two feet in diameter. Steel hand- and footholds stuck out into the shaft, a makeshift ladder. They were old, rusting. But the top ones were holding her. The shaft was rough and ready but it was passable.

It didn't take her long to climb down. The handholds snagged her clothes. She gasped as a sharp edge gashed her forearm, but a few seconds later she was on the ground floor, peering through another pair of spyholes into the library. There was no passage running away along the front of the house, only just space to stand. Glancing up, Maggie felt as if she were in the bottom of a well, the footholds jagging out like a torture device. Or an oubliette; when the executioner throws the prisoner down and turns away. The only trapdoor far out of reach, impossible.

A most casual killing.

Nobody was in the library. They never spent much time in there when they were at Wintercross. Maggie couldn't hear any sounds at all from the house. But the library was a long way from the kitchen and the drawing rooms, and even sounds from the dining room would be muffled.

You have to find a way out.

Maggie ran her fingers over the oak panelling that separated the shaft from the library. Again, nothing. Maggie thumped the wall in frustration, bruising her knuckles. There *had* to be a way out. Ivo must have climbed up this awkward ladder to sneak into her room. But it had been sheer luck that she had found the mechanism to make her way down here in the first place. Chance, nothing more. And it might take hours to find the way out into the bedroom or the library. Days. These secret places had been designed by a brilliant mind. They represented painstaking hours of careful diligence, because any error meant an appalling death. And that brilliant mind was working against her, centuries later. Knowing it was childish, Maggie stamped her foot.

What was that?

She stamped her foot again. A hollow sound. Maggie crouched down. It was awkward bending down in this narrow space, the footholds biting sharply into her shoulder. But once again, she ran her hands over the grimy floorboards, jamming her fingers into the knots in the wood.

Nothing.

Again.

Nothing.

Maggie pointed her torch at the rough old boards.

Nothing.

Nothing.

A gleam caught her eye.

On either side of the bottom of the shaft, two more metal footholds stuck out, partly embedded in the floorboards. Maggie peered at them for a second. Then, moving cautiously, she tucked her phone in her pocket and placed one foot on each hold. Once again, she swept her fingertips over the floorboards.

It seemed to take forever, seconds ticking away agonisingly, but all at once, the boards beneath her were sliding, whispering away until they disappeared under the floor of the library and Maggie was left standing on the footholds. She gasped. In the faint light from the spyholes, she could see that a deep shaft had opened out beneath her. Beneath her feet, there was only a perfect darkness.

A surge of terror. The old mines on Dartmoor. The old ones, long abandoned. She had no idea how to send the floorboards sliding back into place, creating a safe floor under her feet. How far did it fall away, this shaft? How long could she cling on? Would she have to drag herself back up the makeshift ladder, knowing that any slip, any stumble, would send her plunging into a void, down and down?

Maggie forced herself to breathe. These secret places had been designed with care, she reminded herself. The floorboards next to the bedroom: they had only shifted once her weight was safely to one side. The opening below her now had only yawned open when both feet were balanced on the metal footholds. Her weight was the key to unlocking this shaft, and it was only possible when she was secure on the footholds. So she must be safe, for now. Unless this was a place for disposing of your enemies, sending them to a lonely death. Forgotten.

No. Don't think of that.

What, then?

Breathing deeply, Maggie pressed herself against the side of the shaft and felt for a pen in her pocket. Her pen: a journalist's habit. Forcing herself to stay calm, Maggie took a breath and dropped the pen into the shaft. A clatter, audible and almost immediate. Only twenty feet, she guessed. Survivable, at worst. As long as you didn't impale yourself on one of the footholds.

Down, then. It was her only chance.

Moving cautiously, Maggie felt for the next foothold down.

One foot, one hand. The other foot, the other hand.

Slow, slow. Breathe.

Keep going.

It was a shock when she reached the ground, her foot bumping into solid rock. Maggie let the surge of relief flood her body. She reached for her phone, flicking on the torch again. Nothing. All around her, the walls were solid. Maggie heard a gasp of despair escape, the claustrophobia gripping her throat again. She touched the walls. Cold, rocky. She glanced down. The pen glinted up at her, looking outlandish here. Maggie stretched to pick it up, squeezing awkwardly to reach the floor. As she bent down, she saw it. A gap in front of her. A blackness reaching away from her.

A *tunnel*.

Maggie recoiled. An escape, maybe? She straightened up sharply.

No. It was impossible.

For a moment, Maggie stood breathing shallowly. The tunnel was low, there would be barely any headroom at all. She would have to wriggle along. Narrow, too, not much wider than her shoulders. You would have to be desperate. You would have to be fleeing the most agonising of deaths.

A tunnel that led away from the tall walls of Wintercross.

Maybe.

Maggie bent down again. She pointed the torch beam along the narrow pass. The torch lit up a few yards of tunnel and then the beam was lost among the jutting rocks and darkness. Maggie felt the claustrophobia claw at her throat, a physical tearing.

No.

Please no.

How else?

Slowly, Maggie bent down again. She pointed the torchlight along the tunnel again. It must be solid, she told herself firmly. Must be, to stand firm for all these years.

She swallowed.

I can't.

A scuffle above her head. Maggie looked up sharply, tilting her head back to look all the way up the shaft. There was a scraping sound, a muffled curse. 'Maggie?'

Ivo.

Maggie ducked into the tunnel, rat-like. It was just about wide enough. Just about doable. If you were desperate, hunted, frantic, you might…

She was.

Maggie took a deep breath and started crawling along the tunnel on all fours. It was cold down here. Damp. Impossibly narrow. Maggie felt as if the walls of the tunnel were closing in on her, crushing her down. Gripping her phone in her hand, she forced herself along. Behind her, she could hear more muted sounds. She panicked, writhing faster. It was that playground game: coming, ready or not. That primitive horror of someone grabbing her legs, of bringing her to a halt down here under thousands of tonnes of rock and earth. Of hands around her neck.

She struggled on. What was she *thinking*, coming down here? If she got stuck in this tunnel, no one would ever guess, no one would ever know. Ivo could close up the smooth-running trapdoors and at the very best, the police might peer down once, move on in seconds.

A hide within a hide.

She could die down here, her screams deadened by the immutable Dartmoor granite. Because if this was a dead end, she would never be able to make her way backwards all the way to the shaft. There would be no way of turning, no way of…

She had buried herself.

Maggie came to a halt, her breath coming in panicked gasps.

The air down here.

Visions of miners choking, candles sputtering, coffins.

Stop it, Maggie.

Think of something else.

Ivo.

It was a habit.

Why?

I don't know.

Try.

She forced herself to think clearly, precisely. As if she was writing in one of her notebooks, with the clean white paper and the nice, neat lines.

Why were Ayda and Ivo so desperate to silence Lily and Helen?

Rory and Finlay: that would have made sense. Hiding their part in Mike's death.

But there was nothing to link Ivo and Ayda to any of it.

Think about *that* then. Inch forward, think about Ivo and Ayda and what connected them to Helen Jansen.

Nothing connected them to Helen Jansen.

But there must be something. There *has* to be.

There has to be a reason why I'm twenty feet underground, crawling along a makeshift tunnel of granite and mud.

Helen Jansen's brother connected them. The thought was clear as the ring of a bell. Helen to Mike to Ayda and Ivo. That's the link.

But what was it about Mike Jansen?

She tried to picture him. Gingery hair, weak mouth, glasses.

That's all I know. Maggie was panting for breath as she struggled along. *That's all I remember about Mike.*

He's a mathematician. Maggie's brain threw up the fragment of information.

A mathematician like Ivo.

Finlay had known what time Mike would walk back to college across the common. He had known where and when to lie in wait. So maybe it was Ivo, the fellow mathematician, who had told Finlay. Who had helpfully informed Finlay where to lie in wait.

But surely that wasn't a reason to kill Lily and Helen all those years later and—

Maggie hit her head hard on a projecting lump of granite and swore loudly, the tears smarting.

No, there must be more.

It couldn't be about Mike raping Jude either. Ayda, coldly, didn't give a damn about that. Neither did Ivo. Neither of them were motivated by justice or vengeance or any of the storm of emotions that led Finlay out to that riverbank on a dark, dark night.

Keep going.

How much further? Where can this possibly lead? I can't... I'm going to...

No. Don't think about that. Just keep crawling. One hand in front of the other, drag yourself along like a wounded animal.

'Maggie!' Ivo's voice in the tunnel, not far behind her. She almost screamed. Faster, she told herself. *Move faster.* For a second, her thoughts were only fear, only terror.

Her knees were agony now, knees ripped to shreds by the sharp roughness of the granite.

Keep going.

What did Lily know? What did she tell Helen? Lily knew all along about Mike raping Jude. But did she tell Helen about the rape? How would devastated, distraught Helen have reacted to being told her beloved brother was a rapist?

He was kind to people. Thoughtful. Shy, of course, and very naïve. Elizabeth's words echoed in Maggie's head.

Maggie came to a halt.

Water.

Water was trickling along the tunnel.

The tunnel angled downwards. She hadn't wanted to think about it, but relentlessly, unarguably, she was going deeper underground.

And as she went deeper, slowly, slowly, water was seeping from the top of the tunnel.

Rain.

Far above her head, the rain had been falling on Dartmoor for hours.

Maggie had seen the rivers here rising after a storm. She had seen the streams – threads of water picking their way across a field so delicately – turn into roaring torrents. It took only seconds. This tunnel must have been designed to avoid flooding – one of the old tin mines, maybe? – but in this constant rain…

Maggie choked with horror.

She crept forward a few more yards. More water was trickling from the top of the tunnel here. From a few drops to a constant trickle now, chillingly cold beneath her hands.

A beautiful maid, who lay down in the snow.

Back.

She had to go back.

Impossible.

Maggie collapsed onto her front. She was freezing, bleeding, covered in bruises. She lay there for a moment, feeling the tiredness sweep over her.

She would never make it. It was hopeless. Unbearable.

Her surroundings blurred. She could just lie here, just let the horror float away.

A sound behind her.

Maggie's head jerked.

Ivo. Ivo, who would never surrender. Ivo, who would never give up. Ivo, who had everything to lose.

Maggie thrust herself forward again. The water was deeper now, running away ahead of her. She struggled to keep her phone above water. If she dropped it now, if water seeped into its delicate electronics, it would quench its tiny light, and all its precious memories and she would…

Come on.

Maggie dragged herself along.

Ivo was getting closer, she could hear it. Fuelled by rage, fired by his own sort of despair.

Lily. Helen. It must have been something vital to send him on this hunt. Something all-important. Ayda. A rape.

Ivo's size was a disadvantage down here. In any other situation, he would have caught her by now. Grabbed her, smothered her, left her here to rot. But his shoulders would be jamming in the narrow tunnel and slowing him down, just slightly. He was catching up on her, but she was still just ahead. Just. A burst of something like hope. If he was bothering to chase her, maybe he knew that this narrow awkward tunnel led somewhere.

Or guessed.

Maybe.

Ivo was closer now. She could hear him cursing as he scraped past the granite boulders. It was the breadth of his shoulders, the sheer scale of him. That strength would extinguish her with ease.

Ivo. Rohypnol.

Maggie almost missed it. A second tunnel, leading off the first. Branching up. *Up.*

A jolt of hope. Maggie pulled herself up, forced herself forward again. She was dragging herself away from the menacing stream of water now. Up towards light and air and a new day.

Mike. A mathematician.

But behind her, Ivo, had turned up the tunnel. Of course he had. She sensed that he had accelerated. She must reach the surface soon. Had to.

Ayda, and a weighing machine, and a string of bright red numbers.

Was that a hint of a breeze reaching down the tunnel towards her? Clean Dartmoor wind blowing down into this choking hole?

Apparently, Mike was a bit broken-hearted just before he died.

Faster.

Come on.

A mathematician. An algorithm.

A gasp escaped her. Was that light?

It was the palest possible light. And so far away. But it was light all the same.

Hope.

Maggie fought her way along faster.

Mike had a crush on you before he died.

A grille, she realised. There was something barring her way out. Not far now until she reached it. Nearly there. But what if it was locked? Just get there. Then see. Only a few more yards now. Not far. Ivo had fallen behind. Maggie was benefitting from the light above them, she realised. It was easier for her to worm over rocks and squeeze through the narrownesses, while Ivo was still stuck in the darkness. He might not know that she was seeing light, feeling hope.

Not long now.

Nearly there.

Maggie was gasping for breath, completely exhausted. Her fingers were bleeding, her nails torn away.

An algorithm. An algorithm worth billions.

The grille. What if it was locked? What then?

She reached the grille and threw herself against it.

The gate didn't move. It was solid, wrought-iron, heavy. The handle must have rusted, jammed. She hurled herself against it again.

Nothing.

With an animal panic, Maggie rammed her shoulders against the grille, crunching herself against the unyielding metal again and again. There was the faintest movement. Hurry. She threw herself against the iron and this time it gave a protesting screech. Ivo was crawling up the passage behind her. He was nearly on her. She could hear his breath, almost a snarl.

Maggie flung herself at the grille again, crying out at the pain.

He was so close, reaching out.

The grille yielded and Maggie burst out of the passage.

For a moment, she was disorientated. Granite walls, a blur of green overhead, a cool grey sky. Then she realised where she was. The old chapel, the strange folly down by the tin mine. Maggie hurled herself out through the doorway, the wooden door long since rotted away. She sprinted past the bonfire ash and made for the house.

Her thoughts were a blur. Ivo was just behind her. Where were the others? Ayda… what would she—

Behind her, she heard a curse as Ivo fought his way out of the old chapel. He was so much taller, so much stronger. And out in the fresh air, he would be able to run much faster than her. She would never be able to escape. Never.

Lungs searing, Maggie raced up the hill. There was Wintercross, so beautiful in the dawn light. But she could hear Ivo's footsteps behind her. And he was so fast, so ruthless. There was no hope. There was nothing.

There.

Several small figures outside the house. Maggie redoubled her efforts. One of the figures was ahead of the others, and seemed to be looking down towards the chapel.

No air to scream, no air to pray. Maggie struggled up the hill, slower with every step.

But they had seen her. And they were hurrying down the hill, slipping and sliding over the dewy grass. And Ivo must be able to see them. Must know there was help coming. Must be realising that there would be no quiet murder far beneath the ground.

Keep going.

The first figure was carrying something.

Run.

The first figure was Jude, Maggie realised. And she was carrying a gun.

Ivo must have seen Jude at the same time, because Maggie heard his steps slow, stop.

'Maggie!' Jude's words came down with the wind. 'Maggie, we're coming!'

73

Jude, on Rory: Thank you for looking after me.
I don't think I'll ever be able to repay you, but I
hope I find a way.

Ivo and Maggie came to a halt a few feet apart, both too exhausted to move a step further. Jude was holding a gun in a way that showed she had no idea what she was doing, but it was enough.

Enough.

Maggie slumped down on the ground.

'Point the gun at the ground.' Rory had caught up with Jude now. 'It's over, Ivo. It's over.'

'Jude,' Maggie was beyond exhaustion.

'It's okay,' Jude spoke over her shoulder. 'It's alright, Maggie.'

Maggie's thoughts were becoming clearer, sharpening in the dawn light. 'Ivo... he...'

'We'll work it all out, Maggie. The police are on their way now.'

Maggie wasn't looking at Ivo, but she heard the desperation in his voice. 'No,' he gasped. 'No.'

'It's too fucking late, Ivo,' Jude snapped. 'And this time, they'll get to the bottom of whatever the fuck it was that you did.'

Elizabeth and Ollie reached them, sprinting down from the house. Both looked bewildered, both horrified.

'You *can't—*' Ivo took a step towards Jude.

It was Ollie who jumped forward, blocking his path. 'Ivo! What the fuck?'

'I know…' Maggie managed to force out the words. 'I worked out what he did.'

'What?' Jude looked across at Maggie for a second, and then snapped her attention back to Ivo.

'I know what happened.'

'What did he do then? Go on.'

Maggie was lying on the sheep-cropped grass, struggling to get her breath back. She was soaked from head to toe, shivering with cold.

'What the hell's going on?' asked Ollie. 'Ivo, you—'

Jude cut him off him with a gesture. 'Maggie knows something. She's going to tell us.'

'Mike…' Maggie gasped the words. 'Mike had a crush on you, Jude.'

An impatient shake of Jude's head. 'I know that… that doesn't—'

'Ivo knew about it. Ivo knew that Mike was crazy about you. And all those years ago, Mike… Mike was working on an algorithm.'

Jude turned to stare at her, the gun sagging towards the ground. There was a realisation creeping into her eyes.

'So what, Maggie?'

'That prediction about Ayda and Finlay being superheroes together,' said Maggie. 'From that time they found Katia in the flowerbeds in Great Court. Ayda *saw* what someone was like after they'd been roofied. She *knew*.'

'She knew what?' *Don't say it*, said Jude's eyes. *Don't. I can't bear it.*

'I think Ayda got hold of the Rohypnol,' said Maggie. 'And Ivo told Mike that you liked him. That Mike's feelings were reciprocated. And then…'

'Then what?' Jude's voice was empty.

'Then,' Maggie's eyes were on the gun, 'they gave Mike lots to drink and they gave you the Rohypnol.' Maggie could see it so clearly. Jude, reeling, out of control. Mike, shy, nervous. And besotted.

Go on, Mike. She really likes you. She was saying earlier how much she fancies you. Go on, you idiot. Jude's crazy about you. Oh, Christ, look at that. You'd better help her back to her room, anyway. Go on, Mike. Go on.

Jude, stumbling away. And Mike… Mike following.

'Ivo knew that Mike was working on some ground-breaking maths,' Jude said slowly. 'Maths that would change the world. And maybe no one else knew about it yet. Nobody else understood what it might do.'

'Yes,' Maggie nodded. 'Ivo wanted Mike out of the picture. If Mike was discredited, if Mike was jailed… then Ivo could steal the algorithm.'

'That algorithm is the basis of SummerX,' said Ollie. 'The basis of everything.'

'Ayda and Ivo,' Jude, almost wonderingly. 'They did it on purpose.'

'Ivo stole the algorithm.'

'And used it to make his billions.'

'Yes,' said Maggie. 'But it all depended on Mike going to jail for rape. And when the police didn't even try for a conviction, Ivo sent Finlay out to seek revenge. Then Finlay and Rory came back after attacking Mike, saying they'd beaten him up and left him on the common. But that wasn't enough. It wasn't enough at all. It was Ivo who walked out along the river while it was still dark. It was Ivo who shoved Mike into the river. Finlay was the one covered in blood but it was Ivo. Ivo was the one who killed him.'

'You bastard!' Jude's scream made Maggie jump. Jude swung round, raising the gun. 'You pathetic little creep.'

The gun was wavering in the air, pointing at Ivo, pointing at all his cruelties.

'Jude!' Rory leapt forward. 'Don't. For God's sake, don't.'

Ivo was cowering away, quivering on the grass.

'You ruined my life!' Jude bellowed. 'You and fucking Ayda. And for what? For a few more millions? You already had *everything*.'

'Jude.'

'All those years!' Jude shouted. She shook with rage. 'All those fucking years. And you sat in Finlay's room, telling me to go to the police. Telling me that your father would call the Chief Constable. And it was all just to get rid of Mike for your own bloody reasons. It was all because of you.'

'Ivo told Ollie to claim that they'd all been together,' Maggie said quietly. 'Ollie, Rory, Finlay, Ivo, they all said that they were together that night. And of course, by saying that, they were all giving Ivo an alibi too.'

Ollie was shaking his head. 'Ivo,' he was saying. 'I can't believe—'

Useful idiot, Maggie thought. I know just how that feels.

'For all those years,' Rory was shaking his head. 'I believed it was Finlay. That Finlay killed that boy. We've spent *decades* thinking that Fin was a murderer. And it was you, Ivo… all along, it was *you*.'

Ivo got to his feet. The mask was back on his face now. With the splendour of Wintercross behind him, it was only the splashes of mud, the soaking clothes that gave him away. He didn't say a word.

'You ruined so many lives,' bawled Jude. 'You absolute—'

'Don't, Jude,' said Maggie. 'Don't. The police will take him away.'

'And Ayda!' Jude screamed. 'That bitch. Where is she?'

'She's up at the house,' Rory managed to keep his voice calm somehow. 'Finlay is with her. He won't let her get away.'

'I hate her!' Jude yelled. 'I *hate* her.'

'Jude.'

'Why would she do that to me?!' screamed Jude. 'Why?'

'She might not have known what Ivo was going to do to you,' said Maggie. 'She might only have worked it out afterwards.' But even as she spoke, she could remember Ayda's disdain for Jude all those years ago. Cool Jude, who came from nowhere to be best friends with Lily, Ayda's childhood friend. Sexy Jude, who all the boys fancied. Clever Jude, and her undisguised contempt for Ayda and everything she represented. A vicious rage jagging through the gloss.

'Stupid, fucking... how could she do it? How could *anyone*?'

Maggie thought of the layers of secrets and sadness. 'I don't know,' she said quietly.

'And Lily. How could Ayda? How could *she*? Lily was her *friend*.'

'I think Lily knew something,' said Maggie slowly. 'I think Lily knew enough to take Ivo and Ayda down.'

'Even so... to *push* her.'

'Ayda was desperate.'

'I hope she spends the rest of her shitty little life in jail.'

'I think Ayda supplied the Rohypnol to Ivo.' Maggie put it together slowly, piece by piece. 'And that was what started her dependency on him. If that had ever come out, she would have lost her job instantly. But then it became more than that. He handed her the SummerX business, which was crucial to her career, and she became more and more tied in with Ivo, with everything.'

'Yes, but... *Lily*.'

'Ayda was sad, Jude. She was so lost. Lily turning out to be her half-sister, it might have been the last straw.'

'Still.'

'And there was something else, too,' said Maggie. 'The most important thing.'

'What was that?'

'Ayda was in love with Ivo, all the way along,' Maggie said simply. 'She would have done anything for him.' She caught the briefest gleam in Ivo's eye. Even now, even here, he knew his power. Knew it and enjoyed it.

'Ayda...' Jude murmured. 'Loved *him*?'

'It became a habit,' said Maggie. 'A way of life. An addiction.'

Turning away from Ivo, Maggie looked over the cool of the Dartmoor dawn. The breeze was catching the long moorland grass now, a soft sea ripple of green.

'It's *pathetic*.'

'I know how Ayda felt,' Maggie admitted. 'I know how it feels.' She turned back to Ivo, looked him straight in the eye. 'But we all grow up in the end.'

'Why?' asked Ollie. 'Why the hell did you do it, Ivo?'

'His father was a ruthless fucker,' said Rory flatly. 'Take what you want: that was what Ivo was taught from day one.'

'But he already had all this.' Ollie looked around.

'He wanted more,' said Maggie.

She remembered that shock when she first arrived at Trinity. Going from sixth-form star to ordinary undergraduate. Ivo must have been hit by the same bombshell, she guessed, but for him it struck so much harder. The golden boy one moment, unremarkable the next. He must have watched with a cold jealousy as others accelerated, as others danced up against the boundaries of all that is known.

His father, dismissive. Shrugging. *Just as I expected.*

Because it was Mike – ginger, unremarkable, a *nobody* – who had found the key. Mike was the golden boy.

For Ivo, it went against the natural order of things. For Ivo, it was unacceptable.

He had always liked to manipulate. To test. Carrot, *here*, stick, *there*.

And he had Ayda.

Ayda, who adored him.

He could – Maggie admitted to herself – just as easily have chosen Maggie herself to carry out his dirty work.

It was probably just because Ayda was the wilder one, Ayda was the one who could easily tag a few Rohypnol tablets onto her order.

Just one decision.

A sound from the house and they all spun around.

Ayda and Finlay had emerged, Ayda tiny beside Finlay's bulk.

Come down, Rory gestured and when Finlay and Ayda reached them, Rory told his brother, in as few words as possible.

For a moment, Finlay couldn't take it in. 'But I don't understand.' He was shaking his head. 'I don't… it was *Ivo* who killed Mike. Ivo?'

Ivo's face was blank, admitting nothing.

'He'll never admit it,' Jude's voice was contemptuous. 'But we'll always know the truth.'

'Years of my life,' said Finlay slowly. 'For years of my life, I thought I killed Mike.'

'You didn't,' said Rory. 'You didn't kill him.'

'But how could anyone… and Lily. *Lily.*'

'I'm sorry, Fin,' murmured Rory. 'I'm truly sorry.'

'You bastard.' Finlay stepped towards Ivo, the violence bubbling to the surface. 'You unspeakable shit.'

'Don't.' Rory got between them. 'Not now, Finlay.'

Finlay scraped his hands back through his hair, digging his fingers hard into his scalp.

'I can never get that time back.' For once Finlay's physical power seemed to have drained away. 'It's all gone.'

'It's not all gone, Finlay.' Rory insisted. 'There is so much more ahead.'

'Not for you.' Jude stared at Ayda with a molten spite. 'How could you, Ayda? How could you be such a pathetic little *handmaiden* to a man like that?'

Because that was what they had been, Maggie thought. Still, after everything.

Women, disposable.

'Lily,' Maggie murmured. 'Lily. She was your *friend*, Ayda. She'd known you her whole life. She was your *sister*.'

'She knew what you were, didn't she?' Jude said viciously. 'That was why she was dangerous to you. Because she *knew* you.'

'I filmed you,' Maggie said to Ayda. 'I filmed you and Ivo screaming at each other in your bedroom.' Just for a second, the lawyer mask crumbled, a flame of humiliation burning across Ayda's face. Then the mask was back, unreadable.

'You never meant anything to him,' Jude was watching Ayda closely. 'You were just a tool.'

'I wasn't.' The words burst out of Ayda, then her mouth was tight shut again, her lips a thin line.

'You're going to jail, Ayda.' Jude sounded dismissive now. 'Where you belong.'

'I thought we were friends,' said Maggie. 'I thought we were *friends*.'

Just for a second, Ayda glanced at her. 'What,' Ayda asked, 'does that even mean?'

'How did you know to come out here?' Maggie asked Jude. 'How did you guess where I was headed?' The two of them had walked away from the rest of the group, Finlay and Rory standing guard.

'I heard them.' Jude glanced up towards the old house. 'Ayda and Ivo were talking about a passage out to the old chapel. Ivo had opened his gun safe and then he suddenly just disappeared. I couldn't work out where he had gone at all, but I figured it had to have something to do with the chapel. So, I grabbed a gun too and headed out here. It's a bloody arsenal he's got up there. For murdering wildlife, or anything else that might stand in his way.'

'It must have been impossible to get the gun along that tunnel,' said Maggie. 'He must have just abandoned it down there. Impossible to get a shot down there too.'

Fleetingly grateful.

'I suppose so.'

'I'm surprised you didn't gun down Ayda.'

'No,' said Jude. Something caught the corner of Maggie's eye. She looked at Wintercross, dark beneath the dawn. A blue light was flickering up the drive. Jude looked up with a sudden smile. 'I called the police,' she said.

74

Maggie, on Lily: Lily will have learned to be
Lily. And it will be wonderful.

Eight months later, they gathered at Barras Tor. The sky was wide and
blue and there was a sparkle of frost in the air. Early March. Spring,
arriving slowly.

One of the police officers had grudgingly emailed Finlay's solicitors a
photograph of the last scraps of paper. Maggie's real prediction, which
Ayda had stolen and replaced with a page from the hydrangea blue
Moleskine notepad. The police had found the original prediction balled
up in Ayda's room. Evidence, it was now. Rory read the words aloud, and
then turned towards the moor. Grass and heather, gorse and a couple of
scruffy brown ponies.

'Lily,' he said quietly. 'How we wish you were here. It would have been
wonderful. It would have been wonderful indeed.'

In silent agreement, they had skirted Wintercross, and approached
Barras Tor from the north side of the moor. It stood jagged as a broken
tooth, the scree tumbling away on all sides. Far below, Maggie could see
one of the Dartmoor reservoirs glinting in the sun. Helen had abandoned her car beyond one of those reservoirs, over on the west side of
Dartmoor.

That reservoir, surrounded by pine forests, had taken up a lot of the
searchers' time when Helen first went missing. Her mother had raised

the alarm within a day of her daughter disappearing. Had begged, and pleaded and searched on her own. The car was found, silent and alone, not far from the reservoir car park. After a cursory search of the pine woods, the wide expanse of water was the obvious place to start. Sympathetic and pragmatic, the boats and the divers had gone out. Rosemary and Anthony Jansen standing desperate on the banks. Like fishermen's wives when the storms blow in, the rain sheeting across the grey sheen of the water.

Eventually, search and rescue had admitted defeat. Packed up their vans and left. Rosemary was left alone, staring out over the darkness of the reservoir.

And all the time, the rain poured down.

At first, Helen's death looked like an accident. Or a suicide, maybe. Odd, perhaps, that she had walked five miles from where she parked the car. But they all knew she had been distraught about her brother, possibly hypothermic. This was back in February after all. Or March, it was maybe, by then. Nobody was quite sure.

It had been an odd place to abandon a car, perhaps. Beyond the reservoir service road, there was only a bumpy track used occasionally by the Army when they came up to practise killing people. That petered out into heather and low-growing gorse. It was here that Helen had pulled over. She must have climbed out of her car. Left her phone behind and walked out into the Dartmoor darkness wearing only a thin sweatshirt, jeans, trainers.

In the days after she was last seen alive, the temperature fell below zero shortly after nightfall, and nightfall came early. The bogs froze to muddy ice. There was fog, too, the moon blotted out. By the time she was a hundred feet from the car, Helen would have been hopelessly, impossibly lost.

It was madness. Suicide, it had to be.

After the police were summoned to Wintercross, they thought again. Slowly, the jigsaw was put together. They wondered if Helen had been following Ayda's car up that bumpy track. They wondered if Helen had followed Ayda thinking they were nearly at Wintercross, believing that she was so close to knowing – *finally* knowing – the truth about her brother's death.

Perhaps they had passed a parked car. Or maybe it had followed them, gradually drawing closer. And then maybe all three cars came to a sudden jarring halt: an ambush.

Maybe Helen didn't call for help because someone had a gun.

Maybe she scrambled out of the car. Left her phone and ran.

Maybe she still thought then that she might escape.

Helen didn't know Dartmoor.

No, her parents agreed much later. *She'd never been to that part of the country. And she'd been abroad for almost twenty years. You forget what it can be like out there in the wilderness. Even though it's England, it's…*

Helen wouldn't have known about the rocky hillsides where the ground fell away from one step to the next. She wouldn't have known about the icy rivers, roaring, angry from the endless rain. She wouldn't have known about the bogs, every step deeper, until even one more step was impossible.

She didn't know.

'If that's how they did it, they had nerves of steel,' one of the police officers said grudgingly to Maggie. 'Letting her run off into the dark like that. She could have made it all the way across the moor. Maybe. She might have survived.' The police officer shook his head again. 'You couldn't be *sure* she would die.'

After that, Maggie had wondered about Gulliver, the old hunter, bay and unsuspecting. Trudging up to the moor, his head hanging low. In the darkness – in the impenetrable blackness of that long February night – there was nothing to see, nothing to remember. And only hoofprints left behind, up where the ponies ran wild.

Hoofprints, so insignificant, washed away by the rain.

She hasn't come home yet.

Maggie imagined Helen running, as the sleet turned to snow. Clawing her way up the tors, plunging down hillsides. Stumbling, desperate. Followed, all the time, by the clink of the bridle here, the creak of a saddle there. Relentless, remorseless, wherever she ran, wherever she hid. Ivo, who knew every inch of the moor, and was dressed for the weather. Ivo, hunting.

A beautiful maid, who lay down in the snow.

Ivo was riding a horse who knew the way home through rain and through fog. Untiring, determined, with those infrared goggles, perhaps. Maybe Helen thought she was escaping. Maybe she thought she was disappearing, as she ran and ran. While all the time, she was just a blundering shape, bright red against the miles of bitter blue. Bright red as she was nudged further and further into the darkness.

Footsteps in a rose garden. *Who's there? Who's there?*

Maggie imagined the sprint turning to a stagger. She imagined the despair. The slow-growing realisation: *you're not meant to survive this.*

Dartmoor: so lethal.

Which way is it? Where am I?

She stumbles into a stream and now she's soaked through in icy water. And now the cold bites even deeper. Now the thoughts begin to twist and flail.

How is this possible? How? Here? Just a few miles from warmth and safety and blameless modern life?

She limps over uneven ground. The gorse rips blood-stained slashes. There is no way forward, no way back. Another fall on hard, bruising granite and beyond lies the bog. And now every footstep is weighed down by freezing mud and every movement is exhausting.

Not this way, no. Back again, back.

But somewhere there is the ring of metal on granite. A horseshoe clipping a rock.

Him.

Run.

The motions are awkward now, clumsy, broken. Arms and legs no longer follow orders. Another stumble into an icy stream. She drags herself out one final time, battered, bleeding, and collapses by the side of the river.

You have to get up.

A frantic effort.

You can't stay here.

Another desperate struggle.

But it's not enough.

Never enough.

If you stay here…

Standing is unimaginable.

Slowly, the thoughts begin to drift away. Suddenly it's easier to lie here. Easier to listen to the wind whistle through the tors. Easier to watch the fog billow and swirl.

She hasn't come home yet.

And all the time, somewhere in the distance, there is the clink of the bridle as the horse tosses his head and waits.

Where am I… Where am I… How can this be… ?

And further back – so much further back – there is the jangle of empty stirrups, an exhausted horse trotting into the stable yard.

And a small boy looking out over the darkness of the moors.

For another woman, lost in the heart of the moor.

A small boy waiting for his mother.

She hasn't come home yet.

'Why didn't they find her earlier?' Maggie asked, afterwards. And the police officer shrugged, half-embarrassed.

'They sent up a helicopter at the time,' he shrugged. 'But Ms Jansen had died of exposure long before that, so there was no heat signature, you know? And she was a long way from her car, and that tor's got a rocky underhanging part. She'd hidden under there. And she'd got much further than you'd expect, too.' He paused for a second. 'Tough girl.'

That was probably what happened.

Probably.

Probably, because Ayda still wasn't talking.

It took the police a long time to link Ayda to any of it. Helen had definitely gone to Ayda's flat. The police had talked to Ayda last March, it turned out. Ayda was the last person to have seen Helen alive, so naturally, they knocked on her door.

Helen told her mother that she was going to visit you, Miss Nassar. Helen had been all over the place, from what we can make out. Asking about her brother. Mr Michael Jansen.

Oh yes, poor Helen. She was crying when she was here. Just couldn't stop. She was so upset about her brother, poor thing. I should have called her parents and told them she was in such a state. You've got no idea where she is now?

Afraid not. Her mother would like to talk to you. Would you mind if we passed along your number?

What? I guess so. Sure.

Helen's habit of turning up on doorsteps – Finlay's, Elizabeth's – hadn't left much of an electronic fingerprint. Helen hadn't told poor devastated Rose Jensen about any of those visits, so the police never made it to Finlay or Elizabeth. It had been, in hindsight, a half-hearted search. There was not much in the way of publicity, no televised pleas. If a story about a Helen Jansen had ever popped up on the wires, Maggie's eyes must have just floated over it, never drawing the dots to a red-headed mathematician who died all those years ago.

Just another missing person.

The security cameras had picked Helen up as she was buzzed through reception by the concierge at Ayda's mansion block. After an hour or so, Helen left alone. The security cameras had seen that too. Helen had stopped at a petrol station, before driving all the way down to Devon. Cameras monitored her travelling down the M4, the M5, the A30. She was alone in the car, all the way. No one, back then, noticed that the A30 turn-off was four miles from Wintercross.

Helen's car disappeared into the darkness of the lanes.

A few days later, it was noticed not far from the reservoir.

Ayda's phone had stayed in her flat all weekend. Her car never left the underground garage at the mansion block either. The sporty little BMW – scarlet, a present from her father – didn't show up on any of the cameras all the way along the M4, the M5, the A30.

I spent the weekend chilling out and then worked from home on Monday and most of Tuesday. My company's cool with that, nowadays. I didn't get up to much. Reading mostly. It's been a tough time at work, the last few weeks. Knackering, really.

Throwleigh Pearce, actually.

Yes. Yes, I am a lawyer.

The security camera footage the police had collected stayed on file, because Helen was still missing. By June, the rest of the CCTV footage from around the flat had been long overwritten. Thirty days, roughly, they keep it. It was long gone. So they couldn't tie Ayda to the journey down to Devon. The police swore that Ayda could not have travelled down in Helen's old blue Freelander. There were no fingerprints, no DNA, nothing. None of the cameras spotted her.

'It was February,' an officer suggested. 'Maybe she was wearing a coat? Gloves? And sleeping in the back so the cameras just missed her?'

'Not for all that time,' someone else insisted. 'It's what? Three hours? Four? We would have found something. Seen something.'

'Could she have taken the train?'

'The cameras in the mansion block's reception didn't catch her leaving the flat.'

It was just chance that the police had held onto footage taken from the petrol station just down the road from Ayda's flat. Helen had sat in a parking space next to the petrol station for fifteen minutes, staring vacantly into space.

It was only when they looked back through it, and saw a silver Polo hesitate for a moment beside Helen's car that a clever young detective realised. One of Ayda's neighbours had a son. Jaded and nineteen, his car easily borrowed for forty-eight hours. A silver Polo, parked two spaces from the bright red BMW in the underground garage. Swapped for a few lines because old habits die hard. Coke, just one of the many currencies that Ayda had lying around in the flat.

The Polo drove out of the underground car park, the driver ducking her head under a baseball cap. Then Helen's Freelander followed the Polo all the way to Devon, their indicators clicking in unison.

The Polo was home by Monday morning.

The sun came out on Wednesday, briefly, the day that Lily died.

Maggie wondered what Ayda had said to Helen.

We'd better take two cars, because I may need to zoom back to London for work. I'll meet you outside, yeah? By that petrol station.

Or maybe Helen had demanded to be taken down to Ivo and it was all rather less chatty than that.

Ivo had flown back to England on the Saturday afternoon, the police discovered, landing in Exeter while Helen and Ayda were still on the way down to Devon. The private jet had sat on the Stuttgart tarmac while he flew back and forth on commercial flights. Afterwards, Ivo and Ayda probably spent the night at Wintercross, the police guessed. They had to guess because they never found any trace of Ayda's car up at the reservoir, a fact that Ayda's lawyers – criminal lawyers paid for by Ayda's devastated, dying father – leapt upon.

They had to guess because no one saw either of them at the house. Mrs Vereker had stayed down at the gatehouse that weekend. *Ivo said he just wanted downtime. I never go up when he says that. I let myself in after he's gone, give the place a good tidy. He's a good boss.*

'DNA doesn't do well outside,' the police officer told Maggie laconically. They were deep into the off-the-record chats by now. 'Or in the wet. You wouldn't expect to find anything much up there all these months later.'

'And you never thought to check on Ivo's connection to Helen Jansen? The fact that Ayda had been at university with both Mike and Ivo?' asked Maggie. 'You never noticed that Helen's car had been abandoned so close to Wintercross?'

'There was nothing to link Mr Fitzwilliam to Ms Jensen,' he said slightly defensively. 'Not then. The car was abandoned on the other side of the moor from the house.'

'Ayda had claimed she was on the phone to him when Lily died.'

'They were two separate investigations in Ms Jensen's and Ms Blake's deaths,' the police officer said, looking down at the ground. 'London was looking at Lily Blake's death and that investigation knew Ms Nassar had called Mr Fitzwilliam. But Devon and Cornwall were looking at Helen Jensen's death and they never had Mr Fitzwilliam on their radar.'

They never knew what Helen had said to Lily, or what Lily had said to Helen. Maggie guessed that Lily – clever, medically trained Lily – had made the same calculations that she had made deep down in that pitch black tunnel.

Helen, so adamant that Mike never could, never would do anything like that.

Although he had.

He was so *naïve* though. He would never even have heard of Rohypnol.

But Lily had grown up alongside Ayda. Lily knew all about Ayda, and her little weighing machine. And she knew about Katia, collapsed in a flowerbed.

Maybe Lily's mind had followed the right trajectory much faster.

Maybe Lily had suspected all along.

What her old friend and her new sister had done.

Several of Lily's colleagues remembered a woman with auburn hair waiting outside the hospital on the Friday evening before she died. A nurse had left at the same time as Lily. They had been chatting, sharing a bag of crisps, before they were interrupted.

Are you Lily Blake?

Yes. Sorry, who are—

My name is Helen Jansen. Please, I need to speak to you.

By Saturday morning, Helen was outside Ayda's mansion block.

Phone records showed that Lily had called Ayda on Sunday morning.

There had been no answer. The phone must have been left in the flat.

But by then Lily knew too much.

Maggie remembered her own phone call from Lily that weekend, the uncertainty in her voice. *Maggie, I'm scared.*

Lily had spoken to Jude, too. But she hadn't told Jude anything either, not yet. Maybe she would have, eventually.

Maybe not.

Because back then, Helen was only missing.

And perhaps Lily walked out onto that train platform still believing in friendship.

75

Jude, on Ayda: Still Daddy's girl, when she
could be so much more.

Ayda had hidden that prediction too, in a tight ball in her bedroom.
Maggie imagined Ayda picking her way through the Venetian bowl,
confronted by an unfaceable truth.

'She moved on from being a Daddy's girl towards the end.' Jude
acknowledged. 'Money-wise, she could. Doing so well at that law firm.
It's tragic, really.'

Because instead of growing free, she had fallen to Ivo.

'It was a bit mean, that prediction,' said Elizabeth.

Jude laughed mirthlessly, 'She did plot to kill me, Elizabeth.'

'Probably after reading that prediction.'

The wind stung Maggie's eyes and whipped her hair across her face. She
turned to face it, tipping her head back and defying the storm's rage.
When she closed her eyes, she was back in the tunnel. Scrambling,
scrabbling, desperate to survive. With Ivo, so close behind.

The cold, the dark, the terror. It was embedded deep in her bones.

No.

Try and remember seeing that blue flicker of police lights across the
moors: try and hold on, hold on, hold on.

Ayda was in jail, awaiting trial.

Throwleigh Pearce suspended her, without missing a beat.

'Ayda was terrified of losing her job, wasn't she?' said Finlay thoughtfully. 'I think she believed it was all she had.'

'Ivo had made her so dependent on him,' said Maggie. 'Ayda had brought the SummerX business to Throwleigh Pearce and that was a big part of her making partner so young.'

Ayda, the intellectual property lawyer, valuing information, valuing secrets.

'Do you think that was how Ivo got her to...' Elizabeth paused, 'do everything?'

Maggie thought of Ivo whispering down one of the burner phones the police guessed they'd had. *If Lily tells... if Helen tells... we have to stop them, Ayda. We have to, or we'll both be in jail forever. This is what we'll do.*

And, later, Ivo providing her alibi from Devon. A sort of partnership.

'I think that Ivo was the one constant in Ayda's life, and every time she tried to move on from him, he found a way of drawing her back in. He did it to everyone, really.'

All the relationships that never quite stuck.

Not enough.

Never enough.

Maggie had wondered – many times – if Ayda had done it all to save herself.

Or to save Ivo.

'Imagine,' said Jude, 'if work was all you had.'

There was a new light in Jude's eyes. She hadn't had a drink since they left Wintercross.

'Don't laugh,' she had said to Maggie a few weeks into the New Year, 'but I'm going to be a lawyer.'

'You'll be brilliant, Jude.' Delighted, Maggie reached out to touch Jude's hand. Jude glowed, looking younger, happier, hopeful.

'The organisation that Genet used to work for – violence against women and girls – I'm going to work there around my training. Sodding hard work, but it's great.'

'I'm so, so glad.'

Finlay had accepted a caution for assault after the CPS decided that a prosecution for a twenty-year-old GBH was unlikely to succeed.

'I still feel guilty,' Finlay had said to Maggie. 'And I always, always will. If I hadn't attacked Mike, Ivo would never have killed him. But I didn't kill Mike, I know that now.'

Rory was chastened. Demoted to the backbenches in the uproar, but still clinging on. 'Jude saved me, really. Without her...'

That was Jude in an impassioned article in the *Guardian*, dancing very carefully through the contempt laws. Rory and Finlay, the heroes. Young Finlay, hopelessly in love. Impulsive, yes. Headstrong, yes. But not – never – a murderer.

It was understandable, almost. Heroic, according to some.

The debate had rumbled on for weeks.

She was almost unconscious. She never consented. It was rape.

He thought she liked him. And it was different back then. Back then, boys... she didn't even know she'd been raped.

It was rape.

He didn't know she had been drugged.

He knew she was hammered.

He didn't deserve to die though.

Maybe not.

Maybe.

Ivo was dead.

He had broken away from them, Jude jerking the gun in his direction, pointing the gun at his back as he sprinted away towards his house, towards his birthright.

'No!' shouted Rory, grabbing her hand. 'No! Not another murder, Jude!'

After Jude dropped the gun, Finlay grabbed it, handling it with an easy familiarity. In case Ivo came back with another gun, Maggie realised.

But it hadn't been that. As the four of them stared up at Wintercross, there was a single gunshot.

As the blue lights flickered closer, Ivo had made his choice.

Ivo never touched Helen, Maggie thought. When the obvious thing would have been to kill her as she ran across the icy moor and then to bury her somewhere. To drag her to one of the mines that honeycombed this land, his land, and abandon her to an eternal darkness.

But maybe he remembered his own youth. The fourteen-year-olds, the fifteen-year-olds, out on the moor in all weathers. Inquisitive, fearless, wide-eyed.

Or perhaps that sharp mathematical mind simply preferred to leave a question mark to avoid a thousand questions.

Or perhaps it was something else. Not getting your hands dirty. Wintercross, where the maids went tidily out to the hills to die alone in their terror.

Perhaps.

Maybe the boy who had learned manipulation from the cradle just enjoyed puppeteering.

Footsteps in a rose garden.

Lily, pushed sharply by someone else.

Helen, edged to her death.

And a proxy rape.

Only as a last resort did he actually touch his victims.

Coward.

And Ayda left to face justice alone.

'It's almost funny, isn't it?' Jude chucked a small chunk of heather root at a tuft of grass.

'What is?' Maggie was leaning back against Barras Tor. The granite was cold and oddly comforting in its immobility. Elizabeth had brought a Thermos, and was pouring tea for everyone.

'It's just quite funny that Ivo assumed Mike would be jailed for rape,' Jude took a swig of tea.

'What do you mean?'

'It just obviously never, ever occurred to Ivo that Mike would simply go free. That no one would really care that Mike had raped me.'

'In all his scheming, in all his conniving,' Maggie agreed, 'Ivo failed to spot that rape convictions barely exist.'

'Ivo was so entitled, so embedded in the *patriarchy*,' Jude rolled her eyes at the word, 'that it never even crossed his mind that his clever little plan would inevitably fail because no one would believe my word over Mike's.'

'I remember him saying that his father would call the Chief Constable,' Rory was shaking his head, 'and I thought it was so cool to be able to just ring up whoever you wanted like that.'

'That's why Ivo thought there would be a conviction,' said Jude. 'He probably expected my words to be worthless, but it must have been a surprise that even when the Fitzwilliams got involved, still – *still* – nothing was done.'

'Yes,' Elizabeth nodded. 'That was probably it.'

'If Mike had gone to jail,' Jude shook her head, 'he would still be alive today. Helen would be alive. Lily would be alive. And Ivo... Ivo would be alive too.'

SummerX was deep in litigation. The Jansens, shattered all over again, were suing. Mike's algorithm: the root of SummerX's fortunes. SummerX – with a nervous interim CEO in place – was proposing a new foundation to fight violence against women and girls.

Jude and the Jansens would be trustees.

Elizabeth passed around home-made brownies. She and Ollie were – unexpectedly – sitting next to each other. Not holding hands though, a long way to go.

'We grew up together, really.' Elizabeth shrugged. 'Didn't we? That matters. I'm training as a therapist, by the way. I decided at Ivo's funeral.'

'Well.' Jude stuffed a brownie in her mouth. 'You'll certainly be incisive.'

Maggie thought of Ivo inviting Lily and Ollie down for that weekend at Wintercross. Throwing them to each other, knowing what would happen.

Ivo, Cupid, again.

'I'm not being defeated by him,' said Elizabeth. 'I will not be manipulated.'

'And I,' Ollie made it a joke, 'certainly don't want to be Ivo fucking Fitzwilliam any more.'

They had all gone to Ivo's funeral. Awkwardly, almost silently. He had been buried at the Wintercross church, the local vicar soothing his agitated congregation into a sulky acquiescence. Only a small crowd attended, a group drawn to Dartmoor without knowing quite why. A distant cousin organised the funeral, reminding Maggie how few close relatives Ivo had. As the coffin was carried outside, Maggie's eyes had drifted across to Verity Fitzwilliam's grave, *requiescat in pace.*

Ashes to ashes, dust to dust.

And gold to base. A reverse sort of alchemy.

As she wandered back to the house for the wake, Maggie had realised that she was walking next to Luke Russell, Ivo's old school friend. The woman next to him – long blonde hair, elegant black coat, a huge diamond on her finger – must be his wife.

'Maggie,' Luke managed, just before it became awkward. 'It's been years. How are you?'

'Oh. Fine. Thank you, Luke.'

For a moment, they smiled at each other, remembering that night two decades ago. Pills and ghosts and kissing Ayda to Faithless.

'How is Ayda?' Luke's good-looking brow creased.

'I don't know,' said Maggie. 'We haven't spoken.'

'That night,' said Luke. 'That was the night that I…'

'Yes.' Maggie thought for a few seconds. 'Ivo must have used the secret passages to scare us all. Put speakers in them or something, to create his ghost.'

The old house, its secrets like arteries.

A house built around secrets.

'I was really into you back then,' said Luke, his eyes looking backwards to old memories.

'Me?' Maggie was startled. '*Me*?'

'Yes.' Luke laughed. 'I'd told Ivo I thought you were fit.'

'So classy, darling.' Luke's wife smiled, too beautiful to be worried about a past dalliance. Louella, that was her name. Some Duke's daughter.

'I didn't know,' said Maggie. 'I never knew that.'

She could almost hear Ivo's voice in her ear.

Luke thinks Ayda likes me.

Kiss me.

Oh Ivo, she thought. Ivo.

You fool.

Maggie thought about the secret places burrowed out. Those darkest of places, gouged out by sadness and malice and fear and desperation. Wintercross, a house of forgotten secrets.

It was on the market now, its secrets lost forever.

A third cousin in America was going to inherit millions.

They never found Ivo's prediction about Maggie.

And Maggie always wondered.

Far above their heads, a sparrowhawk was riding the wind.

'I miss him,' said Maggie, without thinking. 'I know I shouldn't, but I do.'

Murmurs. Mutters. A sort of assent.

'Pulling out the arrow,' said Jude, 'doesn't cure the wound.'

'It doesn't,' said Maggie. She watched the sparrowhawk rise up through the air. 'But one day, maybe, we'll be who we're meant to be.'

Nothing could ever be proved about the death of Verity Fitzwilliam and Maggie would always wonder what Ivo knew.

Eight-year-old eyes, empty stirrups, and those very oldest of rumours.

And a mind trained from the cradle to think through all the possibilities.

He must have known, in the end.

How the Fitzwilliam men dealt with troublesome women.

But by then there was no one to tell and only secrets to keep.

And Dartmoor, a witch-dark accomplice.

She hasn't come home yet...

A beautiful maid, who lay down in the snow...

And a murder in the dark.

ACKNOWLEDGEMENTS

I thought this book was inspired by a conversation in my final year of university with the phenomenally brilliant Sebastian Isaac. I was *sure* that we had discussed writing down where we would all be in twenty years' time, and reading our predictions over a weekend in the then unimaginable 2023. However, Seb is equally sure that this conversation never happened. And given that he got a double-starred first and is now an *extremely* esteemed KC (yes, the exact trajectory we would all have predicted for him), I am going to have to go with his version of events. If I did, in fact, have this conversation with someone completely different, I am sorry! Third year was... a little wild. But thanks for being a generally wonderful friend, Seb, even if you didn't inspire this book. And thanks for helping out with libel advice on various occasions.

To the rest of my university friends, do re-read that last sentence.

No, seriously, writing this book has forced me to look back over those years with so much affection. It was such a wonderful, magical, unrepeatable time. Thank you – all of you – for sharing that adventure.

More specifically, thank you Collette Lyons, one half of Ellery Lloyd, for your wonderful words of wisdom as I wrote this book. Thank you Felicity Fitzgerald for being such a brilliant friend (and getting that Wellcome Trust funding – wooooooooo – you just told me while I was writing this!).

Harry Wardill, Imogen Collingwood, Cressida Pollock, Laura Stanning, Laura Wood, Adam Lister, Jo Katz, Antonia Williams, Margot Hill-Landolt, Maria Angelicoussis, Linda Zell, Toby Darbyshire; you all bring back particularly fond memories too. Thank you. Well, not you so much, Toby.

Writing this book made me think about friendship in all its different forms. Sarah Mahmud, Alice Wood, Jessica Sheehan, Alex Marrache, Claire Newell, Robert Winnett, Catriona Ward, Miriam Kelly – the word friendship makes me think of you.

Thank you also to Ivo Stourton for being zen about your name being stolen. 'Does he have any redeeming qualities at all?'

'Um.'

Sorry about that...

Thank you to Will Wintercross for being zen about your name being stolen, too. It *is* a cool house, isn't it?

I am also very grateful to the staff and volunteers at the various sites I visited, in particular the teams at Harvington Hall, Coughton Court and Baddesley Clinton. An especially big thank you to Patrick Clifford at Bradford's Builders Merchants for telling me all about the mining sites on Dartmoor and helping me locate the one that became a key inspiration.

For the last few years, I have been lucky enough to live on Dartmoor, and I am so happy here. I am especially happy here because of friends like Becky Knox and Rachel Vanns. Thank you for putting up with me when this book was misbehaving. Thank you also to Rory and Tess Hardick. Without your advice and support, I probably would never have written this book at all.

Thanks once again to Andrew Gordon and everyone at David Higham. The whole team at Bloomsbury astonishes me every time I publish a book, but an especially huge thanks to Alison Hennessey, Therese Keating, Faye Robinson, Emily Jones and Isobel Turton.

This book wouldn't have been written without my children being looked after by a wonderful group of people over the past couple of years, so an especially huge thanks to Tina, Becky, Mrs Lloyd, Mrs Enderson, Miss Coleman and Mr Green.

Thank you to Granny and Pompom for your endless support. And most of all, thank you to my darling Jonny, my beloved Izzie and my scrumptious Jago. You fill every day with happiness.

Finally, our university reunions will now always have the loss of Ian at their heart. Dearest Ian, we will miss you forever. In so many ways you were our sun, and the world is not the same without you.

A NOTE ON THE TYPE

The text of this book is set in Minion, a digital typeface designed by Robert Slimbach in 1990 for Adobe Systems. The name comes from the traditional naming system for type sizes, in which minion is between nonpareil and brevier. It is inspired by late Renaissance-era type.